THE CACHE

"The Cache: Secrets Revealed and Treasures Discovered was an intriguing read and fascinating from the first page."
—Antoinette Wessels, Reader's Favorite

"Davis throws quite a number of curveballs into a captivating plot that keeps surprising you with each turn of the page."
—Pikasho Deka, Reader's Favorite

"The pacing is spot-on and never feels too rushed."
—Sarah Westmoreland, Reader's Favorite

"The Cache is a highly enjoyable work of mystery, romance, and, ultimately, human spirit and ingenuity in the face of great emotional turmoil."
—K.C. Finn, Reader's Favorite

"The plot of The Cache was fun, the characters had plenty of time to develop, and the entertainment factor was off the charts!"
— Rabia Tanveer, Reader's Favorite

Read the full reviews here:

THE CACHE

**Secrets Revealed and
Treasures Discovered**

Lauren Anne Davis

Fourteenth Avenue Press
Ft. Worth, Texas

Prologue

W here's Gary?" asked King closing the shed door.

Gayla was sitting on the mattress, smoking a cigarette. Since Dr. Glasser retired from the Veterinary clinic, Gayla started smoking.

"He's at camp."

"Camp? Wow. How old is he now—ten?"

"Nine. So, I hear you just bought your parent's house?" Gayla asked, surprised. "It's big enough!"

King chose not to ask where she got her information.

"Yes. Business has been good. I can afford it. My parents struggled to maintain the ranch, and since mom likes to clean her house, they needed something smaller."

"You gonna give me a key?"

She extinguished her cigarette on the concrete floor and tapped the threadbare mattress invitingly. King sat beside her, hesitated, then held up a key.

She grabbed it. "Good."

"Bring Gary with you when you come over. That is the only way this works, Gayla. It's time."

She pursed her lips. "We'll see."

Chapter One

Storm whined, and King awoke with a start. The same dream, again—recurring for at least two years—beginning the day after the initial conversation took place. He could not determine what triggered it and the anxiety that always followed.

"Thanks, buddy," he said, patting his sympathetic German Shepherd on the head. It never failed that Storm would wake him during that same dream sequence involving Gary going to camp, Gayla taking his house keys, and not agreeing to allow King to have his son alone. This time felt different somehow. Storm licked the back of King's hand.

"Yeah, there's something wrong," he informed Storm and poured a bowl of food for his dog before cooking dinner for himself. Storm gobbled his food down and rested on the kitchen floor to watch King chop broccoli and skin a substantial portion of Codfish. He seasoned them and slid the tin-foiled pan into the oven. He twisted the cap off a dark beer. The doorbell rang.

King flipped on the front porch light, and no one was there; silence. He looked to the sky and then up and down the country road twenty yards from the house. He picked up the package off the porch.

Hmm. No dust. I answered the door quickly. The only way somebody could have delivered this would have been on foot.

He turned the light off and opened the envelope on his way back to the kitchen. A small piece of paper fell out when he reached into the package. It had a typed message:

You'll know what your family did soon enough, and you'll pay.

He read it, held it briefly, folded it, and returned it to the envelope, double-checking for the sender's address, but there was none. He stood staring out the picture window overlooking the back of the ranch—lost in thought until the oven timer alerted him his dinner was ready. Had he known he would be a target for extortion, he might have picked a different line of work. Strangely, in all his years in the pawn business, his father, Jack, had never been robbed or blackmailed. To date, neither King nor Ace had experienced anything of the like. Perhaps their luck had run out.

Chapter Two

Gayla's family moved into a farmhouse one-half mile down County Road 704 from the Pullman ranch. It was late in the summer before she would begin eighth grade and King the ninth. A few months into the school year, old Mr. Heck, the school bus driver, grabbed King by the arm before he exited the bus.

"That girl is mighty sweet on you. I'd be cautious as a fox if I was you. Mind your P's and Q's, boy," he warned.

King asked, "How do you know?"

Mr. Heck coughed a laugh. "Cuz she sits watching you and makin' a puckerin' mouth and takin' your picture or maybe a movie film of you. Damndest thing. She got it bad fer you."

"Okay," King said quietly, "thanks for telling me. I will steer clear."

Avoiding Gayla had been working fine for three years—until the party. King's senior year of high school, he and Ace threw a Halloween party bonfire on their family's property. Word of the event had spread like a contagion through Hallsville and the neighboring town of Whitehouse. Jack, Kate, and half a dozen other parents had volunteered to chaperone the party.

The night of the event, the adults employed all three of Jack Pullman's Gators to patrol over three hundred kids on the acreage as they roasted s'mores, danced in the fields, and strolled around. Opposite the main barn on the far side of the ranch, students excited about bobbing for apples formed a line and cheered on their friends. Any mischievous teens caught smuggling alcohol onto the property were to have immediate transportation home, and Jack picked up the bill for their Uber ride.

Illegal alcohol played a part in the grievous actions perpetrated against Gayla Adamson that night, and although the chaperones did all they could, no one was there in time to save Gayla.

Buzzing from his Dr. Pepper soda, which, unbeknownst to King, had been spiked with something odorless, he passed a couple of people he knew from school. They asked him to tell Gayla about the karaoke party in the main barn.

"Sure—if I see her—"

"Okay, awesome party, dude!" shouted a deep-voiced teenager.

King dawdled, but when he finally did see Gayla. "Hey," he said to her, "Karaoke in the barn if you—"

"Only if you'll come with me," she said, smiling.

"Sure," King slurred, "in a sec—gotta whiz first."

"Okay," she said, skipping off toward the barn alone.

Later when he noticed people leaving the party and heading to their cars, King remembered Gayla and jogged to the barn. Karaoke was still happening; kids were still screeching out rock song lyrics into the mic with the help of their friends. Gayla was not there. He climbed the stairs to the loft—no Gayla. Stopping a girl King had seen sitting with Gayla on the bus to school the previous year, he asked, straining to be heard, "Hey, where's Gayla?"

"Oh, it's you! Nice party! Is that guy riding around on the horse, your brother?" she asked, pointing past King.

King turned. "Yes!" He ran out of the barn, yelling, "Ace! Over here!"

"What's up?" Ace asked, halting the American Paint Stallion. "You look sick, bro."

"Yeah, well, I need Buster, please. I have to find someone."

Ace hopped off the old spotted horse and handed the reins to his brother. Immediately, King headed to the tractor barn thirty yards away for a flashlight, remounted, and began circling the property.

"Hey! Whaya doin'?" shouted a voice in the dark.

Another said, "Good party KP! See you Monday."

When King flashed his light, he saw a group of guys he thought were his classmates moving toward the house. The crowd was beginning to dwindle.

A quarter-moon dimly lit the ranch, and Karaoke had stopped. King peered through the dark, turning in circles, scanning for Gayla. The last band of budding vocal talent was leaving the main barn. In the distance, King heard the fading voices of his guests and some parents. He guided Buster into the main barn and stopped. The hair on his arms stood when King heard someone whimpering. Quickly, he dismounted and ran outside around the barn where, the day before, he and Ace had transferred ten square bales of hay from the hay barn.

"Gayla?" said King, his mouth agape at the sight of her crouched down, her top torn, jeans and underwear in a pile nearby.

Her hands covered her face. King turned his flashlight off, jammed it in the back pocket of his jeans, and hurried to her side. "Are you okay? What's wrong?" She looked up and took his hand; King helped her stand up.

"I thought you'd never get here!" Gayla cried through her puffy, cracked lip. "Your friend had sex with me. It was awful!"

A lump formed in King's throat, blocking the vomit that threatened to erupt. "Assholes."

He tried but failed to recall the faces of those who had requested her presence in the barn. "You don't know who hurt you? Please, try to remember," King slurred and looked away.

"Someone blindfolded me and then hurt me," she said, shoving her feet into her jeans. She retrieved her underwear, wadded them, and crammed them in her pocket. "My back hurts. Will you look at it?"

King turned around. "Oh wow, Gayla, you are bleeding—the hay lacerated your skin. Let's go to the house. I'll help you clean up the cuts, but you should see a doctor."

Hastily, she put her blouse on, fastened a button, and shoved her bra in another pocket. "Okay, let's go."

As King ushered her into the house, Gayla whimpered into her hands. She heard someone flick the light switch on, and the door to the bathroom closed. Leaning slightly forward, bracing herself against the countertop, she admired the concern on his face in the mirror while he swabbed an antibacterial wash across her back.

"I can't believe I wanted to sleep with you all these years! It's awful!" sobbed Gayla.

King glanced up in the mirror at her twisted expression as tears rolled down her face. He was shocked at the news of her desire for him. He had taken the warning from Mr. Heck, the bus driver, seriously and stopped riding the bus—his motorcycle was quicker anyway. Sweat warmed his scalp.

"With me? Oh, sh— I, ah, don't think it's supposed to be awful."

"Really?" she questioned, still crying, and turned around to lay her head on his chest.

Jack Pullman whipped the bathroom door open as his eldest son secured Gayla in an embrace. King quickly lowered Gayla's blouse over her back, grateful his father could not see her face.

"What the hell are you doing in here? You have five seconds to get her the hell home. Do you hear me, son?"

"Yes, sir," King said uneasily.

Jack slammed the door shut. When King heard his father storm out of the house into the back of the property, he took Gayla's hand and ran down the hall, through the living room, and out the front door. In moments they were a quarter mile down the road, on the way to her house.

King let go of her hand.

"I'm sorry," Gayla began, "I'm sorry for involving you in the crap that happened to me at your party. If you hadn't had the party, maybe I wouldn't have had that awful experience." She paused. "What did you mean when you said it's not supposed to be awful?"

King chose his words carefully. "It makes sense that if sex were terrible, there would not be many people—if any—in the world, right? Because no one would be doing it."

"That seems true, but I still hate it. I will never do it again— Unless maybe with you. Do you even know how?"

"What? Yeah, I know how it works. Do you want to do that? Why." He wiped the moisture from his forehead with the back of his hand. The neck of his T-shirt tightened around his neck like a noose.

Gayla covered her smile. "We have a workshop we don't use; it's a ways behind the house. No one would know. Tomorrow, then? I want you to make this right," she urged.

"Tomorrow?"

Their secret affair promptly began, and by Christmas, King noticed her body changing. Gayla agreed to meet him so they could talk. Jogging across the uneven terrain in a flurry of snow mixed with rain, stomach flipping, he slipped into the back door of the shed at the south end of the Adamson's acreage.

King sat down next to Gayla on the mattress on the floor. "Hey, Gayla. How are you?" he asked.

"I'm fine; what's up?" She plucked the tasteless gum from her mouth and stuck it under the mattress. "Wanna do it?"

"No, I want to ask you if—"

"—If I'm pregnant?"

"Yeah. Are you?" He stared intently at her face.

Gayla reached for the wad of gum and began kneading it with her fingers. "Yes, and you will be a great dad," she said, focused on the gum.

"About that, are you sure it's mine? Remember the party— you didn't know who—have you slept with anyone else?"

King's fists clenched into balls in the front pocket of his hoodie.

"King," Gayla said, "The baby is yours. A woman knows these things. I felt it when it was happening."

"Oh, I didn't know," he admitted, fists loosening, shoulders dropping; he gazed blankly at the floor. "I want you to know that I'm going to quit football and pick up more hours at the Feed Store to give you money for things the baby will need."

Gayla smiled. "That sounds like a good plan." She reached for his hand and placed it on her small but protruding belly.

"Stay for a little while," she said, "I know you love me. One of these days, you will say it to me, right? You know how I feel about you, King."

Chapter Three

"Okay then, I will see him on Monday at eleven. Thanks," Gayla said, ending the phone call. She put her phone face down on the table littered with bills and unopened mail and glared at her mother.

"Who were you talking to?" asked Ms. Adamson rhetorically. "Gayla, you are in the eleventh grade. God in heaven, why did you have unprotected sex? You still have one year left of high school! How far along are you?" she said with one hand on her hip and the other massaging her forehead; eyes closed, she continued, "Do you have any idea how much a baby costs, and do you know who the father is?"

She shook her head, and a thick clump of hair fell to the floor to be immediately attacked by her son's Burmese cat. "Oh god! I am going to kill that cat!" she yelled, throwing a handful of their mail toward the cat, bills flying everywhere.

Gayla watched the cat prance around the living room with the wad of wavy reddish-brown hair hanging from his mouth. "Mom, you're still pulling out your hair! You said you stopped."

She sat on a wooden chair at the kitchen table and listened to her mother whine until she had enough. Standing up, Gayla leaned across the table and shouted, "Just cool it, Mom! I have a plan that includes me still going to college."

Ms. Adamson laughed hysterically. "Sure! Because of our money tree in the backyard? You have screwed up royally this time, Gayla. We are broke. We barely break even every month.

Your brother has been working more hours since the property taxes went up on this place."

"Listen, Mom, if you and Robert can take care of this baby, I will not only pay you for that, but I'm going to be a veterinarian, and things will be much better then. You'll see. I know you can't leave the house, and you won't have to."

Shaking her head in disbelief, Ms. Adamson asked quietly, "Whose baby is it? Somebody with money, I hope. Is the baby a Pullman?"

Gayla shivered and quickly composed herself. "I need you to wean yourself off those anxiety meds, Mom, so you will be okay to babysit next fall. I will finish high school online and start college after the baby is born, but I need you in your right mind, okay?" She stood and walked over to her mother. "I have an appointment Monday. Can I borrow your car?"

Ms. Adamson waved her hand, dismissing the request. "I'm surprised you're asking. Whatever."

"I have an appointment with Mr. Sabeth," Gayla announced to the secretary, who immediately paged the lawyer.

"Thank you, Carolina," said Mr. Sabeth, "Come in, Ms. Adamson? Have a seat. What can I help you with today?"

Gayla sat in one of the burgundy leather club chairs across a huge desk from Conroy Sabeth's father, the managing partner of Sabeth and Gilmore Law Firm. She smoothed her blouse and strategically cradled her belly with her hands. She took a big breath. "Mr. Sabeth, this baby is Conroy's."

A deep crease formed in the center of Mr. Sabeth's forehead. "Oh, I see."

Gayla smiled. "Conroy and I go to the same high school and are friends. I hope you can help me in the short term so I can be independent. That's all I want. Conroy will never know this baby. I will never tell him."

"Hmm." There was a long pause. "Ms. Adamson, you are extorting me and my family. You must be quite confident the child is Conroy's, so you won't mind submitting to a paternity test?"

Gayla licked her lips. "Please, whatever you need. This baby is definitely his. You'll see. I will need money for the test."

"If the child is Conroy's, what are you hoping to gain from me?" Mr. Sabeth studied Gayla's face and movements while tapping ink dots on blank paper with his pen.

"I want you to pay for my college."

There, she had said it. The dream that had been forming in Gayla's mind for years—college—had been spoken out loud.

"I will go to Junior college for two years, then state university, then the College of Veterinary Medicine—in-state. My family will raise this baby."

Mr. Sabeth's eyes widened. "Interesting. Alright. Go for the blood test, and we will talk again when you have the results. In the meantime, I will draft a contract with the arrangement you just laid out. If you change anything, even a comma, regarding your proposition between now and then, everything is off, and you can run off to a primitive love nest with my son—who, for your information, has no money of his own. Not a damn dime. You can live in squaller, eating beans and pumping out more ignorant, poor babies, which is what you both deserve from this family." His jaw clenched.

Gayla promptly stood, heart pounding. "I'll call you."

Mr. Sabeth slammed his pen down and stood. Reaching for a desk drawer, he pulled out a one-hundred-dollar bill. "Here. Get the test," he said, "and see yourself out, Ms. Adamson."

Gary Edison Sabeth entered the world on a sunny Tennessee afternoon in August at the hands of a midwife while Ms. Adamson and Robert waited to hold the swaddled baby. Days later, when the baby's eyes were well opened, Gayla learned that he might have

Strabismus—wandering eye syndrome. She made an appointment with Mr. Sabeth to finalize their arrangement.

"Thank you, Carolina," Mr. Sabeth said. He watched Gayla stride in, lugging her baby in an infant bucket carrier. "How are you?"

"I'm fine, but the baby is not. He's got brain issues; look for yourself."

She set the carrier on Sabeth's expansive desk and touched the baby's cheeks so that he looked up at her blankly with one eye crossed.

The blood test results Mr. Sabeth had received months ago indicated the baby was Conroy's, and this eye condition was just like Conroy had as a baby and was quickly corrected. He closed his eyes and shook his head, lips pursed—the malicious intent of this teenage girl—using her situation and baby this way. Sabeth envisioned the crumbling of his only son's future as an attorney and firm partner at the hands of this stupid girl. His face reddened.

"I see. The child's condition changes nothing, little girl. Don't you play hardball with me. Remember, Conroy is broke, and as we can see here," he pointed to the baby, "my son is as ignorant as you. I want no connection with you or this child, but as I understand your plan—" He placed the contract in front of her on the desk. "Read it, sign it, and I will give you the cash."

Gayla held the contract, but the words faded in importance to what she was hearing; Mr. Sabeth slowly counting and stacking bundles of twenty-dollar bills on the desk—four thousand, ten thousand, twenty thousand—sixty thousand—one-hundred ten thousand—two-hundred sixty thousand dollars."

Twenty neat piles of cash. Gayla swallowed hard and remarked hoarsely, "That's more than I asked for!"

"It is. You apparently do not know the cost of the schooling you say you want. I am funding your education because you will raise this child in secret. No one will learn his identity, ever—not even him. Do we understand each other? If you renege, hell will reign down on you, girl, in ways you have never known. You will prefer to kill yourself, frankly."

She shook her head yes. "I understand."

"Each semester, we will meet in secret—never again in my office. I expect you to bring me a certified copy of your grades, and I will give you another stack of cash. Our contract says that, and I will hold the only copy. Do not test me."

"I don't have anything to put the money in."

"I suspected as much." He pressed the intercom button on his phone. "Carolina, bring me the bag, please."

She responded, "Yes, sir."

Carolina breezed into Sabeth's office with an oversized leather diaper bag. "Here you go," she said, handing the bag to Gayla and promptly leaving.

"Where's the pen?" Gayla signed the contract and loaded thirteen thousand dollars into the fancy tan bag that smelled like a cow. "I will be in touch." With the backpack-style diaper bag strap comfortably on her shoulder, she grasped Gary's carrier by the handle and glided out of Sabeth's office, smiling.

Months ago, Sabeth had decided to ride this situation out with the pushy pregnant girl, fully aware that she could change her mind and go public one day, and the gig would be up. He had taken her bait and swallowed hook, line, and sinker. If she reneged on their deal, there would be nothing he could do except futilely deny her claims. After their first meeting, he investigated Gayla's and her family's credit and financial records and concluded she was truthful about her plan and ability to keep the secret. A girl from a family with that many buried secrets... Sabeth slowly sat down and rocked in his tall, executive leather chair.

King met Gayla and baby Gary in the Adamson shed two days before he departed for college on a partial scholarship to Texas A&M University. Gary was in his carrier on the workshop counter as Gayla and King stood side by side looking at him.

"He looks like you," said Gayla. She tugged the thin, gray coat sweater tightly around herself and crossed her arms to fight off the chill.

"I don't see it." King shoved his hands deep into his jeans' pockets. "His hair is reddish blond and straight. Everyone in my family has darker brown hair with waves."

"Baby hair falls out. His nose looks like yours, and his eyes are blue like yours," she replied defensively.

"My eyes are green, Gayla, and yours are brown."

King abstained from divulging that his mother's eyes were violet blue, not the unusual pale blue of baby Gary's eyes.

"What is your problem, King? Did you come here to accuse me of something that did not happen?"

"No, sorry."

Gayla reached up and put her arms around King's neck while the baby whimpered.

"My father's eyes are blue. That's where he probably gets it. Will you still send me money when you're away at school?"

"Yup. I have a job lined up on campus."

Gayla smiled and moved closer to Gary. "Good, as you can see—the baby has brain issues, so we'll need it."

"Are you sure it's not just an eye problem?"

Gayla softly touched Gary's head. "The eyes are connected to the brain. The neurologist told me he would have problems."

"Oh."

"Thank you for the money you have been paying this year. It helped me so much. I finished high school online while I was pregnant, so I'm starting college next week too. I won't be living in a dorm, though, like you. You're not going to see other girls, are you?"

"Ah, I haven't thought about it." He shrugged his shoulders.

"Mom will babysit Gary, and the money you send will help. I am so glad I can count on you." There was a long silence. "Do you want to do it?"

King jerked his head and looked at her, surprised. "You mean—?" He pointed to the mattress on the floor.

She smiled and removed her sweater. "Yes. You earned it."

Earned it?

Like a wave, heat and nausea passed over his entire body; then, unease settled in his stomach. "Nah, I should go finish packing." He turned to gaze upon the angelic face of the baby. "I'd like to spend some time with Gary at Thanksgiving when I'm home."

Startled, Gayla stammered, "Oh, ah, well, I don't know about that. I like to have him close. But we can meet here again. I'm sorry if that seems overprotective, but he has medical problems and all."

King felt another wave of nausea about to envelop him. "Okay, well, take care, Gayla."

"Geez, at least you could kiss me!"

King stood frozen; Gayla pulled him close and mashed her lips against his. "Okay, I love you. I mean, we love you!"

He left without a word.

It was a warm sunny June day. King sat on the back porch of his parent's ranch house, relieved his business degree was complete and graduation was over. The college segment of his life had been arduous but fulfilling. For four and a half years, King had kept his word to Gayla regarding money; he faithfully sent her an allotment each month, but he had not kept fidelity toward her. A few girls had come and gone each year.

He surveyed the neglected pasture and lack of animals, and a lump formed in his throat. He remembered Ace calling him months ago to share the news of Buster's death—so many great childhood memories on that friendly horse.

Earlier at breakfast, King had noticed how his parents had aged while he had been away in his last year of college. A pang of guilt caused him to lay a hand on his chest; he should have visited more often and seen to his own family's needs rather than devote himself to his dorm RA job to support the secret child he had seen grow only because of photos from Gayla now and then. She had shot down every request King had made to see Gary anywhere but in the shed.

King vowed that once he was settled and earning a decent living, he would hire a lawyer and fix this bizarre, uncomfortable situation with Gayla and maybe even get custody of his son. In the meantime, no rocking the boat. He would accept seeing Gary on Gayla's clandestine terms and sleep with her whenever the mood struck her.

"Do you mind company out here?" Kate asked.

"Hey, son," Jack said. He was arm-in-arm with Kate as they walked over to the iron glider and sat down.

King grinned. "I don't mind at all."

"Been thinkin'," Jack began, "Ace wants to open a pawn shop, so I'll be helping him out. He wants to buy a house too."

"Really?" King said. "That's big news."

Kate said, "Our baby is growing up!"

"Well, I'm not sure about that," Jack added, "but he wants to start makin' money and build equity— Anyway, King, I was wondering if you might be interested in doing the same thing— having a shop of your own. You got the smarts to run a solid business, son. I'll gladly show you the books if you want to see the profitability."

"I need to do something, for sure. The Feed Store I used to work at offered me a management position, but the pay is not great." He considered his father's offer for a moment. "Yeah, Dad, I'd like to know more."

Jack nodded. "We'll go to my office at the shop tomorrow, and I'll show ya the ropes."

"Sounds good."

Chapter Four

The policeman who responded to the break-in call from Meagan had been frank with her when he discovered she had no renter's insurance.

"Well, filing a claim is out. Do you know what is missing? Was it anything valuable? I ask because there are some pawn shops in town, and people love Sell-City and Ebay—that's where I would check. You never know; you may get lucky and see something of yours, depending on what it is. Don't get me wrong; I'll gladly take your statement and keep an eye out for your things, but—"

"I appreciate your honesty and the advice." *More than you know*.

Slipping her fingers under the flap of the breast pocket of her jacket, she extracted the photo again, kissed it, put it back, and patted it, eyes misting. Time was not on her side. With every hour her treasures were still 'out there,' the odds of her recovering them grew dimmer. Meagan slammed the truck door and marched into Ace's Pawnshop, not expecting to drain her checking account to buy back her guns.

The cocky sales guy was in no mood to haggle; he seemed distracted and anxious.

"Are you going to buy these guns or just stare at them?" he said, looking over his shoulder. "I can't take less than six hundred."

"I'll pay your price if you can throw in some ammo—at least for the 9mm." Meagan sucked in a deep breath.

Aside from these guns being hers, the rest of her plan could not transpire without them. Something had to give.

The guy grinned and said, "I can do that."

Having her belongings stolen from her and then having to repurchase them felt like insanely agreeing to lie down on a bed of nails.

It had to be made right.

They were gifts. Paxton had purchased those guns for her and taught her to shoot. The fifty-thousand residents of the town of Whitehouse heartily supported the two gun ranges situated at opposite ends of town. The range managers knew her name, and she knew theirs. After Paxton was assigned overseas, Meagan continued shooting practice regularly.

She was grateful she had come across the guns locally and quickly because they were essential for recapturing the rest of her belongings now that she was flat broke.

Successfully recouping the guns at Ace's Pawnshop had empowered her mentally. She was physically strong, but a firearm changed the equation; it added to her bravado and thrust her to her next target; King's Pawnshop.

The sun had disappeared, and the atmosphere was gray. Meagan glanced at the brown tweed passenger seat; it wasn't funny, but she noted that her pistol was riding shotgun. The cold, black steel weapon was her partner in the crime she was about to commit.

I'm not a criminal. I can't even believe this is my life! But a girl's got to take what's hers.

Her fingers rollicked on the steering wheel. A quick glimpse in the rearview mirror confirmed her thoughts again—she was unrecognizable. She smirked, knowing the gear she sported would cause even her gender to be in question. Wearing Paxton's Army fatigues, tucked into the tan, well-worn Army-issued boots he had died in, she wiggled her toes and smiled. His leather jacket hung awkwardly on her slim figure, revealing his AC/DC rock band t-shirt over a breast-flattening sports bra. Shoulder-length silky flaxen hair perfectly concealed under the cap's neck flap, and no one would ever guess that under the layers of cheap Halloween makeup was flawless skin, the result of her simple lifestyle, bar soap, and good genes.

It's a good day for redemption.

The East Valley shopping center buzzed with activity as the streetlights flickered. A trendy Italian restaurant was the biggest draw. She rolled the pickup to a stop several shops from King's Pawn and slid down from the driver's seat of Paxton's jacked-up, brown Dodge Ram truck.

There was no room for doubt. Meagan was running on instinct and understood that if she looked for her belongings, she would find them. With a spring in her step, she approached the building, tingling with anticipation.

She was in luck; the iron-barred door was open. A neon sign in the window of King's Pawn indicated they closed three minutes ago, but it did not matter. Meagan clenched her teeth and boldly pushed the door.

Surprised, King glanced at the unwanted customer trudging through his shop and quickly muted the country music blaring from his cell phone.

"We're closed," he declared, clenching his jaw.

Expertly, King wrapped up counting the till, zipped the cash bag shut, and set it on a shelf under the register. His curiosity mildly piqued, he checked his Breitling wristwatch, took a deep breath, and eyed the pseudo-military hobo surveying the guitars for sale.

Ordinarily, a late pawn customer was not an issue, but tonight's plan was a talk with Gayla. It was a long overdue conversation, the substance of which he had been contemplating all day.

King swiftly locked the shop door and hurried back to the counter. "Listen," he began, "you apparently did not hear me. We, ah, I—this shop is closed."

The camo-clad bum stood erect and turned slowly toward King and calmly, in a gravelly voice, said, "There's something I need."

He shrugged. "Ah, hell, give me a minute, and I'll be right with you."

He raced to his office with the cash bag and tossed it in the vault. Storm's growl caused King to quicken his pace back to the front counter. He couldn't see the eyes; the aviator sunglasses were too dark, the hair obscured under a black knit cap. The makeup was very overdone, almost comical. Brown lipstick and fake, blue plastic dentures masked the lips and teeth.

He wiped the sweat from his forehead with his rolled-up shirt sleeve. Assessing every detail about the tall vagabond, even the strange gait, it was clear this individual protected their identity with someone else's ill-fitting wardrobe. He peered out the window, wondering if he was part of a television show like Candid Camera or something. He was ready to be punked.

Evening light streamed through a small window; exterior iron security bars cast an image of a jail cell on the wall of instruments, drawing her attention. She moved stealthily toward the smell of carved wood. She swallowed hard and removed a glove, her fingers dusting across the guitar's Hawaiian Koa wood belly.

Furrowed brow, King noted the fine-boned hand with long, tapered fingers—man or a woman—the verdict was still out. His jaw twitched. He sighed loudly.

"Hey, come on, man! Let's get the show on the road. I have somewhere I need to be."

Meagan squinted her eyes and shoved her hand into the torn glove with resignation. She slowly turned and approached the man she was sure was a link to her past.

Without much history or understanding of women, King Pullman's insight into people arose from his decade in the pawn business. If he were a betting man, he would have laid odds this customer wasn't shopping; he was spying, doing recon.

Now standing stick straight twenty inches from the counter, shoulders squared, she met King's calm hazel eyes and scrunched her chin into her neck, throwing her voice deeper. "I'm looking for some jewelry."

He gestured to the extended display case before him. "What we have is all here."

Meagan noted the minor differences between this shop and Ace's Pawn, which she had visited several days before. The other store was smaller than King's Pawn and did not have an intriguing smell like the beckoning scent in this shop. As she neared the scowling bearded man behind the counter, she discovered the pleasing, woodsy aroma was coming from him. It was inviting and familiar, like green tea and spice cake in a forest. A distant memory of her uncle Abe's tobacco pipe floated to mind.

"Would you like to see something in here?" the broad-chested man inquired, causing Meagan to snap back to the present.

She peered at the imposing German Shepherd lying on the floor behind the pleasant-smelling man. His growl escalated as she drew near.

"Storm, hush!" he commanded, and the dog quieted. King watched the suspicious person as she examined a photo in her raggedly gloved hand. Even upside down, King could identify the gems in the snapshot. Nothing good had ever come from a customer discovering their former possessions in his shop.

He coughed. "Ah, could we speed this up? We *are* closed, remember?"

Nothing.

It was a rotten time for King to recall asking Marty to fix the silent alarm button. Screws had loosened, and the control, which once was attached to the back of the counter, lay inconveniently on the floor, in the corner, under the display cabinet.

"They have to be here," she muttered.

King sucked in a deep breath and stole another glance at the alarm button.

There was no sign of her amber ring, a white gold band with four prongs clutching the stunning amber stone. It had been given to her by her father upon his mother's death. She continued to surveil the assortment of jewelry inside the sizeable glass case. Meagan hoped her Grandmother Pearl's signature necklace would be here too.

"Could I see those?" she said hoarsely and pointed to the tray containing a string of pearls and then quickly tucked her hand back in her jacket pocket.

King took the cabinet key from his jeans pocket, unlocked the sliding glass panels, and then set the tray of jewels on the counter while assessing his customer's body language as she examined them, clearly locked on the pearls.

"If you haven't been here before," he coached, "how it works is, you tell me a price you are willing to pay, and we negotiate."

Meagan's eyes glazed over with the discovery of the pearls; bile rose in her throat when she realized there was only one Morris family heirloom in this shop. No Ruby Rose brooch or cameo; no amber ring, opal choker, or pocket watch; and no painting, pheasant, speed bag, or guitar. *My hunt is nowhere near over.*

Her shoulders fell, her lips pursed, and her nostrils flared.

Through her sunglasses, King felt rather than saw the determination in the eyes of his customer. "Oh, no," he muttered.

"Hands up! Right now!" she ordered, extracting the 9mm handgun from the inside pocket of Pax's leather jacket. "I will shoot you, so don't do anything stupid."

"Damn," King mumbled.

As Storm sailed over the counter like a track hurdler, King shouted, "Stand down!"

Storm's toenails scratched across the smooth cement floor before he froze in his tracks—watching Meagan like prey. King worried his nervous assailant might panic and shoot his dog.

Meagan flashed the gun from King to the dog sitting ten feet away at the ready and back to King, whose heart was racing. His face flushed.

"Please! Shooting the dog and, or me, would be stupid. Think of the repercussions," he said, lifting his hands. He eyed the alarm button a final time and stretched his leg out as far as he could without falling, and then stretched—just a bit—more.

"What are you doing?" Meagan demanded in her most resounding voice.

Storm was on her as she lurched forward to see what he was doing behind the counter, taking hold of the seat of her baggy pants and jerking her backward. Stumbling, she fired the gun, which left a new hole in the ceiling.

"Damn!" King spat and hit the small round alarm button with the toe of his cowboy boot. Later, he would discuss shop repairs with Marty and point out the roof damage. The triggered alarm linked the shop to the police station; they were likely already on their way. "Stand down, Storm! Thank you, big guy."

In seconds she was free of the dog's jaw; Meagan scrambled to the counter, her gloved fingers still gripping the pistol. She resumed pointing the gun at King's chest, and he re-hoisted his hands.

With her free hand, Meagan felt the back of the old camo pants, looking for a tear.

King smirked at the bizarre bum. This had to be a woman, the way she yelped when Storm tossed her backward, and then the way she checked her clothing.

"Now, where were we?" he asked her. "Oh, yes, I think you were robbing me."

Meagan glared at the dark-haired, handsome man and was not amused. She lowered her chin to lower her voice, "Yeah, so shut your pie-hole."

"Sure. Whatever you say."

She pulled the plastic grocery store sack from her jeans' back pocket. With the gun still leveled on him, she plucked the long strand of pearls off the tray and gently dropped them into her flimsy bag. The almost-botched plan was now back on track. She smiled, revealing ugly fake teeth.

"I'm outta here," Meagan announced and slung the bag off the counter with a cocky whip of her hand, sending the pearls flying across the shop. "No!" she yelled. "No!"

Storm's teeth had punctured the sack.

King stared toward the shop door and gritted his teeth. He checked his watch.

Where are you, Dell?

Officer Dell and the Pullman family were well acquainted and had maintained a good working relationship over the years—one that included 'no light bar warning lights.' Gripping the wheel, Dell swung the cruiser into the parking lot near King's Pawn. He smirked and shook his head in disbelief that King and his family were still in the pawn business. He recalled breaking up fights among pawn customers and another time when he called an ambulance for Jack after an irate customer had delivered a potent right hook. Those Pullman men must be made of some rather unique grit to put up with all that nonsense. A reality show filmed in their shops would have made them millionaires because people love a good crime drama.

He scanned the parking lot, still teeming with cars—seeking out King's robber would be difficult. Italian music wafted from the Bistro, where aproned servers filled customers' water glasses at small round tables on the tiled outdoor patio.

The evening was dreary, damp, and overcast. Next door to a unisex hair salon, a cluster of men stood talking on the sidewalk in front of the auto parts store. Dell heard all the chatter and sifted through it.

He shoved his car door shut. His pace quickened toward King's Pawn. He felt his belt for equipment he might need. Dell surveyed the parking lot, and only one vehicle commanded his attention—a brown truck with a lift kit and mud-covered license plate. Par for the course—a three-D sticker on the back window read, 'Girls love trucks too.' It was parked remotely and likely belonged to an employee of the restaurant.

The brilliant LED headlights of the cruiser flooded the shop, reflecting off hanging brass instruments in King's place. Dell cupped his hands around his eyes and peered into the shop door, his view hampered by a thin film of reflective sunblock Marty had installed. He dug in his pocket for the shop's supra key King's father had insisted he should keep.

One glance at the cop and Meagan froze like a deer in headlights, then scrambled desperately to compose herself; she threatened King through clenched teeth, "I want my pearls. You get them, or I will shoot your hand—now!"

"You'll—what?" Did he understand her correctly?

He glanced at his currently intact palms and fingers. Why someone would target one of his hands was a mystery to him. He could hear his assailant's heart pounding. The only people he had ever seen sweat like this criminal were drug addicts—suddenly, he knew there would be a fatality in his shop today.

"Storm, fetch!" King commanded.

His dog obeyed and bolted for the string of pearls dangling from the handlebar of a racing bike.

Dell could faintly make out a conversation between the owner and the customer while tugging on the locked door. "Dammit!" He growled, jerked his key out, and opened the shop door. Dell had handcuffed his fair share of women in his career. He recalled yanking two hookers out of King's Pawn not long ago. That was rough; those women were so lovely to him, absolutely the most pleasant, flirtatious criminals he had ever met. Maybe this wouldn't go too badly—if it were a woman—again. He smiled; sometimes, his job was a piece of cake.

Still grinning, Dell entered, drawing his gun, and leveling it at Meagan as she shoved her pistol back into her pocket.

"Officer Delbert Wims! Put your hands up!" he bellowed.

"Hi, Dell," King greeted the friendly, black officer.

Dell nodded.

Meagan's heart dropped to her stomach and pounded harder than ever as she concluded she was about to be taken into custody. Her scalp baked like a pizza oven, sweat trickling down her neck from under the thick knit cap. She thought about running but imagined getting shot in the back and how Grandma Pearl would have hated that and would have lectured Meagan in a sweet but stern way about the pitfalls of stealing and running from the police. Her armpits were swimming. Pumping her elbows up and down for a draft of air, she dreamed of skinny dipping in the Atlantic Ocean. Her breathing became shallow as she listened to the two men.

King studied his robber and snapped, "You just missed him, Dell. Hispanic or Brazilian, I can't be sure. He took off with an iPhone," he lied smoothly while gently taking the pearls from Storm's mouth, patting his head. "Good boy."

Dell's smile melted, and his gun wavered in the air. He knew it had taken him less than four minutes to respond.

"Oh—so everything is good here?" he checked, holstering his gun. He scratched his chin eyeing the lanky customer suspiciously.

"Doubt you'll catch him; he had friends waiting," he explained to Dell.

"Well, hell," Dell mused. "Got any coffee still in the pot back there?"

Meagan stood, mouth agape as the man behind the counter casually wiped the dog slobber off the pearls and arranged them in a necklace case. He put the container in a King's Pawn bag like she had purchased it.

"Here you go. Come back and see me," King instructed, handing the bag to Meagan.

Humiliation heated her cheeks under all the makeup. "Thank you. Excuse me," she whispered, averting her Halloween face and gratefully slipping past the officer at the door.

"Hmm," Dell mumbled and stepped aside, holding the door open for her.

King glanced down and hastily grabbed the photo the robber left behind. He would study it later. In the meantime, it fit nicely into the breast pocket of his buttoned-down shirt.

"These kids, Dell, they think we owe them everything. It makes me want to retire."

"Yup." Dell watched the customer stride across the parking lot toward the brown pickup. He shook his head in agreement and headed for the coffee pot. "I know what you mean." He poured the overcooked remains of the carafe into a Styrofoam cup and turned off the machine. "How much did that punk get away with?"

"About two hundred dollars."

Officer Dell slurped his coffee and strolled toward the exit. "Sorry, I didn't make it in time, King. That man, the one who just left, has he been here before?"

"You mean—him?" King asked, pointing to the door. "Ah, no. I thought it was a woman. Strange person, but I try not to let that influence the deal."

"Strange, fella," Dell grunted when he realized he had jumped to conclusions about the truck and the customer. He had been sure the alarm call had been for the bum in King's shop.

King agreed, "Yes, strange."

"Yep, but ignoring how someone looks would be hard, though," Dell said. "Why'd you get into this business, King? It seems like there are better, I mean safer, things you could do."

"…said the pot to the kettle!" King smiled. "I appreciate your concern, Dell. This business gives me the freedom that I need to do other things. Besides, you know I carry a gun and know how to use it if I ever need to." His lips formed a thin smile at his trusty friend while tapping his foot anxiously.

"Okay then," Officer Dell conceded, "I'm glad you're okay. Be seeing you. Tell Jack and Ace hi for me." He turned and left the shop.

"Will do. Thanks, Dell." He waved.

King hastily bolted the glass door and killed the central lights in the store.

"How about some dinner, buddy?"

Storm's tail wagged. In his office at the back of the shop, King set a dish of dry dog food out and refilled Storm's water bowl.

One desk lamp illuminated the musty room. A wall of painted black shelves held items King thought were too important to sell— a vintage typewriter, Coke Cola, and Disney merchandise, and a 1:29 scale USA train locomotive with two box cars. A thirty-year-old leather-framed photo of Jack and Kate, King's parents, sat next to a wood carving of a German Shepherd, a dead ringer for Storm. Among the myriad treasures pawned to him were several trinkets like watches, rings, and the swap King would never forget—three gold fillings.

Again, he checked the time. The decision to blow off a potentially ugly talk with Gayla was simple, considering his near-death robbery experience. Only the hum of the air filtration motor whirred. The shop was eerily quiet. The 19th-century rustic Railroad chair squeaked as King settled in to examine the picture. He put on a pair of his dad's old round reading glasses. King refused to let anyone know that his vision wasn't perfect anymore. He knew it was silly, but he didn't read anything with small print if other people were around. Thankfully, his manager, Marty, hadn't noticed the increased font size on his cell phone; he would have been the butt of Marty's jokes.

"Hmm," King murmured. *If I had to guess, I'd say the people in the photo were likely the robber's relatives.*

In the picture, a girl about four years old wore a fancy amber ring on her thumb; it was mounted high and appeared expensive. Shifting the image under the sizeable magnifying glass vice-gripped to his desk, he confirmed the thief took the pearls worn by the eldest woman.

If the thief is after anything else in this photo, it must be a Ruby Rose brooch, two necklaces, and an amber ring.

He felt an urgency to check the inventory at his father's and brother's shops. The last thing the Pullman family needed with Kate in the hospital was a homicide because of a deranged person in a military costume.

Chapter Five

The carved sign hanging above the veranda of the old Victorian house read, 'Willoughby B&B.' Meagan turned the brown truck up the curving driveway, coasted to a stop in the rear of the house next to Cousin Andrew's familiar blue jeep, and killed the engine.

The twenty-four-mile drive from King's Pawn to her aunt's bed and breakfast had evaporated under the weight of her emotions; she wiped tears of relief from her cheeks over the shock of her robbery-turned-gift and the kindness the big man behind the counter had exhibited.

What was he thinking? I wish I knew. He should have turned me over to that cop, but he didn't.

Clutching the bag he handed her, she sobbed and groped around inside the sack—no photo. *Great. That's just great—the nice man has my family photo. Whatever.*

Luckily, the thieves who ruined her life had not destroyed her family photo album, the only place her loved ones still resided.

I have other pictures.

The truck lights turned off automatically. In utter silence, Meagan watched moonlight cast its beams through the still branches of several hundred-year-old oak trees and a massive cottonwood in the half-acre backyard. Strange, elongated designs formed a shadow tapestry that Meagan likened to her life. In the first part of her life, there was a sun and a moon, and they revolved around her loving mother and father and Meagan. Then her parents disappeared one day along with the sun. A moonlit life of shadows remained thanks to her best friend's family who took her in—Rhonda and her parents, Dr. and Mrs. Richards.

Meagan moved from the Richards' home when she married Paxton Calvert at eighteen; they used wedding money to buy a modest frame home on the outskirts of town.

After Paxton died, Meagan felt uncomfortable in their home, which she thought odd at the time because while he was alive, she had spent most of her time in the house—alone. Knowing she was "keeping the home fires burning" while her husband fought for this country had been her mission throughout their ten-year marriage. After he died, she held on for one year before depleting her savings, forcing her to sell the house and rent a cheap apartment—robber bait.

A previously unforeseen opportunity, living in a bed and breakfast, materialized quickly after her apartment break-in. Meagan ended up at the B&B with a distant aunt, her husband, and their son, Andrew.

Dragging herself up the creaking back stairs as though wearing shoes of lead, Meagan made her way to her room on the third floor of the B&B. She recalled the horrific events of two weeks earlier when she had a place of her own, and all her memories were where they were supposed to be.

Work had been particularly stressful that day; throwing on a pair of sweats and going to Nate's Gym to work out was the day's remedy. Rounding the corner to her apartment, she knew something horrible had happened. The front door lay open and hanging by one hinge; the door frame shattered from a forced entry. Speechless, she stood with hands covering her mouth, assessing her new loss.

Questions began to circle in her thoughts; *Why me? Why this apartment?*

Taking inventory, she soon had a list of exactly which items had been taken—all heirlooms of infinite value to Meagan. That day would forever be marked by the absence of the moon and its shadows—the only light the cosmos had left for her.

She paused, shook off the images of her trashed apartment, and held the smooth wooden rail at the top of the stairs.

That was then, and this is now.

Antique wall lamps cast soft amber light illuminating the landing, which offered only two bedrooms and a large bathroom for guests to share.

Aunt Agnes had ensured no one occupied the room opposite Meagan's.

"I know you are a private person," she said, patting her niece on the arm, "You'll be okay here. No one will rob you here, dear. There is work to do, and you will be ever so helpful! Besides, we don't have an elevator, and most folks hate all the stairs!"

Meagan gently closed and relocked her room door. She placed the case with the pearls in the top drawer of her dresser, under her pajamas. Her hands fumbled to unlace Paxton's boots and park them in the armoire. She studied her reflection in the washstand mirror and rubbed off the tear-streaked makeup.

What am I going to do? A hundred dollars in my bank account and so much of my life yet to be recovered, which will take money.

Her job at Appliance Warehouse did not allow her time to surf the internet for her belongings; she planned to use the computers in the city library right after work—maybe tomorrow.

On his way to pick up lunch at Sam's Sandwich Shop, King received a text from Ace, "Dad just called me. He said to let you know—Mom is in a coma."

He quickly dialed his younger brother. "Hey, Ace, I called you early this morning. When you didn't answer, I figured you had a late night. What happened?"

"Yeah, I overslept. It was a late night. Doc says Mom's coma is probably not permanent. Dad seems pretty calm about the whole thing, and that's weird."

"Oversleeping? That's not like you. Is everything okay?" asked King.

Fumbling over his words, twenty-eight-year-old Ace responded, "Yep, yup. Yes. No worries. I've got it handled."

"Handled? Ace? Are you going to tell me what needs handling?"

"Nah. I'm good."

King took a deep breath. "Listen, I'm sure Mom is going to be fine. It will just take longer than we thought," he said reassuringly. "I need to ask you about a customer."

"Shoot."

"She's a clown-looking fool with dark glasses, fake teeth, and wears military garb," King said, "Ring a bell?"

The more he reconstructed the character in his head, the more he realized that if the person had been buying car parts, he would have assumed the robber was male. His face flushed over his confusion.

"Actually, Ace, it could have been a guy— with a quiet voice."

Ace coughed, blatantly covering his snicker. "What happened? Your love life sucks so bad that you're going after customers now?"

"Smart ass! Only the ones who rob me."

"Dude!" Ace said, surprised, "You got robbed? What? Wait a second—there was a guy like you described—at least, I think it was a guy. He came into the shop a few days back and bought guns: two rifles and a pistol. He knew what he wanted and paid cash in full."

"Hmm," King responded, "was the pistol a 9mm Glock?"

"As a matter of fact, it was! How did you know?"

"Just a guess. How did you do on the deal?"

"I made triple what I paid for them." Ace's phone beeped with another call. "I gotta go, bro. Tell Mom and Dad hi for me when you see them later. Sorry you got taken, dude."

"Thanks, I'll tell them. Later." King set his cell phone in the console cup holder of his truck and stared blankly at the lunch-hour traffic, contemplating his day.

A shirt-and-tie desk job career would have been fine—for anyone but King Pullman. His finance professor at A&M intimated an expectation that he should be able to whip a necktie into a Full Windsor Knot and claim his desk with pride shortly after graduation. It was not in the cards. Growing up Pullman meant freedom, cattle, and land, not office, housecat, and apartment. Besides, he wasn't interested in learning the fifteen different ways to knot a necktie and choke his life out.

The traffic light turned green, and King proceeded to the hospital parking lot. He tugged at the crew neck of the t-shirt under his buttoned-down plaid shirt and headed for the elevator, then quietly slipped into his mother's room at the end of the sterile hospital corridor. Jack sat a few feet from Kate's bed—far enough away to not disturb her but close enough to read all the machine monitors hooked up to his wife.

King stood beside his dad with his hand on his shoulder. "Hey, Dad, how's Mom doing?" he whispered in the dimly lit space.

"She's in a coma, son. The doc said it's sometimes the brain's way of dealing with a stroke. Her sister—your Aunt Carol, is coming to sit with her so I can go to work the rest of the week. Take a seat."

King leaned over, kissed his mother on the forehead, and then settled into a cold, metal hospital chair beside his father.

"I think she's going to be fine, Dad. I'm not a doctor, but I know Mom, and she will pull through this." Hands clasped as though desperately beseeching the heavens to hear him. King studied the frail-looking form. "She is kind and strong and needed right here. She'll be fine."

Jack cleared his throat and rubbed his eyes. "I sure hope you're right."

"I need to talk to you about something, Dad—about a threat. Beware of a person dressed in camo fatigues and military-issued boots. She'll rob you. Scratch that—he'll rob you," he stated, then closed his eyes to pray for his mom.

"Was Dell working?" inquired Jack.

"Yes, he says, 'Hello,' by the way."

Jack nodded, and King continued, "I couldn't hand her over to a cop—damnedest thing. I couldn't do it. Maybe I've gone soft? Dad, I could have taken her down, but I just let her take the damn thing. I helped her!"

He omitted the part about being at gunpoint and silently scolded himself for labeling the thief a woman.

Eyeing his eldest son, Jack's eyebrows rose. "That's a new one. I remember when Dell hauled those two strippers out of your shop. You handed them over with no questions—didn't give them a chance. They were good-looking, too, and throwing themselves at you. Geez, now you've gone all Greenpeace on me. What's goin' on?"

"Not sure." He recalled the hooker ordeal, jaw clenching. "Yeah, it was bizarre. The big difference between the strippers and my robber, Dad, is that one of the strippers was pawning rhinestone-covered pasties—the problem was she was wearing them."

Jack's eyes went wide, and he laughed. "Oh, that's rich!"

King continued, "While one encouraged a transaction with me, her friend shoved some merch in her purse. Marty was watching and hit the alarm. They had it planned. On the other hand, the costumed robber was looking for something specific, and she found it. I am worried he or she may come looking in your shop."

Jack nodded. "Do you think he'll come back again?"

King yawned and stretched his legs out, crossing them at the ankle. "No. I think he got what he wanted at my place; I'm just concerned about you."

Jack assured his son, "I'll call Mr. Lee tonight and let him know. Just understand this, son; we will not be aiding any thieves at my shop. They will get exactly what they deserve."

King knew the heist did not surprise Jack—but the fact that King helped his assailant astonished his father.

If the thief were to shove a gun in Jack's face, she wouldn't last long. Jack was notorious for his quick and brutal temper, which could be lethal if confronted by the angry person who robbed King. For both their sakes, King couldn't let that happen.

"The robber is bad news, Dad; you need Storm," King said, leaning back and adjusting his cowboy hat to cover his face for badly needed rest.

Before his mother's stroke recently, King had overheard a conversation between his parents. Jack was doing his best to convince Kate to sell that 'bad luck cracker-box house they call a garden home.' They had purchased the property a few years earlier when they sold their ranch to King. It seemed Jack was still interested in having acreage again.

In the quiet of his mother's hospital room, prayers for his parents overshadowed thoughts of the criminal.

"Uh huh," Jack responded, crossing his arms and assuming the same posture as his son.

They fell awkwardly asleep in their chairs at the side of Kate Pullman's bed while hospital machines monitoring her pumped and beeped.

Chapter Six

It was a Thursday at one in the morning. Ten-year-old Meagan was spending the night at her best friend Rhonda's house when Mr. and Mrs. Richards received the phone call that shattered Meagan's world; Ruby and James Morris died, along with the pilot they hired, in a single-engine plane-crash less than seventy-five miles from town. Rhonda became possessive of Meagan like a momma cat trying to protect her kitten from the harsh realities of the universe; it was an extraordinary effort.

Meagan reserved her tears for her pillow. She had been a princess once, but her reign ended with the death of her tender, loving parents. Face buried deep in the duck-down fluff, she cried, "Momma and Daddy, I love you, and I miss you. My heart hurts so bad."

Every pew was at capacity, and the double funeral at St. Alban's Church lasted several hours. The stained glass, arched windows, the scent of ancient wood, and the statues and regalia became etched in her mind. People Meagan had never seen or heard of said beautiful things about her mom and dad. At the mention of her parents' accident, the church is what comes to her mind first, and it has stayed with her.

Meagan recognized her parents' absence occurred at a pivotal point when she struggled for self-assurance and love. She would stare into the bathroom mirror, longing for the sun-lit warmth of loving arms around her and a family to call her own. She wished for the day when love would be a permanent answer, not a passing question.

Her years since their passing have been filled with work and punctuated with stretches of loneliness, introversion, and more loss. Rhonda was at Meagan's side when her Grandmother Pearl passed, and then her Aunt Opal. The girls stayed close through middle and high school.

Rhonda seemed to be constantly on her phone and excitedly planning to go somewhere or do something with friends. She usually invited Meagan along; sometimes she went, but mostly, she stayed home alone in her bedroom opposite the hall from Rhonda's.

Dr. Richards was a successful chiropractor in town, which afforded them a home with plenty of square footage providing ample privacy for all four people. On her double bed in her spacious room, Meagan sat surrounded by sheet music and taught herself to play the acoustic guitar her Uncle Abe Morris had bequeathed to her; it was the only item not relegated to storage. After probating Meagan's parents' will, the Richards put the contents of the Morris estate in a storage facility for Meagan when she became old enough to do something with it. That day had arrived with her wedding; she and Paxton emptied the storage unit and filled their quaint home.

Marriage, college, and jobs took Meagan and Rhonda in separate directions. Despite technology, they hardly kept in touch—only catching up during the holidays. Getting together once a week for lunch began after Paxton's death. Rhonda had seen the news story that Meagan's husband died in Afghanistan. Without hesitation, she drove to Meagan's house to provide emotional support. Their sisterhood resumed as though it had never faltered.

Prolific leafy green vines wove through the lattice of a long arbor shading guests from the midday sun. Soft Mediterranean guitar music flowed through hidden speakers.

"I love this place," Rhonda said, grabbing Meagan's hand and leading her to an iron table on the patio. A lean, clean-shaven waiter placed two glasses of ice water before them.

He handed the girls each a menu. "I'll be right back with your teas," he said, then headed back inside the café.

Meagan watched the door swing shut behind him. "Does the feeling of being violated ever end?" She sipped her water and waited for her friend to respond.

"You mean about your robbery?" I don't think so. Eventually, it won't be so raw. Right now, you should focus on rebuilding your life." She reached across the table and held Meagan's hand. "I wish that blasted apartment had had a security gate."

"Yeah, well. I was flat broke, and I couldn't afford a fancy place. Now I'm even more broke—if that's even possible!" She rolled her eyes skyward.

The waiter set their hot teas on the table. A breeze kicked up, tossing Rhonda's brilliant red hair around like flames licking the air. Smoothing a strand of hair from her mouth and tucking it behind her ear, Rhonda ordered, "Two soups of the day with crusty bread, please." She smiled and batted her eyes at the young man.

He winked at her. "Got it. Thanks. I will get that right out." He picked up the menus and left.

Meagan smirked. "Wow, he winked at you, Ronda. Nice to know you are attractive to boys!"

"Ha. Ha. He is at least—"

"Seventeen!" Meagan blurted with a snicker.

Rhonda sipped her tea. "It's better than nothing!"

"I disagree, but you already know that."

Rhonda shrugged. "So, how's it going at Willoughby's? How did you get them to rent it to you long-term?"

"Just like a realtor to ask about the contract!" Meagan smiled.

"Seriously! What's the deal? I thought that was an odd choice for housing. I mean, I know money is a huge factor, obviously—I mean, I live with my parents for that reason. Of course, that didn't happen until the divorce. I will say that Alex has the best life."

Meagan nodded. "I totally agree. Your parents are the best, and Alex is a great kid. I'm glad you all have each other."

Silence like a vacuum enveloped them, and time stopped, only jump-started by the waiter. "Here you go. French Onion soup and sides of seasoned crusty bread. Anything else?"

Neither friend spoke. They shook their heads no.

Meagan began, "You may not remember, but my dad's second cousin is Agnes Willoughby, and her husband, whom everyone knows as Mr. Willoughby, were both at Paxton's funeral. They approached me after the service, and Aunt Agnes said, 'We are your family, so if you need anything, please let us know. We are here for you.' Mr. Willoughby grabbed my hand and planted their business card in my palm. He said, 'Call us anytime.'"

"Uh, huh," Rhonda mumbled. "You're right. I don't remember them, but that was a nice gesture."

"Anyway," Meagan continued, "After the robbery eight days ago, I called them. I had never been to a B&B before. Aunt Agnes remembered and invited me to lunch at their place. It feels much safer than that apartment, and I can pick up extra money by helping them around the place."

Rhonda nodded as she battled her flailing hair in the wind.

"Why don't you just wear a ponytail?" Meagan suggested bobbing her head and swinging her ponytail. Although Paxton preferred Meagan's hair down, her preference was the efficiency of hair tied back. Since no one at Appliance Warehouse commented either way when Meagan stopped wearing her hair down—the ponytail had become her go-to look.

"Last week, didn't you say Agnes was a bit strange?"

"A bit," Meagan confirmed, "she's snoopy. I'm surprised she climbs those stairs, but I can tell she does because things are—moved. She is also too concerned about my personal life." Meagan smirked. "Yesterday, she introduced me to her son, Andrew, again. I suppose she forgot we had already met. So strange, actually; I do not remember hearing about Andrew or seeing him anywhere before I came to the B&B. The age gap is a mathematical problem. Agnes and Mr. Willoughby had to have been at least fifty when Andrew was born."

Rhonda's eyes widened. "How old is Andrew? Is he living there too? Why are you laughing?"

"It's you! You are guy-crazy. You always have been! Andrew? He travels for work—I don't know what he does, though, and he lives on the second floor." Meagan chuckled again. "And no, he's not hot; warm at best and thirtyish something—not for me."

"Right. I know you, Missy, and unless he's got ab muscles of iron, good teeth, buns of steel, and eyes to match, and—"

"Wait a minute. Am I that superficial? The man must have a heart and a conscience! Rhonda, do you think I'm shallow?" she asked, head cocked to one side, her crisp blue eyes searching.

The waiter was standing close by. "I'm supposed to answer that?" he teased, "I just serve food. Can I get you, ladies, anything else?"

"You are wise. Incredibly wise," Rhonda informed the young man. "How old are you?" She took a bite of crusty bread and waited.

"I'm twenty-seven, but people say I have a baby face." One corner of his mouth pinched back to reveal a deadly dimple.

Rhonda's cheeks protruded like a chipmunk's as she chewed and scanned him from head to toe.

Meagan giggled. She turned to the waiter. "You are being evaluated. Should you choose to accept this assignment, more directions will follow. Otherwise, this situation will self-destruct after we pay our bill."

Feeling the heat of Rhonda's stare, he pulled a napkin from his server apron and mopped the sweat from the back of his neck before escaping to the restaurant kitchen.

Rhonda laughed and said, "Coward!" causing Meagan to choke with laughter. "Now, back to our subject—no, you, my dear friend, are not shallow. Shallow is not your problem."

"My…problem?" Meagan swallowed hard.

"Yes." Rhonda stared into her soup bowl as she stirred it. "I have known you practically our whole lives, and I'm still trying to figure you out. I don't mean to sound 'preachy,' but I feel like you're keeping secrets, Meg, and we said we would never do that. We were each other's maid of honor, remember? Yes, things have changed for us—I'm divorced, and you're a widow, but aren't we still maids of honor? We still have our 'code,' right?"

Meagan slowly nodded in agreement. On the face of it, Rhonda was right; everything she had said was true, but deep down, an alternate reality caused a ripple of guilt as she recalled her decade-long marriage to Paxton Calvert. Each Army mission changed him and changed his sense of humor and tolerance. He eventually lost his compassion and became progressively more competitive with Meagan. He had to be correct; she had to be wrong. He had to be the faster runner, the stronger puncher, and the superior breadwinner. When their next-door neighbor offered her a job earning more than Paxton, she turned it down to keep peace in their home.

If Rhonda had been privy to the inner workings of Meagan's marriage, she would have thought Meagan was crazy and urged her to divorce.

How can I tell my best friend that I was comfortable with a man who rarely talked to me, seemed peeved at me all the time, and had no qualms about telling me to shut up if I sang? Rhonda does not need to know about my plan to recover my stuff—she would not be on board for many reasons. One look at me in my 'thieving clothes' at the pawnshops and Rhonda would call her parents for advice. Rhonda's friendship was a lifeline when I needed it most, but what matters to me are those cherished things handed down to me by my grandparents, aunts, uncles, and my mom and dad; these are what I need most now—their spirits are in those things. My life would be unbearable without the priceless gifts stolen from me. I cannot fathom life without them. Maybe when all my possessions are back where they belong, I might give Rhonda some insight. In the meantime, I will hunt—

"I'm sorry if I seem secretive. I have a lot of stuff—in my head—that I'm processing. You know, with the robbery and having to move again. I feel like I'm stuck in a loop of loss sometimes. I am sorry."

Rhonda dabbed a tear from her round brown eyes. "I don't mean to be insensitive. You have been through so much! Whenever you want to talk, I'm here. Can you still come with me on Saturday night? My mom said she would babysit Alex so that we could try that new bar. I've heard it's super modern and fun—there's dancing too!"

"Yes. I'll go; I haven't been to a club in a long time. Not sure about the dancing, though," said Meagan.

Chapter Seven

"Visiting hours ended thirty minutes ago," declared a perky middle-aged nurse as she tapped King on the shoulder. "Be sure you take him with you." She pointed to Jack, who was snoring under his tilted cowboy hat.

King woke with a start and nearly lost his hat.

"Thank you for letting us know. We'll go. Come on, Dad," he said, patting his father's hand.

Jack sat up straight, rubbing his eyes. "We gotta go now?"

"Yes," King said, "I'm heading out. Keep me posted about the robber." He leaned over and kissed Kate's cheek, then hugged Jack.

By ten thirty PM, King had stopped at his shop, picked up Storm, and drove twenty minutes to let himself in Jack's Pawn Shop. Jack, King, and Ace had keys to each other's shop—in case of emergency, and King believed that zero hour had arrived. He flipped on the main switch illuminating the lengthy front counter loaded with items under glass. Studying the photo from his pocket, King scanned the display cabinet for pieces his assailant hadn't found in his shop.

"Bingo!" he said, spotting the cameo pendant on a stunning gold snake chain. "She will surely want this!" he whispered and closely compared it to the piece in the photo. If the coral and ivory cameo necklace were not there, maybe the thief would leave Jack's shop peacefully, without burglarizing him. Leafing through his wallet, King pulled out three one-hundred-dollar bills and placed them in a cash drop bag with a note for Jack or his manager, Mr. Lee.

> Let me know if this does not cover the
> gold chain necklace with the Lady's
> head pendant. Thanks, BKP.

It was one AM; King was exhausted; he idled up in his driveway, gravel crunching under the tires of his Dooley pick-up. Frustration furrowed his brow—Gayla's SUV was there.

"Damn," he muttered, "I just wanted to be alone. You know what I'm talking about, Storm?"

Ears straight up and eyes riveted on King, Storm placed a paw on King's thigh. King preferred to be alone tonight—there was so much to think about—like what Ace was up to and what was going on with his mother's health. He worried about his dad too. His parents were each other's world. King was also woefully behind on his second-floor building project and craved time to swing a hammer.

He turned off the truck engine and tried not to give his jewelry thief any thought, but his mind saw the person clearly, and he imagined ten possible actions he could have taken during the robbery. Most of the scenarios ended with the tall individual behind bars leaving him very conflicted.

He turned off his truck. Gayla would be in his bed and waiting for him. Once again, King put off the inevitable, necessary talk with her. He patted his jeans pocket where the necklace was.

"Let's go," he ordered, and Storm gracefully hopped out of the truck, following King into the house.

Silently, he set the necklace into a drawer in his bathroom, then dropped his clothes in a pile and slipped into his King-size bed next to Gayla. King lay flat on his back, staring at the soft moonlight shadows on the bedroom walls. Storm swaggered over to his massive, sheepskin therapeutic dog bed in the corner of the bedroom and curled up for the night.

"Hey, babe," Gayla cooed in her raspy voice. "Where have you been?"

"Visiting my parents."

"Oh," she said, rolling over to face him, her fingers combing his chest.

"How's Gary? I Haven't seen him in six months. How's he doing? I'd like to teach him to build things. How about I bring him over here for a day? It seems like he doesn't get out much."

Gayla sighed. "He's fine. He helps his grandma in the house and plays mechanic with my brother. Do not hammer me with that 'deal' you think we made a couple of years ago about me bringing Gary over here. Not going to happen." Gayla's eyes squinted as though he had pinched her. "King, you know we've been homeschooling him. It means a lot to my mother. Gary is not into outdoor stuff or sports if that's what you think. Just let it go. Let's forget our day for a while."

"Do you realize that in ten years, I have hardly seen him? I don't think he would even recognize me."

King's eyes were hollow as he stared past Gayla.

"Not true, King," she countered, knowing he was right. She lied again, "He has a photo of you."

He held her sinewy form on top of him and studied her. Although Gayla's scent had never aroused King, her touch still had some impact. Her skin generally reeked of the countertop antiseptic spray she used at her clinic and cigarettes, something showering did not erase.

"What?" she snapped, searching his hazel eyes. "What's wrong now? You need to let go; de-stress; get out of your head, babe." She craned forward to kiss his lips, but he averted his face. "So that's the game we are playing today? I can tell you about the horse I put down today. The family stood around telling stories about his damn life for an hour before they let me inject him. They were crying and carrying on. I thought they'd never stop. Poor horse. When he finally stopped breathing, guess what happened?"

"I—I really—don't know, Gayla," King stammered. He shook his head. "Maybe we should just sleep. I am tired, and you must be stressed and tired too?"

"What? Let me tell you what happened. This dog, a Brittany Spaniel, walks up to the dead Mustang, licking his face, lying on him, and whining. Man, that shit is so sad— and stressful. You know what else is stressful, babe?"

King gently pushed Gayla over to his side. "What?"

She took a deep breath. "My brother is flat broke again, so I need money. Can you give me some? Work has been slow."

For an accomplished veterinarian, Gayla continually ran short of money. Money was the subject King had been avoiding confronting her about, and his checkbook reflected it. A wave of nausea began to envelop him.

"Something is wrong, I can tell. Whatever. Make love to me, and we can talk about everything later." She took King's hand and placed it on her bare back. "It's been a long time; take me."

King squeezed his eyes shut and then left his bed. "I just remembered I need to check my email. Would you like a drink?" he asked, opening the center cabinet door of his long dresser.

When she noticed the bottle of Whiskey, she sat up in bed. "Make it a double, toss me my cigarettes, and hurry the hell up."

He did her bidding, dumped his drink into hers, and set it on the nightstand before rushing to his home office down the hall. King heard the TV in his bedroom blaring when he quietly closed the office door and paced the room.

The threatening note King received five weeks ago had become the elephant in the room when Gayla was near, making him unable to lie with her. He grabbed his senior high school yearbook off the shelf and began leafing through it while waiting for his computer to power up. His hand moved over the faces of all his buddies in the football team photo; King was absent. He had quit sports and given up a potential football scholarship to work and earn money to give to Gayla, who was pregnant with their love child. That was over a decade ago, yet she was still in his life, and Gary was still a secret.

He studied the happy face of his replacement, quarterback Max Dagget. Next to Max stood Ernie Smith, Shawn Spencer, then Conroy Sabeth— "Sabeth," King repeated and quickly typed Sabeth in the search bar on his computer. *Just what I thought—he's a lawyer now, just like his dad, precisely who I need to talk to.*

King dialed the phone number for Sabeth, Gilmore, and Sabeth Law.

Hallsville Country Club

"Well, if it isn't Hallsville's finest quarterback!" exclaimed Conroy Sabeth. He leaned his club against his monogrammed leather golf bag and embraced King—patting him on the back.

King grinned and returned the hug. "Conroy, the lawyer, who knew? Seriously, congrats!" He set his golf bag down near Conroy's. "I saw those last few practice shots. You look ready to play."

"I am. Let's do this," Conroy replied.

The two men loaded bags of clubs onto the cart and climbed in. Approaching the first hole, Conroy broke the silence. "What's up, King? You didn't call me out of the blue to get beaten at golf today."

"You are right, but I don't expect you to throw your game." They both laughed. "How about we first hit a few, and drink a few?"

"I'm game!" said Conroy. He flipped the lid off the small cooler on the back seat of the golf cart and pulled out two beers. "To renewed friendship—cheers!"

"I'll drink and play to that—cheers!" replied King. He noticed Conroy was wearing his signature Ray Ban sunglasses, just like he wore in high school.

Neither kept close tabs on their score as they talked about high school teachers and football games. On the eleventh hole, Conroy hit his approach shot in the fairway and returned to the cart, watching King search for his ball in a thicket.

"Find it, Sherlock?" Conroy yelled, "The last time you looked that lost was at your Halloween party!" He laughed heartily at the memory. "Just spinning around on your horse in the middle of the pasture with your flashlight."

King stopped, turned, and stared at Conroy momentarily before marching toward the cart. He shoved his iron into the bag. "I'm conceding to this hole. Let's go to the green. At least your shot was good. And what the hell, Conroy? Where were you at that party?"

Conroy pushed the cart's park pedal, removed his sunglasses, and tossed them on the cart's dash; he turned to King. "It figures you don't remember anything; I spiked your favorite Dr. Pepper. Sorry about that, man. I know it was a stupid thing to do, but I was a stupid, desperate guy after a girl who wouldn't give me the time of day. You don't know what I'm talking about because you were the 'quarterback' every girl wanted back in the day." He took off his golf cap with the PGA insignia, tossed it on the dash of the cart, then raked his fingers through his shiny, straight hair. "I'm serious!"

"I have no idea what you are talking about. Conroy, man, everyone knew you were going places. You were the top of our class, if I remember right—not to mention the fastest receiver a team could ask for. Plus—those pale blue eyes and that strawberry hair—" King stopped short to study his friend, his mouth slack. There was a long pause.

"Conroy, ah—ah—" He stared, unable to blink.

"King, you're freaking me out. What's going on?"

"Conroy, who was the girl you were desperate for in high school?" Millions of tiny hairs spiked on the back of King's neck.

"Why?"

"Just—please?"

"Gayla. Cute little thing with brown eyes. Smart too. She was my lab partner in chemistry class and had to explain most things to me. King—what's wrong!" demanded Conroy. He reached out to his friend.

King had leaned out of the cart and puked. He stuck his hand up in the air. "Give me a minute. Please, just drive back to the clubhouse." He wiped his arm across his mouth.

"No problem, man."

Chapter Eight

Meagan arrived at the library as the doors were opening. She called in sick for the first time since beginning her job at Appliance Warehouse. Going to work that day would have cut into her research time.

After four hours of sitting in the same position in the cheap rolling office chair, she stretched and walked up and down inside the spacious library, making mental notes of the items she had already located today on Sell-City. In the website's list of categories and under 'electronics,' she had found her television and surround sound components, which Paxton had purchased and installed in their home. She had texted the seller and arranged to see the items in the nearby town of Rio Vista at a remote spot that Meagan had selected—an abandoned gas station on Frontage Road. She paced and rubbed her hands together, clearly envisioning Paxton's face; he was smiling. A warm feeling of pride enveloped her; another glorious family reunion would occur at seven PM.

With plenty of daylight still, she drove home to the B&B, where she had chores to complete and dinner to help prepare as she had promised Mr. Willoughby.

Meagan put the truck in park, hopped down, and shut the heavy door—whistling.

"Well, look at your happy self!" remarked Aunt Agnes. "I sure do hope you're ready to work. We don't need laziness around here!"

Meagan smiled and ran up the stairs two at a time shouting, "I'll put my sneakers on and be right down."

King sloshed water over his face and dried it with a paper towel, checking himself in the Country Club restroom mirror, his heart hammering in his chest.

There will be a reckoning.

He walked past the formal dining room with its panoramic views of the golf course bordering Railhead River and many tables adorned with vases of fresh wildflowers. ESPN television blared from the Club Sports Bar entrance, where Conroy sat at the long bar, staring at the TV.

Assuming the adjacent stool, King asked, "Hey, not drinking?"

"Yeah, time for water. One beer is my limit. Listen, what happened to you out there?"

King took a deep breath. "You and I will unravel a decade of a mess, Conroy. But my first question is, are you single, married, or engaged?"

"Wow. Why? Are you interested? I mean, I like you, but—" he choked on his laugh at King.

"Very funny. I'm serious."

"Okay, King, I'll bite. After threatening to leave for several years, my fiancée broke it off ten months ago. She said there was a ghost in our relationship that I loved more than her. How's that for 'single'? The truth is—she was right. I had just accepted Jesus as my savior. I'm saved. He was or *is* the ghost, I suppose. She didn't understand or feel the same way."

"Saved?" King asked, "from what?"

"From myself. I became a Christian. That's a testimony for another round of golf. What were you saying about the mess?"

"Wow, you are religious, now? You did a one-eighty. Sorry about your fiancée."

Conroy rubbed his hand over his face. "My life needed the one-eighty. Interestingly, my decision to clean my life up caused my fiancée so much discomfort that she bailed. I appreciate your sentiments. What's eating you, King?"

"Plenty, but like you said, that Pandora's Box can wait for another round of golf." King sucked in a deep breath. "Did you ever go *out* with Gayla Adamson?" He studied Conroy's expressions.

Sorrow washed over Conroy's countenance. "Well, like I said, I had it bad for that girl—monovision. A couple of days before your party, in Chemistry class, I asked her if she was going to your party, and she asked me why I wanted to know. I confessed that I liked her and wanted to hang out with her if she would be at your Halloween bonfire. I was working up my nerve to ask her on a date."

"And—" King encouraged.

"And, at lunch, she asked to talk to me alone in the hall. She said she didn't believe that I liked her. Something about—how could a smart, hot guy like me want her? She seemed confused and did not understand that I thought she was amazing. I told her she didn't have to believe me, but I thought she was smart and beautiful and that I had thought about kissing her in Chemistry class in front of everyone. She laughed but told me she would also look for me at the party." Conroy stared ahead at nothing, reliving those moments. "King, I still think about that girl. It's weird though—I don't know what happened to her—"

"So, you did or did not see her at the party?"

Conroy chuckled. "Am I on trial?"

"Almost," said King, "please answer." He wiped the sweat from his forehead with a napkin from the bar.

Conroy continued, nearly whispering, "I was in the Karaoke barn and saw Gayla; she was gorgeous as usual. All I could think about was being alone with her, so I told the pack of guys I was with to look for her. When they left the barn, I found her, grabbed her hand, and she led me to where those hay bales were all stacked around. She was my first love—I mean it, King."

"So, you were intimate with Gayla?"

Looking down at the bar, Conroy said, "Yes, we had sex. I was like a dog in heat around her. The worst part, though, is Gayla disappeared. I went to her house, and a short guy answered the door and said she had gone to live with her father. Her phone number stopped working. The bottom line is, she dumped me." Conroy's shoulders slumped.

"Why did you leave her there by the barn?"

Conroy looked surprised. "We heard you out there yelling and saw you were spinning around with the flashlight, and Gayla told me to leave before we were both caught. I didn't want to, but she begged me to go. That moment was my biggest regret because I never saw her again. I called, and I even wrote her letters—"

"Wow, Yeah, I understand the regret, Conroy. I'm sorry for you, man, but Gayla never left."

"What?"

"She stayed right here in Hallsville. Fooling us all." King shook his head.

Conroy asked, "But…why?"

"That is the mystery. I do not know how Gayla did what she did because her mother is a single mom, her father is MIA, and her twin brother is a brick short of a load. He is likely the one who told you Gayla went to live with her father." King pulled out his phone, produced a baby photo of Gary, and showed Conroy. "Look familiar?"

Speechless, Conroy held the phone and stared at the incredible likeness to his baby pictures. "No—way—But—why?"

"He's a nice kid, Conroy. Not only did Gayla finish high school, but she also went to college while raising this kid and then

Vet school—she has no student loans, which is odd. She is the managing vet of Whitehouse Animal Clinic. I know that her mother was behind on property taxes for a while—must have found a windfall."

"I have a son." Pain etched Conroy's face. He asked quietly, "King, are you guys an item or something?"

"No! Not at all. I know her—she doesn't live far, Conroy, as you know. Gayla is not my type at all. I wish I could understand why, years ago, she thought I was her type. Something is missing from this picture, don't you think?"

"Absolutely! How did she pull all that off?"

King replied, "I don't know."

Conroy quietly processed King's words. "Hmm. Listen, King. I have a weird feeling about this," he admitted and stood up. "Bud—thanks. I'll be in touch."

King watched Conroy practically skip out of the bar.

Andrew sipped his fourth cup of coffee and slowly raised the old window roller shade. He spied through antique crocheted curtains as Meagan crossed the parking lot and entered the house from the service entrance of the B&B. Quickly, he set his coffee cup on the nightstand in his room and hurried downstairs, seizing the opportunity to talk to her.

"Oh, hi," Meagan said, stiffening.

"Mom told me that you were married," Andrew disclosed. "How old were you when you married?"

Her forehead creased. "Um, I was eighteen. Paxton died seventeen months ago—if that was your next question."

Andrew poked his chest out and proclaimed, "I would like to take you out to dinner."

Meagan started to make her way past Andrew and up the stairs. "Let me think about it, okay? I need to help Aunt Agnes."

"Oh, right. Okay."

Aunt Agnes laid the law down the day after Meagan moved into the B&B with a hearty rent discount. "Mr. Willoughby only cooks, so you can help me clean this place." Since Meagan was out of options and doomed to scour, she embraced it. She found dusting, vacuuming, wiping windows, and power washing the walks and patio—cathartic. Everything deserved a fresh start, in her estimation. Life at the B&B was illuminating; the more Meagan helped and understood the business, the more respect she felt toward Aunt Agnes and Mr. Willoughby.

Being on call twenty-four hours a day took incredible dedication. Mr. Willoughby and Agnes did it all; they booked stayovers, cooked like chefs, cleaned, and were gracious hosts to guests from near and afar. They had befriended hundreds of people over the years. Successfully managing a bed and breakfast required forfeiting privacy, something Meagan could never give up. She was content helping the elderly couple and staying out of the limelight.

By nature, Aunt Agnes was not a quiet person, nor was she complimentary. Recently, she had begun smiling at Meagan, which caused the latter some anxiety.

After checking the appointment book, Meagan dusted and vacuumed each unoccupied room; she headed to the kitchen for a bottle of water and gulped it down. Mr. Willoughby was preparing a beautiful Italian spaghetti dinner, including homemade garlic rolls.

"Smells great in here," noted Meagan.

"You can toss that salad, dear," said Aunt Agnes, holding the tongs. "I need to check on my Tiramisu."

"Sure," said Meagan. "I thought you didn't cook?" She added oil to the salad and tossed it before scooping portions onto salad plates, covering them with plastic wrap, and putting them in the fridge.

Aunt Agnes smiled. "A woman must keep up the practice. Right, Mr. Willoughby?"

"Yes, dear." Mr. Willoughby then asked Meagan, "Did you cook when you were young?" The steam fogged his glasses as he drained the spaghetti water into the sink.

"Not really. I was mostly daddy's girl, and outdoor activities were preferred. But when I lived with the Richards, cooking wasn't a priority. We ate out a lot, had take-out, and ate soup and sandwiches once a week. I found a delicious recipe a few times, cooked it for the Richards, and surprised them."

Aunt Agnes piped up, "That was a thoughtful thing to do. Why didn't you do it more?"

"Because I love music, and there is only so much time in a day." She smiled at her aunt.

Mr. Willoughby stopped to look at Meagan. "Do you play an instrument?"

"Guitar."

My beautiful guitar, which I will find—soon.

"I always thought the piano was a lady's instrument—it's so elegant, right Mr. Willoughby?" Agnes said. "Especially when they hit all the right notes."

"Yes, the piano can be elegant, dear. Are we ready to serve?"

Aunt Agnes peered through the swinging doors' slats that separated the kitchen from the dining room. "The table is set, and the guests are all here. Oh, I do hope they will like my dessert."

"They will," assured Mr. Willoughby.

Meagan helped serve the meal and listened to the banter of a young couple from Wisconsin. They raved to Aunt Agnes about the dinner and shared their desire to start a family. Across the table from the couple sat three sisters from a neighboring state, visiting the town to bury their mother's ashes at Hallsville Cemetery and celebrate her life. Andrew sat at the head of the table, focusing on his cell phone. Opposite Andrew, at the other end of the table, was a traveling businessman from India looking to experience a B&B and bring his family here one day.

When the guests had finished their entrees and raved sufficiently over the beautiful Tiramisu, Aunt Agnes encouraged her guests to enjoy coffee on the front veranda. Meagan collected the dishes and expeditiously cleared the table in anticipation of her Sell-City meeting.

She ran to her room, quickly showered, threw on sweats, and methodically applied her makeup to the extreme. She rolled up her military ensemble, including boots, shoved them into a bag, and then set out on her quest.

Hours earlier, the sun had dropped out of sight, and Meagan was a mile from her destination. In a decrepit gas station bathroom, she changed into her disguise and texted the seller of her TV that she was nearby.

"We're already here," they responded.

She wore military pants, boots, a tactical jacket, clothing she had sported for recovering her guns, and then Grandma Pearl's necklace from King's Pawn. Her hair, pulled tightly back, was hidden under Paxton's black ball cap instead of the knit cap she had sweated profusely in when she thought she was going to jail.

At the meeting spot, two men stood waiting by a Chevy van. Meagan sized up the surrounding area until she could safely make a move with no witnesses. Finally, the coast was clear.

The truck's brakes squeaked when she backed it up to the van.

"You military?" asked the taller of the two sellers.

"Yes, I just got back. How about you?"

"Not us. That shit is cap."

Her hands shoved deep into her pockets Meagan asked, "Can I see the TV and equipment?" A brief examination proved the equipment was hers. "It looks right. Does it work?"

The shorter of the two men replied, "Yes, it works. We wouldn't sell busted equipment."

Meagan shrugged and innocently asked, "Okay, I believe you, but I can't carry it; it looks too heavy for me, and I'm not sure it will fit in my truck."

"We'll help you," said the tall one. "I think it will fit."

They transferred the TV to the bed of Meagan's truck while she hauled the surround sound components and set them in the back seat. In a minute, her vehicle was laden. She slammed the tailgate in place and turned her gun on the two men. "Get the hell out of here before I shoot both of you for trying to sell stolen merchandise!"

"You bitch!" the tall one spat and attempted a front kick. Meagan pulled the trigger, putting a bullet in the bottom of his outstretched foot.

"What the hell! Jay, get me out of here," he yelled while hopping around the parking lot. "Oh my god! She freaking shot me!" He wailed.

The shorter man ran to his friend's side, helped him into their van, then ran around and hopped in the driver's side while Meagan kept her gun trained on them.

"I'm gonna find you," the wounded man screamed, flipping his middle finger and speeding away.

Shaking from the altercation, she settled into the driver's seat, wiped away tears, and drove to the B&B with her TV and sound system. The sun had vanished over the horizon; an occasional streetlight cast a greenish glow. Meagan removed her baseball cap and glasses. She uncrumpled a store receipt from the truck console and used it to rub off the brownish lipstick.

Blanchard Avenue, lined with vast-canopied oak trees, branches waving in the breeze, welcomed Meagan home to the B&B. The driveway was difficult to see at night, but Meagan had learned the narrow turn-in was ten feet from a neon yellow fire hydrant. Aunt Agnes introduced her to that fire hydrant the first day she visited the house. "You'll be the one picking up the dog droppings around the yard, and there is usually a concentration here," she had said, pointing to the shiny hydrant. "Will that be a problem?"

"Poop patrol is not a problem," Meagan had assured her, "I appreciate the reduction on rent."

A single lace-fringed lamp spilled golden light atop the player piano, visible through the living room window of the Willoughby's business. Meagan crept the truck up the driveway and around to the back of the house, where Andrew had just closed his Jeep door. He waved and waited for her to park.

"I could use a hand moving my TV," she said, pointing to the truck bed.

Andrew approached to take a look. "That is a huge TV!" he remarked. "I'll help you if you will have dinner with me."

There was a long pause as Meagan seemed to be weighing her options. "Okay," she agreed, opening the tailgate.

"Why are you dressed like that? Are you in the military? Where did you get this TV?" Andrew pressed.

She leaned against the truck. "No, I'm not in the military. I got robbed not long ago, and they stole most of my clothes." Waving her hand across her torso, she continued, "This is all I have from my husband. The TV is from a warehouse I rent."

"Oh, okay. Yeah, let me help you carry this stuff to your room."

Three trips up and down the stairs, and Meagan's entire TV system was in her room. Andrew checked the time on his phone. "That took thirty minutes." Casually strolling around her suite, he added, "Nice room!"

Meagan sat down on the burgundy crushed velvet tufted bench at the foot of the antique bed and pulled off Paxton's boots. She stretched her toes and then curled them under, causing several toe joints to pop.

"That will give you arthritis in your toes, then your shoes won't fit," Andrew informed her, then grabbed the crystal doorknob of the massive armoire—

"Please don't—"

He ignored her plea, and Meagan observed Andrew taking inventory of the clothes in her closet.

"Why don't you have any clothes, I mean dresses?"

"If you don't mind. I am not a 'dress' person." Moving toward her monstrous television, she added, "I'm a TV person."

Andrew looked her directly in the eyes. "Hmm."

Six feet tall and skinny, Andrew's legs looked unusually long in his tight, flat Chinos. In three steps, he was across the room, his face inches from hers. "I'd be happy to watch TV with you. Just call me."

He held up a business card. Meagan took it and set it on the old hall tree shelf beside the door. At close range, Meagan saw the pockmarked acne scars that littered his face and the tip of a linear scar on his forehead. When he glanced down momentarily, she noticed the line was neat, like an incision, and snaked at least eight inches into his thick, brown hairline.

She lifted a finger to point at it. "Did you have surgery?"

"Ah, I was having headaches. Now they're gone. It was a long time ago."

Andrew moved closer to her, stuck his neck out, and tilted his head, preparing to kiss her. Meagan's eyes bugged out as she realized his intent. He puckered his full lips, and she quickly sidestepped closer to her bedroom door and held it open.

"I'm tired. Thanks for your help. You're quite strong!" Meagan said.

Andrew set his hand on her shoulder. "I could say the same thing about you. Anytime you need help, let me know. How about I take you to dinner this weekend?"

If he had just said something, Meagan did not hear it. Her mind was on the pawn shop she would visit tomorrow to resume hunting.

Andrew squeezed her shoulder to get a response. "Hello?"

Meagan shook her head. "Oh, okay, text me. I'm exhausted," she said, leaning against the open door with her eyes closed.

"Okay, g'night."

Meagan watched Andrew stride down the hall past the communal bathroom before disappearing to the left. The staircase was an echo chamber for his skillful whistling until it faded away, and she closed the door.

Her phone buzzed with a text from Rhonda, "I'm here! Are you ready to go?"

"OMG. I forgot! Be there in five," Meagan texted back. Swiftly, she kicked off her fatigues and slipped on old jeans and a flattering red swing top. Her overdone makeup would have to do. She spritzed her favorite Orchid body spray on and dashed out the door.

Rhonda turned down the music blasting from her car stereo when she saw her friend approaching the car. "Meagan? You look fabulous! I'm glad you started wearing more makeup. Get in, girl! Let's go have some fun!"

"Thanks."

Meagan walked around to the passenger side and slipped into the compact car. "I can't stay out too late. I have things to do tomorrow," Meagan confessed, pushing her hair away from her face.

Rhonda laughed and explained, "Yeah, yeah, yeah. My mom is babysitting Alex, so I'm free and ready for The Electric Panda."

Meagan shivered and stared out the window into the darkness. "No worries, sis, I'll be your designated driver."

Andrew pushed the window roller shade aside, enough to see Meagan sprinting to a car. "Tired? Hmm, right." He gritted his teeth and swirled the ice cubes in his Old Fashioned.

Many women had lied to him but weren't his cousin—however distant. He expected a bit more courtesy from a relative. She is wrong if she thinks she is the only woman I want. Aside from the apparent fact Meagan had model-worthy looks, he could not fathom why his father was so adamant he should date Meagan; she seemed like too much effort.

"Son, a woman like Meagan is hard to come by. You have no idea what you'd be missing if you don't go after her," Mr. Willoughby had advised before reaching into his shirt breast pocket. "I want you to have this silver pocket watch to mark this pact between us." They had shaken hands to seal the understanding.

Still agitated by Meagan getting whisked away earlier that evening, Andrew pushed his head severely to one side and then the other before the vertebrae in his spine popped.

His thoughts wandered from his tough cousin to Justina—the lovely gothic checker from the Piggly Wiggly. He had taken her on a date twice, and each time caused him to have more questions about her. She was a mystery with a raspy voice and silky hands. He knew very little about her because Justina wanted it that way.

"You may think I'm secretive, but I'm not. I hate talking. You should try it," Justina had informed Andrew, kissing him hard on the neck.

Oh, Justina! Now, she's a real woman.

He dialed her number, and when all he could hear was breathing on the other end, he knew it was his speechless Justina, so he asked her to meet him in an hour, and she agreed.

Chapter Nine

Jack's Pawn opened precisely at ten AM, as specified on their website. This shop was older, Meagan presumed, based on the sheer amount of inventory sandwiched everywhere. It would take years to go through everything. Suddenly, she worried her family treasures might be buried somewhere in there. There was a path to follow through the store; it was one-way and wide enough for only one person to pass at a time. A feeling of impending doom fell on her. Silently, she begged the god of possessions to keep hers safe.

"Can I help you?"

"Yes, Mr. ah, Lee?" she asked, noting his nametag. "I'm looking for a cameo necklace with a gold chain, a Ruby Rose brooch, a silver pocket watch, an amber ring, and an opal ribbon choker. Got any of them?"

As the petite Chinese man studied the jewelry on his counter, Meagan searched, also. None of her gems were there.

"Wait a minute!" said Mr. Lee, digging his hand in his pocket. "Ah, yes," he confirmed, reading the note King left. "Mr. Pullman buy it, so it at King Pawn. Maybe you buy for a girl?"

"Yes, ah, no, I am a girl. King's Pawn?" Meagan said.

Mr. Lee wore an apologetic but bewildered look. A hot flash darkened Meagan's vision momentarily while processing the information. She couldn't help it. She had to know if this Mr. Pullman was the man she had robbed. "Do I know him? What does he look like…the man who bought the cameo necklace?"

Please, God, don't be him.

The manager smiled. "He tall, spike hair, beard, and…"

"…mean?" Meagan finished. She felt her cheeks reddening at the thought that he was indeed the same man she had held at gunpoint.

"No! He is not mean. Mr. Pullman, good man." Mr. Lee scowled. "Nobody say that before. You go to King Pawn and find a necklace." He shooed her out of the shop, irritated that someone would comment negatively about Mr. Pullman. He was surprised she did not have glowing words or romantic designs on the dashing man, as most women did. But instead, she seemed disgusted with him. That was a first.

"Thanks." She sighed.

"Sure, you go now," he urged.

In the quiet of her truck, she wondered why the man she held a gun to, who called the police on her and then gave her the pearls, would buy her cameo. She decided whatever his reasoning was, it was screwed up, and she intended to give him a piece of her mind when she got to his shop.

He wasn't there. Back in her truck, she reviewed the facts: The cameo necklace was at Jack's Pawn, but that bearded man she retrieved her pearls from went and bought it. Okay, then it should be at this shop because he would want to sell it—unless he doesn't want to sell it, in which case the necklace would be with him—at his house.

Don't worry, Aunt Camille—I'll get it back.

On her phone, she googled the property tax office and located multiple properties owned by people with the last name of Pullman. Recon would begin with the first name on the list immediately after B&B chores and dinner.

Agnes Willoughby stood on the small back porch, hands on her hips. "Young Lady, why are you dressed like that, and where have you been? Today is a cleaning day!"

"I had to run errands, and these clothes are comfortable. I'll pick up dog poop and then vacuum. Agnes watched as Meagan tucked her t-shirt into the camo pants and shook off the oversized jacket. "And what's wrong with your face?"

Meagan had rubbed most of her 'robber' makeup off while in the truck. "I'm trying to be better about wearing makeup more often."

"I see," Agnes said, "here." She handed Meagan a bucket and a squeegee. "The windows need doing while you're out here."

The back door of the house flung open, and Andrew strode out. Agnes's face brightened. "Oh, hello, Andrew!"

"Hi, Mom," Andrew replied. "Well, soldier, late night last night?" He smirked at Meagan.

"A huh," Meagan said, noticing something stuck in his teeth. She imagined it was a piece of spinach left over from lunch. While planning the next step of the exhausting search for her family and how she would recover them, she forgot to eat. Time had evaporated that morning, and now hunger scratched at her insides, begging for a salad.

"Time to work!" Meagan said and turned away from mother and son. The quiet of her mind was comforting; time to dream of reclaiming her cameo, which she was positive the big man possessed.

"You'll need this," Andrew said, maneuvering a sixteen-foot ladder to the side of the house. "I'll do the third-floor windows."

"Okay, thanks," Meagan said, dropping her wet rag, followed by the squeegee, into the bucket of water; the first-floor windows on the back of the house were clean. She climbed the ladder to the second floor, bucket in one hand, while Andrew watched.

"When did window-washing become a spectator sport?" she asked.

"Since I need the ladder to get to the third-floor windows when you're through. Where did you go last night?"

"I forgot I promised a friend I would go out with her."

"Right," Andrew said, rolling his eyes.

When all eight second-floor windows across the back were clean, Meagan climbed down the ladder cautiously for the last time and faced Andrew.

"Here you go! Thanks for volunteering to do the third floor. I appreciate it," she said, handing him the cleaning supplies.

"Wow, you smiled! You look like a different person."

Meagan disregarded his comment. It was time for vacuuming and then poop patrol. The quicker she could complete these tasks, the faster she would be in the kitchen to help Mr. Willoughby cook a dinner of Salmon and wild rice and whatever side dishes he dreamed up. Her mouth began to water.

The dinner guests were as complimentary of the food as ever, and several asked for the recipe. Mr. Willoughby was possessive of that information, so Meagan disclosed nothing. A lesbian couple from Indiana provided entertainment during the meal. Meagan stood several feet away from the table as the homosexual women shared how they met in the waiting room of a psychotherapist's office. The retired couple across the table stared at the ladies in fascination, stopping short of asking them how they 'did it.' Meagan began bussing the table for Aunt Agnes. The elderly gentleman gently coaxed his curious wife away from the dining room with the suggestion of a stroll before dessert.

The moment the sun disappeared Meagan set her plan in motion. First, she would walk the half-mile to the corner gas station to catch the cab she had called earlier—her truck must not be visible near the Pullman place.

I wouldn't need to pay cab fare if the slimy thieves who ripped my life apart hadn't also stolen my bike.

Paxton was in Afghanistan when Meagan's old car died, requiring one thousand dollars' worth of work, which they did not have, to resurrect. Refusing to risk a long-distance argument by driving his truck, Meagan bought a used bike for twenty-five dollars at a garage sale on her street and began riding it to work. Even after

Paxton's death, she did not drive his truck without a push from Rhonda.

"Come out here," Rhonda had ordered, pulling Meagan by the arm to the driveway. "I saw this and thought of you." She pointed to a sparkling bumper sticker she had affixed to the back window of Pax's truck. It read, 'Girls love trucks too.'

Meagan stood frozen, staring. "Thanks."

"Will you please stop riding that stupid bike? It's dangerous. The truck is yours now," Rhonda pleaded.

"You're right," Meagan said. "I will drive the truck. There. Are you happy?" She straightened herself and apologized to Paxton in her mind, then drove that truck everywhere.

The cab fare to the crossroads near Pullman's ranch was twenty dollars, which Meagan had to scrounge for. She had done a happy dance when she found an old ten-dollar bill folded into a tiny square in the pocket of Paxton's jeans. She began rooting for money in all his clothes and discovered Paxton had numerous hiding places.

"Perfect. Stop here," Meagan said.

Wide-eyed, the cab driver looked around the surrounding fields and warned, "Lady, it's dark, and I don't think you should be walking around here. What are you gonna do if a coyote comes? I'll charge you half-fare to take you back to town right now."

"I'm good, thanks," she responded confidently, stuffing the fare and a small tip into his outstretched hand.

He persisted, "At least let me take you to that house?" He pointed down the road. "Isn't that where you need to go?"

Meagan stepped out of the cab and thought for a moment. "I'm not sure. I am searching for something—I don't want to intrude on anyone—I am fine."

"Suit yourself." He rolled up his window and executed a U-turn on the gravel road.

Standing in the middle of the county road, Meagan inhaled deeply; the air was cool and flavored with hay, maples, oaks, and witch hazel. This picturesque ranch, with the barely visible Blue Ridge Mountains in the distance, was an idyllic oil painting that had come to life.

The gravel crunched under her boots as she made the half-mile trek to a Pullman property, needing clarification about exactly whose home she would be spying on.

Meagan approached the lone, long ranch house; an extensive, half-built second-story addition sprouted up from the center of the home. She picked up her pace and sprinted across the property, keeping on the grass and avoiding the dirt and gravel driveway. No lights shone from inside; the place looked desolate.

Paxton's comfortable, dark canvas camouflage pants made stealthy snooping around easy. The dark ball cap she sported had a connected sheet of black nylon fabric that covered her ears and hung past her neck, concealing her light hair. Paxton wore it often to keep the sun off his neck when he mowed the grass. The hat still smelled like him.

A horse whinnied in the distance, and several far-off dogs barked. Pipe fencing surrounded acres of meadow desperately in need of grazing or mowing. Meagan moved around to the side of the house, where she noticed a jacked-up truck parked next to a gold SUV outside a three-car detached garage. Past the spacious garage, she felt the remoteness of this place. Aside from the house and several barns, the property appeared to go on for miles. Meagan squatted down behind a rock-encased barbeque under an arbor behind the house.

From this spot, she could see the activity inside the well-lit kitchen of Pullman's house. A woman, likely in her thirties, wearing a t-shirt and sweatpants, appeared to be searching for something. Meagan observed the woman whip her long hair into a messy bun on top of her head before pouring two tall glasses of beer. A muscular man entered the room with only a towel around his waist. He raked his hands through his wet hair. His body language indicated he was exhausted.

It's him! The pawn man.

The tension in the room was evident, which Meagan was not a stranger to.

He watched the woman, then she turned to him, and it seemed there was a standoff. The discord between them was evident: he wants her to leave—she wants him to have a drink—he wins—she guzzles the beer and marches out. The broad-shouldered man left the room and returned wearing sweatpants and a hoodie. Meagan squinted but could not make out the writing on the jacket. He rinsed the beer bottles, disposed of them, then rinsed her glass and set it in the sink.

Meagan heard him whistle loudly, and, in a flash, the dog rushed to his side—confirming beyond any doubt that she was at the right place. The golden-faced German Shepherd had been the variable in her attempted robbery-gone-gift episode involving the man she was spying on that very minute.

I held a gun to his head. I should have brought dog treats to this stakeout. Stick to the plan—why did this guy take my cameo necklace? I need to get inside that house. I know it's in there.

The man picked up his glass of beer, tapped the light switch off, and left the kitchen.

A light snapped on in another first-floor room, and the man sat in a wide leather chair. Through wall-height windows across the back of this living room, Meagan saw the man recline the chair and flip open a laptop as the dog curled up on the floor next to the chair. The vertical stripes on the man's pants caused his legs to appear disproportionately long.

Fortunately, the weather cooperated with her investigation. Meagan tiptoed from the outdoor kitchen to the house and stopped short beside the living room windows when the German Shepherd growled. From this new vantage point, with the compact binoculars she had remembered to bring, she could see that Pullman was intently researching something about Comas.

Comas?

Occasionally, Pullman would say something causing the dog's prominent black eyebrows to move oddly. Meagan snickered.

Who protects whom?

The dog prompted the man to close his computer and set it aside. As they left the room, he scratched and petted the dog's head, then the lights went out.

Meagan scurried backward to a cluster of shrubs edging the perimeter of a stone-terraced fire pit surrounded by half a dozen Adirondack chairs. The evergreen shrubs provided an ideal cover for her caper. She waited.

So peaceful out here. To sit in one of these chairs and stare into a blazing fire would be heavenly.

Lights in the next room at the back of the house snapped on. The Holly Bush leaves jabbed her side as she jockeyed for a comfortable position to continue secretly watching the man in his home. There were no blinds or window coverings of any kind.

How can someone care so little about their privacy...asks the woman who is grateful this guy has no window coverings!

Everything outside his windows to the man inside the house was a universal blur with a coating of iridescence thanks to the moon. Conversely, for Meagan, spying on this man had fast become something akin to a dramatic play, and the intrigue was addictive.

The dog curled up by the bed while Pullman went into his bathroom for what seemed like an hour. The well-lit room was dark grey, spacious, and sparsely furnished; taxidermized hunting trophies adorned the walls.

Meagan sat on a slatted wooden ottoman to wait and watch for the bathroom door to open. Then she heard a car door slam and an engine roar to life.

It must be the woman from the kitchen—she's finally leaving.

He emerged from his bathroom, wearing only boxer briefs and holding a load of laundry which he deposited in another room. She focused her binoculars on the boxers' fabric and snickered—*Scooby-Doo!*

Re-entering the bedroom, he turned off the ceiling light, walked up to the plate glass window, and stared out. Meagan fell off the side of the ottoman and lay flat on the ground, grabbing her flashlight as it rolled from her pocket. She stayed like a statue—still peeking between the base of the shrubs. A subtle light gave Pullman a freakishly shadowed appearance as though in a horror movie. He seemed to look right at Meagan, but she did not avert her gaze.

He returned to the bathroom, removed something from a drawer, walked to his bed, and sat down.

Again, she peered through the binoculars, and in the dim light of the lamp on his bedside table, she witnessed him letting the chain with the cameo pendant dangle from his fingers.

Meagan sucked in a breath; her hand shot up to cover her mouth, and she dropped the binoculars and then scrambled for them. He slid a paper out of the night table drawer, then lay down against a pile of pillows and studied it, rubbing his temples. She focused on him again.

What? My photo too? You weirdo! What are you up to with my things?

Meagan felt her pulse quicken and her world tilt. There were bad guys and good guys, and they were easily identifiable, which kept life in balance, but this guy—Pullman—was straddling the line, which was unacceptable. She should have put more thought into the details of the evening's escapade; she was tired, sleeping outside was not her favorite, and she hadn't even brought a bedroll.

The only way I leave this property is with my cameo necklace—and the photo.

The German Shepherd hopped up on the vacant side of the bed and rested his massive head on Pullman's lap. The dog's golden eyebrows danced again as his big brown eyes focused on his master's face when Pullman spoke to him.

When the bedside light went out, and Meagan felt confident Pullman was asleep, she crept over to the windowless, detached garage seeking an entry point. Only the jacked-up gray truck remained parked in front of the building. The gold SUV was gone.

She checked the door on the side and found it unlocked. With her flashlight, she could discern two vehicles and a work area designed for someone knowledgeable about cars. What could have been a third garage bay had been transformed into a crude office with a dorm fridge and bathroom.

She moved into the makeshift office and discovered a cot covered with a sleeping bag. Jackpot! A well-worn desk in the corner of the space was disorganized, littered with papers and various small car parts. A greasy cordless phone sat near the edge. Meagan picked it up, pressed the green button, and discovered it worked. She beat the dust and cobwebs from the bedding and climbed into the heavy-duty sleeping bag. A strong scent of Old Spice and body odor assaulted her. Focusing on her cameo necklace and the photo, she fell asleep remembering the faces of the people who loved her.

Chapter Ten

"Anita, where is Dad?"

"Hi, Conroy. I didn't see you come in. Will you be here for breakfast?"

Hands on his hips, Conroy looked into the eyes of his family's beloved cook and childhood caretaker as she chopped vegetables for a quiche.

"Sit down, sweetie. Something on your mind? I recognize that look."

"I'm good. Where is Dad?"

Anita chuckled. "He is in the gym working out."

"Wow. That's new."

Still smiling, she responded, "Yes. I think it is a blood pressure thing. Your mother is at a bible study," she paused. "What you have done for this family, Conroy—it is a good thing."

Conroy glanced down at the brick floor. "God did it, not me. Well, I can't stay for breakfast. Just thought I would pop in for a sec and chat with Mom and Dad."

"Gimme a hug, Connie," Anita said, reaching for him.

He hugged her, and in moments he was out of the house and in his Porsche, staring at the photo of Gary that King had texted him and rubbing his forehead—*my son.*

As Conroy had been sorting through the events of the party years before, he considered what King had shared about Gayla's life. He vacillated between confronting Gayla and having a face-to-face with his parents and, in the end, decided a talk with his parents would be the best course of action, but since neither of them was home, that solved that. Setting his phone on the car dash, Conroy prayed for peace and guidance. Perhaps he would call his mother tomorrow when he might have the right words and discuss 'the mess.'

He drove to a rent-a-car business, parked the Porsche, and moments later was driving a Chevy Tahoe down the road to Whitehouse Veterinary Clinic for a glimpse into Gayla's life.

King was up before the sun. His sidekick, Storm, paced the front acreage taking care of his morning business. King's phone rang; it was Ace's number, but the voice on the other end was not Ace's.

"Your brother screwed me, and I want my money back. Twenty grand by three PM today, or Jack will have an accident too. Bring it to the Chester Park Amphitheater. Use a lunch pail and be there on time and alone. I'll be calling you again," the breathy anonymous caller said.

"What have you done to Ace?" King demanded.

"He's alive if that's what you want to know," the caller said before ending the call.

"Storm," King said, letting the dog back in the house, "we've got problems."

Mechanically, he called Ace's number back. No answer. Hands shaking, King accelerated his morning routine with nonstop thoughts of Ace's safety while contemplating the caller's orders and possible options.

He dressed quickly, a plaid button-down, a pair of old jeans, and a favorite pair of cowboy boots. The supple black leather jacket was a college graduation gift from Gayla. He had told her he couldn't accept it, but she had insisted.

King stood in the driveway beside his truck, on his phone. "Ace, pick up! Come on, Bud, answer your phone!"

Hearing the pawn man shouting in the driveway, Meagan woke, jumped off the cot, and scrambled to the garage door. With her face pressed against a small crack between the garage door and the wall, she could track the activity outside where the shepherd was sniffing the air.

The gold SUV from the night before veered into the driveway and parked next to Pullman's truck. Pullman ended the phone call and immediately dialed another number. "Hey, Dad, where are you?" Pause. "Okay, I'll pick you up in fifteen minutes."

Meagan saw the woman from last night step out of her gold car.

This ought to be interesting.

She rushed to Pullman and demanded, "We need to talk."

Pullman tossed his phone onto the truck seat and turned to her.

"No, Gayla, I have to go." He whistled sharply, and the pointy-eared dog leaped into the truck. King climbed in behind the wheel. "Gayla, we are not talking now." With a disgusted sigh, he slammed the truck door; jaw muscles twitching, he ordered, "Please leave."

The woman screamed and stomped at the truck as it sped from the ranch. "What is your problem!" Her car kicked up gravel as she raced from the property, taking a different direction than Pullman had.

After witnessing the curious drama, Meagan straightened the sleeping bag on the cot and prepared to break into Pullman's house to get her things. She washed up in the small bathroom sink and was drying her face with her shirt sleeve when she heard gravel crunching under car tires. Peeking through the garage crack again, she saw that it was the gold SUV woman.

Why are you back? The suspense is killing me!

In the sunlight, the strange woman appeared rougher; her jeans and boots thin with wear, and her white lab coat hung loosely over a plaid, buttoned-down shirt. She wore heavy, dark eye makeup. Meagan watched the woman scurry toward the front of the house with keys jingling in her hand.

So, you must be the girlfriend.

Meagan hustled out the garage side door and ran toward the firepit, then to the outdoor kitchen to resume spying on the man's life and patiently wait for an opportunity to enter his house illegally. The woman was snooping for something as she poured through the kitchen drawers. Meagan lost sight of her momentarily then the woman reappeared in the living room, where she began searching under cushions and through cabinets.

Gayla threw her arms up in disgust and stormed out of the room only to appear in Pullman's bedroom. Tentatively, she moved toward the bed then buried her head in Pullman's pillow, smelling it; then she walked around the bed to the other side and smelled the other pillow.

Pullman, news flash—your girlfriend is a loon. What the heck! Everything to do with this guy is weird.

Meagan felt a sharp pain stab at her heart as a memory burned in her mind. A time when she stood close to Paxton just to smell him. Suddenly, Meagan understood—Pullman's intruder was in love with him. Try as she might, Meagan could not tear her eyes away and felt sadness for the woman.

After canvassing the bedroom, the woman made a phone call and departed.

Meagan walked around the house's perimeter, looking for a window to breach. All the windows appeared new, and most were sheets of glass—except the side of the house—these windows were about four feet tall and did not open as one would expect. They required hand-cranking from the inside to pivot open, similar to a door. To her delight, one of the three windows in this room was not completely closed. She returned to the garage and searched for anything to wedge into that window crack.

A tire iron!

She left the garage with the crowbar and a bucket to stand on. With the iron worked into the crack, she could push the crank until the opening was sufficient for her to reach her arm in and extend the window the rest of the way. Meagan shimmied in the window and fell on the carpeted floor.

Dusting herself off, she realized she was in a small bedroom and hurried to the door to get her bearings as she had become somewhat familiar with the home's layout. She marched down the hall toward the man's bedroom and shuffled through his nightstand.

What? It has to be here! Stop. Breathe. Think!

A photo of two handsome, clean-shaven men or boys was sitting atop a tall chest of drawers. Meagan recognized one of the men as a younger version of the clerk who sold her back her guns at Ace's Pawn. In the photo, his arm was over the shoulder of the taller man—the man she had held up at gunpoint. Their jeans were faded, and they wore muddy cowboy boots and t-shirts stained from work. There was a lake in the background and horses. The men squinted in the sun, but Meagan saw how they favored each other in their smiles; she knew they were brothers. To be friends and relatives at the same time is the ultimate gift. She thought of Rhonda, smiled, and put the photo back in its place.

Back to business. Where is my necklace? Last night, Mr. Pullman, you took it out of the drawer, along with the photo— Then—You fell asleep!

She ran to the bed and whipped the sheets and covers back, and there it was. Pullman must have fallen asleep and dropped it and the photo. She immediately put the necklace on, tucked the picture in the back pocket of her pants, and remade the man's bed.

Her stomach had been growling for hours when she pranced to Pullman's kitchen and flung the fridge door wide.

Hmm, lots of good stuff in here.

She took a handful of plump, juicy grapes as an appetizer. Pulling the plastic lid off an irresistible leftover noodle dish, she found a spoon and ate some of it cold.

"Pullman, you're a good cook!"

She washed the meal down with a tall glass of milk. Content, for the moment, with the recovery of her cameo necklace and a belly full of food, Meagan was careful to clean and leave the kitchen as she had found it.

Strange and exciting feelings coursed through her; locating her belongings was rewarding. Her family's legacy: the jewels, the artwork, and the electronics, among other things, were her mission, and with each recovery, she felt more emboldened.

In the clear light of day, she noticed a large red barn and sturdy fencing in various places, which meant, at some point, this was a working ranch with areas for different animals. Standing in his living room, gazing out at the ranch's expanse, Meagan began to understand the draw of living remotely. A red-tailed hawk swooped within ten feet of the window and rode the current toward the barn, where it perched atop a weathervane.

It is beautiful and so quiet.

Turning back to the hallway to the room where she had entered, an office faced the front acreage.

He doesn't use this room much.

A clean, sizeable modern desk sat on a large colorful area rug in the center of the room. Meagan studied the bold, thought-provoking geometric pattern on the carpet, then turned her attention to multiple tastefully framed academic awards and degrees gracing the walls; all belonging to Brandon K. Pullman.

"Brandon?" she mumbled and flopped down into his comfortable swivel executive chair, her hands caressing the leather arms.

Maybe you look like a 'Brandon.'

The view across the driveway and gravel road was serene. Fifty yards ahead, cows gathered at a fence; some black, some blonde. Meagan watched them as they moved gracefully along the fence line. A few stopped to poke their heads through the fence railing to sample grass on the other side.

The grass is the same everywhere, so don't stick out your neck!

At that moment, she thought about her mission and how none of her heirlooms would be home if she had not 'stuck her head out.'

Forget I said that cows; try it all!

She had been dawdling in Pullman's house for over four hours when her phone vibrated in her hand, disrupting her quiet contentment. The number was unknown, so she let it go to voice mail. When she listened to the recording moments later, she discovered it was Andrew calling about dinner.

She texted him, "I'm tied up. Another day?"

He replied, "Okay."

A familiar gold SUV turned into the circular driveway and up to the front porch.

Not you again!

Meagan groaned and scrambled for somewhere to hide. Her options were closets or under a bed. She darted down the long hall to the main bedroom, dived to the carpeted floor, and slid under the bed.

The front door opened, followed by resolute footsteps on the hardwood floor. The steps grew quiet, and Meagan knew Pullman's girlfriend had entered the bedroom. She watched the pointy-toed cowboy boots parade around the room and heard the woman speak.

"What do you want?" she sneered into her phone as she removed her clothes. Hopping around on one foot, she pulled off the boots, and soon all her clothes were piled on the floor. She marched naked to the bathroom, still talking on her phone, "That's fine. I hope it works. Your special delivery note did nothing. We need it. Bye." She set the phone on the bathroom counter.

"What are you doing?" Meagan mouthed as the shower roared to life.

I am one hundred percent sure you should not be here! I should leave, but Mr. Pullman's life and this crazy lady are fascinating—

She closed her eyes and fell asleep.

Chapter Eleven

King tried to reach Ace on the phone again.

"Ha— low."

"Oh, thank God. Ace, are you okay?" King asked.

"Yep. Sore—Really, I'm okay."

"Where are you?"

There was a pause, then Ace's voice cracked, "My house. Don't freak out, King."

"Are you sure?"

"Yes, I'm bruised. That's it. Promise."

"Okay. I will drop Storm off at Dad's shop on the way, then I'm coming for you." King put his phone in his jacket pocket and whistled for Storm, who bounded toward him and leaped in the truck. It was time Jack and Mr. Lee had some additional security.

"Thank you for bring Stohm. Everybody love him. Customa too. He a great dog," Mr. Lee said in his charming broken English.

King sighed. The last thing he wanted to hear was that customers loved his dog. "Mr. Lee, no one feeds Storm except you and Jack, got it?"

"Yes, yes, yes. I rememba."

"Have you talked to Dad about the robber?" asked King.

Mr. Lee's eyebrows rose. "Robba? No. We fine."

King told Mr. Lee about the mysterious phone threat he had received earlier. "I'm on my way to check on Ace.

"Fooish people do that to you and you fam-we," said Mr. Lee, "they in for big hurt. Eveyting be fine, Mista King. Stohm good luck. You good family. You see."

"We'll see," said King.

Mr. Lee was a funny old gentleman who sometimes oozed wisdom like he did today.

Everything be fine, Mr. King. Storm good luck. You good family. You see.

A sense of calm came over King as he drove to Ace's house.

It was quiet. The front door was ajar; the door frame was split. Whoever did this had kicked their way in. "Ace? Ace? Where are you?" King's heart began to pound in his temples.

A groan came from the living room. Ace was lying on the floor with his face bloodied. He appeared semi-conscious. King checked his brother's neck for a pulse, and it was strong.

"Let's go," King ordered. Propping Ace up, King led him to the truck and helped him inside. "I'm not exactly sure how, but we've got to fix this."

"I'm…fine…" whined Ace. "I just hurt like hell. Please don't…take me to…the hospital."

"What? Seriously? What if you've got something broken?"

Ace shook his head, 'no.' "I'm just…bruised. I need a drink and sleep. You should see the other guy."

"Funny. If you're sure…" King had been driving to the hospital. After listening to Ace, he turned the truck around and headed home to the ranch.

There was Gayla's car in his driveway. "Damn!" he said, "She's here again."

He lugged Ace into the house and to the sofa, where he removed his brother's boots. Ace roused and winced in pain as King cleaned and bandaged the cuts on his face.

"Take this," King ordered, handing Ace two pills and a glass of water. "This will help you rest. We'll talk when you wake up."

Meagan woke to heavy footsteps approaching the bedroom, her pulse pounding in her ears.

Oh, God. This is terrible. I wish I had left when cuckoo woman was in the shower.

She buried her face in the carpet.

"Gayla? What are you doing here?" King said. He stood unmoving.

Meagan rolled her eyes. *No kidding!*

Gayla emerged from the bathroom; hands planted firmly on her hips. "You're home early. I'm not even in bed yet," she purred.

Gross. Meagan assumed Gayla was naked, though her view of the couple was limited to the knees down. As Gayla advanced toward Mr. Pullman, he backed up.

"I could use some money," she confessed. "Mamma's bills are high. I thought you might help me again, King."

Wow. Poor woman selling herself out like that. She's using sex as a tool on the man. Who am I to talk—I held a gun to his head, broke into his house, and now I'm a freaking peeping tom! Please, God, wherever you are—keep me out of jail.

"Gayla, why are you not at work right now? You have a business to run."

Meagan blinked hard to clear her vision but saw tracks on the back of the woman's legs.

She's a drug user? I don't know anything about Pullman, but I'd bet he's not involved in drugs.

"What are you implying?" demanded Gayla.

"I'm saying that if you paid attention to your business, you wouldn't need to ask me for money. I have plenty of issues with my own family right now. I'm sorry, but—I can't help you."

Wow. That's pretty clear!

Gayla continued, "We're family, for Christ's sake. Just sell something! Aren't I worth it?" she shouted, slapped his arm hard, and then launched onto the bed. "I'm not leaving, King. I need you right here beside me." She patted the bed.

Oh, no.

"You need to go. Now," he said.

Yes, please.

Mr. Pullman left the room. Gayla shouted as she stomped to the bathroom, 'You're making a mistake!" In a few moments, she emerged fully dressed and sat down to pull on her boots. Meagan watched Gayla slide open one of two ceiling-height mirrored closet doors, causing a velvet ring box to fall on the carpet. She quickly picked it up, closed the door, and exited the room.

How screwed up is this guy's life? He works at a pawn shop all day and comes home to this.

Meagan couldn't fathom the thought of yelling at Paxton. Her emotionally empty roller-coaster, ten-year life with Paxton seemed peaceful next to the melodrama she had just witnessed. The regular boxing matches Paxton insisted on had been for her benefit, so he claimed. The day she inadvertently clocked him with a right hook that sent him sailing to the mat, something changed in her; she had tasted physical power for the first time. Paxton changed, too; he became more and more emotionally closed off. Then his unit was called back to Afghanistan, where his life was taken.

He had anger issues, but at least Paxton never did drugs.

Gayla ran down the hall to the living room, where she saw Ace on the sofa, his face littered with bandages.

"You weren't kidding, King," Gayla shouted, "You have family issues. Good luck. Call me if you want some action. You know I love you."

There was no response from King; the front door slammed shut. Meagan smelled something delicious.

He must be cooking.

She considered bolting out from under Pullman's bed and hiding somewhere else until she heard his footsteps coming down the hall. He was talking on his phone.

"Dad," he warned, "I want you to be careful. Ace has some guy pissed off, and he is threatening our family."

On the speakerphone, Meagan could hear the response. "What the hell! Do you have the details?

King answered, "No, but I will get answers when Ace comes to. "Any sign of the son-of-a-bitch in military garb?"

Meagan shivered. *Oh no.*

"I haven't seen him, son. I will let you know if the scum bag has the balls to show up in my shop. I don't mind spilling a little lead protecting what's mine."

"Thanks, Dad, but please—no gunshots."

Meagan was perspiring profusely.

Me, an outlaw! Her vision was spotty. *This must be what it feels like to have your face plastered on a 'wanted' poster in the town police station.*

A piercing timer bell summoned Mr. Pullman to the kitchen, allowing Meagan to shimmy out from under the bed and run to the bathroom to relieve herself—no flushing, however, as that might attract attention. She took in the sterile atmosphere of the master bathroom, white towels, white shower, and white floor tile. Her fingers feathered across the white marble countertops on her way back into the bedroom.

Mr. Pullman was rattling utensils in the kitchen. Meagan looked toward the bed and hid in the sliding doors closet. Wedging herself back six feet between heavy men's clothes, suitcases, and boxes, she slowly slid the door shut. The closet was deeper and wider than it looked at first. A sliver of light reflected off something metal nearby, a built-in gun safe. With her small flashlight, she peeked around. Through the glass, she examined the polished rifles. Her knowledge of guns did not extend beyond handguns, but she recognized the quality. Lifting the lid off a box like the one she was sitting on, she discovered scads of paperback books. Snickering, she read the covers: Only You, Sleeping with the Prince, A Lady for the Duke, and Spice up Your Marriage in Three Easy Steps.

Perhaps these books belong to Gayla, the slapper?

Meagan selected a Western romance and began reading by flashlight.

King sat at the bar in his kitchen, eating his dinner, and kept an eye on Ace. Gazing out the window to the early evening sun, he romanced the day when cattle would graze the fields again. His daydream was interrupted by thoughts of the people aiming to hurt his family.

He finished his dinner and put a portion of the leftovers in a bowl for Ace when he woke up. When he was done washing the dishes, he checked on the progress of his room addition. He would need some help if the remodel was to be completed before bad weather hit. His phone rang.

"Hi, Mom!" he said, entering his bedroom. "Wow, you're awake! How do you feel? Is Dad there with you?"

Meagan snapped the flashlight off and listened.

"Dad is on his way to you. Well, good. You sound well," he said, "when can you come home?"

After he listened for a while, he said, "I love you, and I'll see you shortly. I'm on my way." Then ended the call.

When King saw that Ace was still sleeping soundly, he left a note for him on the end table next to the sofa and went to visit his mother and father at the hospital.

Now that Ace was safely here with him at the ranch, King knew it was time to inform Jack about the phone call threat for money, which King had ignored today. He had fully expected a phone call from the perpetrators when he did not show up at the Amphitheater earlier, but it had not come—yet.

Chapter Twelve

Based on the fragmented phone conversation she overheard, Meagan surmised Mr. Pullman had gone to visit his parents. The tall door slid open smoothly, and she fumbled out of the closet; her left leg had fallen asleep. Limping down the hall, Meagan stopped short at a bedroom. The door must have been closed earlier, or she surely would have noticed this room—a child's bedroom. Nothing about Mr. Pullman indicated he might be a father; the room seemed an anomaly in this house. The walls were pink and green; a twin sleigh bed sat in the middle of the room next to a baby crib full of stuffed animals. A white rocking chair sat in the corner, worn from hundreds of thousands of precious moments—a child's book left on the seat.

Engine noise in the front of the house commanded her attention and she quickly snuck down the hall to the office with views of the cows and the drive. A strange vehicle was in the driveway a mere twenty feet from the room where Meagan hid.

Her breathing shallow, she listened. Reaching around to her back she was comforted by the feel of her pistol. Car headlights flashed through the office window and then abruptly shut off.

Two men in face coverings stepped out of the car.

This is not good.

In the house, a man hollered, "Shit, ow!" Pans rattled around in the kitchen.

What on earth?

Meagan scurried to hide behind the sofa before the men reached the front door where she could see them. Still not knowing who was in the kitchen, her palms began to sweat.

Seconds later— "Pop! Pop!"

What's that?

There was gunfire. The masked men blasted their way into the house, looking all around and pointing their guns toward someone in the kitchen, which was out of Meagan's line of sight.

"You? You don't live here!" shouted one of the masked men.

The man in the kitchen said, "No shit, Sherlock. You bastards—get out!"

That's not Mr. Pullman's voice!

One assailant was short, and the other tall and fat. Meagan steadied her gun on the sofa and, taking careful aim, she pulled the trigger twice, both shots landing in the fat man's posterior. His knees buckled, and he fell like a crumbling building. His gun sailed across the oak floor.

"Help me!" screamed the fat man clutching his rear. "Call 911! Oh, Jesus, I'm shot. Somebody shot me. What the hell, Rob!"

The short man wheeled around to see his injured partner squirming on the floor, yelling, "What the hell!"

Meagan caught sight of a man with bandages covering his face; he whacked the gun from the short man's hand with a skillet. Then the short man growled and began punching the bandaged man, knocking him to the floor. Meagan stood up fast.

I've got to get out of this house!

She ran for the open front door, crossed through the living room, aiming her last shot at the man who continued to beat up on the bandaged man—her bullet struck him in the rear. His screams rang through the house. She ran through the busted front door at full speed, not stopping until she was back inside the little room in the garage. With so many questions and no one to provide any answers, Meagan seized the greasy garage phone, paced the floor, and dialed 911.

"What is your emergency?" said the operator.

"Shots fired at the Pullman ranch on County Rd," Meagan said and hung up.

She had glimpsed the bandaged man, and it was not Mr. Pullman. She recalled that one of the men called the other "Rob." Meagan snuck around the backside of the garage and considered her options for leaving the ranch. Thoughts of calling a cab to meet her at the crossroads and pulling out of this crazy place were immediately dismissed because another set of car lights pulled into the driveway.

An elderly, bearded man in a plaid jacket emerged from a Hummer. He stopped short of the front door, saying "No, no, no," then hurried into the house yelling, "King? King?"

The police arrived at the same time as the ambulance moments later. Meagan watched through her binoculars as they hauled out the two men she had shot.

Thank goodness they are still alive!

"Somebody shot me! They're still in there!" the fat man screamed from his gurney.

"Get the bastard!" the short man pleaded with the police. "Go in there and get him!"

"We will," one of the officers replied. Looking around the ranch, he added, "They could not have gone too far. Officer Gage, will you canvas the property? I will check the interior."

"Yes, sir, Officer Rhodes," said Gage.

As paramedics loaded the gunshot victims into the ambulance, Officer Rhodes asked, "Weren't you shot in the process of committing felony burglary? Tell me why we should hurry to find the shooter?"

The short man moaned. "Shit! I was collecting debt! That's not against the law! Don't I have rights? Somebody tried to kill me! Jeez!"

Meagan saw the older man escorting the bloody-faced younger man out of the house.

What? He was the target.

Officer Gage approached the two and greeted them, "Hello, Jack," and shook his hand before turning to the bandaged man. "How are you, Ace?"

"I feel like crap, but I'm alive."

Ace? Ace's Pawn. King's Pawn— Oh my. Wow, I have stirred a hornet's nest of pawn people. The older man indeed is Jack from Jack's Pawn.

Meagan continued spying from her position behind the garage. She licked her lips.

The officer continued, "Who shot these men?"

"I wish I knew," said Ace, "I'd like to thank them. I didn't see anyone."

"Darndest thing!" remarked Jack.

Officer Rhodes pressed Ace, "Why were these men after you?"

Ace scratched his head. "Not sure—I, uh, well—it's got to be the same two derelicts who busted into my house about noon. King came and got me—brought me here. He left me a note and went to see our mother at the hospital. I was fixing something to eat when—Bam! They broke in and started beating on me—probably would have killed me too."

"Do you think they were after King?"

Jack said, "Looks like they were after both my boys."

"They want money. I don't owe anyone except my mortgage company, but they think I do. That's all I know," Ace added.

Jack Pullman studied his son's face, then said, "Officer, let us know if there is anything else we can help you with."

"Will do. Mind if we search the house?"

Jack and Ace stepped aside, permitting the officer access to the house.

"Dad, why are you here?" Ace asked, "You could have been shot! King thinks you are on your way to the hospital."

"I stopped by to bring King this." Jack reached into his pocket and presented a ruby jeweled brooch to show his son.

The low evening sun and the porch light illuminated the jeweled piece; Meagan adjusted the focus on her binoculars and saw it was hers. She gasped, heart pounding at the sight of her mother's brooch.

Why does he have that? What on earth?

"King had asked me to bring it to him if it found its way to my shop—he said your mother might like it, something like that."

Ace examined it. "Hmm. Okay. I didn't know he cared about stuff like this."

"Me either," Jack said, nodding and repocketing the piece.

The ambulance was gone. The officers were wrapping up their search and making a beeline to inspect the garage with Jack and Ace; Meagan ran inside and locked the door to stall them. She climbed inside the trunk of a sixty-seven Mustang and quietly pulled the lid shut.

"You gonna let us in the garage, Jack?" asked Officer Gage. "It's locked."

"Well, I'll be," Jack said, fidgeting for the right key. "Here you go." He pushed the door open and turned the fluorescent lights on as the men searched for clues to the mysterious shooter.

"Nice garage," said Rhodes. "Let me know if you want to sell one of these beauties."

Jack smiled. "Don't know that I'll sell, but you can take one for a spin when I'm done."

Searching the makeshift office, Gage asked, "Who lives here?"

"No one. I put that out here years ago for when I was tired and too covered with grease to nap in the house," Jack said. "Lots of good memories in here." He put his hand on Ace's shoulder. "Son, you are coming with me to the hospital. We'll check on your mother, let King know what happened, and get your head looked at, at the same time."

"Well, okay, I think we're through here. Thanks, Jack," Gage said.

Meagan heard the men shuffle out and the garage door close. Breathing deeply, she located her flashlight and popped the trunk release, hunger nipping at her insides.

Through the crack between the garage door and wall, she could see the driveway was finally clear of vehicles.

Empty driveway, empty house—

Meagan evaluated the destruction. The front door hung disjointedly from one hinge; the door handle was in shards.

Shame on them. Mr. Pullman may have a strange life, but he does not deserve this.

The Ruby Rose brooch was with the Pullman family, and Meagan had heard Jack say that King had requested it. To recover the ruby heirloom, Meagan needed to stay at the ranch. She began picking up pieces of glass and wiping blood off floors and counters with paper towels. When the house interior looked normal again, she removed her thin leather gloves, washed her hands, and raided King's fridge, sitting down with the pan and a spoon and eating slowly with eyes closed, finishing the cold noodle casserole.

She stretched her arms wide, stomach full; tiredness had overtaken her. Her options were the garage cot or the floor under Pullman's bed—she chose the latter. Her eyes were heavy.

Maybe Jack left the brooch here in the house. That would make sense. I'm right where I need to be—

Chapter Thirteen

King let go of his mother's hand to answer his phone "Hello."

"Son," Jack began, "you've had a break-in at the ranch, and two men went after Ace. I think they were looking for you."

"Again? Two guys beat him up this morning. Is he okay?" King rubbed his forehead and stared blankly at the wall.

Jack assured, "Yes, he will be fine. Damnedest thing! Someone shot the men and saved Ace. He said he didn't know the guys but said they're the same two idiots who broke into his house this morning."

"Why? Why are these guys after us? And—who else was in the house?" King shook his head. "Who shot them?"

"That's the thing," Jack said, "we have no idea who the shooter was. They claim he owes them money. I'm bringing Ace up to the hospital to get checked out. Storm is still at my shop; he's fine. We'll talk more tomorrow, Son."

King blinked hard. "Okay. I'm going to head home and check out the damage. Thanks, Dad."

Standing close to Kate's bed, King shared the disturbing news; gently, knowing his mother would see through any attempt on his part to soften or alter it. Her recovery from the stroke and subsequent coma had been nothing short of miraculous. King noticed she slurred her speech and appeared to be thinking more about each word before she spoke it, but for her to speak at all after a stroke was terrific.

King checked his watch and noted the late hour. "I'm expecting a livestock delivery in the morning." He kissed his mother on the cheek.

"I—understand," Kate said, "P—please be care—careful. I—love—y—you."

"I love you, Mom," King replied, closing the heavy hospital room door behind him.

Except for the bullet-ravaged lockset, the front door was salvageable, which was a relief since it was an expensive, special-order, solid-core door. King exhaled, prepared himself for the disaster he would find in his home, and stepped inside the living room.

His jaw dropped. He could not fit his father's description of the crime with what he was seeing; his home was immaculate. Without a wrecked front door and if Ace had no additional injuries, he might have thought Jack had made the whole story up. There was no evidence of a shooting in his house. He flipped open the kitchen trash lid and noted the bag was fresh.

What? Who would— He shook his head.

King marched out to the garage and returned with an electric drill. Until he could find time to fix the front door properly, he screwed the entrance door to the jamb, then grabbed a cold beer. He removed his boots and rummaged through his fridge, stomach growling. Ace must have eaten the noodle casserole—the empty container was clean and sitting in the sink.

He decided to cook a frittata and began setting ingredients on the counter. He whipped half a dozen eggs and added chopped mushrooms, peppers, and a cup of cooked turkey sausage and cheese.

While the frittata baked, he headed back to his bedroom. The house seemed barren without Storm. He stripped his clothes off, except his black jockeys, and tossed them into a large black hamper across the room. It was his custom to spot exercise; King dropped to the carpet, facing the moonlit rear acreage, executing one hundred pushups before showering.

"…ninety-eight, ninety-nine, one hundred," he gritted, resting on the carpet momentarily. Subtle snoring caught his attention, and he turned toward his bed, repeatedly blinking at the sight. From his prone position on the floor, he stared—mouth agape—at the form under his bed. He could not see the face, but the head covering, camo pants, and military boots were a dead giveaway. It was the robber from his shop.

"Holy crap!" he whispered. Endorphins coursed through his veins; he resumed his pushups.

Who are you? Since you did not get shot here today, you must be the mystery shooter who saved Ace, whoever you are. Did you also clean up the mess in my house? Why?

He zeroed in on the delicate wrist, hand, and long, tapered fingers in cutoff gloves, the hand of a woman. He stopped working out.

Why is she here? What is she doing?

His mind raced—the photo—the necklace. When an answer did not come, he hurried to shower before the oven timer buzzed.

Unbelievable.

King ate three slices of frittata, and the remainder would make great leftovers for Ace or the helpful robber person hiding in his house.

Strange how just yesterday I was worried the robber might cause a fatality in our family, and today I'm grateful she took the shots, and now she is under my bed with a loaded gun, snoring.

The myriad of things King should have been thinking about took a backseat to contemplating the events involving jewels, pearls, and other items he noted in the photo the thief had left behind at his shop.

Ah, heck, she can deal with the results of her actions.

King put the sealed container of leftover frittata in his fridge. Yes, he had given her the pearls, but she had more than returned the favor by saving Ace's life. The decision became simple; let her intrusion into his house slide because he was now in her debt.

After checking his email for up-dates regarding the impending livestock delivery, King went to his bedroom, slid open the tall closet door, and removed his handy Ruger pistol from its safe spot. The disarray caught his attention; one of the boxes of books was open, and it had to be the intruder who had extracted a book, The Cowboy and His Damsel. He snickered, shrugged, returned the book, and slid the door shut. Climbing into bed, he discreetly stashed the pistol under his pillow. Sleep was an elusive island on which King finally landed for six hours.

Meagan stirred, body aching from too much time spent in one position on her stomach. She heard deep breathing.

The dog? Where's the dog?

She recalled the day's events and momentarily imagined Mr. Pullman likely sleeping a few feet above her. She inched her way out from under his bed, wincing with the thought that a German Shepherd may attack her at any moment. Staying low, she continued to scuttle along the carpet and down the long hall like a sand crab until she rounded the corner into the living room. A quick inventory of her pockets was reassuring; her handgun, phone, flashlight, and binoculars were still with her. Grateful for the absence of the growling dog, she made her way to the kitchen.

I need food.

The fridge had new leftovers.

Hmm. He's been busy.

She helped herself to a large piece of frittata, wrapped it in a paper towel, and headed for the front door.

Nailed shut? Great.

After a few minutes of tiptoeing around, Meagan found the house's back door conveniently on the far side of the kitchen in a small hall across from a half bathroom—a godsend. She slipped out the back door and walked diagonally across the property to the main barn, then strolled the perimeter for an entry and found one on the south side, not visible from the house.

Unlocked! Everything around here is unlocked!

She was in another office; a rectangular rug depicting a gathering of horses at a river covered a smooth, concrete floor. Photos of Mr. Pullman and his brother blanketed the walls. She turned her attention to a computer on the desk, turned it on, and while it powered up, Meagan toured the empty tack room and horse stalls before returning to the computer.

The swivel desk chair creaked as she rocked. The monitor glowed with promises as Meagan searched on Sell-City for more of her heirlooms. She perused hundreds of artwork postings, and then—there it was—her painting. Light played off the cowboys and their horses in the early morning rain; Meagan's eyes misted with gratitude. The personally signed G. Harvey painting had been bestowed to her by her Aunt Opal's husband, Uncle Gerald, and now it was about to be returned.

Don't worry. I'm bringing you home. Meagan promised, tapping the screen with a pen.

In a quick text to the seller, she requested a meeting time for the next day at nine PM.

A vehicle was approaching the barn.

What?

Meagan logged off, shut the computer off, and hurried up the ladder to the loft to hide.

Twelve-foot-tall double barn doors opened simultaneously, and Pullman hollered, "Back 'er up! Okay. That's good!"

Hand over her mouth, Meagan stifled a snicker when the truck driver grabbed the heads of four alpacas and a donkey and ushered the wild bunch out of the trailer. She had imagined fine quarter horses on this land, not a half-dozen one-hundred-fifty-pound ugly sheep and a jackass.

She had never seen alpacas before that day, and as she observed them, she became more curious about Mr. Pullman's interest in these animals. They had camel faces with big lips atop a long neck attached to a sheep's body but with long legs.

They are very comical creatures. At least the donkey is regular.

"They need to graze in a fenced area," the driver stated. "They can run at a pretty good clip, so you don't want to chase 'em."

"Got it," Pullman assured him and saluted the departing delivery man. "Have a good day."

With the alpacas' leashes in one hand and the donkeys in the other, he guided them to a fenced field with a lean-to next to the barn.

From high in the loft where Meagan hid, ignoring the straw poking through her clothes, she had a clear view out the barn doors. The rising sun twinkled off the dew on the meadow, doubling its brilliance. When she checked the time on her phone, she realized she had already been up there for hours.

The alpacas made loud humming sounds. Meagan's eyes widened, and she rolled onto her side, holding the laughter in her belly when she witnessed Pullman get a swift kick in the calf by one of his new funky sheep on their way to the east acreage.

This is the best!

Her phone alerted her to a text—the sellers of the G-Harvey agreed to a nine PM meeting in the parking lot of a closed accounting firm. *Good!*

With Mr. Pullman occupied with his creatures, Meagan jumped at the opportunity to scramble back to the house, through the mudroom, down the hall, and into his bedroom. She sat on his bed and watched him through her binoculars as he tended to his herd. Rubbing her eyes and yawning, her body weaving from side to side, Meagan moved to lean against the wall. When she spotted Mr. Pullman walking into the barn, she ran for the garage, where the smelly old spring bed was a welcome sight. She emptied her pockets of all tools and weapons and set them on the floor under the cot.

Hammering sounds ended her cozy nap; in a flash, she was at the lookout crack beside the garage door. He was shirtless, on his roof, swinging a hammer at his house. Mr. Pullman stopped pounding to sit on the rooftop, eat lunch, and drink from a gallon jug. Meagan wet her lips. Her stomach growled as she thought about the man's fridge.

He suddenly bolted to his feet on the roof and yelled, "No! Shit!" Standing and nearly losing his balance. "Come back!" he shouted.

The object of Mr. Pullman's distress galloped past the crack beside the garage door. He quickly shed his toolbelt and hopped off his roof like a monkey to chase the fluffy, runaway alpaca. Meagan estimated he was chasing the beast far down the country road when his yelling became faint in the distance.

She bent over at the waist, laughing, trying to catch her breath, then gathered her tools and weapon to sneak back into the house. Ignoring her hunger momentarily, she searched his home for her precious things; no cabinet or drawer escaped her digging.

Time had flown. Her shoulders slumped; she covered her face with both hands. Nothing.

I thought I would find the brooch. I found nothing.

Another evening at Pullman's house, Meagan was back in his sliding doors closet. She could hear him mumbling to himself while he marched across the bedroom to dump an armload of clothes into his hamper.

King casually glanced back to the mirrored closet where, from his spot in the corner of the room, he would be able to see her reflection under his bed. She was not there. The thief-turned-hero could be anywhere in his house.

Wherever you are, your deadly game will kill you. After all, you are trespassing.

Wearing only his boxer shorts, he headed to the bathroom to shower.

Naked, in front of the bathroom mirror, he ruffled a thick towel through his short, chestnut hair. In the bedroom, he quickly pulled boxer shorts from his dresser.

I would bet an alpaca you are in my closet. You're probably hungry too.

Assuming the trespasser had burrowed to the back where the books were, King slid a closet door open to enable her escape before he climbed into his bed, exhausted. He rubbed his aching legs and tried to recall the last time he had sprinted anywhere before today.

It must have been in high school.

Meagan racked her brain for a plan that did not include shooting Mr. Pullman for her jewels. Before leaving the house to retrieve her painting, she planned to conduct another brief search for her brooch. Finding it meant she would not need to return to Pullman's home. Perched on a stack of bagged sweaters atop a book box in the corner of the closet, Meagan listened and smiled. A deafening silence amplified the man's subtle snoring. Strategically situating herself with her flashlight under a long hanging coat, she picked up where she had left off in the book, The Cowboy and His Damsel until she finally dozed off.

A heavenly aroma nudged her from her slumber. Meagan reached for her phone to check the time; five AM. She had fallen asleep in an awkward position and grimaced with the feeling of pins and needles as she straightened her legs. When she moved her feet, light streamed between the hanging clothes allowing her glimpses of the room.

Pullman ambled barefoot down the hall toward his bedroom. His phone rang—it was Ace. King said, "Sure, that's a good idea; see you later. We'll look around." He ended the call, glanced toward the mirrored doors, and shuddered.

Meagan had not thought of Mr. Pullman in any way other than the odd pawnshop man who did not turn her over to the police. Now that the bearded annoyed face with green eyes was peering in her direction, other adjectives came to mind like strapping, provocative and complex; descriptive words she had never attributed to a man. No man had ever made her sweat with his smile until that moment. For a split second, she wished he would catch her in his closet. She removed her head covering, swept her hands over her face, through her hair, and breathed deeply.

When Mr. Pullman left his house, Meagan ran to the kitchen, forming a plan as she went. She would get food, run to the crossroads, and call Rhonda for a lift. As she shoved fruit, some frittata, and pancakes into a bag, she noticed coffee in the pot, and the machine was still on. Her mouth watered.

He won't miss a cup.

She half-filled a mug with coffee, practically skipped to the front door, and stopped short. The door was operational, and there was a new lockset. She turned the knob, gently pulled the door open to peek out, and saw that Mr. Pullman's truck was in the circle drive. Meagan closed the door and headed to the living room to scan the back pastures. Dawn was breaking and spilling a golden-pink haze over the country scene before her. Mr. Pullman, sporting a dark cowboy hat, was tending to his flock. What little Meagan had gleaned about Pullman and his critters suggested he would be out there a while, so she fled, breakfast and coffee in hand, to the garage to eat in peace and rethink her plan.

Yum.

Mr. Pullman's frittata put Mr. Willoughby's egg efforts to shame, and that was saying a lot as Mr. Willoughby had been cooking his entire life. She folded a warm banana pancake in half and savored each bite, noting spices that had been added, such as cinnamon, nutmeg, and vanilla. The more satiated she became, the more slowly she ate, peeling grapes with her teeth before chewing them with her eyes closed.

Stuffed, she snuggled into the sleeping bag on the creaky cot and napped like the dead until crunching gravel and many voices woke her hours later.

Meagan ran to observe through the crack; Pullman was greeting the same two men from yesterday. She recognized the older man, who had her brooch the last time she saw him—Mr. Pullman's father.

Meagan recognized the younger man as Mr. Pullman's brother, who ironically sold her back her guns for a stiff price, and whose attackers Meagan had shot.

The German shepherd happily trotted around the vehicle, sniffing, while King assisted a feeble woman out of the couple's camouflage Hum-V. Meagan was sure the woman was Mr. Pullman's mother.

If he's having a dinner party, the food will be good!

"I'd like to see your livestock, son," his father said.

Meagan snickered at the memory of Mr. Pullman corralling his animals.

The direness of Meagan's circumstances did not escape her. She was in danger of being found—guilty of various crimes she did not care to list. She squeezed her eyes shut, wishing for the life she had before getting robbed. Her shoulders slumped as she stared through the crack. The scene was compelling; she couldn't pull her gaze away. The coolness of the cameo pendant necklace against her chest reminded her that she was not alone on her mission and had accomplished what she had come to the ranch for. But things had changed, evolved, and now she knew her ruby brooch was somewhere in that house; a knot formed in her stomach. The radiant G. Harvey painting was awaiting its rightful owner, and she would be there soon; then Meagan would return to this ranch and get her brooch back. Just then, her phone vibrated in her pocket.

Storm turned toward the garage and growled.

Curiously, King cocked his head to one side and watched Storm, who was keen to search the garage. "Stop," King commanded, and Storm redirected his attention toward Mrs. Pullman.

Meagan sighed. It was a text from Andrew, "Where are you? Mom is worried. You did not come home last night."

She responded, "Out of town. Back later."

The mention of Aunt Agnes brought the B&B to mind.

I need a long, hot bubble bath in the old claw foot tub—but first, my painting.

Ace escorted his mother into the house, Storm at their side, while Mr. Pullman and his father headed for the side door entrance to the garage.

Oh no!

Meagan quickly straightened the cot and hid behind the door, barely breathing.

She heard the men walk into the building.

"I wanted to talk to you privately," said Jack.

"I'm glad you brought Mom here," King said, scrutinizing the area, "Is everything okay?"

"I think she'll heal faster here, son. As easy as that garden home of ours is to keep up, your mother doesn't stop working. She needs a calm environment and good food—thanks for helping us. I know she feels safe here too." Jack's voice was low and solemn.

"Calm? Not today. I used to think this place was safe, but Ace—the shooting—"

Jack put his hand on King's shoulder. "We'll get to the bottom of that mess soon enough."

"I'll do whatever I can for Mom," King said.

"I know you will. There's something else, King; I will hire some help. I need someone to care for your mother while she continues to recover. I also want you to have help with the house."

"Dad, I don't need—" King started to explain.

"This will make it easier on all of us. Let me do this, King. You shouldn't do it all. I'll advertise in the town newspaper for someone close by."

King imagined Gayla would pitch a fit if she thought he was spending money on a caretaker-housekeeper when he told her he had no money to give her.

King nodded. "Sounds fine, Dad."

"We don't want to be a burden," added Jack, emotion thickening his tone.

King pulled his dad into an embrace. "You're not."

"Thanks." Jack stepped back, wiped his hand over his moist eyes, reached for his hanky, and blew his nose. "Are you enjoying the ranch?"

"I am. It's great." King smiled and shoved his hands in his jeans' pockets.

"Yeah, it is. It is."

The two men strolled over to the Mustang and discussed the work left to be done on it before heading out the garage's side door.

When Meagan heard the door shut, she exhaled a sigh of relief and rubbed her temples, tilting her head slowly from side to side and smiling when several vertebrae in her neck popped.

Sitting on the rickety office chair beside the cot, Meagan called for a cab to meet her at eight-thirty at the crossroads.

Chapter Fourteen

"Where to?" asked the cab driver smiling at Meagan.

"Arndell Accounting on Center Avenue," Meagan responded, climbing into the backseat of the yellow cab. She peered into the cloudless black sky in the rural darkness of the crossroads half a mile from King Pullman's house. This night a full silver moon shone with hundreds of sparkling stars surrounding it like a theater in the round.

A plan formed as Meagan thought about her current job at The Warehouse and the pay raises she had turned down over the years. The position Mr. Pullman's father would post for, a helper-housekeeper, would be a convenient—and legal—way to get her brooch back, not to mention the heavenly food and all. A shiver rippled through her body.

"Hey, this place looks closed," the Cabbie said, craning his head in search of human activity.

"Pull over to the right in a less conspicuous spot. I'm meeting some people, and you are to stay here for three minutes and wait for me. Please? It's just a quick surprise for them."

"Ah, okay—meter's running."

Meagan installed her fake teeth, carefully tucked her stray hair underneath her cap, and exited the cab. She marched across the parking lot in the dim light of the street lamps. Ahead, she could see a heavyset woman, likely in her thirties.

"You here for the painting?" she asked, scanning Meagan from head to toe and slurping her coke.

"Yes."

The seller rocked from foot to foot and squeaked her straw up and down through the plastic lid on the Whataburger cup. "Are you in the military or something?" Her beady eyes focused on Meagan's large black boots.

"No."

Meagan approached the woman's open trunk, where the artwork was propped up for display. She flipped on her flashlight to examine the painting.

The seller cleared her throat. "You must know art?"

"Sort of," Meagan admitted, tilting the painting to see her family name on the back. "I do know when it's stolen." She lifted the framed canvas out of the trunk and held it with one hand as she pointed her gun at the woman. "You better get lost fast because I don't feel merciful today."

"How did you know?"

"See here," Meagan said, balancing the artwork on the top of her foot, pistol in one hand and flashlight in the other, illuminating the name on the back of the painting. "That's my family name."

The woman threw her hands in the air, yelling, "Oh my god! Dammit, I didn't know! My brother gave it to me. Please don't shoot me! Shit, shit!"

Awkwardly, the woman clamored into her car and squealed out of the parking lot with her window down, cursing her brother.

Meagan tucked her pistol back into the waistband of her pants. Holding the thirty-two-inch painting securely, she shuffled across the parking lot to the cab.

"We can go now. One thousand Blanchard Avenue," Meagan informed the Cabbie, the 'G. Harvey on the seat next to her.

The driver whipped his head around to the backseat. "Nice painting," he said, "why did that woman run from you?"

Meagan removed her plastic teeth. "Thanks. She developed a sudden case of diarrhea."

"Oh, bummer."

They drove the rest of the way to the B&B in silence.

Dark tint on the windows of the rented SUV, coupled with the onyx night, provided ideal spy cover for Conroy Sabeth as he watched and waited across the street from the Whitehouse Animal Clinic. He had done enough reconnaissance to know that Gayla was working that day, and the clinic closed at seven that evening. Assistant veterinarians had left shortly after closing, but there was no sign of Gayla, and her gold SUV was still in the parking lot.

It had been a week since his revealing golf game with his high school friend, King Pullman—when he learned he had fathered a child with Gayla. The day his investigation began.

He had been watching Gayla from afar and recognized her right away, she looked the same, but something about her mannerisms was unsettling.

Conroy leaned back against the headrest and closed his eyes for a moment. He recalled a disturbing exchange with Natalie, his former fiancée. While Conroy worked as a file clerk in his last year at law school, a friend invited him on a whitewater rafting trip he and his girlfriend planned to take.

"Check with your girlfriend and let me know," he had said.

Natalie pummeled Conroy with questions about the trip. She wanted to know who was going, who was sponsoring it, who else would be there, and where they would be sleeping—

"Just forget it, Nat. I'm going," said Conroy. "You don't have to come."

A church group near campus had sponsored the trip, but Conroy didn't care. Why should he? He was going for the river and the camaraderie with his friend from work. They spent five exhilarating hours each day navigating the rapids, and the evenings consisted of quiet music around a firepit near the two-story cabin. Conroy was surprised the first night when a man younger than himself told stories from the bible and asked the group if they could transfer that information to the present and what it might look like if those tenets were applied today.

Conroy found that he enjoyed thinking that challenged him on a moral level. It was different from any philosophy class he had ever taken. The conversations intrigued him and left him wanting more. When he returned home and shared what he had learned with her, Nat threw her hands up.

"Let me guess," she shouted, "a church sponsored the trip?"

"So what?" Conroy asked.

"So, you lied. I knew this would happen. You are already changing! I hate this!"

Conroy inhaled deeply. "Can we just *not* overreact? Please, Nat. I'm just saying I thought the talks were interesting, and the river was amazing—like you—"

He moved toward her and embraced her tenderly, and she let him. "We don't have to talk about this anymore."

"Okay," she said.

His head bobbed and jerked, and he woke himself up. Startled, Conroy sat up straight. He had fallen asleep in the SUV. He checked his watch, grabbed the half-eaten club sandwich from the sack on the passenger seat, and finished the meal with another bottle of water.

Suddenly, headlights appeared and moved down the street toward the clinic; it was a compact car. Conroy stopped chewing, put his sandwich on the dash, and grabbed his binoculars. He observed the driver in sagging, baggy blue jeans amble to the clinic door and knock. Gayla opened the door for him. It was a friendly meeting.

With the image of Gayla's visitor in his mind, he wrote down the car's license plate number. It was time for him to up his game. He began an internet search for listening devices and quickly realized he was getting in over his head. He was desperate to complete the "Gayla puzzle" and acknowledged his need for a professional. He searched his contacts for Calvin Cobb, a private investigator Sabeth Gilmore and Sabeth Law Firm had recommended to clients occasionally.

What the future held was uncertain, but with Calvin's help, Conroy would finally learn about the events in Gayla's past that led her to the bizarre life with a secret child that resulted in her present deceptive existence. With his new plan, he dialed Calvin Cobb's number, started the truck engine, and left his surveillance post in Whitehouse.

When Meagan left the yellow cab with her painting, the B&B was dead quiet, with only one car in the rear parking lot. No blue Jeep. With any luck, Andrew would not be home.

The Cabbie lowered his window. "You *live* here?" He rolled his eyes and then grinned. "Why didn't I guess that?"

Meagan put the cash for the fare in his outstretched hand and said, "Yes, why *didn't* you guess that?"

The cab driver reversed the car and said, "See ya."

"I was wondering when I would see you again," said a voice in the dark.

"Is that you, Andrew?"

"Yes, where have you been? What's with the cab? You weren't at work." His voice tinged with disgust.

He was leaning against the old oak tree, hidden from the light.

Meagan marched past Andrew. "I was off today. I'm thinking about changing jobs—" She glanced around the parking lot. "Hey, where's your jeep?"

Ignoring her question, Andrew focused on the painting. "Have you been late-night shopping again? Into artwork now? Hmm?"

"I told you already. I have a warehouse unit, and I'm redecorating my room. Remember? Late night shopping—think what you will—whatever," she quipped. "The interrogation is over, Andrew. I'm exhausted. Good night."

Andrew coughed. "Ah, did you ask Mom about that?

Meagan froze at the back door of the house. "About what?"

"The decorating."

"About decorating? Not yet."

Asking Aunt Agnes for permission to put her things in the room she was renting had not occurred to her.

What business was it of hers anyway?

"Yeah, you should probably ask Mom about—all that stuff— from your—warehouse." There was a smile in his voice.

Meagan squinted. "Are you smoking?"

"You want to join me?"

"No."

Andrew inhaled the smoke deeply and exhaled with his mouth wide open, creating a barrier cloud of smoke between them. "How about dinner Friday night at Angelo's?" There was a new-found confidence in his voice. "We are cousins, after all."

"True," Meagan responded, resting the bottom edge of the painting on her foot. Although he could be annoying at times, it was clear that Andrew held sway over his mother.

"I'm waiting—six o'clock?" Andrew said.

"Sure." She could tell he was still smiling, but what did it matter? She could use an ally. One dinner with a distant relative couldn't hurt, and since she wasn't swimming in relatives to have dinner with, she would go.

Somberly, she added, "I'll meet you there."

"Awesome!" Andrew said and flicked his cigarette butt onto the parking lot. "Let me carry your paint—"

"No, I've got it."

Andrew shrugged. "Okay. Don't forget!"

Moments later, Meagan was in the comfort and quiet of her bedroom. Suppose the homey antique room could tell the secrets stained within its walls— lovers separated by war, newlyweds, and maybe a widow or widower traveling with an urn. Meagan imagined a tall, thin woman in a long skirt standing by the window and peering through the delicate lace curtains toward a distant ocean. A man like Mr. Pullman would have offered to light a fire for her because he noticed her shiver. But Meagan understood the woman at the window was not chilled but rather frozen to the bone because of her loss. She couldn't cry because tears were useless; they would not bring her lover back.

There was no woman at the window. Meagan's jaw muscles flexed involuntarily over the unexplained separation. The imaginary scene left her heartsick for her parents, gone because of the plane crash. If her speed bag were mounted in this room, she would punch it for an hour like she used to before thieves took it.

Now the room harbored new secrets, dangerous ones at a higher price. Who would understand that she was a cipher following orders from the grave? She laid the painting on the bed and sat down next to it. Her fingers caressed the perimeter of the embellished wooden frame as she gazed at the cowboys drenched in the rain in the early morning light.

"Are you glad to be back, G. Harvey? I'm glad you're back."

The sound of a revving motor from the parking lot drew Meagan to her window. The towering oak trees limited her view, but she recognized Mr. Willoughby in a Corvette, his abdomen pressed against the steering wheel.

Presently, Andrew stepped out of the shadows and approached Mr. Willoughby.

What are you up to?

"It's fast," Mr. Willoughby warned, struggling to free himself from the cockpit.

Andrew grinned. "Perfect," he said, taking the keys from his father. He slid into the driver's seat, slammed the door, and sped away from the B&B.

Was this some sort of transaction?

Meagan observed Mr. Willoughby stretching, likely because of his recent cramped driving experience in the Corvette.

I would have pegged Andrew as a Volvo sedan person or a Saab owner; they're unusual, well-groomed, and snobbish.

The unreserved, sporty red Corvette belonged to Andrew. Where he went in that car at that late hour was not an issue worthy of Meagan's time. Dismissing the scene with a wave of her hand, she returned to the painting, which elevated her mood. Another one of her soldiers was home. She wrapped the large, wooden framed canvas in a blanket and set it in the closet, praying Agnes would not find it.

Now, time for that soaking bath.

Water shot into the tub in the communal hallway bathroom, rattling the pipes in the walls. Meagan knew it was late, but she didn't care; she felt covered in the grime of several days of rural criminality. She stepped out of her costume and lowered herself gently into the steaming bath, searing her skin as she formed a plan to recover her ruby brooch and opal choker and others among the lost.

Mother's brooch and Aunt's Opal will be home soon—I can feel it.

It was comforting to have his parents and brother home at the ranch. Apart from a few years in a dorm in Texas and his apartment, the farm was the only home King had known.

Jack Pullman had insisted they grill steaks outside for dinner to celebrate Kate's release from the hospital. Standing around the grill, drinking beer, and talking politics, the three men reminisced about the days when the ranch was home to several breeds of cows.

From her seat inside the house at the kitchen table, Kate watched the flames from the fire light up the faces of the three men she loved most. She loved being Jack's wife and mother to King and Ace.

King asked, "Dad, would you bring the salad? It's in the fridge."

"Sure, I'll bring the rabbit food."

"Bacon-wrapped filet mignon," King announced. He set the covered platter on the table before his mother.

"And twice-baked potatoes," Ace said, placing potato halves on each plate.

Jack had plenty of questions for King during dinner about his new herd. Ace and Kate listened attentively, each having their physical challenges to overcome.

With the meal finished, King put a pot of decaf coffee on. "Mom," he said, "why don't you sit in the living room with Dad? Ace and I can handle the dishes."

"Dude," Ace whined, "I'm hurt! Look at my face, for god's sake! I can barely see out of my right eye! I'm gonna lay on the couch. Sorry."

King smiled. "Fine."

He didn't mind taking care of the after-dinner dishes; he found it cathartic. He scooped leftovers into a plastic container thinking about Storm. Jack would have the pleasure of surprising the dog with a rare treat of steak and potatoes.

I wonder if she is watching us now?

It had been a while since his pearl thief had pilfered food from his fridge; he questioned how she was faring. Although he had come to grips with the fact that she could be anywhere on his property, her charade was wearing thin. What was the worst thing that could happen if he rousted her out from underneath his bed or inside his closet and made her talk? His gratitude toward her ran deep; after all, she saved his brother, but for what? To live like a stowaway on this ranch until when? He would not let her escape again as she did in his shop—with his assistance. His heartbeat quickened with his parents and Ace here with him and knowing the stranger was nearby. King was an accomplished marksman, ready to end her game. He wiped his hands on the kitchen towel.

"Kitchen is clean. I'm going to shower," he said, passing through the living room. He marched past his half-asleep family to boot the criminal out of his house.

Sweat began to bead on his forehead. He tucked his pistol into the back waistband of his jeans. No more hiding in his house with his family here—not going to happen. It had to end; whoever the robber girl is, her gig is up.

He flung the tall mirrored closet door open and rifled through the contents, shoving clothes aside and pushing boxes out of the way until it was clear she wasn't there.

"You shoot like a man, but apparently, you enjoy Mom's romance novels," he stated through clenched teeth.

Quickly, he dropped to the carpet to check under his bed, fully expecting her to be there. She was not.

He stood with arms crossed. "You will not win."

There was nothing he could do to locate her unless he chose to involve the police. Any way King sliced it, he would have appeared a fool to investigators for giving her the pearls at gunpoint and not turning her over to Dell. Now that she likely had the lady's head pendant and probably the photo, she might not return.

"Trust your gut," Jack had always said.

Chapter Fifteen

Searching through the Hallsville News online, Meagan reread the ad: Caretaker wanted; must be a hard worker, honest, and kind: Personal helper needed, with light housekeeping.

Discreetly, she sipped her MacDonald's coffee, set it beside the library computer, and imagined herself legally at Mr. Pullman's as she stared at her phone. She wiped the perspiration from her forehead before dialing the number in the ad and asking for Jack.

"Jack, here," came the response. He put down his newspaper.

'Hi," Meagan said, clearing her throat and looking around the library. "I'm calling about the ad in the paper for a caretaker."

"Ah," Jack said. He had not thought a response to his ad would come so quickly, but he would not kick a gift horse in the mouth. "What are your qualifications?"

Pen in hand, Meagan absent-mindedly sketched pictures of her heirlooms on a scratchpad. No hubris lacking, she responded, "I'm honest, hardworking, and strong, and I can start right away."

"We'll see about that. Meet me at 107 Ranch Road at four today for an interview," Jack instructed. "It's the house where you would be working."

"Okay, thanks," Meagan said, "I'll be there."

"Who were you t-talking to?" asked Kate upon entering the living room.

"Kate!" Jack said, "Let me help you." He hurried to her side to escort her to her favorite chair. "You are supposed to ring that bell connected to your rollator-walker. Please let us help you."

"I-I am no-not an in-va-lid. Dear," Kate replied with a smile.

Having only ever worked at The Appliance Warehouse office, which necessitated jeans, Meagan was still deciding what to wear for the interview. She searched the internet for information regarding appropriate clothing for an interview for the caretaker position. She learned that the few clothes she owned were unsuitable for the job.

A text came in from Rhonda, "Hi, how about Karaoke tonight?"

"I can't," Meagan explained, "Help! I have a job interview. What should I wear?"

Rhonda responded, "Is your interviewer a man or a woman?"

"A man."

"Wear a short skirt, tight sweater, and heels, and wear your hair down and fluffy. You'll get the job. How about karaoke Tuesday, then? I want to hear all about your job."

Meagan understood the logic regarding the tight clothes, but it seemed like cheating.

"Tuesday is fine. I can meet you at the Electric Panda at nine o'clock."

"The karaoke starts at eight. Please be there before eight, Meagan, please?"

"I don't see the difference an hour will make, but ok." "I've got to go. Tell you about the job tomorrow."

Immediately, Meagan returned to searching for the best interview practices as she needed more personal experience with interviewing. Years ago, The Appliance Warehouse took her application, showed her the desk she would be working at, and told her to arrive at nine the following day. That was twelve years ago.

Everything surrounding the caretaker position was different because rather than a place to go to work, it was more like a central command—a place to work from. Her family heirlooms were still out there, and the Ruby Rose brooch had to be in Mr. Pullman's house. She logged off the computer and gulped the rest of her coffee before leaving the library. The clock was ticking; she had to prepare for the interview, regaining her family depended on it.

Meagan hopped down from the brown pickup, clutching several large bags from her rapid shopping spree, and looked into the eyes of Aunt Agnes.

"I heard you leave this morning at eight. Just where have you been, Meagan?"

"I'm in a bit of a hurry, Aunt Agnes. I am meeting someone this afternoon."

Aunt Agnes waved her hand, indicating Meagan should walk past. "Andrew, I suppose?"

"Ah, no."

'Well, then who?" Aunt Agnes persisted.

"Sorry, I'm in a hurry." Meagan shuffled up the stairs of the B&B with her packages and tossed them on her bed. After a quick shower, she began dressing as she practiced her responses to possible questions Jack might ask.

Stepping back from the full-length mirror mounted on the inside of the armoire, Meagan assessed herself.

Makeup is not overdone; hair is down and fluffy, as Rhonda suggested. The shoes—oh god help me, these shoes! This pink, scoop-neck sweater was the only sweater I could find under one-hundred-twenty dollars and matched this twenty-dollar skirt.

Meagan had never worn heels. Because she was the same height as Paxton, heels would have diminished Paxton in his own eyes, and she was conscious of that fact. She slipped her feet into the pink heels and turned around to view her backside as much as she could twist herself.

I never thought I would know a day when I would be trying to get a job with my looks and want the position so much that I would wear three-inch pink heels.

Unsure about the shoes, she had texted Rhonda a photo of the pumps, and her response was, *"BUY THEM!"*

Here I go—

She knew the way to the Pullman Ranch by heart. Her hands were shaking on the steering wheel. She swallowed hard and entered the driveway next to King Pullman's truck. The black tube skirt needed frequent 'tugging down,' mainly when she slid out of the truck seat. She negotiated the gravel driveway carefully, skirting stones, her heels sliding in the shoes.

Meagan paused halfway to the front door to regain her posture and push hair away from her face. The hot rollers and firm hairspray had worked; her head felt huge, with cascading curls to the middle of her back. She patted her hair as though ensuring it would not exceed the width of Pullman's front door.

Her credit card needed this job desperately. She spent more on the pink Angora sweater than on her wedding dress, money she did not have.

She rang the doorbell.

"Just a second," King shouted.

A fabulous aroma wafted through the home, and Meagan closed her eyes and inhaled, wishing she was eating whatever Mr. Pullman was cooking.

The door flew open. "Oh, hi," King said, his forehead creased and head cocked to the side. "Can I help you?"

"Hi, I hope so. I am here about the caretaker position. I talked to Jack earlier today. Should I come back?"

Remembering the interviewing, helpful hints article online, Meagan immediately added a broad smile and looked King Pullman directly in the face.

King's perplexed appearance suddenly shifted, eyes squinting as he studied her. "Ok, sure, come on in. Have a seat in the living room. I'll be right back." He rushed to the kitchen to remove something from the oven.

"Who is it, d-dear?" Mrs. Pullman asked from her seat at the kitchen table.

King sidled up to his mother. "Where is Dad?"

"He went to the b-bank. What's going on?"

"I'm going to text Dad. I have a question for him." King pulled his phone from the back pocket of his jeans and asked Jack, "Where are you? We have company. She says she talked to you earlier today about the job."

Jack texted back, "I came to the bank, and my truck oil light kicked on. It shouldn't be much longer. I'm at JB's Garage. You know what I'm looking for. Go ahead and interview her. Mom does not need to know this is for her."

King peeked into the living room at the tall blond. "Got it," he responded and repocketed his phone.

"Come with me, Mom; I'm about to interview someone for a job. She's in the living room."

Kate rose from her chair with the assistance of her cane and gladly held onto King's arm.

"Sorry, I didn't catch your name—" King said to his guest.

Meagan quickly stood. "I'm Meagan Cal…Morris. I'm here about—"

"The housekeeping job," injected King. Turning to his mother, he smiled. "I need the help."

Kate's mouth hung open. "Y—you mean she's a maid?" she said, pointing to Meagan with her cane before sitting in her favorite club chair a few feet from Meagan's side.

A stern look from her red-faced son and Kate shook her head in disbelief. "Go ahead with y-your interview, King. Don't—mind me. That's a b-beautiful sweater, dear," declared Mrs. Pullman.

"Thank you," replied Meagan quietly, lowering her eyes.

"Meagan, please have a seat. I am King Pullman, and this is my mother, Kate Pullman—Mrs. Pullman."

Meagan sat on the sofa while King occupied a club chair across from the soft pink sweater.

Unaccustomed to mascara, the eyelashes of Meagan's left eye tangled at the outer edge, limiting her view. She began to blink rapidly to free the hairs.

Recalling his father's words, King excused himself to locate an application for the prospective employee in his house. He returned promptly with the form attached to a clipboard and handed it, along with a pen, to Meagan.

"Here you go. We'll need you to fill out this basic information."

"Ok, thanks," Meagan said, setting the clipboard on her lap.

"Ms. Morris," King began, "Do you have any experience with this type of work?"

Meagan looked from Kate to King to Kate. "Yes, I love to clean—and help—with anything. I've been cleaning and helping for years!" She looked back to King, and remembering the article, she offered a wide smile.

King and his mother exchanged glances. He watched Meagan's glossy full pink lips move as she continued to speak, then shook his head, having not heard a word. When the lips stopped moving, King said, "Ok. Do you live nearby?"

"D, dear? King, she asked you—a question," Kate said.

"Oh, sorry. What did you ask, Ms. Morris?"

"How much is the pay?"

King pulled a hanky from his shirt pocket and wiped his forehead. "How much do you want?"

Kate snickered at the scene unfolding before her. "Name your price, h-honey!"

The heat of embarrassment colored Meagan's face to match her sweater. Sweat dripped from her armpits as Mr. Pullman evaluated her with his green eyes.

It smells like he's cooking seasoned pork. I sure hope I get this job. Rhonda would kidnap this man and tie him up if she could see how Mr. Pullman wears his jeans.

"Incredible," Kate said, "Sweetheart, that b-blushing makes you even prettier. My son might never recover."

King broke his silence, "Please ignore my mother. Would thirty-five thousand dollars work for you?"

That is more than Appliance Warehouse and the B&B combined, and to think I would be eating his cooking and seeing his face and helping the delightful, forthright Mrs. Pullman. To be in this house—legally—to collect the pieces of my family.

Meagan smiled and bolted to her feet. "It works for me. When shall I start?"

"Y-you can start by staying for dinner," Kate said matter-of-factly. "My eldest son is an accomplished c-cook. Aren't you d-dear?" She turned to Meagan. "How tall are you, Meagan?"

"I'm almost six feet tall."

King stood, his head bobbing up and down. "Yes, stay for dinner—if you can; herb and garlic pork loin with honey mustard sauce, roasted vegetables—" his voice faded.

"Dinner smells wonderful, thank you."

Ace swaggered into the living room, scratching his head. "What have I missed?"

Mrs. Pullman answered, "Ace, this is Mea-gan. She is King's new housekeeper."

Rubbing the afternoon nap from his eyes, Ace stopped and looked Meagan up and down. "Ok, this isn't weird." He laughed. "You can start by climbing into my bed before you make it."

"Ace! That was uncalled for!" King growled. "I'm sorry, Ms. Morris. My brother is unfamiliar with the female kind—er, ladies."

"No problem," Meagan replied.

"Whatever, dude," Ace retorted with a slug to King's arm. "I don't see a bunch of ladies waitin' in line for you. She's your maid. Get real!" He sat down in the only rocking chair in the room.

Men like Ace were all too common in Meagan's experience. His quick temper and lack of respect toward King, who was, after all, kind enough not to send her to jail, was ignorant. Clowns who act like Ace are a dime a dozen; Mr. Pullman, on the other hand, was different. She couldn't say precisely what made him more of a man, but it was something tangible. No man alive could make himself appealing to her by insinuating he would enjoy sex with her. She believed a man like that could have sex with anything and like it.

Meagan had put men in their place before, and she hoped she would not lose this housekeeping opportunity over irreconcilable differences either. Several salespeople at The Appliance Warehouse tried to get her fired after she shut down their advances with a bet that she could beat them arm wrestling. She won, and they didn't like it. Thankfully, Mr. Chang, owner of The Appliance Warehouse, had great instincts and warned the fellows to behave themselves. Meagan's co-workers stopped harassing her.

Jack Pullman threw open the door, swept in, and kissed his wife on the cheek. "Hello," he said, turning to Meagan. "Are you here for the job?"

"Yes, I think I've been hired."

"Y-you have, dear," Kate assured her.

King said, "Ms. Morris, meet my dad, Jack Pullman—Dad, meet Meagan."

The two shook hands.

"Ms. Morris is joining us for dinner," King said, "Dad, would you take the Gator and check on the herd? I'm going to finish dinner."

"I can help set the table if that's ok," asked Meagan.

Ace chuckled. "I'll watch."

Kate ordered, "No, y-you won't, Ace. You can help me take my s-shoes off."

Meagan wobbled a bit on her heels, causing King to flinch and grab her by the elbow.

"Thank you," she said.

Managing warily in her new heels, she set the table for five and poured wine for King and Mr. and Mrs. Pullman; Ace preferred beer.

"This pork is amazing! where did you learn to cook, Mr. Pullman?" Meagan inquired.

"Thanks; I started cooking for survival in college and liked it. I thought about starting a restaurant, but the pawn business was a better fit for me. Would you like some wine? Please call me King."

"No, I don't drink; I never have."

"That needs to change," popped Ace. "Is she going to live here? I might have to move in."

Meagan smiled kindly. She remembered when Paxton talked like that back before the punching when he wasn't scared of her.

She asked, "King, what kinds of animals do you have?"

"Alpacas," he said, "a farmer pawned them. I paid fifty dollars a head; they seemed interesting. I like their coats—er, fleece."

King was somber through most of the dinner. Mrs. Pullman concluded that since her son had never talked about a woman, he was mulling over his new hire. A helper is precisely what Mrs. Pullman thought King needed since he was breaking into the ranching business. With all his other responsibilities, hiring a Maid was a wise decision.

Ace talked incessantly about a woman he met several years ago—how beautiful she was. He switched to sports when he exhausted his long list of female conquests. His mother was familiar with the calculating look on Ace's face, it meant trouble, and Mrs. Pullman didn't want trouble between her boys, so she redirected his conversation.

"Ace t-tell me again how your face became so banged up?" asked Kate.

"Mom, I've told you several times now. A few guys I don't know barged into my house, making false accusations. They threatened me and punched me a few times before they left." Ace paused to chew, then continued, "King came, got me, brought me here, and bandaged my face. While I was crashing on his couch, I believe the same two guys showed up here—only this time, they had guns. I was in the kitchen looking for something to eat whenever they came around the corner and attacked me." He glanced over to Meagan; she was looking down at her hands.

Kate prompted, "Well, wow w-what happened after that?"

"It's the strangest thing, Mom," Ace said, "someone shot them both, and it was not me, and it wasn't King."

"Don't look at me," Jack said.

Kate's eyes went wide. "The L-Lord works in mysterious ways."

After dinner, when King cleared the table, Meagan jumped up to help, and Ace followed. Ace set his plate down on the counter at the sink and pressed his hand to Meagan's rear.

"Oh!" she yelped, raised her right foot, and stabbed her heel onto Ace's barefoot.

"Owl! Shit!" Ace yelled, "What the hell!" He hopped around the kitchen, checking his foot for blood.

"I'm sorry," Meagan apologized demurely. "I must have lost my balance again. These shoes were a gift, and I'm not used to them." She continued scraping the plates.

Jack Pullman witnessed the ordeal and kept his mouth shut. He did not approve of a fighting woman or a rude man.

Ace hobbled back to the table under King's disapproving glare. Since no one was severely hurt, King ignored Ace's drama and cleaned the kitchen.

As Meagan was leaving, King walked her to the door. "Ms. Morris, it was nice to meet you," he said, shaking her hand.

His warm hand enveloped hers. When he finally let go, Meagan remembered the article and smiled at him. The new pumps elevated her, placing her face within inches of King's. She held his gaze for seconds, promptly pulled her hand from his, and turned away.

"Thank you for a wonderful dinner. I will be here in the morning at eight sharp." Extracting her keys from her small shoulder bag, she walked gingerly toward the truck, skirting the driveway rocks.

King shouted, "You may want to wear different shoes."

"Roger that!" she replied, waving from her truck window.

Jack fell back onto the sofa and rested his legs on the coffee table. "Well, I have to say I'm not sure I would have hired her, King, she looks like trouble, but you made the decision, so I'm good with it."

Mrs. Pullman poked her husband in the ribs. "She's fine dear, and sh-she seems to need the job. What King w-wants to do in his home is not our b-business."

King listened to his parents' comments about Meagan and shrugged. "We'll see. She drives an eight-cylinder truck."

"Yeah, but those spiky shoes—" Jack shook his head at the tall girl's odd choice in footwear.

Kate nodded in agreement with King—she understood the language of working country people. A truck signified labor, and the Pullmans appreciated and were grateful for labor.

"Oh, I think King liked th-those spiky shoes. He could about l-look her in the eye. Right King?"

Her question went unanswered. King rubbed his temples. Something was bothering him, and Kate wished he would say it. Instead, he retreated to the kitchen and scoured the sink reflectively.

Chapter Sixteen

On her drive back to the Willoughby's after dinner with the Pullman family, Meagan texted Rhonda, "I need different clothes."

Thrilled about the significant change in Meagan's career, Rhonda dialed Meagan's number and asked, "Did you get the job? Where is it? How's the pay?"

Meagan responded, "Yes, I got the job. I'll be a housekeeper and personal assistant, and the pay is great."

There was so much more that Meagan wished she could tell Rhonda. She dreamed of having no secrets, which meant telling her about the things that made her life feel whole, things that were now gone. Things like the Ruby Rose brooch she had yet to reclaim and—King—she would want to describe the man who showed such kindness when he protected her at his pawnshop.

Meagan planned to return his decency with compassion for his family, particularly toward Kate. Getting her possessions back was too essential to gossip about her boss and how he made her sweat when he was near. Her secrets would remain hers—it was no one else's business.

"The atmosphere is good, and the people are nice," Meagan added, fanning her steaming armpits with her free hand.

"Wow, I didn't know it was *that* kind of job."

Here was the Rhonda that Meagan knew, who was passing judgment right then. Rhonda had five careers to Meagan's only job. Her tone told Meagan she was disappointed with her choice to work in someone's home rather than the business world.

"Are you going to have to— wipe someone's—you know—" Rhonda asked cautiously.

Meagan imagined Rhonda rolling her eyes over the possibility that Meagan might care for someone's personal needs. Rhonda became queasy over such things and rarely changed her son's diaper. Instead, she drove Alex to her mother's house, claiming her mother was better at it. Meagan recalled several occasions where Rhonda's gag reflex kicked in over a simple discussion about Alex's wet diaper.

"Probably not," said Meagan, "but I would if the need arose for this job."

"Maybe you should have gone into nursing. I didn't know you'd like to help on such a personal level, but whatever. Hey, I've got some shirts you can borrow for your job until you can buy some. My jeans are too short for you, though."

Rhonda asked, "Are we still good for tomorrow at eight?"

"Yes. I will see you then. Will you bring the clothes with you?"

Meagan's driving matched her reflective mood as she slowed the truck to a stop at the B&B. It was too late to shop for the right first day of work clothes. Meagan would have to wear whatever she could find in her closet until she could borrow Rhonda's things and get to a store to spend more money she did not have.

Morning painted the ranch in shades of amber rose, the grass a more vivid, velvety green than yesterday. The cows across the road were not reaching beyond the fence. Meagan smiled when she read the note taped to King's front door:

You don't have to knock.
On the counter is a list of things to do today.
King

Not knowing what or who to expect, Meagan let herself in the house, making a beeline to the kitchen. She rolled the sleeves of Paxton's plaid shirt up to her elbows and tucked it into her jeans. Her jeans were much looser than they had been a month ago. Mentally running through the stressors in her life, it hit her that she had not eaten breakfast. *Nerves.* Remembering the beautiful meal from the evening before, her stomach moaned. She knew she needed to focus more on eating regularly and working out to keep her muscles healthy. It would be devastating if Mr. Pullman fired her because he thought her too weak to handle the job.

"Another list!" she said appreciatively. In her decade with Paxton Calvert, she could not remember a note ever being written, and here she had received two messages in one day. What that indicated, if anything, she was unable to ascertain.

Grimacing in pain, Kate Pullman took the final step into the kitchen to lean against the fridge. She studied Meagan at the kitchen counter. "King w-wanted to make sure you were all set," she said, pointing to the note.

"Yes, and I'm glad. Mr., ah, King left no stone unturned. Where is he?" Meagan inquired.

"The men are working in their s-shops today." Kate moved to lean on the counter next to Meagan for balance.

Meagan noticed the older woman was only wearing a sock on one foot. "Ms. Kate, let's go back to your room. I'll strip your bed and help you with your compression socks."

"Oh!" Kate did not expect the angelic young woman to anticipate her needs. "If y-you don't mind. That would b-be nice."

Once the bedding was in the washing machine and Meagan had assisted Kate with her socks and hair, she discovered that the country woman hated to miss her television shows; Jeopardy and The Price is Right. She worked on word searches when she wasn't watching her TV shows. Kate occasionally struggled with her words which frustrated her, but she did not give up, and Meagan respected that. Coping with the aftereffects of a stroke could be maddening; Meagan's Uncle Abe had suffered that way.

King's fridge brimmed with a fantastic array of items and prepared dishes. Meagan was beginning to realize what a planner the man was. When she opened a container of chicken salad, she knew Mr. Willoughby would die for the recipe; there were crumples of bacon, raisins, and chopped cashews; it smelled heavenly. Croissant rolls on the counter were the perfect bread for sandwiches. While Meagan assembled everything for their lunch, Kate added a bit of sugar to the pitcher of homemade Sun Tea.

Over lunch, Kate spoke romantically about her youth and growing up in Texas. She told of a best friend, Carla Denton, and their many good times in high school. Meagan could almost feel the West Texas wind on her skin.

"It's s-sad," Kate shared, "but when Jack a-asked me out on our first date, th-that was the last time Carla and I talked."

"What happened to her?"

"Her momma said she went to live with a re-la-tive."

Meagan put her hand on Kate's. "Sometimes life turns out that way."

When Kate couldn't fight back her yawning anymore, she excused herself to lie down for her afternoon nap and happily held Meagan's arm until she reached the queen bed in King's guest room.

Meagan washed and dried the dishes and put them away before taking a break in the living room to enjoy the acreage view. The alpacas were testing the donkey's patience with their antics. A knock at the front door disrupted her quiet time.

A disheveled cowboy smiled charmingly at her, revealing bits of tobacco stuck to his teeth. "Ms., I got a delivery for Mr. King Pullman."

"Oh! Okay, what is it?"

"Alpacas. You got a corral or something for them? This eighteen-wheeler' oud make a mess a yer land."

"You're right," she replied, looking over his shoulder, "your truck does look too heavy to drive on the pasture. I'll be right back."

"Okay, Ms."

Meagan closed the door and stood frozen in thought; should she stay put in case Ms. Kate called for her or help with this delivery that she knew was unexpected but important. She estimated this 'unloading' would take only thirty minutes while Kate snoozed.

Meagan ran to the garage side door, knowing exactly what she needed, rope. Stringing those animals along one rope was no different than beading a necklace, she imagined, and she'd made plenty of those for extra money. She hurried back to the trucker, toting a forty-pound coil of rope.

She yelled, "Okay, let 'em out!"

"Yes, ma'am," Cowboy answered, removing his weathered cowboy hat. He climbed up the heavy corrugated metal ramp to the back end of the truck and raised the roll-up door of the semi.

Meagan approached quickly and was stupefied when hundreds of chickens responding to the bright midday sun began clucking frenetically and disturbing a chocolate brown donkey with enlarged white nostrils. The donkey started hee-hawing, which upset a dozen llamas and alpacas. As chaos ensued, Cowboy waved Meagan up to the truck.

She climbed up the ramp and asked, "Which ones?"

A nosy female alpaca shoved her furry face in Meagan's ear, allowing her to quickly loop the rope around the inquisitive girl's neck.

"These eight fat woolies, ma'am," Cowboy said, pointing them out to her. The shaved ones go 'ta diff'rent rancher.

"Eight?"

"You sure you wanna do this?" he checked.

"Not going to quit now." With six feet of slack in the rope, she threw a loop around another jittery alpaca and talked herself through the tying of a second perfect Alpine Butterfly knot. "Yes, let's go, ladies and gentlemen," Meagan crooned in a sing-song voice while shaking out six more feet of rope and executing another Butterfly knot on a third alpaca.

Cowboy watched, enthralled. "In all my days, Lady," he shouted over the choral circus, "I ain't never seen no knot-tyin' the likes a yourn!" He whipped out his cell phone and began recording Meagan tying knots around the remaining anxious alpacas while she sang a song called, 'You're Going to Love Me.'

"Holy crap!" Cowboy shouted, "You did it!"

In all the racket, Meagan hadn't noticed Cowboy laughing so hard he was coughing, wheezing, and blowing his nose.

"Hold these last four in rope order, please," Meagan ordered, scurrying down the ramp with the first four animals while Cowboy methodically released the last four to follow. Meagan had all eight alpacas secured by one rope into a line.

"Thank you," she said, then jogged to the side of the house toward the main corral. "Oh, did Mr. Pullman pay you?"

Cowboy scratched his head and smiled. "Yup, bye now."

He had initially thought she might ask him to carry the fat buggers to the corral, and that would have been a no-go. Instead, Cowboy had just witnessed the finest hilarity this side of Jupiter. Excited, he published the video on YouTube before climbing into his rig, still grinning.

"Marty, if you've got this, I'm going to take off and work at home," King said.

"No problem," Marty assured him. "Did I hear you talking about a housekeeper?"

"Yes. Mom and Dad are living with me temporarily, and Dad thought it would be a good idea."

Marty gave King a 'thumbs up.' "I agree."

"I've got to go. I'll tell you more about the new hire tomorrow. Thanks."

King left Marty in charge at the shop; he planned to get home early and pound some nails on the second-floor addition before bad weather might hit, which it usually did this time of year. While navigating his truck toward the ranch, his mind wandered to Gayla, Gary, his mother, her stroke, his dad and the robber, Ace's two attackers, and the house addition. He was careful not to include the new maid in the list he worried over.

Much to King's relief, Ace had returned to his own house. He loved his brother, but Ace resembled a dog in heat when in Meagan's company. Before returning to his place, he had his security system checked, motion sensors and night vision cameras added. King doubted the two men mysteriously shot in King's house would press their luck a third time, but if they did, Ace's response would surely cure them of their life of crime.

Guiding his truck down County Road, Meagan popped into his thoughts. Admittedly, his new domestic employee had his attention. With plenty of daylight left, King turned onto his driveway.

Uh oh. She's not here.

Meagan's truck was not in his driveway; it was only four in the afternoon. She had agreed to stay until five-thirty each day. King buried his face in his hands. He could not move; a stab of panic for his mother, who could not be left alone, pierced his gut.

"Shit."

King slammed the truck door and entered his house.

The pink sweater had shown up for work because the note on the front door and the second note on the kitchen counter were gone.

"Hello?" he shouted. He sprinted through the house when no answer came, calling for his mother. "Dammit!" Suddenly, his phone vibrated through the thin leather jacket lining. "Hello?"

"King, it's Dad. Your mother had a fall. I'm here with her at the hospital."

How quickly Meagan's first day on the job had deteriorated.

"What? What happened? Is she going to be okay? How bad is it?"

"She's gonna be okay. I fired that maid. I know she was a looker, Son, but I didn't trust her. Your mother wouldn't have fallen if the helper had been in the house. She was irresponsible, and I will look for someone new, maybe from an agency."

His jaw went slack. King knew his father was wise not to trust the strange, beautiful woman who answered the ad, but it all happened so fast.

"Yeah, hmm, you're probably right. We didn't know her. When will Mom come home?"

"Doc said tomorrow morning. She has a sprained ankle. By the way, thanks for loaning out Storm," Jack added; he's a great dog. He eats a lot but hasn't crapped in the store."

"And he won't as long as you and Mr. Lee don't forget about him," King said. "Are you bringing Mom back to the ranch tomorrow?"

"Yes, if that's okay. Kate eats better at your house."

"Good," replied King, "I'm glad Mom is doing well. Tell her I love her."

"Will do."

King sank into a club chair facing the back acreage and the low afternoon sun. His father's assertions about his pretty maid seemed reasonable, but they did not feel reasonable.

What the hell happened?

In his line of work, reading people well was essential. Disconcerted that he misjudged Meagan, which endangered his mother, he wondered if he was losing his discernment ability with people.

He checked the time on his phone and headed into the kitchen to sort through his deep freeze. There was a shrimp and sausage medley he had made several weeks ago. There would be plenty of time to work while it baked in the oven.

Maybe he would clear his mind of today's events by putting up some walls in his addition.

Hours later, King had to stop working. The sun had completely disappeared over the horizon, and he hadn't noticed; he had been so engrossed hammering nails into sheetrock. Using the bottom of his T-shirt, King wiped the sweat from his face and neck and surveyed his building progress.

With ten minutes left on the casserole, he drove the Gator out to check on his animals. How badly he had misjudged his new employee! He had put that duty on Meagan's list and suggested she check the herd with his mother, but she probably didn't.

As he made his way to the alpacas' corral, his heart rate jumped at the number of animals; it had more than doubled. He braked the Gator hard and hopped out.

"What the Dickens?" he muttered to the curious faces approaching him. "How...well...hello there, little lady."

The tallest of the new group of alpacas was a friendly girl. She boldly poked her head at King's chest and was rewarded with a good head rubbing. He scrutinized his fields for the tire tracks through his land that should have been there, and there were none.

Hmm.

King immediately dialed Dawson's delivery service.

"Yeah, Mr. Pullman, I done dropped those woollies off earlier this afternoon," reported the cowboy.

King raked his fingers through his hair. "How?"

Cowboy suspended his laughing long enough to share. "Well, that pretty wife a yorn, she's something. I'm gonna send you the video. It's great."

King heard him fidgeting with his phone while speaking.

"Wife?"

"Yeah, I didn't know you was married, but if she got a sister who looks that purty, then hook me up! I don't care if she cay'nt cook nor dance!"

"Ah." King realized Cowboy thought Meagan was his wife and that Dawson dealt with Meagan regarding the delivery of the animals, and there was a video.

"What video?"

"I just sent it. I gotta go." He coughed while laughing. "Thank ya for your business, Mr. Pullman."

"You bet," King replied absently.

He wandered into the barn office, eager for a place to sit down and process the information about Meagan. He tapped play.

This Meagan was very different; she was a country girl in the video. Her worn jeans and plaid shirt suited her, he thought. Her hair was in a ponytail on the top of her head, and she was roping his livestock!

"What?"

He grabbed a pair of reading glasses and leaned closer to his phone to see her better. Meagan cooed to the alpacas as they spouted their guttural bleating. She smiled and sang the words to "Only my Sweetheart" while the tall alpaca kept nuzzling her neck, another nuzzle, and an ear lick.

That crazy alpaca has a long tongue!

Meagan cheered because she remembered her knot-tying skills, then she roped another, and switched songs. A nearby male alpaca didn't care to be that close to Meagan and spat in her face.

"Oh no! Ha, ha, ha!"

King could not keep himself from laughing; Meagan's face dripped with undigested grain-infused spittle fragments. Friendly alpaca girl had Meagan's ponytail in her mouth and was jerking Meagan's head back, but she hung on and continued to sing, "Sweetheart, my sweetheart, I'm in love with you…." Refusing to let go of her crazy not tying scheme—on the sixth creature, on she sang, "Kiss me and hold me near, say the words I long to hear…."

"Oh no! Jeez, this is funny!"

King scrolled down and noted that the video, Hot Naughty Woman with Woolies, had over ten thousand views. He smiled.

So, Meagan roped them so she could corral them for me. What a dynamic woman.

Pride surged through him, along with a renewed zeal to find Meagan and rehire her. Jack had not taken the time to learn why Meagan had not been in the house. That may or may not make a difference to Jack, but it was significant, nonetheless.

The casserole!

He quickly raced the Gator to the house, appetite lost. He turned the oven off, set the casserole to cool on the cooktop, and retrieved Meagan's employment application from the file cabinet in his office.

Any woman who was as resourceful as Meagan, well, she shouldn't have been fired. "I don't care how pretty she is...."

He threw on his old college hoodie, antsy to get to her before the night was gone.

King's anxiety over apologizing to Meagan as soon as possible messed with his rationale; he should have showered and eaten, for that matter. He was lucky he remembered to turn off the oven and put the casserole in the fridge. If he had thought it through, as he did with other areas of his life, King wouldn't have chased Meagan down while he was starving and smelling like sweat and lumber.

Blanchard Avenue could do with more lighting, but thankfully the three-story Victorian B&B was hard to miss. He rolled into the small parking lot before the building and rubbed his temples. He was about to lose his nerve when he noticed lights coming down the driveway from the back of the building; it was the big brown truck she drove. The decision to follow her was simple.

Meagan drifted down Blanchard Avenue and turned onto Highway Ninety for several miles before exiting northwest. King kept a discreet distance, but he bet she was too preoccupied with where she was going to notice his headlights behind her anyway.

"The Electric Panda?" He had never heard of the establishment, but apparently, many other people had. The place was hopping, and Meagan immediately veered away from the valet service; therefore, she had no choice but to park in the far back corner and hike to the bar.

Watching Meagan walk alone through the vast parking lot in her wispy dress, cowboy boots, glossy hair down in waves, troubled him. She appeared utterly unaware of her vulnerability. King knew her peril was real. He waited until she was inside the building before pulling his truck up to the valet; He tossed the attendant his keys and then slipped inside The Electric Panda.

King could have been mistaken for an air conditioning serviceman in the sterile bar, among two generations of people who clothes shop in places with names he could not pronounce. The waitstaff dressed in white gave the bar a clinical air. The volume of the music vibrated the floor, making small talk impossible. Places like this weren't for talking, and King knew it; the sleek people here were done talking; they wanted action. A shiver went through him.

Abruptly, the music stopped, and a throng of people applauded. Venturing farther into the monstrous room, he realized the music was live.

The DJ announced, "Registration is closed. Five minutes until the contest. Back for more abuse, here is Don Canter with a song by Dreadfully Dead. Show him some love!"

A handful of people clapped, and some yelled, "Sing it, captain!"

It was a raised stage suitable for a star. King decided to hang back by the bar and listen to Don sing. Following Don, an older woman built like a man and sporting a fur vest belted out, 'Like A Bridge Over Troubled Water,' the husky way Disturbed sings it.

The crowd loved it. King's opinion of the establishment shifted with the impressive talent he was witnessing.

The dim, atmospheric lighting was sufficient to spotlight Meagan's blonde hair, creating an angelic glow aura. King could easily track her from his seat at the bar.

"Jack and Coke," he called to the bartender.

Meagan embraced a red-haired woman, and King assumed they were friends.

"Thanks, Don, and thank you, Lisa," the DJ announced. "To start the contest, please welcome Meagan Amber!"

King choked on his drink.

"Are you okay?" shouted the bartender over the applause.

Nodding his head, King remained glued to the drama unfolding at the stage where there was a disagreement between Meagan and her friend, as the friend pushed Meagan toward the stage. She reluctantly climbed the stairs, encouraged by the crowd.

A stagehand set a tall barstool near the mic stand, and Meagan sat down on it, hooking one boot heel on the lower rung of the stool. The bartender stopped his work to see what Meagan would do.

The red-headed friend used sign language to communicate with the indignant DJ, then hurried back to the stage and handed Meagan a small black guitar. The crowd cheered wildly in anticipation; Meagan snuggled comfortably under the guitar strap. Her floral chiffon dress stopped several inches short of the light tan cowboy boots she wore.

King's heart was hammering in his chest as war raged within him. His desire to sweep Meagan out of this place battled his concern and morbid curiosity about her upcoming performance— the stress of the situation compounded by her name, something about her name.

She strummed and purred into the mic, "How are you all doing tonight?"

The audience responded with whistling and catcalls.

"That's what I thought," she added, causing a surge of laughter among the throng.

The long fingers of her left hand curled around the neck of the guitar as she seamlessly reached notes and chords. She smiled. "Beatles for you tonight."

The DJ stood, arms crossed, like a sentry at the palace gate, appearing none too pleased with Meagan. This performance was not Karaoke; it was real. Meagan commanded the stage now.

Making eye contact with the barkeep, King held one finger up, and quickly, another Jack and Coke arrived.

"She's hot. Do you know her?" asked the bartender.

His attention riveted on Meagan; King vaguely heard the question.

"Huh?" he asked. "Yeah, I know her."

Radiant was the word King was looking for; she looked radiant.

"So, he checked, "You haven't seen her in here before?"

The bartender shrugged his shoulders. "Nope, I would have remembered her, a babe like that? Whew."

What a thirty-year-old barman with plugs in his earlobes thought about Meagan shouldn't have irritated King, but it did. The leggy beauty on the stage corralled eight alpacas all by herself; she was not the girl for lobes, in his opinion.

It was subtle, but as Meagan sang and glanced out over the crowd, King noticed her countenance changed. It was as though a completely different person had possessed her body, and the real Meagan had just left the building. Astonished, King wondered if anyone else had witnessed the transformation. Her fingers sailed over the frets delighting every ear with her version of George Harrison's song, My Guitar Gently Weeps.

If he hadn't observed Meagan with his own eyes, he would not have believed that voice belonged to her; it was ladened with searing emotion. The clear resonant vocal sparkling with uncried tears shoved the arrow deeper into his heart. When she strummed the last chord, King wiped his forehead, downed the remainder of his drink, and slapped thirty dollars on the bar with a salute to the barkeep.

Back in his truck, he smiled and texted her, then set the phone on the passenger seat of his Ford and steered back to the ranch, lost in thought. This time he was trying to unravel the confounding puzzle that was Meagan.

"Meagan Amber, hmm."

"What was that all about?" Meagan shouted, inches from Rhonda's face. "Huh? Since when do you think I can sing or play the guitar? That, in there on stage, could have been a disaster!"

Rhonda had never known Meagan to spit fire like that.

"I'm sorry, but I'm not. Look, Meg, you are much more than a desk job or a caretaker; you have real talent! A few times when we were kids, you thought I was going somewhere, but I didn't. I sat on the floor outside your bedroom door and listened to you play."

"Why? You had no right. You were spying. This is really because my choice of employment embarrasses you, isn't it?"

Rhonda defended her position. "What? No. I knew you would never actually play your music for my parents or me because all your songs were about sadness and loss, and I don't blame you. But they were beautiful, and sometimes you would cry when you sang. I cried too. You have real talent, and I'm sorry I waited over twenty years to tell you."

Meagan softened. "Whose guitar is this?"

"Alex's. He doesn't know I borrowed it."

"Excuse me," Meagan shouted. Her phone buzzed with a text from King.

"Meagan, thank you for what you did today. You're on my payroll, not Jack's. Please come back to work. Mom gets home tomorrow and would like it if you were here."

Meagan responded, "Thanks, I will be there."

"Who was it?" Rhonda snooped.

"My new boss. I should go. I have to be at work early." Emotionally drained from her firing, the surprise performance, the rehiring, and frustration with Rhonda, she was done with The Electric Panda.

"Okay," Rhonda said, "No secrets, right?"

"Right."

The friends embraced, and Meagan quickly left.

Andrew raced to his second-floor bedroom window, nearly spilling his latte. He frowned at the morning fog. He had hoped to see pretty Meagan scurrying to her truck. Since his room was directly under Meagan's and the floor squeaked, he was alerted to her comings and goings. This morning she had escaped him, which left him perplexed. He sipped his brew, ruminating over their date. She promised to meet him for dinner at Angelo's Italian restaurant on Friday evening.

The thought of cruising with Meagan in his convertible Corvette sent a shiver of excitement through his body. He knew they would have a great time and end with a kiss. Andrew had imagined that kiss and where it would lead hundreds of times since she moved into the B&B.

Justina had studied psychology and told Andrew when he moved in close for a kiss, "A kiss could reveal too much about a person. It would ruin the mystery." She had made it clear to Andrew that their relationship would involve no kissing as she believed in keeping her kissing secrets to herself. The status of their connection satisfied Andrew, but what Justina would not make available to him, he would get from Meagan soon.

His mind reeled with thoughts of Meagan's kiss. Reaching for his iPad, he searched for beach vacation packages; that was the obvious way to get her in a bikini which Mr. Willoughby would be impressed with. He would bring her flowers at her work tomorrow to grease the skids and get things off on the right foot.

Chapter Seventeen

The scent of freshly ground coffee wafted through King's tidy kitchen. Kate hobbled in on a walker. "I am s-so glad you came back, Meagan! I'm th-the first one to ad-mit, Jack's temper can make him un, un-reasonable sometimes. How are you, dear?"

"I'm glad to be back, thank you. Your speech is going great! How about your foot?" Meagan's peripheral vision caught movement by the barn where King worked with the animals.

Kate smiled. "My ankle will be fine. Y-you know we were both so har-ried yesterday, I want to ask you; how is it you c-carried me, like a man, to your truck, and into the hos-pital? I think it was a miracle."

Meagan could see Kate was bewildered. "Well, I work out regularly," she shared nonchalantly. "Let me help you get your socks on, and we'll have breakfast and then visit the alpacas."

"Sounds lov-lovely."

In the barn, King used his brand-new clippers to shear an alpaca for the first time. Nosy Girl seemed the most agreeable to the process. She calmly stood muzzled in the corner of a stall in the barn while King meticulously razored off her fleece.

When Nosy Girl was devoid of her fluff and returned to the pen, Meagan and Kate arrived in the Gator, much to King's amazement.

"Definitely not the girl for lobes," he muttered. The Gator had a tricky gear-shifting system which Meagan had figured out. "Hi." He smiled and waved.

Although they were only a few feet from the corral, Kate elected to stay in her seat.

"Nice to see you both!" He greeted them with a wink to Meagan.

"Thank you," Meagan mouthed as she approached him.

He nodded in understanding that she was grateful to be back on her job.

"Oh d-dear, these animals are big!" Kate exclaimed. "Are they dan-ger-ous?"

King stifled a laugh, remembering Meagan's interaction with the alpacas in the video. "Not really. None of these are over one-hundred-eighty pounds and generally are not aggressive."

"She looks good," Meagan said, pointing toward the friendly, freshly shorn animal.

King explained his struggle with some of the alpacas," They are unruly and somewhat skittish. Except for the tall, amorous girl, she was agreeable." He winked at Meagan again, causing her face to turn beet red.

Kate enjoyed witnessing King more engaged than she had ever seen him. His eyes sparkled as he talked about his alpacas and the ranch.

Gayla shaded her eyes from the bright morning sun as she drove to work at the clinic, passing King's house. She stopped and backed up when she noticed the strange, clean brown truck. A closer look revealed a window sticker that read, 'Girls love trucks too.' It was parked next to King's. She knew the vehicles associated with the Pullman businesses and family; that brown truck was not one of them. She slammed the gear shift into park and sprinted to King's house.

Gayla was pleasantly surprised to find his front door unlocked.

"Hello!" she shouted, marching through the living room to the windows.

There was King in the distance, down by the animals. "There are women here," she snarled. In a flash, she was running uncontrollably toward the pasture. "What the hell, King!" she screamed.

Kate Pullman's hand covered her heart, distressed that the woman was yelling at King. She leaned over to Meagan in the Gator and whispered, "Will she hurt him?"

"I hope not," Meagan answered, surprised. King was an intelligent, tall, strapping man with evident strength, yet his mother was worried for his safety.

Gayla jerked open the corral gate, yelling, "Who is she?" and pointing to Meagan.

"You have no business here, Gayla. I have already told you that!" King snapped.

Gayla lunged toward King with her fist straight out and slugged him in the neck, sending him stumbling backward to the fence.

Donkey scurried over, spun a half-turn, and caught Gayla on the buttock with a hard swift hoof kick causing her to turn and twist her ankle. She grabbed her rear, wailing in pain and hopping on one foot. She screamed, "You hurt me, King!" Then she fell to the ground and lay on her back, gasping for breath and whining.

Nosy Girl pranced close to Gayla and spat a meaty wad of cud directly at her, fragments scattered across Gayla's chest and face.

"No! Shit!" she screamed in disgust, wiping the slime from her eyes while wincing in pain.

"We can take you to your car," Meagan offered.

"My car? I can't sit down, you idiot. Just shut up, will you? I need to lie down. I'm bruised, and my ankle is likely broken."

She rubbed her rear as King helped her off the ground.

"Get in," Meagan ordered, directing Gayla to the small Gator bed.

Gayla asked, "King, tell her to shut up?"

"Just go, Gayla."

Never before had Meagan beheld a man not defending himself against a woman. She had seen the punch coming for King and knew the potential life-altering disastrous consequences if a throat punch was delivered correctly and had held her breath until King could stand. She couldn't understand why he hadn't even put up his guard. Meagan reasoned that Mrs. Pullman's concern was valid; maybe her son couldn't defend himself. Perhaps he never learned how. Some men only knew how to fight with a gun, but she had assumed King would be the kind of man who knew how to do it all. She guessed wrong.

Gayla lay on her side in the bed of the Gator whimpering while King felt her ankle for damage.

"You scraped the skin. You'll be fine," King assured her, then informed Meagan and his mother, "I'll be done in a couple of hours."

Meagan noticed King rubbing his neck and stretching his head slowly from side to side as though he was trying to correct something. He was clearly in pain.

The volatile girlfriend had caused some damage, after all.

"No, I won't be fine, King! You owe me!" Gayla bellowed in outrage.

Kate's eyes widened, and she asked, "You owe her, King?"

In the house, Gayla hobbled straight to the master bedroom and sprawled out on King's bed, yelling for an ice pack for her buttock, which Meagan promptly delivered and ran out before further requests could be made.

While Mrs. Pullman and Gayla took their respective naps, Meagan searched the kitchen drawers for the ruby brooch, but no luck. Since Mr. Pullman had brought the piece to King, she felt sure King had it, and she would find it soon.

She paused at the kitchen window with her glass of tea and watched her employer check the corral fence. When he paused to wipe his face, Meagan knew he was tired and hot. She filled a large tumbler with frosty tea and drove it to him.

He saw her coming and flashed a grin; it was addictive, she thought. Every time he smiled, she wanted another one.

"I thought you might like this." She held up the tumbler of tea.

He took the glass and sat down on a bale of hay, craning his neck this way and that and wincing.

"I can't be out here long. Would you like some help with your neck?" Meagan asked.

"Only if it doesn't involve a rope."

There was that grin again.

Meagan smiled back. "No, it doesn't. If you lay down flat, it would help." She stepped out of the Gator and walked over to King.

When Gayla punched him, he heard something pop in his neck, followed by a stabbing sensation in his upper back with every slight turn of his head. He was game for anything that might bring him some relief. He set his tea on the hay bale, laid back on a patch of grass by the barn, and announced, "I'm ready! Are you gonna walk on my chest or something?"

"No, but hopefully, I can help you."

Meagan dropped to her knees at his head, and they peered at each other upside down. She reached under King's upper back, pushing her fingers and massaging in deep circles. He groaned appreciatively.

"How do you know how to do this, Meagan?"

"I think there are times when we all need it. My best friend's dad was a chiropractor, and occasionally I would get adjustments. I also watched him do this. Just relax," she urged and continued massaging until it was clear King was putty in her hands. She studied his face. Her fingers moved toward his well-muscled neck and stroked hard.

In a dream state, King opened his eyes for a moment. Meagan noted the family's remarkable resemblance among the Pullman men. Although Kate's eyes were ocean blue, her husband and two sons had green eyes tinged with gray, high cheekbones, and dark hair.

King sighed contentedly as Meagan's knuckles pushed into muscles at the sides of his upper spine. She applied pressure with her palms to his clavicle, then moved gently, placing her hands on the sides of his head. He wasn't expecting what would happen next.

Bracing her fingers gently under his chin, she pulled hard, wrenching his head up from his back. His eyes flew open when his neck popped twice. Meagan let go and patted his shoulder softly.

"All better?"

"Not sure…"

He lay there, eyes closed, motionless, and deeply concerned he could be paralyzed. He checked for movement in his extremities, and when everything felt operational, he slowly moved his head from side to side; the pain was gone.

When he glanced up to thank her, Meagan was halfway back to the house.

"Lovely Meagan Amber," he spoke to the sky, "she ropes alpacas and brings music, beauty, and healing."

Yes, she did that, which was great, but it was what she wasn't doing. That's what was getting under King's skin. Meagan wasn't falling all over him. He had only had to imagine a woman kissing him in his entire life, and the universe obliged; the stars aligned, and then it happened. Something was going awry.

During her interview in the pink sweater, he couldn't stop imagining himself holding her. Kate had asked Meagan a question, and although she was responding, King could not hear anything; his dream commandeered his mind.

Meagan ignored my mother's question. She locked eyes with me and came to me. "Thank you for hiring me," she said dreamily, and with her hands on the sides of my chair, she lowered her face to mine and kissed me softly. I began to sweat uncontrollably, and recognizing that I was in a dream state of consciousness, I changed my vision and pictured Gayla's face; immediately, I could hear Meagan again speaking to Mom.

He stood by the barn, picked up his sweet tea, and gulped it gratefully, wondering how to step up his game and make his dream a reality.

Meagan smiled, content that she could help ease her nice boss's pain, and immediately attended to her maid duties. After expertly cleaning the bathrooms, she checked for King's whereabouts and noticed he was still in the corral with the alpacas. She knew she would have time to search for her possessions quickly, and no one would be the wiser. The computer on the desk in King's office was already on.

She began perusing Sell City, there were a million things for sale, and it seemed time was evaporating. Under the 'Sports and Outdoor' category, she zeroed in on a posting of a pheasant. Focusing on the details, she whispered, "Bingo!"

King shucked his work boots in the mudroom. He quietly headed to his bedroom, aware that his convalescing mother may still be napping.

"Damn," he groaned. The last person he wanted to see in his home was Gayla, lying on his bed again.

In his stocking feet, he turned and approached the guest bedroom. Peeking through the open door, he saw that his mother was not napping, and there was no sign of Meagan either. Someone turned on a water faucet in the guest bathroom, and he presumed it was Kate, but the ticking sound captured his attention; he tiptoed to his office.

Meagan was at his computer, engrossed, sitting with her back to King, facing the front of the property and the cows across County Road. He instinctively took out his phone, held it up high, and quietly snapped the photo of the screen she studied. He disappeared before she noticed he was there.

The sound of something falling in the bathroom alerted Meagan, and she wrapped up her investigation in a second to check on Ms. Kate.

"I'm s-sorry about that noise. I dropped a can of hairspray into the bathroom sink," Kate explained.

"Let me comb your hair for you, Ms. Kate," Meagan said, taking the brush from the rumpled, stressed elderly lady.

Patiently she brushed Kate's thick gray hair into a twist and secured it with a long barrette and a dash of hairspray.

"Thank you, d-dear. I napped all over that pillow today!"

King stood out of sight, listening to their conversation. His mother seemed to get along well with Meagan; what's not to like? King reviewed his few moments in Meagan's company, and it was absurd to realize that he knew virtually nothing about the beauty in his employ. Aside from some apparent talents she had, she was a stranger. His gut told him she was up to something. He knew he needed some answers, or he would never rest. He flipped his laptop open on the kitchen counter and turned the oven on to bake the chicken that had been marinating for hours. Foam as thick as a steak crested the ale in his frosted beer glass; he sipped and surfed the Internet.

He searched "Meagan Morris" and was shocked to learn that she had won boxing trophies at a fight club in the city under the name Meagan Morris Calvert. The referee in the article was holding her hand in the air as the winner of the match. Her opponent was a Honduran woman who looked worse for the wear.

The more King investigated her fighting history, the more photos surfaced of her in different garb; *black skull cap, fingerless gloves…lips covered in dark, dried blood…*

Something horrible niggled at his brain; King felt his blood pressure rising as his heart rate kicked up then it dawned on him.

It was her! Oh shit, it's her—the robber with the gun! Holy crap, and she works for me now. I'm sure of it!

"This is insane." A woman with no issues pointing a gun at people would have no problem punching them. Pieces of the puzzle were beginning to converge. "Yes, it's her."

He took a deep breath and vowed to get to the bottom of it. His jaw fell open in awe over his unbelievably complicated situation; the thief from his shop who shot the intruders in his home and saved his brother was the same woman doing his mother's hair. A tingling sensation rippled through him—the theatrics of being secretly watched by her in his bedroom had become a creepy stalker calamity.

An article about her husband, Paxton Calvert, stole King's attention online. He was surprised to learn Meagan was married but more surprised that she was widowed and hadn't remarried.

"Meagan, what are you trying to do?" He questioned the face on the screen.

He began reviewing his first meeting with Meagan; she intended to rob him at gunpoint for a string of pearls in a photo she carried.

The photo! Could she be after another bauble worn by the ladies in that photo?

He was positive that she now had the cameo necklace and picture since they were both missing from his room. He recalled other jewels from the photo.

Neither Jack nor Ace had encountered any of the pieces King told them to look out for; they hadn't mentioned anything yet.

Looking at his worried reflection in the oven door, he wondered if his growing fascination with Meagan was reasonable or lunacy. King doubted Meagan would tell him the truth if he were to ask her what she had been doing on his computer. His intuition steered him away from that conversation.

The timer on the oven beeped. It was time to insert the chicken and put wild rice on to cook. He continued to ponder Meagan. Should he trust her with his mother? The answer was yes because he knew she had fired the shots that saved his brother. It wasn't self-defense on her part because the men who broke into his house could not identify her. He considered asking her point blank if she shot Ace's attackers, but she would likely lie because she was in his home illegally when she fired. It didn't matter anyway because Dell had already solved the mystery for King. Ballistics had confirmed the bullets in Ace's assailants' posteriors came from a 9-millimeter gun, just like the shell lodged in the roof of the pawnshop. It all pointed to Meagan.

Another factor in his maid's favor was that she fixed King's neck; a nice person would do that. The truth was, he was on to her now, and she didn't know it. He now felt he had an advantage: being one up on her felt good. His curiosity was at an all-time high. He enlarged the page on his laptop to look at the photos he had taken behind Meagan's back.

Was it a photo of a pheasant?

"I thought she had a better work ethic than to peruse the Internet on paid time." He smirked, wondering why a person who robs another at gunpoint would have ethics in the first place. "I'm an idiot; she is shopping for a stuffed bird. Why would any woman want a taxidermy pheasant?"

Bewildered by his discovery, he sat on the counter, tapping a spoon against his leg, thinking. Then he texted the seller of the bird, "Still have the stuffed bird for sale?"

The reply came quickly, "Sort of. Got someone looking at it tonight; I'll let you know if they don't show."

"If I could see it at the same time, you might get us bidding for it and make double."

The seller responded, "Whatever, I'm game. George Street bakery parking lot nine PM cash only."

"Tonight?"

"Yes," the seller confirmed.

"Will do then. Thanks," replied King.

He closed his laptop and took out his frustrations on the vegetables he was chopping while considering the possible scope of her war and the battle he was about to engage in—if the buyer was indeed his maid.

Conroy slowed his pace to a walk and picked up his cell phone. "Hello."

"Hello, Mr. Sabeth. This is Calvin Cobb. I have an update for you regarding the case. I am waiting for a call and a set of documents to confirm two things, and the job will be complete. We can set up a meeting if you'd like. If everything goes as planned, I should have a package for you in a few days. Can I call you for a meeting on short notice?"

Veering from the jogging path in the park, Conroy leaned against a tree. "That will be fine." He pocketed his phone and closed his eyes to pray for the enigmatic girl of his youth and their child.

Chapter Eighteen

What are you c-cooking, King?" asked Kate as she maneuvered her walker to the breakfast table. "I used to c-cook," she whispered to Meagan.

"Chicken," grunted King.

Kate's tone was nostalgic and touched Meagan. "What was your favorite dish to prepare, Mrs. Pullman?"

As Kate shared her favorite recipes and their origins, Meagan washed her hands and set the table for the Pullman family. She sensed something was amiss regarding King. Though his neck appeared to be fine now, his attitude was not.

With the water and wine glasses filled and the table set for dinner, Meagan announced, "It's five thirty."

"Yes, d-dear," said Kate.

Meagan gaped at King, flummoxed that he was so lost in his thoughts that he had not heard his mother's conversation or that it was five-thirty.

"Hello?" Meagan said again as she neared her boss.

King shook off his thoughts. "Oh, did I miss something?" He looked Meagan in the eyes. "I tend to miss things here lately… yes, it's five thirty; see you later."

Jack arrived home from work and strolled into the kitchen to kiss his wife. "Hello," he said, then scowled at Meagan.

"She was just leaving, Dad," King said, wishing his father would not carry a grudge against his maid.

Kate waved to Meagan. "Bye, h-honey."

Awakened from her lengthy nap, Gayla stomped into the living room and stopped abruptly before Meagan.

"Who the hell are you? Who?" She snapped angrily, her hands on her hips.

"She is King's maid," said Jack.

"You can w-walk!" Kate exclaimed, noting Gayla's absent limp.

"Yeah, right. Gayla marched, her limp restored, to the kitchen where King served the food. "Which agency is she with?"

"No agency," replied Jack.

Guilt hammered at King. He met his father's glare; they knew Meagan was a calculated employment risk.

"And just who are you?" Jack asked.

"Gayla. I'm King's girlfriend."

Instantly Gayla straightened and smiled.

Jack's eyebrows flew up in surprise. "Nice to meet you." He quickly looked to King for a denial of the woman's statement, and none came.

"It's ready," King announced, ignoring the suspicious look from his father. "Dig in while it's hot. That includes you, Gayla."

"Well, it's about time, King. Thank you," she purred contentedly.

Meagan rolled her eyes, closed the front door, and quietly walked to her truck, grateful that Gayla hadn't parked behind her. She had more important things to do tonight than listen to Gayla beg for money and attempt to have sex with King.

Once she turned off the County Road, she concentrated on the pheasant, and the memory came alive.

She had just turned six years old and had gone with her dad on a hunting trip. She was taking pictures with his phone when she wasn't playing a game on it. Since her dad did not have a bird dog, Meagan knew she had to be vigilant and help her dad visually track the fowl once he shot it. It was an incredible stroke of luck that she had his phone set to movie mode. Mr. Morris kicked up some underbrush causing several large birds to scuttle out and take flight. Meagan pressed 'record.' Her father aimed and shot a bird, which she captured on film. Her effort was a huge success, and her father took every opportunity to praise her.

"Meagan was so clever to film the descent of the pheasant," he would tell people. "We watched the clip, and it took us right to our kill." The best part for Meagan was the hug and the pat on the head, followed by "I Love you, Meggie."

"…and I'm home," she mumbled, saddened her trip down memory lane had concluded.

The Corvette convertible was not in the rear parking lot, which relieved Meagan. She wasn't interested in talking to Andrew. She had a pheasant mission to complete in a couple of hours. She was taking the stairs two at a time to her room, mentally preparing for the recovery operation.

Contentedly lying on her bed, she stared at the custom ceiling, the work of an expert mason who had probably been dead for several decades.

Thoughts of Paxton returned; they were more frequent since moving into the Willoughby B&B.

Maybe it's this place; it's old and probably haunted. I should have asked Aunt Agnes if anyone ever died in this house.

Sleep overtook her; however, she awoke in a panic twenty minutes before her meeting time with the seller of the pheasant. Meagan removed her work clothes and donned the camo pants, black lace-up military boots, AC-DC t-shirt, and Pax's leather jacket. There was no time to fiddle with overdoing the makeup for a better disguise. She grabbed sunglasses and a ski hat and sailed down the creaky wooden stairs to her truck.

Kate sensed King needed space and was not surprised when he told them he would run an errand.

"At this hour? asked his father. "Sun's gone down."

"He's g-got things he needs to do," Kate said, patting Jack on the arm. "Let him be."

"I'm going to pick up a file from the shop," King volunteered.

"Okay, son," said Jack.

King kissed his mother on the cheek and hurried to shower and dress to bid on a bird and hopefully not get shot by Meagan. "I need a Kevlar vest and a lobotomy," he whispered, adjusting the shower water temperature. He would count it a win if he could survive the night.

Jack and Kate sat in the living room enjoying their evening decaf coffee. Kate worked on a word search puzzle book while Jack manned the television remote, flipping channels for a suitable news station.

Gayla entered the room and sat in a club chair across from them.

"So," she said, interrupting the mood, "Why did King hire that maid?"

"He has too much on his plate and needs help," informed Jack.

A thousand times, Gayla had fantasized about the day King would properly introduce her to his parents; it was always a sweet vision, and she always felt proud. Not now. This was going terribly. No one had spoken at the dinner table except to compliment King on his cooking ability. Gayla thought she and King would grow closer over the years, but the past year had been anything but close. Her patience was running out, and earlier, that woman or maid, or whatever she was, stretched Gayla's last nerve. There was something between her and King; Gayla sensed it and loathed it. It needed to stop, and she intended to put the kibosh on the maid.

"Is it okay if I call you Mom and Dad?" asked Gayla.

Jack's eyes cut suspiciously over to his son's guest. "Why? You can call me Jack."

"And I, I'm Kate."

"Well, I thought since King and I have a child together, we should start acting like a family," Gayla drawled innocently. "Right?"

Kate's eyes darted to her husband; she was concerned about his blood pressure. The information about their eldest son having a child was a shock. If the nervous, accusing woman before them wasn't careful, she might be the recipient of Jack's hot temper.

"How old is your child?" demanded Jack.

"Twelve," she said, beaming, and he looks like King and you!"

There was something…it was years ago… a story, maybe a rumor, that was gaining traction in Kate's memory. She cocked her head inquisitively and asked, "What's y-your last name?"

"Adamson. Why?"

"What do you do for a living?" Jack persisted as though, at any second, Gayla would change her story, and some other poor sonofabitch would be named the father.

"I'm a veterinarian," she reported.

Something was off, according to Kate. Little hairs standing at attention on the back of her neck added to her discomfort. "D-did you at-tend the University of Tennessee?"

"Yes! "Did King tell you about it?" Gayla was pleased that King's parents were familiar with her education.

"No, he didn't. I can't remember ex-actly who told me. I seem to re-call hearing about you, and you're a-aspirations when I worked at the bank."

Gayla shifted position in the chair. "What did you do at the bank, Mom?"

"Not too much. I worked there for four years to help with King's c-college costs. He works so hard, you know, I wanted to help. I managed s-some personal accounts for wealthy clients of the bank and assis-ted with financial planning. More of it comes back to me as we sit here and talk," Kate admitted pensively.

Gayla shot to her feet. "Okay then, Mom and Dad, I'm going to head home to your grandson, and I'll talk to you tomorrow!"

She collected her boots on her way out the door.

"Funny thing..." Jack growled, "Kate did you notice she didn't limp? There's nothing wrong with that girl physically. "What do you know about her?"

"Nothing really; I just have a feeling, dear." Kate strongly suspected that King was in a mess, but she needed to check on her old information before saying anything definite.

King reentered the room, freshly showered and yanking an old college hoodie over his head. "I don't know what time I'll be home. Please don't wait up." He cautiously peered around the room.

Jack cleared his throat. "Your girlfriend went home."

"Oh, good. She's not my girlfriend. Never was."

"King, do what you need t-to do," Kate said softly, "we love you."

Chapter Nineteen

The George Street Bakery closed hours before King arrived. It was a moonless night, perfect for his maid's heist. The bakery at the far end of the building, near a heavily treed area with a drainage culvert provided seclusion. The strip shopping center contained eight businesses; two remained open: a dry cleaner and a Yoga Hut.

"My God is it really you?" he said, spotting Meagan's dark truck approaching the bakery to wait for the seller to show.

The dark window tint on her vehicle made it impossible for King to see exactly who was behind the wheel. He slowed his Ford pickup and parked at the adjacent hair salon business. King snuck out with numerous cars between them, edging closer to Meagan's vehicle and hiding behind a minivan to observe her.

A small SUV whipped into the parking lot. King felt his chest constrict when Meagan stepped from her truck.

"Shit!" he whispered.

She was in her military clothing again with her hands in her pockets.

"Not good."

He noticed she had a swagger that was not present when she had robbed him.

Her thieving confidence has increased. She is more dangerous than ever.

A young man wearing sneakers and smoking a cigarette was carrying the fowl.

"You here for the bird," he asked Meagan.

"Yes, please set it on my tailgate."

"Okay."

King wiped his face with his hand, wishing the vision would disappear. His heart raced when he witnessed her fumbling with something in her pocket and feared she was about to use her gun. He dashed to the scene, coming up behind her and bracing her. His hand clamped down on hers. He noticed the safety was on. His body pressed against her back, one arm sealed around her waist.

Meagan could not move; his body was a vice grip holding hers, trapped.

"Dang, a gun! Whoa! Wait a second," shouted the seller, ducking behind the truck to watch the customers wrestle. "Are you the other interested party?" He emerged with his hands up. "Don't shoot!"

"Yes, I am the interested party." King breathed hard next to Meagan's ear. "Get your finger off the trigger."

"Get off me!" she ordered.

"And miss this dance? Not a chance."

"This is jacked up!" said the seller, flicking his cigarette to the pavement and squishing out the flame with his shoe. He exhaled a puff of smoke. Peeking over the truck bed, he said, "Listen, looks like you all have issues. I'll take two hundred bucks. Who's paying? I gotta go."

"I'll pay your price," said King.

"No!" screamed Meagan. "No, you won't! It's mine!"

"Yours? Really? I don't think so." King jerked the gun from her grip and dropped it on the concrete.

The seller's eyes widened. He fidgeted in his jacket pocket, produced a lighter, and lit the fresh cigarette bobbing nervously from his lips. "Hey, do I know you?" he asked King. "Look, I'll take a hundred fifty."

"No, you won't!" Meagan said through gritted teeth. "You rotten thief! The pheasant was never yours. You stole it!"

She screamed and stomped on King's foot and only succeeded in bruising her heel on the steel-reinforced toe of his work boot.

King felt Meagan's body trembling. His hot breath steamed her ear through the knit cap fueling her anger. He continued to dominate her physically, and there was no wiggle room.

"Whose bird is it?" King demanded.

Astounded and embarrassed that her employer caught her red-handed, trying to recover her father's pheasant, she said, "It's mine. I told you, it's mine."

"Just like the lady's head necklace?" he asked.

"Yes. It's a cameo." Her voice wavered, and on the edge of tears, she added, "And Daddy's pocket watch, my punching bag, and my guitar...." I was robbed! Aunt Opal's..."

"...opal neck ribbon?" King finished with a nod of comprehension.

Meagan gulped, nodding also. "Yes."

King did not see her eyes, but he knew there were tears. His mind spun a mile a minute over her mission to acquire the things she felt were hers. She hadn't mentioned the ruby pin he recalled from the photo she had in his shop the day she robbed him.

His voice went soft, "Meagan, why are you working for me?"

She sniffed. "I need the money, and I want Mother's brooch."

"Ah." Instantly, he released her. "I see. And you think I have it?"

Her reasons for taking the job had nothing to do with the work. She could have at least pretended to care for King's family.

"I know you have it."

The seller sighed. "Very touching, but I'm done here." He picked up the bird and turned to leave.

Simultaneously, King and Meagan shouted, "No!"

The seller scrambled to his car. King recovered the pistol and chased them both. "Stop, or I'll shoot!"

Meagan stopped. The seller stopped, dropped the bird, and shot his hands into the air, slowly turning around.

"Get in your car and go. This transaction never happened," ordered King.

"What about my money?"

"This bird belongs to her," King said, pointing to Meagan.

Hurriedly flipping through her phone, Meagan produced a photo of a photo and showed the seller and King. She and her father were in the woods, smiling as he held up the dead pheasant.

"How nice," the seller said smartly. "Proves nothing."

"Proves everything unless you have a similar picture of yourself," King said.

"Okay, okay, I'm going."

Mouth agape, Meagan could not have anticipated King's actions; he had just helped her again.

Wagging the gun toward the bird, he told Meagan, "Just get it and go."

As the seller's SUV burned rubber speeding from the parking lot, Meagan put the pheasant in her truck.

"See you," King said sorrowfully and handed her the gun.

When she did not respond, he turned to go. This beautiful, confused woman practicing vigilante justice over stuff he saw in his shop daily had tied his heart into a painful knot.

Eyeing the pheasant on the passenger seat as she drove to the B&B, she attempted to sort out her feelings.

How dare King insert himself into my quest! I was getting back what belonged to me!

Now that her boss knew her secret, surely, he would give her the brooch. She would probably also get another job where people wouldn't follow her. The fact that she had not told King the truth of her situation before he hired her had come back to bite her.

Why would I have told him anything? It's my private business.

Thoughts of leaving her job at the Pullman place as Kate's helper pained her. She imagined King's face in her mind and could hear his voice in her ear, not to mention Ms. Kate would be disappointed and at the mercy of whoever Jack or King picked next. There would be other jobs for her. She must stop giving King Pullman power over her actions.

No man needs to know the power they possess.

She texted King, "Do not follow me again."

He returned, "I don't care if you think everything is yours. Don't steal again."

"Am I fired?"

"Ah, shit," he groaned.

Part of him wished she, her gun, and her problems wouldn't show up for work tomorrow. The other part hoped she would stick with her job helping his mother so he wouldn't worry for either woman.

"No," he texted and added a wink.

A wink! What is that for? Is he smiling because he knows my secret?

Disgusted, she tossed her phone on the seat and concentrated on the road.

Chapter Twenty

Good to see you," James Cobb said and stood to shake Conroy Sabeth's hand.

"It's nice to see you too. Thank you, sorry that I'm running a little late. I'm not familiar with this area of town. It sounds like you've been very busy with my case."

"Yes, I have been. Can we order before discussing the information in this envelope?"

"Sure; what do you recommend on the menu?"

"I've been coming to The Daylight Diner for at least ten years, and I can tell you that everything on the menu is good. I like their halibut or cod fish tacos."

"Then fish tacos it is," said Conroy. "So, tell me what you have learned."

While waiting for their lunch to be delivered, James slipped some paperwork from the large Manila envelope. He set a photo on the table before Conroy.

"It starts with her," he began, "This is Carla Denton. She had a twin sister named Carol, and they lived in Nashville. When the girls were seniors in high school, Carla witnessed Carol's boyfriend, Tim, beating on her in the backyard. Carla picked up a board; I presume it had large nails in it because the autopsy report on Tim indicated he was stabbed to death with a large nail in the back of the head, repeatedly."

"And this woman is…." asked Conroy.

"The beating victim was Gayla Adamson's mother, Carol."

"The sister, Carla, went to jail, and Tim's family threatened Carol bodily harm as justice for the loss of their brother. Carla committed suicide in prison, and Carol began years of running and psychotherapy."

"Good Lord! Then what happened?"

"Carol's immediate family changed their last name to Hobart and went one direction in this country, while Carol Denton, now Carol Hobart, pregnant at the time with Gayla, and her twin brother Robert, went the other direction. Tim, the deceased, is Gayla's and Robert's father."

"Here are your lunches, gentlemen," announced the middle-aged waitress.

James quickly swept all the paperwork back into the envelope. "If you would leave a pitcher of water here and...."

"...not disturb you until you stand up to leave?" the waitress said. "I remember, Mr. Cobb."

James smiled. "Wonderful. Thank you, Kim."

Conroy sorted his napkin on his lap and eagerly bit into a fish taco. "This is good food! Tell me more."

"I will warn you, Mr. Sabeth, it gets sticky, the whole thing is a prickly pear affair, and I admit I haven't figured out some of it yet. I'm hoping you can fill in some blanks," he spoke while chewing his food.

Conroy's eyebrows rose at James' request. "Possibly."

James continued, "Carol Hobart married a computer salesman named Bill Jakes when Gayla and Robert were three, and they moved to another city in Tennessee. Jakes died of a burst appendix when the kids were about fourteen. Carol was the beneficiary of a life insurance policy valued at a quarter million. She then changed her last name to Adamson and moved with the kids to where she currently resides, a half mile from King Pullman's place. Robert continued homeschooling, but Gayla attended the same high school as you. Did you know her?"

"Vaguely. What else?" Conroy asked.

"I'll tell you, those midwives for hire know a lot," James said, shaking his head. "Gayla has a kid. It's a boy, and he's about twelve now." Old Mrs. Adamson homeschools him. His name is Gary Edison Adamson."

Conroy choked and coughed into his napkin. "Did you say, Edison?"

"Yes, funny, isn't it? I know a woman who named her daughter Einstein!"

"Yeah, funny." Conroy had not known that Gayla knew his middle name. He never shared it because although his mother thought it was incredibly original, it embarrassed Conroy. He always said his middle name was Ed. Now, his son has the same cross to bear.

Cobb placed a photo of a young boy on the table.

"Is this her son?" Conroy asked. How did you get this picture?"

"With a high-powered lens, after a very long wait. Yes, it's Gary Adamson, looking out an upstairs window."

"Interesting. You are a patient man."

"I like to think so," responded Cobb.

Finishing his last bite of fish taco, Conroy wiped his mouth and smiled. "That's a virtue—patience."

"Here's where things go off the rails; Gayla's mother has never worked outside the home. Carol Adamson homeschooled Gayla and Robert until they started high school." James set a photo of Robert before Conroy. "He is an interesting fellow, currently in the hospital due to a gunshot wound. I have a friend in the local police." He revealed a photo of badly beaten Ace Pullman being escorted by his brother to a truck."

Conroy's mouth hung open as he listened.

Cobb continued, "Robert and a friend assaulted Ace Pullman at his home. Then hours later, the same duo broke into King Pullman's house and again attacked Ace."

"Who shot Robert?" Conroy asked.

James smiled. "No one knows. My theory is that Ace is the dead-beat father of Gayla's child."

"Oh," Conroy said. "That's an interesting theory. Anything else? What did they want?"

"My friend at the station says they were after money."

"What does the brother, Robert, do for work?"

"He works for Pickering Warehouses. Stocks shelves, ships stuff." James watched Conroy's facial expressions morph. "What do you know about this family?"

Since Conroy's father had a good working relationship with James Cobb, he could not divulge any information about his child, regardless of how tight-lipped James Cobb claimed to be.

"Only that she works as a veterinarian in Whitehouse."

"True. She does work there. The big question is, why are there no school loans? Vet school is not cheap. Neither she nor her brother or mother has outstanding loans. Here is where intuition prevails, Mr. Sabeth; Whoever the child's father is probably paid for Gayla's education so that she would keep everything hush-hush. I suspect Gayla's brother was trying to make Ace pay if he is the father. My second theory is that the father is King Pullman."

"Hmm."

James added, "She dated King Pullman for many years. It was an on-again, off-again type of deal. His is the only money trail, and it wasn't nearly enough to pay her bills. He sent her money regularly for a decade, beginning when he was a senior in high school."

Could this be why King quit the football team, to give her money to help raise my son? Why?

"I could try to get paternity information for you."

"Oh, that's not necessary." Conroy's expression became strained.

"Here is an interesting altercation," James said, adding another photo to the collage before Conroy. "Again, this was taken with a long-distance lens. Our subject, Gayla Adamson, delivers a punch to the throat of King Pullman."

"Oh, wow!" Conroy said, rubbing his eyes. "Why? And who are the other people there?"

Cobb pointed to the blond woman. "This is Pullman's maid, Ms. Morris, and the woman in the vehicle is Mrs. Pullman."

Head cocked to one side, Conroy asked, "Mr. Cobb can you sum up the relationship between the Adamson family and the Pullmans with one word?"

James looked thoughtfully out the diner window as he processed the question.

"Money."

"I agree." Conroy nodded. "I thank you so much for your work. You've revealed more than I anticipated. You are right, the entire situation is sticky, but I believe it is, at its core, quite simple. As you have surmised, it's money."

"You are welcome. If you need assistance again, I'm happy to help."

After reinserting all the photos into the envelope, James stood, and the waitress hurried over to give him the bill.

"I've got it," Conroy said, taking the bill from James and handing her a fifty-dollar bill. "Thank you. Please keep the change."

She smiled, nodded, and said, "Thanks. Come back soon!"

"I appreciate you picking up lunch," James said. "Do you want more information?"

Absently, Conroy looked pensively over his car at the tire shop across the street. "No, thanks. I think I'm all set. I know I can count on your discretion with this case."

"Absolutely. I wouldn't be in business otherwise," James said, handing the manila envelope to Conroy. "This belongs to you."

Before slipping into his car, Conroy watched James Cobb drive away from the diner.

What an execrable circumstance the Adamson family has. No doubt of their own making; however, based on all Cobb just shared regarding the flow of money from King Pullman to Gayla, it appears Mr. and Mrs. Pullman funded Gayla's education. They must have all believed Gayla's child was King's. This explains King's reaction to seeing me and learning about my history with Gayla, not to mention the likeness between Gary and myself. Something is still not right. Why secrecy? Why didn't the Pullmans write checks to Gayla and keep everything above board?

Some people believe money is the root of all evil, not Conroy. He understood that evil is the root of all evil and that anything in the world could be perverted by evil people to perpetuate evil.

Navigating his way through afternoon traffic, Conroy pulled into the Gateway Church parking lot, and using a side entrance, he entered the sanctuary. He stood before a twenty-foot-tall wooden cross on the wall and prayed.

Lord, I am forever grateful for your love. I know the plan you have for us is good. Please help me to understand my place in Gary's life and boldly take on whatever responsibility you have for me in that family. Use me, God, to love and lead them to you. Please clarify the truth so I can know how to approach Gayla. Lord, I will wait on you and continue to pray for direction. Amen

Chapter Twenty-One

Squaring her shoulders, Meagan let herself into King's house at eight-thirty AM, then she texted him, "I'm here."

"With or without a weapon?" responded King.

"You asked me that yesterday. It's still in my truck. Am I fired?" Meagan texted.

"You said that yesterday," King quipped.

His maid was not one to be trifled with; the conversation felt full of fire. As he thought about the recoupment of her pheasant and her body pressed against his, he knew it was time to throw a little water on the flame. She needed to come to him. He wanted her to kiss him so he could kiss her back, childish as it was. His quandary was how to bait her, and she wasn't like any other fish.

"No, you're not fired," he texted, "My mom likes you, and you're the only ranch hand I have. Please stay."

"No note today?" She texted.

She completely blew off his begging with not even a 'thank you' for not being fired.

"Miss my notes?"

"No," she snapped back, irritated, but she couldn't pinpoint exactly why she was annoyed. This sarcastic side of King was different. She had never known a man like him. She wondered what else he had up his sleeve.

"Okay, good. I'll be home at three to work on the house," he replied, ending their text jousting.

Meagan tapped on Jack and Kate's bedroom door. "Good morning."

Kate looked up from where she sat on the side of the bed, "Good m-morning."

Kneeling before Kate, Meagan took over the chore of putting on Kate's compression socks.

"Thank you, dear. It's just us for b-breakfast today. King and Jack have gone to work in the shops. Can we take a walk today?"

"Absolutely," said Meagan, elated that Ms. Kate enjoyed the outings to see the alpacas as much as she did.

Watching Meagan across the table during their morning meal, Kate stirred her coffee and set her spoon down. "Meagan, tell me about y-you."

"Hmm, well," Meagan began, "I'm boring. I was an average student in school, average athlete on the track team, average decade marriage to an average guy. He died in Afghanistan almost two years ago."

"Oh, I'm sorry to hear that. But, d-dear, there is nothing a-average about you. It a astonishes me that you don't see it." Kate shook her head, disappointed with the people in Meagan's life who did not help her know her value. She set a warm wrinkled hand on Meagan's.

"You are an amazing woman, and I-I want to know w-what you plan to do with your life?"

"I'm working here and getting myself together, alone."

"That is h-hardly a plan for the future. That's g-good old survival! You need to dream! Dream about all the things that make you happy and b-bring you joy, great joy, Meagan. What makes your heart leap, dear?"

Getting my stuff back. "I'll let you know what I come up with, Ms. Kate."

Meagan's thoughts were interrupted by the recollection of King's text commanding her not to steal again.

"I look for-ward to that."

While Kate worked on her puzzles, Meagan sanitized the kitchen and bathroom counters and washed the kitchen floor before preparing a light lunch. A thorough search of King's fridge yielded ham and cheese sliders, and soup.

"King n-never asks for help in the kitchen even when I know he needs it," Kate commented.

Meagan listened while Kate talked about the early days of her marriage and how King was a wonderful surprise, then how they planned for Ace. Her voice grew soft, her eyes distant. A tapestry of the Pullman family formed for Meagan, rich with love and work.

When Kate laid down for her afternoon nap, Meagan searched again for her ruby brooch. She scoured King's closet and determined the brooch was not there. Tomorrow she would dig in more cabinets and drawers. Why King had not returned it to her was another irritation. In the meantime, she searched the internet and found nothing of hers on Sell City. Her frustration with the situation made her want to punch her stolen speed bag.

"Pity the fool who tries to sell me back my bag," she muttered, giving up her search temporarily when King appeared in the hallway.

Meagan looked up to see King. "I was just tidying your room."

His eyes steady, he stood unmoving. "Sure, you were. Should we talk about the pheasant night?"

"No."

Her phone alerted her to a text from Andrew, "Hi, bad news. Mom said to let you know a plumbing pipe broke. Two guests had to leave. No water. Plummer says it could be fixed by morning. Would you like to stay at a hotel with me tonight?"

"Ugh, no!" She moaned.

"What is it?" King asked.

"Uh, would it be okay if I stayed here tonight? I'll take the couch?" A pipe broke where I live. No water till tomorrow."

She threw her hands up, exasperated.

"Uh," he said, nodding.

King was surprised she asked. While his brain was adamantly saying no, his mouth said, "Sure, use the baby's room." It couldn't hurt; he reasoned it was just for one night, and his mother liked her.

"Thank you," she beamed. "I'll take care of the dinner you planned."

"Okay, well, excuse me," he said, passing by her to get to his bedroom.

King was grateful for her offer; he needed to work on the addition. He was glad he seasoned pieces of roast beef last night. Maybe she wouldn't screw up dinner.

Fresh from her long nap and feeling springier than she had been in a while, Kate helped Meagan set the table early. They talked about the news they heard from the TV in the living room.

Meagan snooped around the kitchen and found all the ingredients necessary to surprise the Pullmans with homemade rolls to sop up the roast gravy. The thought made her mouth water.

"Is someone at the d-door?" Kate questioned when she heard odd noises coming from outside.

Meagan smiled. "No, your son has been hammering on the upstairs addition for the last two hours. Do you know what that remodel is going to be?"

"You know, dear, I have no idea. King just g-got it in his head that he needed an extra room. I think Jack is home."

"He sure is, honey," Jack said, strolling directly to his wife for a hug and a kiss. "She cooks?" he asked, peering over at Meagan as she tossed flour on the counter.

"Yes, she does," Meagan fired back. The oven beeped, and she inserted a sheet of dinner rolls and texted King," dinner is ready in fifteen minutes."

"Can't wait," he replied.

The aroma of King's herb roast and vegetables wafted through the house. Meagan checked her watch and realized it was quitting time, but she didn't need to leave, which made her glad. She would rather be at the ranch with Ms. Kate than anywhere else, even considering her irritation toward King. Secretly, she thanked Aunt Agnes for her plumbing issues.

King entered the mud room and shucked his boots. Meagan was ladling stew into large bowls with dinner rolls on the side in the kitchen. He scanned the length of her knowing he should have talked to her about her clothes, but King wasn't sure exactly what he would say. She went from a seductive secretary in her soft pink sweater and short skirt at her interview to a sexy cowgirl in her jeans and plaid shirts. The more thought King gave the problem, the more it became a nonissue because there was nothing she could wear, save a tent, that would make her not appear seductive. That was the rub. She was too hot, and he shouldn't have hired her back, not to mention she was a vigilante. He knew he was a sucker.

Kate informed him, "Homemade rolls b-by Meagan."

Imagining Meagan punching down the dough for rolls drew erotic thoughts. King recognized his vision was taking off in a ludicrous direction, considering she probably couldn't stand him. "I'll bet they're even better with a little honey," he said with a smile.

Meagan tried to ignore King, but with his honey on the rolls comment, she wondered if it was some double entendre. The way he said it felt provocative, and it made her sweat.

As they all proceeded to enjoy their meal, the doorbell rang. King locked eyes with Jack, suspicious of who might be calling. He hoped it wasn't Gayla.

A slim thirty-year-old man wearing intense cologne asked, "Is Meagan here?"

"Why," probed King, craning his head for a better view of the Corvette in his driveway.

"We have a date. I'm Andrew."

"Oh," King smirked at the terrible start to this poor chap's date. "Come on in. You can join us for dinner."

Never having been on an actual date his entire life, King pondered the man's choice of clothing. He wore several layers of shirts topped with an army-green mountain climber's vest. His jeans were tight resembling denim skin. King noticed his reflection in the man's light brown shiny shoes."

"We're in the kitchen," King said, "this way."

King would only let Meagan out the door with Mr. Shiny shoes once he knew more about him. To say that he was thrilled with the opportunity to present Meagan with the date she forgot was an understatement; he was giddy.

Jack and Kate stopped eating to focus on the unexpected scene. King grinned like he had won the Lotto as he watched Meagan's mouth move slowly.

"Oh, Hi, Andrew," she said mechanically. "How did you find me?"

"I brought you flowers at work," Andrew said, "and they told me you had quit. Mom didn't even know where you were working! So then, I followed you here the other day out of concern for your well-being. I'm glad I did follow you because nowadays, anything could happen."

"That's t-true," agreed Kate, "he's right about that. You never know."

Andrew added, "So when you didn't show up for our date at the restaurant tonight, I had to come here."

Meagan groaned. "I completely forgot it's Friday. I'm sorry."

Andrew moved around the table nearer to Meagan, staring at Jack as he walked. "You look familiar."

"A lot of people say that" Jack said. "What's your last name, Andrew?

"Willoughby."

"How did you meet Meagan?" inquired Kate.

"Wow," Andrew laughed and shot a look at Meagan as she set a bowl of stew at the empty place at the table. "Did you arrange this inquisition?"

No one laughed.

"We met at a funeral, "he disclosed. "I was adopted, so it's not like we're related. Technically Meagan has no relatives except my mother, Agnes. All her people are dead."

"Oh, dear!" Kate exclaimed, reaching to cover Meagan's hand with her own. "I'm sorry, I know…."

"I'm fine, thank you," Meagan whispered, squeezing Kate's hand.

King knew she wasn't fine. She replaced people with things long ago and wanted them back. Meagan wasn't okay. She was delusional.

"I thought we could go see a movie," Andrew suggested. "The Assassin is playing at eight." He refused to abandon what was left of their date, knowing his parents were waiting on a report of his and Meagan's outing, and he didn't want to let them down.

Meagan shoved a big chunk of beef in her mouth, buying precious seconds to consider his request. The fact that he followed her to her new employment was weird. He distrusted her as Paxton had.

Andrew remembered the antique watch recently given to him and dug it out of the side pocket of his canvas vest. He flicked the silver case open to check the time.

"This thing keeps perfect time," he said, smiling smugly and thinking himself a gentleman.

King's heart skipped a few beats when he noticed the alarming look in Meagan's eyes.

"Nice watch; mind if I take a look at it?" asked King, feigning nonchalance, trying to avoid a possible murder in his home.

Jack cleared his throat. "Now I remember you! You tried to pawn that watch in my store."

"No. I'm sorry. I didn't go into your pawn shop," Andrew stammered.

The gut-wrenching pain etched on Meagan's face knocked the wind out of King. As he examined the quality pocket watch, Meagan reached to turn it over in his palm, subtly pointing to the inscribed initials GM.

"George Morris," she shared in a whisper.

"I'd like to own something like this, Andrew," King said. "Will you sell it to me now?"

Meagan's eyes went wide, perspiration beading on her neck. Her boss attempting to purchase it made the stress over the battle for the pocket watch nearly unbearable. How Andrew came to have the watch was an enigma.

Andrew smirked. "I don't think so. I mean, probably not. It was a gift, and I should probably keep it."

"How about two hundred?" suggested King.

A guttural growl escaped Jack, indicating his disapproval of King's transaction at their dinner table. He had hired back that pretty fake maid, has a child somewhere with a violent woman, and was now pawning at his dinner table. Jack supposed King was losing it. He needed to sit his son down and talk with him soon.

King tried again, "Two hundred fifty?"

"King!" snapped Jack. "What is going on here?"

Kate patted Jack's arm. "He's bu-busy, dear."

"Ah, maybe three," said Andrew reaching for the pocket watch in King's hand.

Meagan gritted her teeth, "You are a liar and a thief!" She could not move toward Andrew, King's vice grip on her forearm kept her stationary.

"Please, you three, sit down!" demanded Kate. "No more na-name-calling in this home."

Slowly, King, Meagan, and Andrew obliged.

Unnerved, Jack shoved a forkful of dinner into his mouth and chewed hard.

Andrew watched King extract his money clip, one-hundred-dollar bills spilling out, and changed his mind. "I think four hundred would be a fairer price."

Meagan lunged for him. King wasn't fast enough to stop her. She came off her seat in one fluid movement, and her right fist shot straight into Andrew's face, knocking him backward in his chair.

"Holy shit, woman!" Jack yelled in a deep, astonished tone, simultaneously choking on his stew. "Are you okay, son?" he asked Andrew, coughing.

"He's not innocent!" Meagan defended.

King was up and pressing himself against her, again with his arm around her waist to keep her from finishing off her cousin.

"I think you should take the three hundred," Jack advised their unintended guest, with a reprimanding glare toward Meagan. "That was more than a fair offer."

"Shut up, you old fuck," Andrew spewed, regaining his footing. "You wouldn't give me nearly what it's worth."

"You will not speak to these nice people like that!" warned Meagan.

Every protective atom in her body wanted her rude cousin on the ground. She twisted in King's arms and executed a perfect sidekick to Andrew's ribs knocking him to the floor again.

Kate clapped her hands like she had bought a ticket for the fight.

Sufficiently defended and righted by the fighting woman, Jack helped Andrew off the floor. "You are leaving now," he ordered."

"A word to the wise," admonished King, "Do not, under any circumstances, touch anything, and I mean anything in her room, do you understand?"

"Do you understand?" Jack repeated, patting Andrew on the back. "You don't mess with our family."

"Ha, she's not your family. She's no one's," Andrew shouted, wiping blood from his cheek.

Kate stood. "Just a moment, Jack; I want to say something to this ig-ignorant young man. Andrew, that special, beautiful woman," she said, pointing an arthritic finger at Meagan, "has more character in her p-pinky than you will ever know. She is caring and helpful, industrious, and creative. She is precious to us; now we understand how precious we are to her. Thank you for bringing me a d-daughter." Kate smiled at Meagan and said to Jack, "Now you can throw him out, dear."

King felt a lump in his throat at the realization that Meagan was as fiercely protective of his family as anything she hunted. Still holding her to him, he leaned down to her ear, his lips touching her silky hair; he begged, "If I buy you a guitar will you stay?"

Kate overheard King and quirked her head in surprise. King had never cared about learning a musical instrument or listening to the radio. He had always worked his tail off chasing the almighty dollar since his senior year in high school.

Meagan's emotions were scattered. She peeled King's fingers from her waist and then ran to the bathroom to cry privately. In her entire life, she had never been offered a bribe so painful. She knew what a wonderful man King was, and the fact that he felt he needed to lure her to stay with a guitar was too much. She sat on the commode to bawl. Her heart wanted to tell King she didn't need a guitar to stay. On the other hand, she was angry and wanted the classic Martin guitar given to her by her uncle. It was only right.

Kate and King cleaned up the dishes and straightened the kitchen while Jack took his bourbon outside and sat behind the wheel of the parked Gator to relax and ponder King's maid.

Admittedly he knew he had been hard on her. When Meagan protected and defended him, he became riddled with guilt at that moment; his indigestion flared up.

Jack considered himself a good judge of character. He had the beauty queen maid pegged as a money-grabbing wench; his judgment was off. She had shown she was not a money grabber or a wench but more of a goddess-badass-vigilante. He had never met one of those before. He shook his head in disbelief. The last gulp of the expensive silky bourbon hit his gut. He asked himself if what Andrew said justified Meagan's response. Smiling, he headed back inside for the Evening News.

There was a soft tap on the bathroom door. "Meagan d-dear, can I show you something?"

The door opened slowly, and Meagan emerged, her eyes puffy and red.

"I'm sorry I brought trouble to your home."

"Don't worry dear, see this room?" Kate asked, leading Meagan by the elbow. "It's yours. The year after King was born, we b-brought Maddie into the world. She lived for four months. We had four months of j-joy with her. I imagine she would have been like you. I hope you will move in with us. It would help if you had a safe place, far away from Andrew."

Suppressing the urge to cry again, Meagan looked around the airy room and hugged Kate.

"I had no idea you had a daughter. I'm so sorry that she passed. Thank you for your offer. I appreciate it, and the room is lovely, but I have my place. The plumber says the burst water pipe will be fixed by tomorrow, and then I'll go back."

Down the hall, King listened to the conversation with disgust. The thoughts he'd entertained about Meagan were not brotherly by any stretch of the imagination. He cringed as he heard his mother try to adopt a sister for him in the last hour.

He cranked out one hundred push-ups on his bedroom floor, pushing out the evening's frustrations. King was relieved Meagan's stay was only for one night despite his mother's efforts to convince Meagan to move into his house. As he processed that he almost had a sister bestowed on him, he worried about his mother. Maybe she was aging faster than he cared to admit, and her mind was slipping. His bicep muscles burned with the one-hundredth push-up. He jumped in the shower dismissing the intruding thoughts of dancing cheek-to-cheek with his overnight guest.

Kate leaned close to Meagan, whispering, "Would you take me to run an errand tomorrow b-before you go home? Jack will be at the shop."

"Anything serious?" Meagan asked.

"Maybe not," Kate replied with a wink. "We'll see."

Chapter Twenty-Two

King's manager Marty was already at work when he arrived.

"How's it going, King?"

"The condensed version is my life is not my own, Marty." King poured them each a cup of coffee. "When I'm down here at the shop, I'm worried about everything at the house. There was a shooting in my house, and two men took bullets in their posteriors in my kitchen. Can you believe that? My mom sprained her ankle, and I'm behind on finishing my edition and shearing my alpacas. I haven't seen Storm in weeks, and Dad fired my maid. I rehired her, but I wish she weren't so good-looking." He sipped his coffee pensively. "All the usual stuff. How about you? How's your wife?"

"Damn, King," said Marty, "That's a lot of shit going on in your life; it makes my life look like a breeze. Hey, ain't nothing wrong with a good-lookin' maid as long as you both are single. Is she?"

"Yes, far as I can tell. She's a widow."

"Ah, heck, you'll be fine," Marty encouraged. "Noreen wants another kid."

"Marty, how old is your wife?" King wondered; he knew Marty was at least sixty.

"She's fifty-one. I told her it wasn't a good idea. I think I got her talked into a dog," Marty confided. "Hopefully, she'll agree to the dog; you know she loves Storm as much as I do."

"That's nice, but you're not getting my dog, just so we're clear."

"Yeah, I'll figure out something. I'm thinking of a smaller dog anyway," Marty responded.

Customers began trickling into the shop, throwing King's day into full swing before ten-thirty AM. He hadn't slept well the night before with Meagan down the hall in Maddie's room. Instead of counting sheep, King wondered what his maid wore for pajamas. Maybe he should have offered her a T-shirt or something, but he didn't. Knowing she was wearing something of his with probably nothing underneath would have driven him batty. She wasn't in the room when he passed her bedroom that morning at five-thirty. He found her in the kitchen. She had already made coffee, set the table, and was flipping banana pancakes when she noticed him.

"I can do more than herd alpacas," she said. She knew better than to give her boss more than a glance because her deodorant would not have held up, and she couldn't very well fan her armpits with him standing there, brooding.

Amused by her mood, King pursed his lips and nodded.

"We'll see. Excuse me," King said, reaching past her to the spice rack. He sprinkled a bit more cinnamon into her pancake batter. "I like things spicy."

"What do you mean by that?" Meagan asked.

"I'll be back in ten minutes," he said, going out the door and heading to the main corral.

King was happy to check on the animals and breathe before enjoying Meagan's cooking. He was sure his clothes would have caught fire if he had stayed in the kitchen next to her for a few more minutes.

What the heck is wrong with me? I thought I was going to burn up in there.

"She makes my blood boil. "What do you think, Nosy Girl? Do you think she feels the same? How will I ever know?"

Since he would never make the first move, King had a dilemma.

"The pancakes are delicious," Kate commented, looking over at King across the breakfast table.

"Yes, they are. I can taste that spice!" He grinned and winked at Meagan. "Don't look at me, Mom; Meagan cooked this morning."

When Jack and Kate glanced at Meagan, her face turned crimson.

Could that be a sign that she was on fire too?

The men shuffled out the door to work shortly after their morning meal, and Meagan checked with Kate regarding her plan. "Are we still running errands this morning?"

Kate assured her, "Absolute-ly, we must do this and early."

Whatever Kate thought had to be done had such an air of mystery and secrecy that Meagan knew not to ask any questions yet. After tidying the kitchen, Meagan assisted Kate with her compression socks, brushing her hair, and a lift into the passenger seat of Meagan's pickup. The vehicle's navigation system confirmed the address, and in thirty minutes, they reached The Allegiant Community for Seniors.

Grand Magnolias edged the wide circular driveway of the magnificent property. Meagan gawked like a tourist at the sailboats on the sparkling blue waters of Lake Hast. The sprawling one-story Chicago brick building with its tall narrow windows could have been the setting for an 18th-century English love story. The country castle rose bushes were beginning to flower, daffodils bloomed, and Ivy ground cover climbed up the side of the building near the entrance.

"I remember ch-charting out the cost of this place for Maydelle. She knew thirty years ago that she wanted to live here eventually. She was adamant about not living un-under her childrens' rooves," Kate disclosed as they stepped into the grand foyer.

A staff worker approached, pushing the wheelchair of a crumpled little woman in a light blue pantsuit.

She immediately recognized her friend's mischievous sparkling brown eyes. "Hello, Maydelle!"

"I know you! How are you, Kate? I was so surprised to get your call! I'm glad to see you. What did I do to deserve this wonderful visit?" Maydelle asked, then pointed to Kate's foot brace. "What happened?"

"I twisted my ankle at King's house, but I'm healing and fine. Maydelle, this is my fr-friend Meagan. Meagan, this is my friend and past client, Mrs. Sabeth."

Being called Kate's friend warmed Meagan inside like gourmet hot chocolate at Christmas, comforting and sweet. "It's nice to meet you, Mrs. Sabeth."

Maydelle smiled prettily. "You as well, dear."

Kate cleared her throat. "I just hoped we could talk for a few minutes."

"My family might tell you a few minutes is all I have!" Maydelle said with a snicker. "Now, Jesus, I think He has another plan for me because I feel better than an eighty-two-year-old woman should. What would you like to talk about, Kate?"

Kate turned to Meagan. "Could you give us a few minutes alone?"

"Of course. I noticed a coffee shop down the hall. I'll wait over there," she said, waving to the old friends.

Kate got right to her point, "I am trying to remember something you shared with me years ago when you made a substantial withdrawal at the bank. Maydelle, do you know anything about the Adamson family?"

Maydelle squinted and bit her lip as if dragging a painful memory from the deepest part of her mind. "I'm not familiar with that family," she replied slowly, "I'm sorry. Why exactly do you ask?"

Kate spoke softly. "There is a girl, Gayla Adamson. She mistakenly believes that King is her boyfriend. It's terrible for him. She is very aggressive."

"Gayla?"

"Yes, Gayla," Kate said.

"Can you tell me what this is about?"

"It's about a baby out of wedlock."

Maydelle's eyes misted. "What baby?"

"All I know," Kate began, "is the mother went to school with King and your grandson, Conroy. Ring any bells?"

"Oh, that name is unfamiliar to me. I'm sorry." She paused, then asked, "Didn't I come and see you so you could help me decide which accounts to access for a large payout a decade ago?"

"Yes! That's what I remember. I can't recall the reason for it."

Maydelle licked her lips. "My son, Brently, came to me for a lot of money."

Kate smiled, "Yes, I remember the amount, and you s-said the money was payment for something personal. You said you could not discuss it; it was only a family matter. Can you tell me now?"

"I suppose it is all water under the bridge now," Maydelle said, wringing her arthritic hands. I don't know what this could mean to you, Kate, but Brently said it was to make a 'bastard child go away.' I never learned the name or gender, such a travesty. I don't even know which of my children is the cause of that child; it could be Brently, his younger sister Annette, or any of their children. Brently was about to explain, and I raised my hand to make him stop. I remember telling him not to place his burden on me, and I gave him the money. You know, Kate, life is a precious gift, and what we do with it most of the time is a travesty of justice to the soul."

"I can see that this is a d-distressing memory for you, and I am sorry. It is so important that the truth is known. Is there anything else you can tell me about the child?" Kate pressed.

"Hmm," Maydelle said, "Yes. I brought it up several years after the payout. I asked Brently for an update on the baby. He told me a nice young couple in Pennsylvania had adopted the child. That was that, until today; until you. That's not to say I haven't thought about that child millions of times."

Sadness fell on the woman's intelligent brown eyes like a haze of fog.

Kate reached out to hold her hand. "Thank you for sh-sharing the information. May I come and visit you again soon? Do you mi-mind?"

"I don't mind at all. Let's have a cheerier visit next time. My ticker can only take so much sadness. I don't stand anymore, so you'll have to come down to my level so I can hug you."

"Okay. I'll be back again," Kate said.

Maydelle signaled for an attendant who appeared at the same time as Meagan, and the parties departed.

"Where to now?" Meagan said, smiling at Kate. "This has been interesting so far. This place is beautiful, and they have the best coffee. Would you like to go on a boat ride?"

Gripping Meagan's arm with her own for support, Kate smiled. "Maybe we'll all go boating soon. In the meantime, dear, we must s-spy while Gayla works. You must get into that house and take movies or photos of that young b-boy. A movie would be b-best."

"Hmm. Nothing too illegal, I hope?" "Where will this mission take place?" Meagan suspected this assignment affected King somehow since it involved Gayla, which was unsettling.

"Next door," Kate said. "The white two-story house up the road from King's place. Gayla lives there."

Silence thickened the cab of the truck. Meagan felt her lungs constricting with the knowledge that Gayla lives nearby. It was apparent Kate was thinking and plotting, and Meagan sensed trouble. The last thing she wanted was Jack Pullman on her case for being irresponsible, but she would do anything Kate asked her to do, so she jumped right in.

"How old is the boy?"

"Twelve."

Kate knew better than to say anything more about the child. If her suspicions were correct, several people would be humbled, but more importantly, things could be made right. She would not tell

Jack until she had the proof, which she planned to get with Meagan's help.

Kate and Meagan discussed ways to execute the task of capturing time with the boy.

"Please get a video, Meagan."

"I'll do my best. Veterinary clinics are open on the weekend, right? And Gayla works today, so today may work for the recording; I think you're right," Meagan responded slowly; her swirling thoughts echoed—King telling Gayla she had to work more.

What if Gayla wasn't at work? Based on the strange times she showed up at King's place, she might not be at work, and she could very well catch Meagan, which would botch Kate's plan. It seemed to Meagan that getting to the boy might require acting skills she did not possess.

"You know I can't act," she confessed.

"It would be better if you didn't. Just be yourself, and g-get the boy on film. You can do it; you'll be great, and Maydelle will love you for it."

Ms. Kate had quickly become one of the nicest people Meagan had ever met, except for her parents. Meagan felt taller, if that was possible. Just being in Kate's company empowered her.

The ladies arrived at the ranch with a burn to execute their plan for Maydelle. Kate was too anxious to take a nap, and Meagan wanted the ordeal over with, so she trekked to the main corral with the rope to leash Nosy Girl to take her for a walk across the east pasture to the rear of the Adamson property where she had seen a child several times. This instant urge to complete Kate's plan felt risky. Meagan calculated that where she had seen a child, near an outbuilding, was far enough from Gayla's house that if Gayla came running out screaming, Meagan and Nosy Girl would have time to high tail it back to King's house before Gayla could attempt another throat punch.

The weather was a brisk sixty-two degrees; gray stratus clouds hid the sun, which was still high in the sky. Meagan came upon the dilapidated wood split rail fence which bordered the Adamson's place. She casually gave Nosy Girl attention and a good neck scratch as she surveyed the property. A car stopped far ahead on the main road, letting out a boy.

"Thanks, Doctor Lou," he shouted happily to the car driver then skipped towards Gayla's house.

Seconds after the car drove off, the boy spotted Meagan and the alpaca, froze in his tracks, then quickly changed his direction. Rather than going to the front door of the Adamson house, he ran at top speed toward Meagan.

"Is that a camel or something?" He quizzed, dropping his backpack in the dirt.

Meagan could not believe her luck; angels were indeed overseeing this mission of Kate's. Discretely, she began recording with her phone.

"No, she's an alpaca. Typically, they are not very friendly; however, this girl is easygoing, which is why I walk her," Meagan answered.

"I'm going to pet her like you're doing," the boy stated, reaching to feel Nosy Girl's long neck; she rewarded him with a long, sloppy lick along the side of his sweet face. "Her name should be tongue thrasher!" He decided as he wiped his face.

Meagan kept recording.

"What's your name," he asked.

"I'm Ms. Morris. What's your name?"

"My name is Gary Adamson. I don't have a dad, just an uncle and a gramma, and she's sick."

"Oh, I'm sorry," Meagan empathized, keenly aware that he didn't mention he had a mother. "Why is she sick?"

"Gramma says she's heartsick and takes pills. She cries a lot too." His mood became somber and then changed quickly. "Hey, can this girl learn a trick like a dog?"

"I don't know; she's pretty stubborn. Gary, I have to get back to my house way over there. Can we talk again sometime?"

"Sure." He shrugged. "If you're out here, we can talk."

"Okay then, bye."

Meagan steered Nosy Girl west for the hike back to the main corral. She stopped cold in her tracks for a moment.

Why didn't I think of this; that boy is probably King's child.

Meagan's feet suddenly weighed one hundred pounds each, making each step a strain. As she reviewed the words she had heard exchanged between Gayla and King, she derided herself for not considering the possibility that they had a child together. A contradiction existed, however, because the man Meagan had been learning about over the past weeks seemed unlikely to abandon his own.

"Hmm." She picked up her pace.

With Nosy Girl back in the pen, Meagan met Kate at the back door of King's house.

Rubbing her hands together like the temperature was freezing, Kate said, "You were gone so long I was w-worried that maybe you got caught."

"I'm not sure exactly what you were hoping for, Ms. Kate, but here it is," Meagan said, tapping play on her phone. "He's a sweet boy."

Kate watched the recording and nearly collapsed. Meagan quickly wrapped an arm around the weak, shaking woman.

"This is amazing. We have to go back to Maydelle, Meagan. Can we go now?" She begged. "Maydelle was right. This is a travesty!"

"Of course, Ms. Kate, let's go see Maydelle."

Maydelle was intrigued; she hadn't seen Kate in several years, and when she stopped in to visit this morning, it was to talk about the child that her family wrote off for reasons of illegitimacy. She had learned so little about the circumstances surrounding the matter when Brentley had asked her for money to silence the involved parties; Maydelle's heart sank. Since Maydelle's time with her family was already scarce, any less time would have been too painful.

To keep her relationship with her children, she handed the money to Brentley and kept her mouth shut about the baby. Somewhere in the world was her great-grandchild, her blood. The past twelve years had been the hardest in her life. She remembered the ominous visit to the bank many years ago and discussing the withdrawal with her financial advisor. Under duress by her family to quelch 'an obstacle' as Brently had put it, Maydelle had offered a sparse explanation to Kate for the withdrawal; "It is a private family affair, and the funds will safeguard our family name."

Kate had always enjoyed sleuthing stories, and mystery novels intrigued her. Still, she had not appreciated what she had gleaned from Maydelle's secret during the financial consultation on the day of the withdrawal. Kate kept the secret, never telling a soul, not even Jack, about safeguarding the Sabeth family name to the tune of two hundred and fifty thousand dollars. Over the years, she would revisit Maydelle's words and dismiss the thoughts out of respect for Mrs. Sabeth. However, now that it seemed Maydelle's mystery could impact King negatively, it had to be addressed. Kate would not stand by and watch anyone hurt her family.

Maydelle's attendant stood by her side while waiting anxiously in the foyer. When Kate had called a second time this day, Maydelle thought her tone was off; she seemed worried about something and desperate for another visit this afternoon; it couldn't wait.

"Thank you for seeing me again today," Kate said gratefully. "This is so important. Meagan has a v-video I want you to see."

Maydelle instructed her helper to wheel her to her private room, and her guests followed.

"Now, what is this video?" Maydelle asked, causing Meagan to touch 'play' and hand her the phone.

Maydelle laid eyes on Gary, and her mouth dropped open in shock.

"That's, that's...Oh, my good God in heaven above!"

Her eyes filled with tears as she rewatched the video multiple times, finally begging, "I must see him. Please?"

Meagan met Kate's eyes and asked, "How do we go about this?"

Kate shrugged. "If the L-Lord is willin' and the creek don't rise."

Dabbing at her eyes with a tissue, Maydelle explained, "I would like to call an emergency meeting tomorrow afternoon at four with my family, Kate." Studying Meagan, Maydelle asked, "Can you bring that boy to me here tomorrow afternoon?"

"Four o'clock should be a good time. I will be here," Kate said, "It's r-really up to Meagan whether or not she can bring Gary here. Do you think you will be able to bring him?"

Maydelle interrupted, "Let me tell you something, young woman," she spoke to Meagan, "I may not have known the baby was a boy, but I have loved that child since I learned of his existence. Now I see that he is Sabeth through and through. Looking at his face, I see my eyes, Mr. Sabeth's smile, God rest his soul, and Conroy's inquisitive nature. I realize I'm asking a lot, but please bring him to me. I may not live much longer." She smiled tenderly at Meagan.

"Did you just play the age card?" Meagan laughingly accused her. "I knew I was going to get him before you said anything. I have become as curious about this story as a person can be. I will do my best to get Gary here. I promise."

"That'll be fine, thank you," Maydelle said. "Thank you so much for coming today. I will see you both tomorrow."

On the drive back to King's ranch, Kate remained quietly lost in thought while Meagan was dreaming of a variety of possible mission-related avenues which could result in the apprehension and delivery of one Gary Adamson to Maydelle Sabeth at the Allegiant.

The surest idea she could think of to make Maydelle's dream a reality involved Rhonda and her son. If Rhonda agreed with Meagan's plan, maybe she would bring Gary to the Senior Center. Meagan quickly texted her at the first traffic light, "I need a huge favor tomorrow. Please bring Alex and be at my work: Ranch Road 704, it's on the left, at three in the afternoon."

"No details? How important is this? I don't have any clients lined up yet."

Meagan responded, "Super important. Just tell Alex it's a fun surprise with his Aunt Meagan."

"You owe me."

"I know."

Chapter Twenty-Three

I am calling an emergency family meeting. Tomorrow afternoon at four o'clock, I will have important things to discuss here at the Allegiant in the Nautical Mile meeting room."

"What's going on, Mother? This isn't like you. Are you sick?" asked Annette.

"Arthur Conan Doyle himself could write this story. Bring your husband and three children. Don't be late. I am calling your brother and his family next."

Assuming her mother's emergency meeting was regarding the disposition of her estate, Annette quickly responded, "We'll be there."

Meagan checked the time on her watch as she paced the driveway. Jack turned to Meagan and asked, "Can you tell me what this is all about?"

Meagan said, "You'll have to wait and see."

"That's right!" Kate exclaimed, "Now let's go see my friend, Jack."

With Jack's help, Kate climbed into the Hummer, waving to Meagan as they ambled down County Road.

Jack had left his shop early to spend the afternoon with Kate because she told him there would be a surprise. They had arrived at the Allegiant by two-thirty. The shroud of secrecy was still intact.

Rhonda pulled her white sedan into King's driveway. "You have a lot of explaining to do, my friend. So, this is where you work?" Rhonda asked. When Meagan nodded, Rhonda continued sarcastically, "Could you have picked a place more remote? Uh, no."

Hugging her friend, Meagan said, "You're funny. Look, this is super important. Hi Alex! You are so tall now! How old are you, eleven?" Meagan hugged him tight." I am so glad you're here. We are going to have fun today."

"I'm eleven and a half." Alex smiled. "Do you have horses?"

"No, no horses," Meagan explained, "Mr. Pullman raises other creatures. I'll show you, but not today. This afternoon we have a critical mission. Are you ready to be a detective?"

Still thinking about the animals, Rhonda rolled her eyes at the thought of livestock, and the stink involved but listened to Meagan as she laid out a plan.

"Rhonda, you're going to park a block away from the next ranch." She pointed down the road illustrating the direction. "Alex will go to the door with me and ask if Gary can come to play and look at the animals. With any luck, he'll come. We need him in the car with us. He will have a huge surprise, but we shouldn't tell him that. Can you convince Gary to hang out with you, Alex?"

Alex replied, "Maybe. I can try."

"Are we…kind of kidnapping him," whispered Rhonda. "You didn't mention his mother. I'm sensing this operation might be criminal. Where exactly are we taking him?"

Meagan sucked in a deep breath. "The Allegiant community for the elderly, and we kind of have to hurry." She checked the time on her phone; it was already after three. Meagan's lips formed a thin smile. "Thanks for helping." She hugged Rhonda again. "I have a feeling the criminal activity happened years ago…but we'll find out soon enough. Let's go!"

"What?" Rhonda asked. "Seriously, this does not seem right. Why don't you call the police?"

Meagan was out of time and options, so she changed tactics.

"Rhonda, have I ever asked you for anything?"

"No. Oh, no, you don't! Meagan Morris, don't even pull that on me! Alex and I will help you deliver the kid to that place. You don't have to guilt me—that is reserved for my mother," Rhonda said, snickering. "Just get in the car already!"

"Thanks, you are wonderful." Meagan beamed.

Rhonda rolled her eyes, and Alex giggled from the back seat.

As Meagan had directed, Rhonda dropped her and Alex off so they could walk about fifty yards to the Adamson's place. When there wasn't any sign of Gayla's SUV, Meagan sighed and shuffled her fingers through Alex's hair. "You ready?"

"I guess."

She knocked on the front door, and Gary opened it a sliver.

"Hello, hey, you're the elpaco animal lady!" said Gary.

"Yes, I am," Meagan said nervously, and I brought someone who would like to meet you." She shifted her gaze to Alex.

Alex stuck his hand out, very adult-like, and shook Gary's hand. "You wanna hang out and maybe see elpacos?" he asked, "My name is Alex."

Gary lit up like the fourth of July, eyes twinkling, grinning from ear to ear, and shuffling from foot to foot.

"I'm Gary. Sure!" He stepped onto the porch, momentarily leaning back into the house, yelling, "Gramma, I'm going out to play."

The situation felt like a bank heist to Meagan as she hustled the boys to Rhonda's car.

"Let's have Alex's mom drive us to the alpacas," she suggested, and Gary willingly climbed into Rhonda's vehicle.

"Hey, we passed your ranch!" Gary informed them, panic lacing his voice over how fast they were cruising away from his home.

Sensing Gary's trauma, Alex explained, "Oh, there's something cool in town. You have got to see it, and then we'll see those elpacos."

"Okay, cool," said Gary with a shrug.

Rhonda drove, biting her lip. She knew nothing about the boy they had just ripped from his home under false pretenses. The boys' conversation in the back seat dulled her negative feelings about the crime. They had so much in common; it forced a smile to her lips. Gary volunteered that he didn't have a dad, and Alex shared that he didn't know his dad very well because of the divorce. Their subjects were everywhere, from home life to life on other planets. They were having a great time, but Rhonda still planned to give Meagan a piece of her mind privately and soon. Then Her navigation system alerted her to the Allegiant community on the right-hand side of the road, and Rhonda was stunned.

"This place is amazing!"

Disappointed, Gary asked, "How is this place better than the elpacos, Alex?"

"Well, there's supposed to be a surprise in there for you," Alex answered, knowing his aunt may not be thrilled with the disclosure.

"Okay. I guess I like surprises. I hope it's a good one, and then we go see the pacos, right?"

Rhonda parked the car in a spot overlooking Hast Lake. Meagan noted they had made good time; it was three-fifty-three.

"Alex, do you know how to fish?" Gary asked.

"Nope. Do you?"

"Nope, but we should try it sometime," suggested Gary.

"I would be glad to show you what I can remember about fishing, guys," Meagan offered. "How about we get on with the surprise and talk about fishing later?"

A cold chill ran down Rhonda's spine at the thought of a hook in a fish's mouth. There was a reason God put restaurants on the earth; not everyone cared to fish.

The four paraded through the marble-floored foyer down the hall, where a sign read: 'Sabeth Family Meeting.'

The Nautical Mile meeting room was an impeccably decorated reception room with massive ornate area rugs gracing the floors. A dozen occasional chairs paired together created numerous places to sit and visit semi-privately. Twelve-foot floor-to-ceiling windows were adorned with crisp blue and yellow striped valances; sunshine yellow draperies held open with massive blue rope tasseled tiebacks. The room offered a fantastic view of the lake and low mountains in the distance. The calming scent of Jasmine permeated the air.

Kate spotted Meagan and said, "Jack, let's go quickly to Meagan and her friend before they enter the room."

In the hallway, Kate studied the group and smiled at Meagan. "You did it!"

Meagan introduced, "Mr. And Mrs. Pullman, this is my childhood friend Rhonda Richards, her son Alex, and our friend Gary Adamson."

"Well, I'll be," said Jack, glancing suspiciously toward Kate.

"Maydelle thinks it would be best to have you wait in the next empty room until four-fifteen. Will you do that?" asked Kate.

All four nodded and moved to the empty room.

In the Nautical Mile room, Brentley Sabbath refused to sit. Frustrated with his mother's antics, he paced the room, occasionally being told to calm down by his wife, Conroy's mother, Gwyneth.

Casually entertaining himself with a copy of National Geographic, Conroy sat on one end of a plush sofa in the center of the room, an end table away from his grandmother, Maydelle, in her wheelchair. He had been pleased to receive the invitation to visit his loving grandmother, who taught him to play Gin Rummy and Yahtzee. He noticed she seemed jittery this day.

"Hello, Mother, hello, nephew," said Annette. "Has anyone figured out why we are here yet?"

"Hi, Aunt Annette," countered Conroy as he greeted his three female cousins, Justina, Janice, and Jett.

"Please, sit down," Maydelle instructed her daughter, "This shouldn't take too long," she said, then waved Kate over.

"Who is she?" asked Annette, pointing to Kate.

Maydelle shook her head. "She is, was my financial planner. For the love of all that is Holy, please sit down and don't talk."

Conroy turned Maydelle's wheelchair as she requested to see everyone's face.

"Hello, family," Maydelle began, "I invited you here for a visit. It's been so long since we have had any sort of family reunion. Today is a great day for just that. I apologize for my many mistakes as a mother, grandmother, and person. I now understand how grievous those mistakes were because of the loss of a relationship they have caused."

Conroy shifted his position on the sofa and glanced around the room.

"Mother, just get to the point!" growled Brently.

Maydelle raised her hand and pointed to the entrance where Meagan, Rhonda, and the boys stood, causing all to look at the four strangers.

"Wow, this place is gorgeous," remarked Rhonda.

"Look at the big TV!" exclaimed Gary. It's a good surprise. Can we go now?"

"Hello, Gary," Maydelle said. "Please come in and meet your relatives."

Suddenly frightened, Gary admitted, "I shouldn't be here. I already have relatives who don't know I'm here."

"Oh, son, they will now!" Maydelle reassured him, genuine tenderness evident on her face. "Would you like to meet your father?" she asked, pointing to Conroy.

There was a collective gasp in the room. Gwyneth Sabeth fainted; her sister-in-law quickly dug for smelling salts from her purse. Brentley Sabeth, a hand to his chest, was speechless.

Meagan and Rhonda inhaled their shock at the woman's words as well. Rhonda pulled Alex closer to her as the drama unfolded.

Gary took three giant steps toward the man by the sofa. "My... Father? Ah…"

Conroy stood unmoving beside his grandmother, and Gary asked, "Are you really my father? Do you hate me?" His soft intelligent, blue eyes evaluated the unusual man with the Internet wristwatch.

Something akin to a vice grip clamped around Conroy's heart. Taken aback by the bright-eyed direct child, he blurted, "No." There was so much to say, but what should he say, if anything should be said? "My name is Conroy Sabbath. Your mother, Gayla, was my girlfriend in high school."

"Wow," said Gary, shaking Conroy's outstretched hand.

From the corner of the room, Annette was heard counseling Gwyneth, "Just rest here, sister; this will all be over soon."

"I want to see him. I want to meet him," Gwyneth said. "Brentley, help me up."

Brently cleared his throat and went to his wife's side. Together they approached their son and the young boy sitting side by side on the sofa.

Awed, Gwyneth Sabeth said, "My goodness, Brently, do you see what I see?"

"God dammit, yes, Gwen. We all see it. Of course, we see it."

For a moment, the room had no air. Then innocently, Gary asked, "What do we see?"

Gwyneth began to shuffle through her designer handbag until she found what she was looking for and showed it to Gary. "Who do you see here?"

Confused, Gary studied the photo. "Looks like me, but it's probably him." He pointed to Conroy.

"Exactly," Maydelle said with a smile. "This photo means you have been a secret waiting for us to discover, and someone in this room has some explaining to do." She glared at Brently.

As he observed his mother's shock and Jack and Kate Pullman's aloofness regarding Gary, Conroy turned his attention to his father, who was disturbed rather than surprised. His mind was reeling and heart racing, Conroy had come full circle with his analysis of Gayla's secret; his father must be the secret manager.

Meagan looked to Alex and Rhonda and whispered, "Why don't we get a latte at the café here while they discuss things?"

"Sounds good, Meg. I have so many questions," Rhonda said.

"Me too," chimed in Alex, which brought a snicker to his mother and Meagan.

Chapter Twenty-Four

Gayla arrived home from work shortly after five PM. Gary wasn't in his usual spot in front of the computer, and when she drilled her mother about it, Gayla discovered she was clueless. She called for Gary.

Mrs. Adamson had taken one of her mood pills and then napped. Thankful for her pills, she couldn't bring herself to worry. It was nice never to worry. When Gary had shouted his plan to her before running out of the house, she slowly got up, but by the time Carol had reached the door, he was gone.

"When I looked out the window," Mrs. Adamson told her daughter, "He was walking with a tall blonde woman and another boy."

"A tall blonde? Oh no. Not that maid bitch! I know who it was. The only Amazon that would know about Gary."

Gayla immediately dialed King's phone number.

"King? Your maid kidnapped my son—I mean our son. What are you going to do about it? Should I call the police?"

"Wow. Okay. Calm down, Gayla. Let me think about this for a second," he said, "I'll call you back in a minute." Quickly, he texted Meagan, "Where are you? Do you have Gary, and where's my mom?"

"Hello to you too." Meagan texted back. "Gary, your mom, your dad, and I are at the Allegiant Senior Community."

"What? Why? Never mind. Okay, I'll be there soon."

King immediately texted Gayla Gary's location and assured her he would meet her there. Then he messaged Ace and asked him to come.

Ace responded, "Busy tonight. See you tomorrow. Picking up chicks at a Senior Center now? Lol."

King was not too surprised when he arrived at the retirement center, and Gayla's SUV was already there; that's how she operated, like a bat out of hell. Stepping into the foyer, King's curiosity hit critical mass. Soft Jazz music from the Allegiant's ceilings became smothered by shouting and crying. Then, he heard Meagan's laugh as he neared the coffee shop, so he ducked inside to see her and asked, "What is going on?"

"Hello, King," Kate and Jack said in unison, hugging King.

"Rhonda, Alex, this is my boss, King Pullman," Meagan introduced, then warned King, "I wouldn't go into the reception room until all the yelling is over."

Kate added, "Gary Adamson just met his secret family… and they love him."

A noticeable shiver shook King. He reached out to shake Alex's hand first. "Good to meet you both."

"Nice to meet you too," Rhonda cooed, "wait a minute, Meagan, did you say he's your boss?" She scanned King head to toe, flipped her red hair over her shoulder, and added, "So you work in his house?" Her eyes became huge, her face animated and red.

King ignored the sexual innuendo in Rhonda's questions. He stood quietly near his parents and spoke with them.

"Yes, Rhonda," Meagan snapped, humiliated by her implication. "I don't want to be preached to about my job choice, please. Not right now."

"No, yeah, I mean... Sure, later, whatever," Rhonda stumbled over her words, her hormones reacting involuntarily to King's presence. Her imagination took a flying leap into bed with him. "Why don't you sit with us, King?" She invited, tapping the booth bench next to her.

Hearing Rhonda call King by his first name was like fingernails scraping down a chalkboard to Meagan.

Jack located two chairs and moved them to the end of the booth for himself and Kate. King glanced at Meagan for approval to sit beside her at their table and was relieved when she granted him the spot next to her. King's move put a smirk on Rhonda's face.

Alex was about to ask King a question when an ear-piercing scream came from the hallway inside the Nautical Mile room. "No!"

In unison, Bentley and Gwyneth shouted, "Yes," in response then the door to the reception room flew open. Gayla was running away, pulling Gary by the hand.

"Is Gary in trouble?" asked Alex.

Rhonda patted Alex's leg. "I think Gary will be okay."

"Stop, Mom, stop!" Gary shouted, "Stop. I want to tell them something, but where's Alex?"

"Over here!" said Alex, waving to Gary.

Jack, Kate, King, Meagan, Rhonda, and Alex left their booth in the café to join the loud conversation in the hall while several guards of the Allegiant appeared, ready to kick people out.

Gayla abruptly stopped in the middle of the hall for her son. "You better not say you want to live with these people. I told you someday a family might try this. Remember?" she said through gritted teeth.

"I just met them, Mom. I have a great-grandmother!" he excitedly informed her and pointed to Maydelle Sabeth. "She's even older than Gramma! And I have another grandma and grandpa, don't I?" he questioned, and Gwyneth Sabeth nodded enthusiastically and smiled, while Brently cut his eyes over to Gayla and frowned. "But mostly, I have a father and want to know him. He said he doesn't hate me, Mom."

Gayla let go of Gary's hand to cover her face as she bawled. Then she marched over to Brentley Sabeth, yelling, "I guess you want your money back?"

"Dad, what's going on?" Conroy asked, "An explanation now would be good."

Brently shook his head and remained speechless.

Maydelle had listened long enough. She had had her fill of the entire affair. "Here's what we're not going to do; we're *not* going to sue Gayla," she informed her clan, "Here's what we *are* going to do. We're going to appreciate her, and we're going to love our Gary if it's okay with him?"

"Yay, Gary," Alex cheered.

Gary looked at Conroy and eagerly asked, "Can Alex and me finally go see them elpacos now?"

Conroy looked at Gayla, who was non-communicative and staring at the floor. Mascara-laden tears had stained valleys in her makeup; she chose to say nothing.

Conroy replied, "Maybe, but under two conditions."

Both boys asked, "What conditions?"

Conroy steadied his gaze upon Gayla. "Gary, your mom has to come, and you have to tell me where these pacos are."

"My place," said King from down the hall. "Conroy, how about y'all come over tomorrow afternoon?"

"Sure. Would two o'clock work?" Conroy smiled appreciatively.

"Absolutely," added Rhonda, which gained her a suspicious look from Kate, but Alex and Gary high-fived one another.

King asked, "Is anyone else hungry for dinner right now? I'm starving!"

"We're going to Caspian's for dinner," said Jack, "why don't you all join us?"

Several of the cousins said they would come along to the restaurant.

Gayla whispered something to Gary, and he quietly approached Maydelle to hug her goodbye, then Brently and Gwyneth, and lastly, his father, Conroy. Shoulders slumped, still in her lab coat, Gayla took him by the hand. They left the Allegiant and went home.

Soon all the goodbyes were said, and Maydelle tearfully thanked Kate for her tenacity regarding her sensitive family matter.

When King noticed Meagan striding towards Rhonda's car, he volunteered loudly, "Meagan, I can take you back to the house for your truck."

"Well, I was going to get a bite with Rhonda and Alex first," she replied.

Kate cringed when she heard King say, "We're going to Caspian's. Why don't you all come with us?"

Reluctant to spend the time socializing with all that needed her attention at the B&B and online, Meagan stammered, "Well...."

At that exact moment, Rhonda spouted, "Okay! We'll come!" nudging Meagan with an elbow to her side, excitedly hissing in Meagan's ear, "he has got to be the hottest man on the planet! He's taller than guys I usually date, but still hot."

"Yeah, he's nice."

Chapter Twenty-Five

A short, curvaceous woman with two-inch eyelashes and black hair to her waist, accompanied by a bald, heavily tattooed white man, strolled into Ace's Pawn. The woman extracted a gemstone choker from her pocket.

"I might part with this today," she announced.

"Okay, well, I might take that necklace off your hands today," Ace told the young woman. "How much do you want for it?"

It was an Opal stone on a black velvet ribbon, a very unusual item. Ace was sure that particular piece was one that King told him about.

"It means a lot to me," she admitted, batting her eyelashes. "I hate to part with it. It's a real Opal. How about three hundred?"

Ace could have hard balled her, convinced her that the Opal was substandard and would be difficult for him to sell, but he skipped it.

"I'll give two hundred."

She smiled sweetly. "Two-fifty, and we have a deal."

"You drive a hard bargain. I'll be right back." He returned to his office, where his personal cash box was stored. The shop radio volume was low, which allowed Ace to overhear his customer's excited phone conversation.

"This was so easy. It went just like you said. What's next for the movers?" She snickered. "I'm getting two-fifty for the piece."

She strolled around the shop talking while Ace continued eavesdropping.

"Nah, I like hawking jewelry more," she answered and pocketed her phone.

Her side of the dialogue smacked of something illicit, Ace thought. When she was out the door, he texted King, "I just bought the Opal piece you described. You owe me two-fifty, bro."

"Here," he said, handing the pawn customer the money for her necklace.

King returned a text, "Great, thanks. Who pawned it?"

"Little Hispanic woman in her twenties. There was a white, bald guy who drove and hung around, but he didn't talk. He had major neck art! I heard her say something about what the movers are doing next. Any idea what that is?"

"No. Interesting. Good work, Ace. I'll call you later."

Everything surrounding Meagan made King's headache lately. He didn't want to be an accessory to a murder she might commit, but he didn't want to lose her from his employ either. She refused to speak openly about her episodes of recapturing her belongings, and he stopped asking.

Movers. Hmm. What if...

He massaged the bridge of his nose and texted Meagan, "What moving company did you use to move into your apartment?"

The suspense was killing him as the minutes ticked by, and he waited for her response.

"Before the B&B?" she asked.

"Yes."

"Apple Orchard Movers. Why?"

"I'm thinking about moving something," King responded. He jotted down the name and began to research the company.

Meagan was exhausted mentally and physically as she reviewed the events of the evening. She parked the brown truck in the back of the B&B and made her way through the back door, glad the outing to Caspians was over.

Dinner with the Pullmans, Rhonda, and Alex was pleasant but stressful. The seating arrangement was strange; King had requested a booth, and when Meagan slid in first, Rhonda quickly sidled in next to her. Kate Pullman scooted onto the bench across from Meagan, leaving Jack Pullman directly across from Rhonda. Alex was about to sit next to Rhonda when she suggested he sit across from her, next to Jack Pullman. This left King at the end of the same bench as Meagan; only Rhonda was between them.

Meagan gathered that Kate disliked Rhonda, which was upsetting, and Jack Pullman repeatedly grunted his disapproval over various comments from Rhonda during the meal. King discussed alpacas with Alex while fending off Rhonda's advances. More than once, Kate cut her eyes over to her son when Rhonda laid her hand on his arm or his back.

The last thing Meagan expected when she got home was Aunt Agnes—madder than a wet hen and waiting for her in the parlor room.

"Young lady, where the devil have you been?" Agnes demanded. "Andrew went home yesterday, I'll have you know—with a black eye! That's what he gets for hanging around with you. Where have you been? Answer me!"

Meagan suddenly realized that her arrangement with the Willoughbys was on thin ice.

"I'm sorry, Aunt, I should have called you."

"That would have been nice since we had people checking out today and more due tomorrow. You must help me clean tomorrow since you were gone the last two days. We'll start early. I'm tired. Goodnight!"

"Goodnight," Meagan returned.

She wasn't in the mood to argue with Aunt Agnes; Her mind was still on the Caspian's dinner outing. Paxton's face appeared, and she was reminded of how she and her husband ate dinner together faithfully twice a week whenever he was not deployed. He was always so busy and often preferred to eat out by himself.

She tried to reason with herself. Moments like this are likely why people drink—just to stop the thoughts!

Rhonda went on and on about King and clarified that she wanted him; her comments about King's appearance or smooth baritone voice confused Meagan. King was her boss, and she had never thought about crossing that line which technically made him fair game for Rhonda, and that unnerved her. The thought of potentially working as a maid for King and Rhonda if they became a couple was too strange to dwell on.

To make matters more awkward, King made a point to invite Meagan to the ranch the next day when Conroy Sabeth was to be bringing Gary to see the animals.

"Meagan, please join us tomorrow when Alex and Gary visit the 'pacos,'" said King. "I know it's your day off, but we would like you to be there?"

"If King had not been insistent, Meagan would not have said yes. It would be a long day of intense house cleaning for Agnes, followed by social pressure at the ranch, and she'd rather not deal with the latter. The sooner she could get to bed and fall asleep, the sooner her problems would be behind her.

As Meagan showered, the pipes knocked and groaned in the old house's walls. She let the hot water beat the day's stress from her body and tried not to think of how Agnes would complain about it in the morning.

Meagan snuggled between the sheets in her tall antique bed and prayed into the darkness, "God are you there? Please keep me from sweating around King Pullman if you can hear me, and bring my family heirlooms back."

"Hi, Meagan. Are you going to be ready to go to King's ranch soon? Alex and I are ready, and he's super excited!"

"Sorry, Rhonda, I'm house cleaning and not nearly done. You guys should probably go since you're ready, and I'll see you later."

Rhonda could hear the exhaustion in Meagan's voice. "You do realize that this is a habit of yours now?" She scolded Meagan impatiently. "Too much cleaning will ruin your social life. See you when you get there."

"Bye."

And Agnes wasn't kidding when she said she was behind on the cleaning; Meagan cleaned nonstop for over five hours before finally declaring victory over the dirt.

In the kitchen, she poured herself a tall glass of water and drank it under her aunt's scrutiny. Early that morning, she sensed Agnes's irritation went deeper than a dusty house.

"Meagan asked her, "Is everything okay?"

"No. No, it's not, Meagan," Agnes admitted. Andrew said he's not coming back home while you're living here. I'm sorry. You know I hate to choose."

Meagan tamped down her rising panic. Aunt Agnes was indeed her last relative. She had felt safer on the third floor of the Willoughby B&B than anywhere else except the Pullman's, but there was no winning a conversation with Aunt Agnes—only surviving it. Andrew was the higher rank, making Meagan the disposable relative. Ms. Kate kindly offered her a room, but Meagan thought she had already pushed her luck with King. She would have to be creative and find a place to live, somewhere and fast. Rhonda's parents' house had four bedrooms. She would talk to Rhonda about it later.

"I understand, Aunt Agnes."

"I knew you would, dear. Please be out by Tuesday at the latest."

Meagan's eyes widened. "Uh, will do." There was no point in arguing; she needed to shower and get to the ranch.

Gayla was silent and stern-faced when Conroy arrived to pick up Gary. The tension in the air was thick enough to cut with a knife. A distance of ten feet separated them, with Gary in the middle. Innocent, intelligent, and caring, Gary invited his mother to join them on their alpaca field trip. Gayla was in no mood to rub elbows with Conway Sabbath or the Pullmans, not to mention the whore who had kidnapped her son and started this train wreck family situation.

"You go have fun with your… father," Gayla encouraged Gary.

Gayla hurried up the stairs to the second floor of the modest home, and checked out the activity in King's driveway from the bedroom window through binoculars. No sign of the maid's brown truck, and it was after two PM. She breathed a deep sigh and wondered what she would have felt compelled to do if Blondie's truck had been there.

One thing was for sure after the talk she overheard between Gary and Gramma Anderson yesterday, she would not ever want to embarrass her child again. When his grandmother asked him what it had been like to meet those people at the old folk's home,

Gary replied, "It was great, but Mom made me scared because she was mean."

Until that news, Gayla had never imagined herself as mean. A stabbing pain in her heart kept her from barging to the Pullman's.

On the short ride over to King's ranch, Gary talked to Conroy, and two things were made clear to Conroy; Gary believed Gayla was in financial distress and that Gary loved her very much. Conroy appreciated Gayla's position in his son's life and wondered how he could fit in.

'That's it!" Gary recognized Rhonda's car at Mr. Pullman's house. He was ecstatic that he had broken his mom's rule about talking to strangers yesterday. He would never forget meeting his father and grandparents; it was the biggest surprise of his life.

Rhonda and Alex sat at the table in King's kitchen drinking iced tea for about an hour when Conroy and Gary arrived.

"Hi, Mr. Pullman," shouted Gary as they entered King's house.

In the living room, Kate worked a crossword in her chair while Jack snoozed in a club chair near her; an episode of Bonanza blared on the television.

King asked, "Are we ready to go?"

Alex and Gary jumped up and down.

"Absolutely," said Rhonda.

King and his guests trekked down to the main corral near the barn. Alex and Gary were full of questions which King did his best to answer.

"Aren't these animals in the camelid family?" inquired Conroy.

King knew Conroy was never much of a biology student; he must have brushed up on alpacas for their outing. "Yes, they are, but they are not beasts of burden like camels—they aren't big enough," said King. "Guys, would you like to help me fetch hay for their fence buckets?"

Alex and Gary beamed enthusiastically and followed King into the barn while Rhonda stood with one foot on the lower rung of the piped fence, next to Conroy. She milked him for information about King. She would use anything she could learn about the standoffish, bearded man to win him. Like everything else, she studied her subject and dove in, prepared to win. After all, how much different could hot men be from desirable properties—the principle of the thing was the same.

Striving for a second wind upon her arrival at the Pullman ranch, Meagan couldn't recall the drive there; thoughts of her living situation clouded everything else. She paused to knock on King's front door.

Jack answered, "Hi Meagan, come in. The misses and I fell asleep for a few minutes. King and everyone are down at the barn."

"Okay, thanks," said Meagan, and upon spotting Ms. Kate, she waved and walked into the living room. Then she froze, speechless at the sight of Kate wearing her Ruby Rose brooch. It was pinned to her right side, exactly how her mother, Ruby Rose, wore it—high and right.

"Hi dear, you look so beautiful, Meagan. That pink sweater is lovely. I'm sure King will remember it too!"

Meagan's words came out slowly, "Thank you. Lovely brooch. It looks... Perfect… on you."

Ace appeared in the foyer like a gust of wind. "I know, I should knock, but I need to talk to King." He was surprised to see his mother wearing the red flower. "Nice flower thing, Mom."

"Thank you, Ace! Your father was going to surprise me with it, but I found it first," she disclosed with a wink to her red-faced husband.

"I know I don't surprise you like I should," admitted Jack.

Earlier, when Jack encountered Kate in the bathroom admiring the brooch on her lapel, he lost all nerve. He struggled to remember another time when he was responsible for her pleasure over a gift and couldn't.

Kate hugged him, saying, "I love it, dear, and I love you."

Until then, Jack had forgotten he stuffed the ruby brooch in his jacket pocket, intending to give it to King. He hadn't imagined Kate would borrow his jacket and discover it. Jack figured King wouldn't mind when he saw his mother's delight with it, and all would be forgiven.

"We'll take the Gator to the corral," Jack informed Ace. He was pleased when Meagan assisted Kate to her seat in the all-terrain vehicle.

The mid-afternoon sun mingling with the gentle cool breeze made it the perfect day for a farm outing. As they approached, Ace began to laugh.

"Man, these are some freaky sheep!" King's terrible shave job on some of the animals cracked Ace up. "Where's their crazy shepherd?" he asked with a grin.

Rhonda whipped her head around to see the cocky man ridiculing King. She locked eyes with Ace for a moment. The intensity of his green-eyed stare reduced her to a puddle of nerves; she quickly averted her gaze. Prickly hairs on her neck stiffened in response to the wild-looking alpha male.

Conroy snickered at Ace and his amusement over King. "He's in the barn with the boys. Hey, Ace, before you run off, let me introduce you to Rhonda Richards. Rhonda, this is Ace Pullman, King's brother."

Ace hopped off the Gator, feeling her gaze on him like a hurricane, and cocked his head to sweep his golden-brown hair away from his eyes.

"Hi."

"Hi," Rhonda shot back and turned her back on him to resume her conversation with Conroy.

Ace chuckled and spat, "Yeah, okay, Red," then marched to the barn. "King, how's it going?" he asked.

King led Ace a few yards away from the boys to speak privately with him and explained, "I researched Apple Orchard Movers, and the owner's brother was in jail for robbing a church in town."

Hands in his jeans pockets, Ace said, "So? A moving company run by ex-cons or employing them is not news, bro. It's an easy business to 'break into,' no pun."

"Funny guy. You are right, though."

"What are you going to do with the information?" Ace questioned.

"Not sure. I will let you know if I find anything pertinent regarding the company."

King had the moving company's address and planned to spy on their truck business. He needed to watch their operation. "…they may have something they shouldn't. That's what I'll be checking for."

He hoped that apple orchard movers would yield badly needed answers for him… and Meagan.

"Let me know what you find. Why are you into jewelry now, King? Oh, by the way, here's that Opal choker thing." Ace cleared his throat. "How do you know the hot redhead out there talking to Conroy?"

"Why?" King pressed. "Are you interested?"

"Ah. Only if you're not, dude. She's at your place. I don't want to interrupt anything."

"That's rich little brother! Since when do you care about interrupting love?" King laughed. "Listen. Go for it. She's Meagan's friend. I think you may get along great! Hell, I'll be your best man!"

"And I'll be yours when you marry your maid—if you can corral her." Ace laughed so hard he was holding his side. Alex and Gary began laughing at the sight of him. "Seriously, bro, if you can tame an alpaca, you may have a chance with that woman!"

The hilarious imagery Ace created caused King to laugh as well. His brother was more accurate than he knew.

"Hey, King, grab a rope," Ace said, chuckling, "she's in the Gator, dude."

King's countenance immediately became grave. "Okay, boys, let's take her back to the corral so she can visit with our company."

Alex and Gary led Nosy Girl to the corral, followed by King and Ace. Ace immediately approached Rhonda and Conroy. King headed toward the Gator and stopped short. He stood dumbfounded at the ruby brooch pinned to his mother's jacket.

"Hey, Mom. Hi Dad," King said, approaching his mother's side of the Gator, heart rate doubling at the sight of Meagan.

His memory of the military hobo pointing a gun at his chest made him instinctively move to stand between Meagan and his mother. If she did pull a gun, he'd rip it from her hands.

As Meagan stepped from the Gator, her silky-smooth hair wisped across King's forearm like caressing fingers… and that pink sweater… the air was suddenly too hot and dense for King to breathe easily. Today she wore something new. Her faded blue jeans were tucked into mid-calf pink Roper boots that matched the pink sweater. He remembered the soft pink interview sweater, that short skirt, and those high-heeled shoes.

Shaking off the vision, he glanced again at the brooch, tapped his shoulder area, met Jack's stare and mouthed, "What happened?"

Jack mouthed back, "I'm sorry," and shrugged.

He remained in the vehicle seat with Kate, reminiscing about the ranch when they bought the land and built the house King purchased from them. Before King and Ace were old enough to attend school, they rode horses and fished on that land. The couple agreed their life was not easy, but it had been excellent. To see King take over the property and raise livestock pleased them immensely. Jack noticed Kate dab at her eyes.

"You still love this place, don't you?" he asked. Choking a quiet sob, Kate nodded sorrowfully while Jack rubbed her back. "I'm sorry we didn't hang on to it longer, Kate. I thought we were ready to move into something less demanding."

Kate dried her tears; she was not in the habit of crying over spilled milk. It was done. They had sold it. She would learn to appreciate their garden home in town.

"I'm fine," she said. "There are just so many memories here; it's hard to let go."

Meagan took a spot at the fence next to Ronda, and they watched Conroy study his son in amazement while Alex and Ace helped King tote some hay.

Rhonda's country look was something Meagan had never seen before; her tight skinny jeans were tucked into tall black boots, and because Rhonda was short, the man's flannel shirt she wore was practically a dress. A wide black belt cinched the oversized shirt and accentuated her tiny waist. To top it off, her shoulder-length red hair had been teased at the crown, and she looked like she had just crawled out of bed. The look was sexy country.

When an alpaca neared the fence, Rhonda jumped back; she was skittish about the animals but enjoyed her view of King and his brother; they had her undivided attention. Although Meagan was talking, Rhonda hadn't heard a word. She was lost in her own thoughts surrounding the Pullman men.

Chapter Twenty-Six

Conroy had quickly become obsessed with righting his wrong. His pleasure was evident as he observed the boy learning about the animals and asking questions. Being there on the Pullman property provided a connection, like a thick thread that had just woven him full circle. He intended to make good use of that tie that was binding them.

Alex tapped Gary's shoulder to turn his attention to an old bush hog tractor, prompting Gary to ask. "Mr. King, may we ride that tractor?"

"No, unfortunately, it needs some more work before it's drivable."

"We can have smores at the fire pit," announced Ace. He pointed to the cluster of evergreens and Adirondack chairs in the distance. The boys were thrilled and high-fived each other.

Jack started the engine on the Gator to take Kate back to the house to gather all the items needed for smores.

Meagan jumped in the back seat. "I'll help."

After depositing Kate and Meagan at the house, Jack headed to the fire pit with lighter fluid and matches. Soon there was a blazing fire in the stone pit. King and Conroy walked across the property with Alex and Gary between them. Ace and Rhonda followed closely behind, making small talk.

When they arrived at the bonfire, King told Jack, "I'll go get Meagan and Mom." He didn't wait for a reply; he worried about his mother wearing the brooch. King slid into the driver's seat of the Gator and left.

"Where's Mom?" King quizzed Meagan, startling her.

"In the bathroom."

In one giant step, King stood directly before her. "Why is my mom wearing your brooch?"

Meagan's face reddened at the thought that King knew about her secret mission to regain her possessions.

"She said Jack gave it to her. Please don't say anything to her, Mr. Pullman. I would like her to have it."

King was speechless as he searched her beautiful blue eyes, gauging her sincerity. "That's very kind of you, Ms. Morris."

His sudden formality with her name signaled his caution.

"I'm ready," Kate announced as she emerged from the hallway carrying a sack of old quilts.

"And I have the cold items for smores," added Meagan.

King loaded the blankets into the Gator, and the trio made their way to the fire pit. He had forgotten how chilly it could get sitting outside in the shade of the soaring Evergreen trees.

"This is awesome," exclaimed Gary poking a marshmallow onto his metal toasting stick. "Have you done this before, Alex?"

"No, but it's cool."

Conroy hoped that Gary would not ask him that question. In this exact spot, he had a friend tell King to send Gayla to the barn many years ago. Remorse, thick as sludge, choked him for a moment. Glancing at Gary's profile, he saw Gayla's face. She was smiling at him and telling him it felt fine. If he had only known thirteen years ago that Gary would be the result of his desperate actions, Conroy would not have given up on Gayla—no matter how many unanswered letters or how many times he was told she wasn't home when he knocked on their door.

The memories returned flooding, and Conroy unearthed the reason for his behavior toward his high school crush. It was King. That's why he felt desperation toward Gayla. The buzz around school was that Gayla was crazy about King.

In Conroy's eyes, Gayla may have been socially awkward, but she was beautiful and intelligent. When he mentioned her to his parents, there was immediate disapproval and bad-mouthing of her family. Conroy couldn't give up on her, at least not for a few months.

Kate passed Graham crackers and chocolate around, and everyone indulged.

Ace began to hum a song. "We need some music out here."

"Hey, Mom," Alex reported, "My guitar is in the car. She can play good music!" he pointed to Meagan.

Ace's face registered surprise. "Really?" He chuckled.

He found it amusing that the mean woman who drove a spiked heel into the top of his foot had the sensibilities to play the guitar.

Rhonda stuffed a generous bite of smores in her mouth to avoid speaking. Although she was happy to help Meagan win money and gain fans at The Electric Panda, this was too personal. With Ace next to her, Rhonda experienced uncomfortable jealousy. She preferred to be the sole recipient of Ace's attention. Everyone's eyes were on Rhonda as they waited for the verdict; would she or would she not bring the guitar from her car?

"Oh, I don't know..." Meagan began dismissively. "I'm not that good."

"Yeah, probably not," Ace jabbed.

King nearly choked on his soda. "Rhonda, throw me your car keys!" He demanded. "This is happening right now."

Rhonda jumped to her feet, dug for her car keys in the tiny tight pocket of her skinny jeans, and tossed them to him.

In moments after King returned with the black guitar, Jack Pullman was the most surprised. He was pleasantly taken aback by Meagan's interest in the guitar and gained a new appreciation for her. As a young man, he dabbled in music, but that gene did not surface in either of his boys.

"Are you cold?" Ace asked Rhonda. "Mom brought blankets."

He handed her a quilt to cover up with. The electric redhead struck him as a seductive Scottish maiden, free-spirited and shrewd, with fiery eyes to match her hair. He would like nothing more than to be captured by her; for the first time, Ace wondered what surrendering to a woman would feel like. His hands got clammy, and his heart raced with the desire to impress her. That wasn't normal Ace behavior.

"Can I get you a beer?"

Rhonda smiled warmly. "That would be great. Thank you, Ace."

Perched on the edge of a weathered Adirondack chase lounge, Meagan alternated between strumming and picking while thinking of songs.

"Know any love songs?" King prodded as he recalled her singing to the alpacas in Cowboy's video.

"Yes." She smiled.

With the sun dipping behind the house and a crisp chill in the air, Meagan sang about unrequited love. Her cadence was slower this time, and her tone melancholy edged with pain.

All eyes were on the fire while Meagan poured her feelings into the song. Only King could not keep his eyes off of her. When she looked out over the barn, he knew she was gone again, just like when she sang at that club. Her body and voice were there, but her heart and mind had jumped ship.

He thought about what kissing her would be like as he tried to remember the last woman he kissed. It wasn't Gayla. It might have been the last girl he slept with before leaving college. Her name eluded him. Thoughts of his lips touching hers, like a caffeine overdose, messed with his heart rate. King knew the optimal circumstance would be for Meagan to kiss him as he had never instigated a romantic kiss in his life, and he wasn't about to change. Yes, that was precisely what needed to happen. He decided to cast his best line and reel her in until she planted her lips on his. Adjusting his position on the creaky wooden patio chair, King concentrated on Apple Orchard Movers and what significance they may have.

"Last one, buddy," Conroy announced as he poked another marshmallow onto Gary's stick.

Alex aimed his stick at Ace. "Can I have one more too?"

Ace deferred to Rhonda with a look, then happily stabbed a marshmallow on Alex's stick; anything to get a smile from the auburn-haired lassie at his side.

Never had such a quandary plagued Rhonda; two amazing men in the same sphere. She gazed at King while he watched and listened to Meagan. He oozed confidence and was elusive enough to cause Rhonda to chase, which she felt she excelled at.

She closed her eyes to blot out King and envisioned the scruffy face of the gentleman sitting next to her. Here is another self-assured Pullman man—attractive, with sparkling green eyes, not to mention his lean muscular form. What he did to her sensibilities was unbearable. Her life seemingly went from famine to feast. All the moisture had left her mouth. Ace unknowingly sent chill bumps down her spine. As manly and in control as King was, there was no question in Rhonda's mind Ace was the man for her.

Meagan strummed her last chord.

"Ace?" Rhonda asked quietly, "Would you like to come for dinner with Alex and me?"

"I would." Ace gently patted Rhonda on the leg and joined the applause for Meagan.

Jack and Kate were pleased with their boys and their exciting guests. In all the years on this ranch, this was their first time enjoying live talent around the fire pit; Meagan's guitar skills were terrific.

With an hour a day of practice, Jack was confident he would play his acoustic guitar the next time King entertained.

"Thank you, Mr. and Mrs. Pullman. I appreciate everything you have done." Conroy touched Gary's back, indicating it was time to say goodbye. Gary thanked the group for a great time and skipped to Conroy's car.

Ace volunteered to walk Rhonda and Alex to her car after she and Meagan promised to get together for lunch next week.

King spread sand on the low blaze with the fire shovel and mixed it around until it was extinguished. Jack helped Kate into the Gator and drove her a dozen yards to the house. Meagan stayed behind to help King tidy up.

"You're very talented, Meagan," King said.

"Thanks. I don't play like I used to; there isn't enough time. Do you play an instrument?"

"I wish. Work always came first for me," he shared honestly while gathering the fire pit equipment. They began their trek to the house, and it occurred to him that he had never walked with a woman like that—just walking and talking. He recalled half a dozen women and confirmed that he had never strolled with them. "Thanks for playing. I know everyone enjoyed it."

"My pleasure."

"Is Andrew giving you any more trouble after his knockdown?" King asked in a serious tone.

Unsure if she should share that she was being pressured to leave the B&B, Meagan did not mention it.

"No, he left, so I haven't seen him around." She sighed.

"Well, good."

They deposited items in the kitchen. Meagan looked at King. "Thanks, today was nice. I need to go."

In the driveway, Meagan started the truck engine when King deterred her with a question about her truck.

"Meagan, have you checked these tires?" He squatted down, examining one. "Check the other back tire."

When she hopped out to do as he suggested, he quickly tossed her opal choker on the passenger seat near a backpack, then hurried over to examine the tread with her and avoid suspicion.

"I don't see anything unusual," Meagan said.

King assured her it was likely a tire manufacturer irregularity that wouldn't be dangerous. He started toward the house and sniffed the air.

"We smell like the fire pit." He grinned.

Meagan smiled back, amused and perspiring harder as she imagined him heading to the shower. She hadn't noticed a pit smell on him, just the killer fragrance she recognized as King.

With a boyish grin, King patted himself on the back for staying a step ahead of Meagan. He was exceedingly pleased with himself for having recovered the Opal choker before she did. In this strange game of 'finding the heirloom,' he was positive he was now in the lead.

Chapter Twenty-Seven

"Mr. Conroy, thanks for a super great time with the alpacas, and I'm glad you're my dad," said Gary as he stepped out of the Porsche.

"You bet. Please call me Dad. I'd like to talk to your mom. Is she home?"

"I'll get her," yelled Gary, already running to the front door. "Mom, Mr. uh, Dad wants to talk to you. I had fun with the alpacas at the ranch."

"That's nice, sweetie." Gayla had been crying. Her eyes were swollen and red. "What? Talk to me?"

"Yes, go…" Gary gently pushed her from behind.

"Okay!"

She forced herself to walk outside, hands covering her stomach as she prepared for the gut-wrenching news that Conroy would surely rip her son out of her life.

Conroy leaned against his car, ankles crossed, and arms folded, waiting. Meeting Gary in person yesterday at the retirement home elicited profound elation mingled with agonizing remorse. Pleased to have a young son, Conroy fought feelings of betrayal by his father and Gayla. Yesterday had eclipsed Gayla entirely. Conroy was compartmentalizing Gary and Gayla to deal with each puzzling person, one at a time. He was overwhelmed.

Sorrow engulfed him for the years he missed with his flesh and blood and the hurt over not knowing about Gary. Although his emotions vacillated between happiness and confusion, learning the truth and meeting his son brought immense joy. What Conroy didn't expect was the mental torture and misery regarding Gayla. He thought he had wiped out that painful memory for good. At the Allegiant yesterday, when he saw her for the first time since high school, he couldn't bring himself to be angry that she had rejected him all those years before. Meeting his wonderful son had pierced his impenetrable heart and left him vulnerable to Gayla again.

Yesterday Gary was the focal point. Today, a sense of calm prevailed. Spending time with Gary was heart-warming. Conroy saw in the energetic, clear blue-eyed boy so much of himself. Gayla was not a priority but rather an obstacle to be worked around.

Today was different. After a decent night's sleep and today's outing with Gary, Conroy was ready to face the woman approaching him.

She's sexy, and she knows it. She's cunning and intelligent, and based on what Gary said about her, she's obviously loyal to her son. All good qualities. Could he forgive her for extorting his family by lying about his son? While Conroy prayed about the situation, the jury was still out.

Gayla stopped five feet before him and leaned against the giant oak tree beside the sidewalk, mirroring his posture.

"What do you want, Conroy?"

He craned his head to ensure Gary was not within earshot. "Gayla, I want us to be honest."

"Ha, great, you first, please. This should be interesting. Are you going to take Gary away from me?"

He sighed. "No, I want to revisit the night he was conceived. I would like you to tell me everything you remember, please?"

"Oh."

"I ask because you wouldn't talk to me after that night." Hands buried deep in his slacks pockets, he continued, "I came to your house looking for you so we could talk. Your brother told me you had moved. I wrote you letter after letter and nothing. After several months went by. I was embarrassed and felt like a heel.

Then my dad said I was never ever to speak to you again. He claimed I was acting like a baby and letting my feelings destroy my college education." He paused. "I let my father convince me to give up on you, and that was wrong."

Gayla stared at his shoes reflectively and began, "At the party, King told me someone wanted to see me by the barn, so I went walking alone."

"Yes, that was me."

She nodded. "You came up behind me as I was listening to karaoke music. You said you always liked me and thought I was perfect." She lifted her eyes and looked at Conroy's face expecting to see him laughing at her. Instead, he was dead serious.

"Go on," he urged.

"I asked you if you were drunk, and you said, 'Maybe a little,' but I thought it was a lot at the time. You stayed behind me, talking to the back of my head and holding my hands. It felt so bizarrely intimate, far away yet so close. I know that must sound strange."

"Not at all, Gayla. I was coming on to you as hard as I could."

She cleared her throat. "I asked you if you wanted to go for a walk, and you said you would, but only if it was somewhere private so you could…kiss me."

"I remember all that. Keep going."

"We uh, we went to the backside of Pullman's barn where they kept all that hay. It was like a hay cave. We kissed." Gayla's fingers touched her lips as the memory came alive. "I remember kissing you a lot. I cut my lip on your braces."

"Yes," Conroy recalled tasting blood, but neither was ready to quit.

She began twisting her fingers and rubbing her hands uncomfortably. "I may have asked you if you would please have sex with me… but understand that my hormones were raging… no one had ever said things to me like that before. I was very hot and bothered and made an error in judgment."

"No, you didn't make a judgment error," Conroy corrected her, "I did. I should never have left you there like that. You were my first love Gayla, and I was a horny son of a gun because of you. When we heard King shouting, you told me to go, and I panicked. I didn't want him or anyone to see you lying on that bale of hay looking like I hurt you, so I pulled up my pants and ran out, and then I left with Elias and the guys. I've been sorry ever since."

Abashed, Gayla buried her face in her hands. Considering what they shared together, the fact that she had never believed him and never had given him a chance now seemed perverse. He would have known his son from day one if Gayla had truly believed the beautiful things he said that night. The truth was that she wanted to hear those words from King. Her fascination with King Pullman wrecked her logic.

"I thought you were lying to me in the barn," she confessed to Conroy.

"Why"

"Because you were the only person who ever said anything like that to me," Gayla replied softly.

"That's a shame," Conroy said, "because it was and still is true. You have made a great life for yourself and raised a great boy. I think you're astute, dedicated, and alluring. Will you let me take you to dinner?"

Gayla covered her heart with her hand in preparation for the heart attack she would have any second. "My life is not great, Conroy. You should know my business is down, and it's been hard. Why would you want to go out with me?" she asked, head tilted and measuring Conroy. "Aren't you furious with me?"

"I'm not angry…at all. I'm fascinated by you. We'll go to a restaurant on a date someplace where there's no hay," said Conroy, "I'd like to know about the last twelve years of your life."

Shaking her head, she smiled at the crazy turn of events and asked, "When?"

"Tomorrow at seven. I'll pick you up."

"Gary, please go up to your room, Gramma and I are going to have a talk."

Surprised, Gary obeyed and ran up the stairs while Carol Adamson sat at the kitchen table smoking a cigarette. "What's this about?" she asked.

Too anxious to sit down, Gayla paced the length of the galley kitchen.

"There are some things I need to sort out. Mom, where are the letters Conroy sent to me?"

Carol tapped the ashes from the end of her cigarette and watched them crumble into the tin ashtray.

"What letters?"

"Letters, Mom. Letters. Where the hell are they?"

"I need a drink."

Gayla grunted her disgust. "You don't need a drink. Remember, you quit drinking! Where are the damn letters?"

"I don't know exactly," Carol said, inhaling a puff of smoke.

"What is THAT supposed to mean? Aren't they here in this house?" Gayla stopped pacing to stare in awe at her mother.

"Oh, God help me. Brently Sabeth…may have them."

"What?"

"You heard me."

Gayla waved her hands in the air. "Yes. I heard you. Of course. You didn't need to tell me that I heard you. Why do you do that? I hate this conversation."

"I know you do," agreed Carol.

"How do you know? Oh, because you are the all-knowing mother?"

"Because I hate it too," Carol confessed. "I was blackmailed by Brently."

Gayla sat down across from her mother.

"Christ, put out the cancer stick, please? Tell me what stupid thing you did to get into a bribe with the devil himself."

Carol put out her cigarette in the tin.

"I found out you went to him, and I figured it was to pull something over on him about the baby. I was right, wasn't I?

Anyway, after I intercepted a letter from Conroy to you, I went to Brently's office and told him about it."

"Mom!" Gayla spat, "You could have ruined my education! I can't believe you did that!"

"…anyway, we were behind on property taxes, and you know how I can't go out to work…so, I said I would sell Sabeth the letter for five thousand dollars."

"Oh, God." Gayla dropped her head to the table with a clunk.

"Here's what happened. The ass snatched the letter from my hand and said, 'If you try this again, I will not pay your stupid daughter, Gayla, another cent, and you can tell her why you took away her education plans.' He told me that I would bring him each letter and not say anything about it to anyone or, 'poof, you are poor and uneducated forever.'"

Gayla looked up, shoulders slumped. "That sounds like him."

Elbows on the table, Carol buried her face in her hands, mumbling, "I'm sorry."

The cat jumped up on the table, looked at Carol, and then at the cigarette butt in the ashtray.

"I know, Mom."

Gayla swung her hand at the feline and missed.

Swiftly, the cat bit into the cigarette butt and carried it off the table.

"How many letters did you give that lawyer?" Gayla asked.

"Seven."

Processing the information about Conroy, Gayla evaluated what he had said about coming here, looking for her, and sending her letters. She decided he was being truthful. Could she believe other things he was saying, for example, that he wouldn't take Gary away? There seemed to be no way to make Conroy go away, so Gayla decided on a plan of action. She would accept his platonic invitation, and so long as he was nice to her, she could play nice too, to keep Gary at home.

Rhonda rushed to the door at six-fifty PM.

"Hi, Ace! Come in."

"For you, Rhonda." Ace produced a bundle of wildflowers from behind his back.

"Who is it?" shouted Alex as he barreled into the foyer. "Oh, hi, Ace!"

Ace followed Rhonda to the kitchen as he rumpled Alex's hair. "Hi, buddy!"

"Ace, Alex, and I live with my mom and dad; they're out of town until tomorrow. The table is set in the dining room."

"Thanks for the invitation. Dinner smells great, but we forgot something," said Ace. "Alex, will you close your eyes and count to fifty?"

Rhonda stopped, wiped her hands on a dish towel, fluffed her hair, and looked blankly at Ace.

Alex slapped his hands over his eyes and began counting while Ace moved toward Rhonda until he stood right before her. "I want to give you a 'thank you for inviting me here' hug. May I?"

The second Ace saw Rhonda's grin, he wrapped her in his arms and held her.

"Alex, you're peeking!" Ace said smiling.

"Sorry!" he said, giggling.

The three enjoyed Rhonda's preparation of stuffed pork loin, scalloped potatoes, seasoned vegetables, and steamed dinner rolls.

"This is amazing, Rhonda, delicious," Ace said. "King's maid cooks like this too. He'll probably marry her."

Rhonda coughed into her napkin. "What?"

"King—he's got a thing for his maid."

"Oh, I had no idea. How long has that been the case?"

"Since her interview!" Ace replied, laughing. "I've never seen a maid dressed like that; pink sweater, short black skirt—"

Rhonda finished Ace's sentence, "Pink heels?"

"Yes. King was a goner from the first second."

"What about Meagan? Does she know? How long has she known?"

"She's probably sweet on him; it's hard to tell with her working for him. She's different, the kind of different that works for King. Does that make sense?"

"Actually," Rhonda said, "it makes a lot of sense. So, Meagan did not have the same effect on *you* at the interview?"

Unfamiliar emotions regarding Meagan coursed in Rhonda's veins. Was it irritation, anger, or jealousy? She could not differentiate.

Ace's face reddened. "No. She is not my type. I sense danger around that girl. I heard her say she doesn't dance. Who doesn't dance?"

Rhonda snickered. "Meagan absolutely does not dance. I have personally seen her attempt it, and it's tragic. People would rather hear her sing and play the guitar."

"That's true."

"Aunt Meagan is awesome!" Alex added. "She's gonna show me and Gary how to fish."

"Alex," Ace said, "You and Gary can come fishing at King's place. I know he wouldn't mind. There is a huge tank, and it's stocked with largemouth bass, bluegill, and some catfish."

Turning to Rhonda, he asked, "If you'll come and cast a line, I will bait your hook and remove and clean your catches. Will you come?"

"Oh, come on, Mom?" begged Alex.

"Well, I guess I'll be doing some fishing!" Rhonda admitted. "I'm meeting Meagan for lunch this week. I'll let her know our plans."

"And I'll talk to King," said Ace.

Alex smiled. "This is so cool."

Chapter Twenty-Eight

Since King began the second-floor room edition, he knew he was tempting the rain gods. While he was not superstitious, he knew dragging out finishing the project would be a mistake. Frustrated with his lack of progress, King called an old friend, a builder, Dale Clements, who would be starting the job early this morning. Per the architect's design for the upstairs room, the elevator subcontractor would also arrive that day.

Hiring a contractor should have been comforting, and Dale was one of the best, but King had hit an impasse. His need to work upstairs challenged his desire to find answers for Meagan and her belongings; Meagan's troubles won; therefore, he had private detective work to do.

After researching Apple Orchard Moving, King decided to investigate their address personally. He hoped his detective work would prove fruitful. Something had to give; Meagan looked exhausted when she got to the house that morning. So many things regarding his lovely maid were such a mystery. She had not been forthcoming about her personal items unless under duress. It was clear to King that she would not give up the search. Adding to her mystery was King's impression that she was hiding other significant secrets. He needed more answers.

"You have reached your destination." His GPS led him directly to Apple Orchard Moving, and to his surprise, it wasn't a home-based business; it was more of a trucker's repository in a run-down warehouse district. If King's gut was right, an illegal stockpile was tucked away in a unit somewhere.

Through his binoculars, King saw the two men. The driver was a Hispanic man with a ball cap and goatee. The other fellow was heavy with plenty of angry tattoo art on his white neck.

As the moving truck left the parking lot, King idled passed bay number forty to see what sort of lock he would be dealing with when he returned. He would need a heavy-duty cutting tool to break the shrouded shackle padlock on Apple Orchard's unit.

With both hands gripping the steering wheel, King vacillated between digging deeper into Meagan's world and the ramifications of that versus going to work at the shop. He headed straight for the B&B to probe. It was long overdue. Any new information he might glean about Meagan would be welcome.

King thought about Meagan at his house, assisting his mother, checking on his herd, and cleaning his place. Precisely what caused his heart to dance regarding her was an enigma. Was it the intrigue surrounding her? Could it be pheromones? He had recently watched a documentary that explained that hormones are secreted by one person and picked up by another: like the transmittal and reception of a signal from ship to ship. Could he just be the lucky recipient of her transmission? It occurred to King that those transmissions might be intercepted. In a flash, Andrew's face appeared in his mind. "No way," he said. "Not in my lifetime."

Half a dozen cars filled the front parking lot of the B&B. King parked in the back where the red Corvette sat. He recognized that car as belonging to the date Meagan forgot.

And she told me he was gone, hmm.

More than a little dismayed by the sight of Andrew's Corvette, King followed a cobblestone path to the oak-stained double front doors and let himself in.

"Busy day today?" he remarked to Agnes Willoughby.

She was a roly-poly of a woman with fluffy hair, which she tinted yellow. It amused him that she scanned him from head to toe before speaking to him. King concluded he was an acceptable guest should he decide to stay.

"We have several rooms left. That group meeting in the formal dining room is my son and his business partners," Agnes touted. "Do you need a room?"

King tilted his brown leather Stetson cowboy hat to obscure his face from the group in the dining room. The last thing he wanted was a fight with Andrew. He settled into private detective mode.

"Actually, I'm here to ask you about Meagan Morris?"

"Who are you?" she demanded.

"Well, she came to me about a job... At my store and put you down as a reference."

The heat of his lie crept up his neck, and he regretted having dashed over there in haste. He would hate it if he had unwittingly made things difficult for Meagan.

"Meagan? She's my third or fourth cousin, works hard—she cleans this place okay." Agnes craned her head around as though searching for areas Meagan failed to scour.

"Has Ms. Morris worked here long?"

Agnes Willoughby yawned.

"No. Meagan's apartment was broken into not too long ago, so she needed a safe place to live. We give her a reduction on rent because she cleans...sometimes."

The news was disturbing. Meagan cleaned at his house and cared for his mother, then she came home to the B&B to knock out more hours of cleaning.

"She's moving out before Tuesday," Agnes continued. "She hasn't said where she's going."

That's only a couple of days from now. Why is Ms. Morris moving out?

Agnes glanced toward the commotion in the meeting room. "Andrew Willoughby will be the new owner of this B&B next week. He has plans to renovate and needed her room vacant. We are very proud of him."

"I see. Congratulations to your family, and thank you for your reference." He tipped his head in her direction with a touch to the brim of his hat, smiled, and slipped out the door, feeling dreadful.

As helpful and kind as Meagan was, it distressed King that Mrs. Willoughby couldn't bring herself to speak of her cousin with more kindness. If Meagan had stood before him that minute, he believed he would have hugged her in appreciation. King wouldn't kiss her, though; That was hallowed territory, and sticking his neck out for a kiss was beyond the pale for him. Maybe he would tell her that not everyone is on the take, and then perhaps she would hug *him*. A few women had embraced King whenever the opportunity arose—generally, he was agreeable to the hugs.

Meagan only hugged his mother. That would need to change. All that thinking about his new renter prompted King to check on things at the ranch.

"Hi, how's everything?" He texted Meagan.

"Fine. Thank you for my opal choker. Your mom is enjoying Mr. Clements' flirting." Meagan smirked at the thought of Mr. Clements' jokes.

"What? What do you mean, flirting?" King's blood pressure was on the move. He did not feel well.

"You know, chatting and being sweet," she replied.

Having to explain flirting to a grown man was odd. Besides, Mr. Pullman should have known the definition; He struck Meagan as an accomplished flirt.

King had never known Dale Clements to be a talker. He was a year or two ahead of King in school and not much of a socialite.

"It's probably more for your benefit, Meagan. I think his wife, Arlene, left him a few months back."

To keep her guessing, he did not admit to returning her opal choker; He was enjoying the game.

Meagan considered what King had just texted and remembered how smoothly he handled Andrew when he showed up looking for her at the ranch. He knew what to do in various situations, and she needed good advice at that moment and King's input would be appreciated.

"Dale likes cats, bowling, and building houses, And his daughters are in middle school. Do you think I should go out with him?"

There was no way King would respond to what felt like Meagan goading him. Of course, she should not go out with Dale, but he wouldn't tell her that for all the alpacas in South America. If there was one thing Jack Pullman taught his boys, it was to keep your cards to yourself, so he elected to ignore her question.

Shifting the truck into park, phone in hand, King reviewed his and Meagan's texting conversation.

His shop was abuzz with customers, keeping Marty and the part-time clerk on their toes.

King had a firm grip on his morning coffee cup; with each sip, his annoyance with Dale's newfound flirting abilities began to subside. As was his habit, he reviewed the inventory list in his office at the back of the shop. He liked being prepared for a transaction and memorized the items and the shop's price. Nothing said 'sucker' louder than having to check your bottom line mid-negotiation. Everything looked normal on today's list; A watch, stereo equipment, two leather coats, a drone, a tuba, a wedding ring set, a golf cart, and an ivory chess set... he sipped his coffee and continued reading until he saw the words, 'amber ring.'

Could that be it?

Setting the cup on his desk, he closed his eyes and imagined Meagan's photo. It was a high-set with detailed mounting—sterling silver with an ornamental design that embraced the gem. The stone had various amber tones.

He was ready to see and hold that ring and examine it.

"Marty," King said, approaching the front, "Where is this?" He pointed to line number twenty-two of the items list.

Reaching into his pocket, Marty pulled out a small ring case. "Right here, why?"

"I need to see it. I'm pretty sure it belongs to someone who was robbed."

Marty held the case firmly. "Describe it."

Surprised, King said, "What?"

"I left you an envelope with a note and money for this. I was going to give it to Noreen as a peace offering. We have been going around and around about a kid."

"Oh, sorry. That ring has sterling silver ornate scrollwork and holds an unusual round Cabochon Baltic Amber stone."

Marty quirked his head, eyeing King suspiciously. "What the hell, boss. Where'd you learn all that stuff?" He grabbed King's hand and planted the ring case in his palm. "Where's my cash?"

"Check my desk. I haven't touched it."

"Okay. Now I've got to rethink this thing for Noreen," said Marty.

"What happened to getting a dog?"

"It's still a possibility."

Momentarily paralyzed with the drama surrounding the jewel, his hand unable to open, or was he unwilling to release his grip? Was the heat coming from the ring real or imagined? Aware of the pending onerous task, King sighed and opened the velvet box.

"You look happier than a tick on a fat dog. That must be it?" Marty asked.

King nodded, grinning from ear to ear. He slipped the case into his pocket and placed two one-hundred-dollar bills into the cash drop bag.

"Marty," King whispered, "What did the seller look like?"

"Let me think," he said, bagging a sporting knife for a customer. "About six feet tall, heavy set. Tattoos on his neck, lots of them."

"White guy? Bald?"

Marty glanced back up at King in surprise. "How did you know?"

"Thanks."

The depth of the mess King had stumbled upon, he could not fathom. The only thing he felt absolutely sure of was the credibility of his maid. If King's suspicions were correct, the driver of Apple Orchard movers had pawned the amber ring; He fit the description.

A flurry of customers required King's attention; He patted his ring pocket and focused on the business at hand.

"What can I help you with?" He asked an elderly man.

The gentleman leaned heavily on his cane. "Well, I was robbed, son, and I'm looking for things they took. That's all. The thing I really want to find is my wife's wedding set. God rest her soul." His eyes misted as he looked in the display cabinet.

A lump formed in King's throat. "Well, Sir, sometimes those precious items do show up. Do you have a photo of it?"

He nodded slowly. "It's not a photo, but since I had time, I drew it," the gentleman said, placing an eleven by fourteen penciled sketch on the counter.

The ring was on a young woman's finger. Her smooth hands and tapered fingers gently cradled a coffee cup. The artist hadn't missed a detail. She was a woman who worked with her hands. The fingernails were short and not perfectly manicured. It was drawn so meticulously that it emanated love; the hands were as lovely as the elegantly set four-carat Marquis diamond wedding set on her finger.

"Incredible," King admitted, referring to the ring.

"Yes, she was," the man responded. The only woman I ever loved. God made her just for me... and I miss her every minute."

Never had a piece of art so moved King; He snapped a picture of the sketch and asked the man for his name and phone number. If he came across the ring, he would call the widower to let him know.

"I do have one question. You said it was stolen; where was this set taken from you?"

Folding his artwork gently, the man responded, "Thieves broke into my home while I was at a doctor's appointment."

"Do you mind if I ask where you live?"

"I wrote my address on that paper you gave me. Thank you," the gentleman said, shaking King's hand.

"You bet," Mr. Callan."

King watched the man leave this shop before returning to his office and the comfort of his banker's chair. Burying his face in his hands, he moaned and quelled the tears that yearned to flow. Unknowingly, the man had embarrassed King. A realization settled into King's bones that maybe he didn't know love, and it bothered him. He collected himself and vowed to someday be someone who mattered most to a woman because he didn't want to miss out on love—profound love.

He assisted customers behind the counter, and his business day zipped by. When he looked at the antique wall clock, it was four-thirty.

"I'm going to take off, Marty. Are you good?"

"Yep, I've got it. See you, King."

King was pleasantly surprised to see the progress made on the addition to his house. Dale and his crew had completed running the electrical and applied the insulation.

"Nice work, Dale," King complimented him as they shook hands.

"Thanks, King. I appreciate you calling me for this job. That's going to be quite the room! Tomorrow we'll throw up some sheetrock and tape and bed. How did you come across Ms. Morris?"

"And there you have it," King mumbled, "Damn."

Meagan hadn't been taunting him after all. She likely asked for his opinion because Dale had expressed a keen interest in her. King wanted any discussions involving Dale's preoccupation with Meagan to disappear. However, if he must talk about her, so be it.

"Yeah, I needed a maid. It's that 'give a felon a job' program," King told him recklessly.

"Oh, wow," Dale commented with zero enthusiasm. He wasn't thinking about marriage; his divorce was still too fresh to consider anything serious. Considering all the lectures he had given his children over the years about not getting caught up with the law, bringing home a felon would have demolished his credibility as a parent. Still, Dale imagined how great it would be to look at Meagan daily.

King persisted with the lie, "She's on parole and can't leave the country; heck, she can't leave the state." It was full speed ahead. He was on a roll—now that he had defamed Meagan and disappointed Dale, he couldn't stop himself.

"Well, I wasn't talking about marriage, King. I wondered if she would go to dinner with me... and maybe go bowling."

King gained confidence and momentum like a snowball rolling downhill though the conversation became precarious. "Meagan's caseworker might let her go—if she wore an ankle monitor." King cringed. "You would have to make sure you had no money on you or jewelry. Not sure it's worth risking your safety over, Dale."

King had shown up at the house fifty points down in the middle of the fourth quarter, and now, miraculously, he was up twenty points with one minute left to play. The look on Dale's face told King that he had hit a nerve.

"She's nice, though, and helpful," King persisted. "The whole thing embarrasses her, and she hates talking about it."

Dale scratched his chin. "Yeah, I can understand that. Well, I should go, see you tomorrow. Thanks."

The two men shook hands, then, frowning, Dale and his men left.

Meagan was preparing dinner, and the scent of herb-roasted chicken met him in the foyer.

With a spring in his step, King kissed his mother on the cheek and greeted Meagan, "Hi! It smells great. You're staying for dinner, right?"

Meagan met his eyes and smiled appreciatively, weary of his perky expression.

"Sure, thank you. If you want to check the 'pacas,' it still has to cook for a while, so you have time."

He was impressed with her selection from his freezer. Soon, he would have to restock it with meat and fish. He would like her input for that shopping trip.

With a quick nod, King was out the door, on the Gator, suddenly feeling terrible. When Meagan smiled so appealingly at him, all he could think about was how crushed she would be by his lies to Dale. He reasoned it was all for her safety but still felt like a chump.

Several of his alpacas scampered over to the fence to greet him; Nosey girl was at the front of the pack. Only half the flock was sheared, and the fleece had already been sold. When Meagan's problem was addressed, he would set aside time to finish the shearing. He was counting on a successful trip to the warehouse where he had seen the Apple Orchard truck earlier.

Meagan deserves some peace.

He packed four hanging fence feeders with hay, replenished both water troughs, and watched the animals eat. Leaning against the railing, King beheld his ranch-style home. Through the expansive, clear windows lining the back, he saw Meagan chatting with his mother and tending to her cooking.

"She is so beautiful," he told the animals. "How did I get so lucky to have her here?"

Jack entered the house, kissed Kate on the cheek, and poured himself a drink.

"I want what they have," he continued, "my parents never gave up. They loved each other, hell or high water."

He could not recall a time when his parents stayed angry for more than a few hours. There was usually a bouquet of flowers from Dad or an apple pie from Mom as a peace offering, and then everyday life resumed. Meagan set a glass of wine before his mother and King's chest constricted. An abnormal ache had plagued him since the evening Andrew showed up for a date with Meagan, and now the unique vision materialized again; King had never cared a wit about dancing, but he could see himself dancing with Meagan in the kitchen; It was so real. He held her close, and they moved synchronously.

"Huh," he muttered with a shrug, dislodging the image with a grin, and zipped back to the house on the Gator.

One drink would be just what King needed to numb the regret he was experiencing regarding his deceit about the woman who had lit a fire in his heart. He kicked off his farm boots in the mud room.

"Animals are fine," he informed his parents and Meagan. "Hopefully, I can finish the shearing this weekend."

Meagan dished the food and set the plates on the table. "That should be fun." She smirked.

"Oh, we have some good news, don't we?" Kate announced with a wink to Meagan. "Meagan is going to live here for a while. She'll be in Maddie's room if that's okay with you, King?"

Desperate for temporary housing, Meagan added, "I'll be paying rent."

King's appetite crashed. No, it was not alright. His mother was not thinking clearly.

"Sure. Why not," King said sarcastically, baffled that he was going along with this nonsense.

The last thing he wanted to do was make Meagan feel unwelcome, but it was an awful idea. He did not wish to have Meagan live here as his maid and Kate's helper, sleeping in his deceased baby sister's room.

He would have to fix the arrangement to suit himself; after all, it was his house.

"Let me hire some moving help for you," he told her. "Some companies are not trustworthy."

He gently combed his hand over his short, groomed beard and waited for her to answer.

"King's right," confirmed Jack. "You never know who's moving your stuff. Half of those companies don't do background checks."

The lump of food stuck in her esophagus felt like a basketball. Meagan was guilty of knowing absolutely nothing about the moving company she hired last.

"Okay, thanks, but I don't have much," she managed.

Why she hadn't examined moving companies more closely was a mystery to her in hindsight because it was obviously the smart thing to do. When she owned her home, she recalled vetting plumbing companies before hiring them. Meagan concluded her life minus Paxton, her financial duress, and her mental state had affected her reasoning. She was depressed, and Apple Orchard Movers was cheap. No one needs to know about that dreary part of her life—it's under wraps.

Chapter Twenty-Nine

You seem pretty pleased with yourself, Conroy," said Gayla.

"I am. You're here. I'm having dinner with a beautiful woman who happens to be the mother of my child. What can I say? I'm fortunate." He beamed.

The neurons in Gayla's brain were moving at the speed of light over Conroy's reappearance in her life less than four days ago.

The conversation she had with her brother, Robert, yesterday was humiliating. It wasn't a secret that her business had dropped off in the last couple of years.

Conroy perused the menu while Gayla dwelt upon yesterday's heated conversation with her brother.

Desirous of the best education money could buy for her son, Gayla's fear for Gary's future, admittedly, drove her to desperate measures. A good parent should provide a college education, and she would do that, no matter the route. Until a couple of years ago, King was more than willing to give her the money she requested. Not recently, though, things had changed between them, and Gary was growing up so fast.

Infuriated, Robert demanded, "You want us to give up trying to get the money from the Pullmans? Why? They owe you, right?"

"Just stop, Robert! Don't go after the Pullmans anymore."

"This better be good because Jim and I got shot over that deal, Gayla! Jimmy is pissed because he took a bullet in the ass cheek, and you never paid him for his effort."

Gayla responded, "The deal was, you would each get a percentage of whatever you get the Pullman family to cough up. Since you and Jimmy couldn't get any cash, I don't owe you anything. I'm dropping the cause because I have a date with Conroy Sabeth." She paused, took a deep breath, and admitted, "He's Gary's father. I'm sure the Sabeth family will ensure Gary has the best education money can buy. So, you see, it's all working out! I don't need you or your buddy."

Shocked, Robert shouted, "Conroy is Gary's father? Damn, Gayla. Conroy Sabeth? Then why did you stalk the Pullmans all these years?" He questioned, shaking his head and limping toward her. "You are an idiot—a stupid sister."

Gayla stood glaring at the floor, refusing to answer.

Robert stormed out of the room, disgusted with Gayla's dismissive attitude toward him and his injured friend.

Her ear against the wall, Carol Adamson listened attentively to her children's heated conversation. She knew exactly why her daughter stalked King Pullman and then Ace.

As a young woman, Carol fell in love with a brood of a boy, heavily disliked by her sister. He was not the love of her life he wished to be, which angered him. Yes, Carol understood passion and the damage it could cause. He was someone to fill the space in her heart temporarily.

After reflecting on Gayla's admission and hearing the nervous anticipation in her daughter's voice, happiness flooded her. Carol dumped her mood pills down the toilet, put the harness on her Burmese, and went for a walk.

"Gayla? Gayla? Yoo hoo?" Conway said, laughing. I hope you don't mind; I ordered the Chilean Sea Bass for you. You were preoccupied and in a daze. Mind sharing your daydream?"

"Thank you. I'm flustered... Aren't you?"

She studied his blonde hair, and a memory surfaced—that thin silky straight hair. A flurry of thoughts…scenes…moves. Conroy held her hands; she led him to the side of the barn. Her legs wrapped tightly around his hips, and she clung to him, her hands moving through his hair and cupping the sides of his square-jawed face.

Casually yanking up the bodice of her dress, she sipped the glass of Bordeaux Conroy had ordered for her. Reflexively, she picked up her napkin and fanned herself. Was she exposed?

He studied pensively before responding. "To answer your question, Gayla, I was flustered when I met Gary. I'm not flustered with you, though. Not now. There are only blue skies ahead…if you and Gary will have me in your life someday. I'm good with whatever you'll allow."

Gayla imagined Gary's face and held her glass up.

"To blue skies and allowances!"

Conroy smiled and set his glass down slowly.

"Please don't make me ask you questions. I would like you to do all the talking. Tell me all about you and what you have been doing these last ten years. Help me to understand you, Gayla."

Her wine glass hadn't left the comfort of her lips as she evaluated the clever man across the table. Did Conroy-the-lawyer really not know who funded her life? Why probe for information now?

Holding her glass by the stem, she admired the beauty of the Bordeaux blend—how the light coaxed the colors from the wine. Were there three or four varieties of grapes in there? She wasn't sure. One thing she was sure of, Conroy Sabeth wasn't getting any information from her.

"You should have a long talk with your dad, Conroy."

The waiter approached with their food. "I'm starving," she said, "Can we eat?"

"Sure, but I would like to ask God for His blessing first."

The blankest expression Conroy had ever witnessed covered her face as Conroy reached across the table, held Gayla's hands, and bowed his head to pray.

"Father in Heaven, we humbly thank You for Your goodness. Help us today, Lord; mend the fences in our lives, and heal our hearts with honesty. You know us intimately, God; teach us to love more deeply. Guide our decisions in this relationship as we get to know one another. We ask Your blessing on this meal and for our lives. Amen.

Checking her wristwatch as she rounded the corner, Meagan stepped through the restaurant door to the patio where Rhonda waited. She was right on time for their lunch at the Bistro.

"What's wrong?" Meagan asked, taking a seat across from Rhonda.

"That obvious?"

The outdoor space was collapsing on Meagan, the air suddenly too hot to breathe deeply. "Seriously, are you okay?"

This version of Rhonda was prickly and caused Meagan to itch.

Rhonda put both hands, palms down, on the table. "You lied to me, Meagan."

"What are you talking about?" She scratched her arms.

"I'm talking about your boss, King. You led me to think he was single when he was not. I made advances on him in front of you and his mother. Good grief. How embarrassing!" exclaimed Rhonda. "A sister would have told me the truth, a friend would have said something to me, but you didn't. You also didn't tell me about Ace."

Meagan's hands cupped the sides of her neck as though keeping a check on her jugular vein.

"What do you mean, King's not single? Rhonda! I don't know what you're talking about."

"He's got his sights on someone, so no other woman has a chance with him."

The waiter appeared, setting sweet teas on the table. "Your order will be out soon," he said.

Rhonda smiled weakly. "Thanks." Turning to Meagan, she said, "I ordered the ham sandwich and soup special for both of us."

"Thanks." Meagan stirred her tea, sipped it, and set it down slowly. "This stuff with the Pullman family doesn't have to be weird, Rhonda. You have my blessing to go after whomever you want. I'm not interested. I still think about Paxton."

"Oh, my God! Meagan." Rhonda shook her head in disbelief. "Can you not see what is going on?"

"What do you mean? I like my job for several reasons; Mrs. Pullman is very nice, the pay is good, and King is a good boss. He writes notes…." She grinned. "He makes me laugh, but, if you are interested in him, I wouldn't stop you; it would just be weird."

'He's into you," Rhonda blurted. "Can't you tell? It seems like everyone sees it but you…and me. I was blinded by that man's aura; it blotted out everything else. Including you. Do you hate me?"

"No."

Meagan froze, processing Rhonda's words. *"He's into you."* The phrase hit her like mother nature's trifecta; a lightning strike followed by a cleansing rain, then the warmth of the sun on her face.

"You're really not mad? Rhonda checked, "Because I think Ace is great. We plan to fish at King's place in a couple of weeks. Ace is going to teach Alex and Gary how to fish. I wanted to make sure you and I are okay with everything. You look sick!"

"Sorry, I'm not sick, just in shock. Mr. Pullman is not my type, but fishing will be fun."

Chapter Thirty

Meagan showed up for work in a new sweater and jeans. It was a thin, black, fuzzy sweater with a lower neck than the pink one. King made a mental note to look into purchasing stock in that sweater company.

Meagan had prepared dinner, and the table was set when he returned home from work, but she was not there.

"She went back to her place," Kate said. "I asked her to stay for dinner, but she said she had things to do."

"When does she plan to move in here?"

Kate smiled. "She called the movers you suggested, and I th-think she's planning on moving in a couple of days."

"Okay," King said, looking at both his parents. "Let's have that dinner she made."

They shared a quiet meal while King concentrated on the adventure awaiting him at the mover's warehouse.

He was as prepared as he could be. After encountering the grieving Mr. Callan, King checked the man's address and pinpointed it on a map. He was not surprised to learn that the apartment complex Meagan moved from was across the street from Mr. Callan's place, which was also pinned on the map on his desk. The third pin was stuck on the address of the Warehouse district where Apple Orchard Movers parked their trucks in front of the bay. The three pins formed a neat tiny triangle. What this meant, he could not say.

Fatigue, plus two beers after his meal, relaxed him to a deep sleep. His parents didn't wake him to say good night either, so he slept soundly.

At one AM, he woke and prepared for a night of intelligence gathering. Quiet as a church mouse, King grabbed his jacket, flashlight, and a brand-new pair of bolt cutters. In moments he was on his way to the warehouse district. His criminality confused him. He generally had no regard for people who broke the law, but he was forging ahead with a sketchy plan based on sketchy evidence. Hopefully, the police would be otherwise occupied and not be in the vicinity. He was as prepared as he could be for a narrow swath of dangerous possibilities.

King parked thirty yards away from the bay and nowhere near a streetlight. The parking lot was bare, except for a few semi-trucks positioned at loading docks, ready to accept their morning shipments. One of the old, white, twenty-foot-long Apple Orchard moving trucks hid the unit from the street. He eyed the bolt cutters on the seat next to him. According to the sales clerk, those cutters would slice through the brass body of a padlock on the metal warehouse door like a hot knife through butter, but with any luck, it wouldn't come to that.

Thoughts of his maid flitted in and out. How pleased she would be if he could locate some of the things she was prepared to kill for.

Then he saw him, the bald white man slathered with tattoos, exiting the door next to the bay. Through his binoculars, King saw that the guy had something in his hand that he put in the truck's front seat. He noted that the man was talking on his phone as he shut the truck door and went back up the short flight of stairs and through the small door.

Now or never!

King threw his truck in gear and zipped over to the Mover's truck. Mr. Tattoos had left the boxtruck unlocked. Disappointment fell on him when he saw the small package was not jewelry but something electronic and unfamiliar. He left it, turned his vehicle around, and snuck up the steps to the small door, unlocked.

He slipped inside and froze, listening. There was the shuffling of squeaky sneakers on the slippery concrete floor and a light turned on in the back section. The phone conversation was still taking place.

"Yes," the tattoo man said, "I have looked, but I don't see anything like that. Okay, I'll keep looking."

King began to sweat as his eyes darted from one object to another. But nothing was familiar. He was in a race to find something, anything of Meagan's. A race he had haphazardly signed up for.

"Okay, okay, okay, Jake. I'll go right now, "the man continued, "I'll let you know when I find it."

When the overhead lights shut off, and King heard footsteps moving in his direction, he spun around and flew out the door as quietly as he had entered and ran to his truck. The moment the large man was in his moving truck rolling down the street, King kept a fair distance and followed him out of Hallsville.

Fifty minutes down Highway fifty-seven, the Apple Orchard Moving truck turned into Baker Estates in the meager town of Wells, with King still tailing them. The neighborhood consisted of trailers, single and double-wides, all shanty; busted blinds hung carelessly in grimy windows. Notable was the lack of trees suggesting the land once belonged to a farmer. The road was not paved and had no street lights. The only illumination came from occasional yellow light streaming from the mobile homes.

The Dooley bounced and swayed, zigged and zagged, and finally turned into a makeshift dirt driveway next to an abandoned metal structure the size of a three-car garage. Tracking far enough behind the mover to avoid suspicion, King veered away from the target property and shut the headlights off. Armed with a flashlight, he parked and jogged toward the moving van. He was inside the building in seconds, feeling his way through the darkness. King stalled until his eyes could see a trickle of light yards away. "Amazing," he whispered, astounded by the interior space, which extended back approximately seventy feet and appeared well organized.

There was fumbling and cursing as the tattooed man dug for something and was unsuccessful. An overhead light flicked on as King passed the section labeled furniture and another area with the heading 'personal.'

There were various musical instruments in the personal section, including guitars. Still, only one guitar brought Meagan to mind: a honey-colored Martin twelve-string guitar with an amber pickguard. Looking closer, King noticed the initials AM were carved into the back of the slender mahogany neck. Beyond the shadow of a doubt, it was Meagan's.

Standing in the middle of the jammed warehouse, King rubbed the ache in his chest again. A red speed bag caught his eye when he turned down another row of neatly stacked items. It was lying on a table stacked with sports equipment; Happy birthday, Pax, was written on it with a magic marker.

"You were privileged to have Meagan as your wife," he whispered to the bag as though it were Paxton himself.

He began to gather as many things as possible. "Meagan, it's Christmas for you!" he exclaimed, hustling down the road to his truck, arms full. Then he set the guitar and punching bag by the front passenger seat and turned around.

"Well, if it ain't the pawn man," said a Hispanic man in his twenties sporting a heavy silver necklace with Mother Mary's face on the pendant.

"So, you are the partner in crime," said King. "What!" he yelled.

Whack!

The man swung a bat. King ducked, and the bat connected with the edge of the truck door and bounced to the ground.

The tattooed man appeared tire iron in hand and saw his buddy scrambling on the ground for his bat. "What the hell, Carlos?"

Before Carlos could reach the bat, King kicked him in the head, and he went still.

The heavyset friend aimed for King's head with the tire iron but hit the roof of his truck instead. King launched a right hook and clipped the man's jaw. The assailant wobbled and swung the tire iron again, striking King's left arm. Something in his arm snapped, skyrocketing his blood pressure. On the third pass of the tire iron, King grabbed it with his operational hand, pulled the man close, head-butted him, and watched him fall unconscious to the dirt.

"No way, man," growled the Hispanic man.

He sustained a cut on his head from the heel of King's cowboy boot, but he had recovered his weapon and was coming toward King. First, throwing his bat at King and then his fist. King returned a punch. The man teetered but came back with a swing to King's head, splitting his cheek and then kicking King in the abdomen. King's left arm was useless, but he scooped up the tire iron as a shield to block the attacker's kick. His shinbone snapped, and he dropped onto the ground crying in pain.

"Damn!" King exclaimed, wiping away the blood blinding his left eye; he had to get to a hospital. "Do you want me to call the police?" he asked the bleeding, crying man lying on the road.

"No. Shit, no, don't call the police!" The man begged. "Just take me to the hospital."

King yanked the man off the ground with his good arm and growled, "Get in!"

"Thank you, thank you," he cried. "I know who you are, Mr. King. You want cash too. I get it. I will not tell the boss."

"I wasn't stealing," King informed the thief, "the stuff I picked up in your warehouse, you guys stole from my friend."

"Oh, sorry, man. I didn't know! You broke my freaking leg!" Carlos began wailing.

"Would you shut up!" King yelled, "I need help for your criminal friend."

"Oh, my god, is Ricky dead? He's my stepbrother. Oh, Jesus, help me."

Wincing in pain and protecting his left arm, King started the truck and dialed 911. "A man is injured and laying on the ground; Baker Estates in Wells, back of the neighborhood. He seems unconscious." He ended the call quickly and looked in the back seat. "We're heading to the hospital."

"You gonna pay for it?" Carlos shouted.

"No. We're square, period. I won't pay for your leg because you broke my damn arm. Now shut up, or I will call the police."

He drove, agonizing over the names of the broken bones. "Humerus, ulna, radius," he spouted, proudly having paid attention in biology class.

"What, Radius? No, man, my name is Carlos."

"Well, Carlos, why are you a damn criminal?"

"I don't want to talk about it, man. I think I'm going to be sick!"

King slammed on the brakes, diving toward the back door. He reached across Carlos with his good arm and opened the truck door. Carlos leaned out and puked. The smell of vomit and King's blood loss were sinking him fast.

Carlos sat up and wiped his face. "Man, puking is good. I feel good. Man. You don't look so good, but I can't drive, so man, wake up!" "Mr. King!" Carlos shouted, grabbing King's upper arm and shaking him. He squeezed King's arm until he roused and put the truck in gear. "I don't want to die out here, man; let's go. You can do it, Mr. King!"

King had no idea how he got to the hospital, let alone what happened in the next five hours.

When he opened his eyes, a doctor and nurse discussed something at the foot of his bed. The attending physician explained to King that he could not drive home because of the narcotics in his system.

"Meagan," King repeated, "Meagan." He pointed to his phone with a finger-swipe motion.

"Can do," the nurse said, placing King's finger on the screen for access. Then she found Meagan in his contacts and called.

"Hello, this is Nurse Janette at Medical South Hospital, and my patient, Mr. Brandon Pullman, requires a ride home."

"Oh," Meagan said, "Sure, I'll be there in thirty minutes."

"Great. Come to the Day Surgery center on Medical Street." The nurse set the phone back on the table and told King, "She'll be here shortly."

"My Meagan is coming," King assured the nurse with a lopsided grin and eyes half shut.

At six o'clock in the morning, when Meagan arrived, Medical South Hospital was bustling with activity. Her frantic worry turned to shock when she saw her boss.

"Hey, honey," he slurred, "you made it."

"What happened to Mr. Pullman," Meagan asked the nurse.

"No, no, no, no. Meagan, it's King!" he mumbled.

The nurse pushing his wheelchair noticed the surprise and embarrassment on Meagan's face and said, "Mr. Pullman is on heavy painkillers. He came in with a broken forearm. We pinned and cast his arm; as you can see, he has ten stitches in his left cheek. At least he's happy; painkillers often make a patient indifferent and sleepy."

The nurse handed Meagan a tote bag with hospital insignia. "Here is the post-op medical care paperwork and follow-up appointment information."

"Thanks. My truck is right outside the door."

"Good," the nurse said, lifting King's good arm over her shoulder. Meagan flanked King's other side and held onto his waist. Together they guided King up into the truck.

Nurse Janette shut the door and promptly left.

Meagan climbed into the driver's seat, and King slurred, "Can't leave. My truck is over there," he pointed feebly. "Go back, front seat, honey."

"Where are your keys?"

Meagan felt King's jeans pockets for the keys, but they were not there. She reached for the tote bag on the floorboard, and there were his personal items, wallet, phone, and keys. King shrugged and fell asleep.

She parked her truck next to his, unlocked the driver's door, and stood staring. The smell of vomit assaulted her, and she pinched her nose, but her uncle Abe's guitar and Pax's speed bag were home!

"How," she whispered, "Where?"

She moved them to her truck and returned to the driver's seat. King was sound asleep and breathing deeply. She studied him; his cast, his battered face, his drug-induced term of endearment. No one had ever called her "Honey" before.

Meagan had come to grips with the fact that King had caught her mid-mission and that he likely had figured out her end game, but this fascinating man snoring in her truck had fought to bring her family to her, which was incredible.

The sun was coming up when Meagan pulled up King's driveway. Jack was leaving for work and about to get in his vehicle. He stopped short at seeing his eldest son in an arm cast and a bandaged face.

"What happened?"

"He had an accident, best I can tell," Meagan said, walking around to the passenger side. With King's arm draped over her shoulder, her arm around his hips, she steadied him. "Are you ready, King?"

"Yes, honey, ready," he blurted incoherently.

Jack smiled and shook his head. "It looks like you've got things under control. I'm going to the shop. Call me if you need my help."

"Thanks, I will," said Meagan.

"No, no, no, no," said King, "not I will. I do, I do."

Meagan could hear Jack Pullman laughing heartily even after he shut the door to his Hummer.

"Are you hungry?" she asked King.

He turned to look at her and snapped his teeth. "Yeah, I'm gonna eat you up. Woah!" His knees buckled.

"Okie, dokie. Well then, you can sleep."

Meagan lugged King into the house, directed him to his bed, and placed his cell phone on the nightstand. "You should sleep this off, King."

He lay on the bed and moaned.

Worried, Meagan asked, "What is it. What do you need?"

He whispered quietly, causing her to move in close to hear him. He whispered again until she was inches from his face, then tapped his bandaged cheek.

"Hurts." Then he puckered his lips.

Did she misunderstand? Her boss appeared to be requesting a…kiss.

Peering into his honest, dilated eyes, she cautiously questioned, "Do you want me to kiss you? Will that help?"

Her surprise at his request turned to amusement when he nodded and puckered again. Would her employer remember any of this when he regained his sanity? Meagan leaned down and pressed her lips gently on his.

Her eyes fluttered and shut briefly before she popped up, asking, "Is that better?"

Eyes closed, King smiled weakly. "My pants…"

"Oh, right." She pulled off his boots, undid his jeans, and slid them down his legs, leaving him in tight, black boxer briefs and a plain white t-shirt. "How's that?" she checked.

He was already sound asleep again.

Kate emerged from her room down the hall as Meagan closed King's door with red-hot embarrassment blotching her face.

Meagan understood how this might look to Kate; the maid leaving the boss in bed at seven in the morning wasn't good.

"Good morning, Ms. Kate."

"Good morning, dear. Is everything alright?"

"Mr. Pullman broke his arm. He had some kind of accident during the night," Meagan stammered. "I picked him up at the hospital and helped him to bed. He's on some strong narcotics."

"Oh," responded Kate, "I wonder what happened?"

"It's hard to tell. Sleep is the best thing for him since Mr. Pullman is in a fog and slurring his words. I'll fix us some breakfast, and we can go check on the animals if you're up to it?".

Before venturing to the main corral, they enjoyed coffee, fruit, and warm sweet rolls.

Nosy Girl clamored for Meagan's attention until Kate maneuvered herself with her cane to the fence. She was itching to pet the adorable-natured alpaca.

"She's delightful," Kate commented, petting her soft, freshly shorn coat. Nosy Girl responded with a sloppy lick over Kate's right eye.

"She really is."

Meagan's phone buzzed with a text from King, "Need help."

"Kate, would you mind if I ran back to the house? Mr. Pullman needs something. I'll be right back!"

"You go, dear. I'll wait. It's a beautiful morning."

Out of breath with frustration rising over leaving Kate at the corral, Meagan stood by King.

"What is it?"

King whispered again until she moved in close, and he pointed to his bandaged sutures again. She rolled her eyes. He closed his eyes and puckered his lips. This time his hand pressed lightly on her back as she leaned near. He pulled her closer, stroked her silky hair, and waited for her lips on his.

There was only the sound of their breathing when Meagan kissed him gently at first. To Meagan's surprise, his lips were operating just fine for a drugged, half-asleep man. The intensity of their kiss felt like hurling through outer space, sucking her in like a stray planet being pulled into orbit by the sun—hot and fast.

What she tried to brush off as a silly kiss early this morning didn't feel ridiculous now. It felt dangerous and unprecedented.

King pulled away from their kiss, looked longingly at her, and reported, "I just need the bathroom."

"What?" she said, panicked that she had overstepped or misunderstood his initial request. "Sure, ah, okay."

King sat up with her help, and she put an arm around him. He threw his good arm over her shoulders, still wobbly. Reaching into his jockeys at the toilet, aware she was likely looking, he didn't care. He would have been flattered if she did look.

Since one of King's arms was trapped in a cast and sling, Meagan turned on the faucet and washed his hand with hers. She ushered him back to bed, and quickly returned to Kate. Meagan was relieved to find her contentedly sitting in the Gator, resting.

"Mr. Pullman is fine, just too drugged to walk properly."

"Oh," Kate said, "I want to know how he broke his arm."

"Me too."

"They made their way back to the house. Meagan suspected that King's arm was broken in a fight over her guitar and speed bag, which caused her feelings of guilt. Add to that fact that she kissed her doped-up boss—she felt like an idiot, A guilty idiot. She hoped he would forgive her.

"I'm going to have a second cup of coffee and work on some puzzles," stated Kate.

Meagan smiled. "Okay, I'll figure something out for dinner this evening."

King was a planner and a thorough grocery shopper. His deep freeze was stocked for World War III. Meagan reached down deep and found Mahi fish fillets. She selected asparagus from the fridge crisper and decided risotto would be the perfect side dish. It had been a while since she had made a pie, but since his pantry contained all the ingredients needed for a Key Lime Pie, she couldn't stop herself.

While the fish was marinating and the pie was setting up in the fridge, Kate laid down for her nap. Meagan set about doing some light house cleaning and readied the table for dinner, then took some time to bring her guitar and speed bag into the bedroom she would rent soon.

Hours later, Jack came through the door, pecked Kate on the cheek, and poured himself a bourbon and coke before sitting down to watch the news with his wife.

"Meagan, dinner smells great. How's King?"

"Hello, Mr. Pullman, King... Mr. Pullman is... disoriented."

Incredulous, Jack responded, "Hmm. It must have been a heck of an accident. King has never broken a bone before."

That news was unsettling and caused Meagan worse guilt.

"Dinner is almost ready. I'll go tell Mr. Pullman," she announced on her way through the living room.

"Dinner is ready," Meagan said and knocked lightly on King's bedroom door before opening it. She found him lying there wide-eyed. He studied her.

King thought he had imagined it, but now that she was standing there, he was sure she kissed him. Had he enticed her? He couldn't remember, but he wanted her lips on his. He closed his eyes and moaned, barely audible, "It hurts."

Slowly, he touched the large bandage covering half his head.

When she moved to the side of his bed, he knew that's what happened earlier. He was sure of it.

King whispered again, "Hurts."

She advanced like a moth to a flame, and he knew he had her—this time. He puckered, and she pressed her lips to his, no questions asked. They had pushed away from shore, adrift on a kiss. Soon there was no land in sight, and their breathing was labored. Her sweater felt like a parka, and King's skin like a fireplace.

King pulled away gently. "Did you say dinner?"

"What? Yes," she replied, discombobulated.

"I'll need my pants." He pointed to his lower extremities—naked except for underwear.

"Oh, yes, sorry."

Over the last hour, King had been analyzing his predicament. The living arrangement mess his mother created needed to be rectified and fast. He believed he had come up with a way to fix it. If it didn't work, nothing would. He was amused by his sexy maid and felt confident his idea would work.

Meagan helped him to his feet, pulled his jeans up, and fastened them. She was about to leave the room ahead of him when he intentionally wobbled and nearly fell. He yelped in fear and gave her an innocent look. In a flash, she was back by his side with her arm around him and his good arm over her shoulders.

He sniffed her hair. "Mmm, you smell great."

"Hmm." She helped him to his chair and realized King intended for her to stay for dinner again, so she set a place for herself and served dinner.

"Mahi, nice," King said, smiling.

He shook another painkiller from the bottle and popped it in his mouth.

Kate and Jack were confounded by their ecstatic son. A broad white bandage covering most of the left side of his face did not mask King's pleasure. The last time Kate saw that expression on his face, he was sixteen and had gotten his first motorcycle. Kate reminded her husband that King was on hard drugs, and Jack nodded in understanding. They soon realized the idiotic joyful look was not going away.

"What happened, Son? Can you talk about it?" asked Jack.

"I slipped off an eight-foot truck dock and landed on my arm. The guy in the warehouse took me to the emergency room in my truck." He lied within reason. "How's the shop?"

Jack was happy to tell several stories involving Mr. Lee and Storm. "They are best friends, those two. Storm takes treats out of Lee's mouth. Damn, best thing! That dog is an excellent deterrent for theft."

King felt a twinge of jealousy. He knew what a great dog Storm was and wanted him back now that the criminals who tried to extort money from Ace were caught. More than anything, King wanted his peaceful life back, a life that included Storm, his family, a ranch, and a woman who kissed like an angel.

Meagan began to clear the table, and Kate got up to help; her ankle was healing well; Some days, Kate used her cane, and on other days, she relied on her walker. She happily maneuvered the metal contraption into the kitchen to assist Meagan.

The moment had come for King to implement his plan.

Meagan leaned in to pick up King's plate. He turned away from his parents and toward her, closed his eyes, and puckered. Meagan froze for a moment and did not take her eyes off King. The man was her boss. Yes, he was doped, incoherent, and flirtatious, but he had also recovered Uncle Abe's guitar and Pax's bag. Adding to his charm, she knew he had put the opal choker in her truck. It had to have been him. Overwhelmed with gratitude, she kissed him.

Euphoria swept over King. His perfect maid voluntarily kissed him.

Nothing else mattered to King or Meagan then; both were consumed with appreciation and desire for the other. Neither heard Jack clear his throat the first time.

King hoped his mother and father would see that renting a room to his employee was a bad idea because she liked kissing him, which was a no-no for a woman planning to rent a room in his home.

Jack smirked and coughed again, but Kate was aghast. "King!" she cried in shock.

Meagan jerked away from King like his lips were hot coals.

"What?" King said innocently, "She kissed me!"

"She did. I saw it," Jack said.

Meagan groaned, "Oh, no," and returned to clearing the dishes.

Jack covered Kate's hand with his. "Oh, leave them be, Kate. They're old enough to know better."

"No, Jack, this is a problem because she's moving in, in a few days. It's in-inappropriate, don't you think?"

Kate was very familiar with King's inability to maintain a relationship with a competent woman. Kate had grown attached to Meagan and knew she could count on her for anything she needed help with. If King allowed her to kiss him, then she could very well lose her valuable helper. If King blew it with Meagan, he would ruin a good thing, and her angelic helper would be gone. There should be no kissing; according to Kate, it was too risky.

Jack shrugged his shoulders and looked at his glowing son. "Kate, I think you're right. Meagan works here. King," he continued, "you have put your maid in a compromising position because of your actions. You allowed her to kiss you. What on earth were you thinking?"

Whatever antiperspirant Meagan had left was failing her. She had never felt so ridiculous. If only King hadn't moaned, his parents would not have known.

"I'm sorry, I thought…." Meagan began trying to explain herself and salvage her job and a place to live. "He said—he said he felt better…"

Jack bellowed with laughter. "Really? King, did a kiss from Meagan make you feel better? Ha, ha…"

King's face was as red as Meagan's. His parents' comments reduced him to an awkward teenager. He couldn't recall another time in his life when he felt humiliated and jubilant at the same time. Kate covered her mouth to hide her amusement as they looked at King, guilty but still beaming.

It hit Meagan that King played her for kisses. His reason eluded her. Any way she sliced it, her participation in his ruse meant she would be out of a job and homeless. She announced, "I should go now; it's late."

"No, no! Meagan," King said firmly. He stood up quickly and wobbled. Meagan hurried to his side and put her arm around his hips.

"Please stay?" he asked gently. "Will you take me to the corral? Gotta check on my woolies."

Jack and Kate observed their interaction through the kitchen windows facing the acreage, speechless at the ignorance of their blissful son and his heavenly maid.

"She loves him," Jack said quietly as they watched Meagan help King into the Gator, though he was perfectly capable.

"No, he loves her," Kate contradicted. "That's obvious."

Chapter Thirty-One

The sun melted the dew over the ranch edging out the chilly morning. King lay on his bed thinking about Meagan. He played her for a fool at last night's dinner, hoping his mother would realize Meagan desired him and, therefore, she shouldn't be renting a room in his house. In his desperation to have his mother recognize the attraction between him and Meagan, he freaked her out.

Now his mother thought Meagan shouldn't live in his house at all. He hadn't contemplated the plan all the way through because where the hell would she go? King didn't want her to rent from him. He would have refused her money anyway. He didn't want her in Mattie's room either. Unable to say it out loud, King wanted Meagan in *his* room. The question that plagued him was, why wasn't Meagan throwing herself at him? The entire situation was gummed up.

Even the sun's brilliance streaming into his room could not keep King awake. His head throbbed; his exhaustion acute. The last time he fought similar tiredness was in high school when he had mono. Finally, he fell into a deep, long sleep.

Still sporting yesterday's clothes, Meagan assisted Kate with her hair as Jack helped himself to coffee, quiche, and fruit. When Kate was comfortably settled at the breakfast table with Jack, there was a light knock on the front door. Dale Clements and his building crew had arrived.

"Hi, Meagan," said Dale.

"Hi, come in, Mr. Clements. Can I get you anything? Cup of coffee?"

"Yes, that would be nice. I take it black," Dale replied, following her to the kitchen. He tipped his head to Mrs. Pullman and shook Jack's hand. "How are you this fine morning, Sir?"

"Just glad the good Lord saw fit to give me another day," responded Jack.

Dale accepted the freshly brewed coffee from Meagan. "Mind if we talk?"

Curious but frustrated that Mr. Clements would draw her away from Mr. and Mrs. Pullman, she followed Dale to the front porch.

"What is it?"

"Well, I thought about this for several days, and I don't care…"

"Pardon me?"

"I don't care that you are a felon. It truly does not bother me that you went to prison, and I don't want to know the specifics. It really does not matter. I just want you to go out with me."

"What? I mean, how, who?" Meagan scrambled for clarity. Were hands choking her neck? Breathing was difficult.

With a sheepish look on his reddened face, Dale confessed, "King, let me know because I mentioned to him that I asked you out. Please don't be embarrassed. I just want us to be open with each other."

Focusing on Dale's work boots, Meagan gritted her teeth while collecting her thoughts.

"Oh, yes, my record," she said slowly. "Hmm, Mr. Pullman told you about that? No one was supposed to know. That was an employer-criminal privilege."

Her hands clenched into fists; fury flowed through her veins over the reality that King Pullman smeared her good name with such an outlandish lie. Was she now in the same camp as the felons and degenerates who robbed her and left her with nothing?

Dale continued, "Your boss only told me because he thought it mattered to me. That's all, but it doesn't." He smiled with his arms crossed, proud of his assertion.

I don't have a clue about criminal consequences from the courts, but Dale needs to keep this conversation to himself.

"I understand but be aware that when I tell my parole officer about this, he will pull me from this job because that information got out. This is bad. I will be immediately placed in a facility…extradited…probably, and I will never…."

"Oh, man! I'm so sorry. I had no idea…"

"Why would you, Mr. Clements? You are a model citizen, like Mr. Pullman. You don't have skeletons to hide like…theft…brutality, er, battery, and dare I say, murder. I'm awful, but I deserve a chance to…go out with you, right?"

She stood up straighter, batted her eyelashes, and smiled sweetly.

"Oh, yes. Absolutely," Dale said, "how can I help?"

"Discussing my affairs must stop immediately. My life, er, my dating life with you, depends on it."

Dale made a zipper-like move with his fingers across his lips. "They are sealed."

Meagan moved close, took his face in her hands, and kissed his cheek. "Thank you."

"Ah…sure." He felt his cheek.

"Dale. I should talk to my criminal therapist about you first and our date." She smirked. "I hope you understand."

Her skin burned with anger. King must have viewed her as a criminal since day one when she held a gun to his head, then he followed her to the Sell City pickup of her pheasant and told her not to rob anymore.

The gall of that man to say things like that to Mr. Clements!

Dale cleared his throat. "No, no. I don't mind. That's fine. Just let me know." He smiled hopefully and waved to his crew to follow him to the upstairs addition.

Meagan spun around on her heels and headed back into the kitchen to collect the morning dishes and clean the kitchen.

When Jack left for work, Meagan asked Brenda, "Would you mind if I ran an errand shortly? I hate to leave you for a few hours, but King is here, and his narcotics have probably worn off."

Intrigued, Kate eyed Meagan.

"Also," Meagan continued, "I think it would be nice to have Ace and Rhonda over for dinner tonight as well. They seem compatible."

"Ah, sure." Kate saw anger in Meagan's eyes. Her face resembled a pot left to boil for too long. "Is everything okay?"

"Oh, yes! It's going to be great," she said and texted Rhonda and Ace an invitation to dinner that night at six thirty.

Rhonda texted back, "Yes! Thanks! Mom will babysit Alex."

Ace texted back, "Why?"

"Just dinner together. Thought it would be nice," Meagan explained. Then her phone dinged with a text from King; he needed help.

Kate enjoyed her second cup of coffee and worked a word search at the breakfast table while Meagan tended to King. She entered his bedroom, asking, "What do you need?"

Like lemon squeezed onto a cut, the slander incident stung Meagan. He began whispering again as though he'd forgotten how he humiliated her in front of his family at dinner the night before. He continued to whisper, and she moved in for the kiss; completely guarded; the information Dale shared was her catalyst.

Their lips touched. Meagan focused on Dale's words, and when she sensed King's arousal, she pulled back first.

"I thought you might like to take a shower before breakfast?"

He searched her eyes, but they were cold. "Oh, okay, but I need your help."

King stood reluctantly. Meagan steadied him as they walked to the bathroom. He grinned and pointed to his jockeys, causing her to briskly whip them down his legs. She vowed to remove that crazy, happy look from his handsome bearded face.

"All set," she said, helping her naked boss into the stall.

He sat on the shower bench, and Meagan casually reached for the faucet and cranked the cold-water handle to the max, then quickly slid the gray glass door shut and left.

"Hey!" King yelled, hoisting his cast up high to avoid getting water into it. "Meagan?"

She'd already left the bedroom.

"Gotta run an errand; we're having company for dinner," she called back.

On her way through the living room, she waved to Kate. "Call me if you need anything, Ms. Kate. I won't be gone long."

"Okay, dear." Kate sincerely hoped the kissing incident at dinner hadn't already reached the breaking point between Meagan and King. Kate was looking forward to the helper-maid moving to the ranch, but with her present mood, Kate could not tell if Meagan was.

Dale peered through one of the upstairs windows and waved to Meagan in the circle drive.

She mouthed back, "Bye."

The appalling things Kings said to Dale weighed on Meagan like a yoke with hundred-pound water buckets, crippling her ability to act or think quickly. In her evaluation and reevaluation of her boss, he did not seem like the kind of man to turn on someone for no reason. Had she given him a reason? It was too much to process when she needed to be getting her ducks in a row about this evening's dinner. After picking up the items that would help her 'teach King a lesson in kindness,' she bought a pair of white jeans and a spring sweater, then stopped for groceries. She was back at the ranch in less than two hours.

Kate had fallen asleep in her chair, and King was upstairs discussing the addition with Dale when Meagan returned. She put the groceries away and hid the other items under the bed in Mattie's room before doing the prep work for dinner.

"Cooking already?" Kate asked.

"Yes, it's an exceptional meal. Everything has to be perfect!"

Kate's eyebrows rose. Last night King's face was stuck on euphoric, and today Meagan was short-tempered and decided to throw a dinner party. She shook her head; glad she was not in the dating world like her boys. Managing carefully without her walker, Kate uncorked a bottle of red wine from King's collection and poured herself a glass. The way things had been going lately with her health and her family's perils, Kate wondered if this was what it would feel like to live in a soap opera.

"You're walking without your walker again?" Meagan noted, impressed at the sight, but shocked that Kate was drinking at two thirty in the afternoon.

Kate smiled and took a swig of her Cabernet. "Yes, now, maybe I can be more help around here. What are we making?"

Meagan grinned, "Beef Wellington. Kate, your speech is amazing! You are healing quickly."

"It's the good Lord. I don't think I have ever had that Beef Wellington. What can I do?" Kate lifted her hands up in surrender. "I'm your helper!"

"Here, you can halve these new potatoes."

Meagan set one oven to four-hundred-twenty-five degrees and seasoned the tenderloin before placing it in the fridge. "I hope you will like it. It's so tasty with the Duxelles!" Meagan exclaimed.

Kate looked to the heavens. "Too fancy for me!"

She stared wide-eyed at Meagan's preparation skill as she tossed mushrooms, onions, and shallots into a skillet and then added butter and cream. After it thickened a bit, she set it aside.

Meagan noticed Kate with her mouth agape, and she smiled. "Now I'm going to make the pastry which the beef will cook in."

"I see," Kate said and added small, prepared bowls of spices to the chopped potatoes: thyme, rosemary, sage, and garlic. Then she poured in a half cup of olive oil and stirred. "This already smells so delicious!" She checked the time on the kitchen wall clock.

Taking further instruction from Meagan, Kate dumped the potato mixture onto a baking sheet, covered it and slid it into the fridge, dusted her hands off, and sipped her wine while marveling at Meagan's artistry. She watched in awe as her son's hired help rolled the browned, seasoned beef and the 'Dux' paste into the pastry and set it in the fridge.

"You have such talent."

"I hadn't considered cooking a talent, but thank you, Ms. Kate. If you don't mind, I will shower and get ready."

"Go, go, go!" Kate shooed Meagan out of the kitchen and sat at the table to enjoy the view of the animals. Something was bothering King. He was driving the Gator around aimlessly with a broken arm. Kate wondered if maybe he went in circles because he could only see from one eye. After a time, she phoned him to remind him to come in for the fancy dinner Meagan had prepared.

Once King had showered and dressed for dinner, Kate met him in the hallway. "Son, something is off with Meagan. I hope she'll be alright."

"I noticed that too."

Chapter Thirty-Two

At six PM, Ace and Rhonda appeared at the front door. Meagan hugged Rhonda and extended her hand to Ace. He was skeptical about touching her, even if it was only a handshake, but he did not want to let Rhonda down, so he shook Meagan's outstretched hand. Instantly, he noticed her stern look and a confidence in her eyes that wasn't there before, which spooked him, and he looked away.

Rhonda said, "Thanks for inviting me. I wasn't sure I would get a second date with this amazing guy." She smiled at Ace, and he put his arm around her.

"Hi," King said, entering the living room.

In a second, he had taken in the sight of Meagan; her crisp white jeans tucked into pink cowboy boots and stunning short-sleeved floral pink and white sweater set with a plunging neckline. Her hair was twisted up and pinned in the back with a poof of a ponytail on the top of her head. He inhaled deeply.

Ace turned to look at King with his head bandaged and arm in a sling and registered surprise. "What the hell happened to you?"

"I fell off an eight-foot loading dock," he said, hugging his brother. He whispered to Ace, "Apple Orchard."

"Oh, wow," Ace muttered, putting the pieces together. "You're lucky. You should have called me."

It disturbed Ace that King was alone and got beat up when they had always had each other's back growing up. He decided to have a long talk with King and patch things up. Life was better when he and King were a team.

"Hi, glad you could make it," King said to Rhonda shaking her hand. "Make yourself comfortable."

The conversation became livelier when Kate entered the living room, and everyone helped themselves to wine and beer. Meagan accepted King's one-armed help, and he set the beautiful plates of food on the table.

"Wow, Meagan, this is great. Are those walnuts on the salads?" asked King.

"Yes, is there a problem?"

"Nope, I just love a creative woman."

"Hmm."

As they were seated, King proposed a toast to Meagan, "The most talented woman I have ever met."

Like she had blown a fuse, Meagan's irritation with his lie to Dale disabled her ability to blush. "Thank you. That can't be true."

Ace laughed. "Yeah, well, it's not much of a compliment, considering he only knows two women."

Rhonda spoke with a wad of salad bulging in her cheek, "Oh, yes, she is! This is beautiful! I know you have always cooked, but this is so…good! Where did you learn to cook like this?"

"It's one of the recipes Mr. Willoughby was willing to teach me because he needed my help."

Jack, Kate, and King remained silent about the B&B and Meagan's living arrangements although her move-out date was quickly approaching.

Ace entertained the group with stories of customers in his shop, and the meal progressed quickly. When they were through, Kate and Rhonda helped to clear the table, and King made coffee.

"So, King," Rhonda asked, "what is the big thing you are building on this house?"

"Yeah, Ace added. "You've been super secretive. Can we see your big thing now?" He laughed. "I mean the addition?"

Kate gave Ace a stern look, and Jack piped up, "Ace, you need to rein it in now, Son."

"Yeah, Ace, rein it in," King grinned. "I guess I can show you," he said, preparing to lead the group upstairs. "Are you coming?" he asked Meagan.

"No, go ahead; I'll get dessert ready."

"Okay." King pushed aside heavy sheets of foggy plastic separating the undisturbed part of the house from that section still under construction, although the elevator was complete.

"An elevator!" exclaimed Jack with a glance toward Kate. "Did you know about this?"

Kate shook her head. "No."

"Dude, this is nice!" exclaimed Ace, "but why an elevator? Wouldn't building out on the first floor be cheaper?"

"Yes," King said," "There is a staircase as well. It's around back." They all rode to the second floor. "But this wouldn't have happened on ground level...."

The elevator door opened on the second floor; the group stepped out and gasped.

"Holy smokes," Jack said. "This is unreal."

Kate tightened her grip on Jack's arm. "Dear, did you ever? Look at the view of the back acreage from these lovely windows!"

Rhonda took stock of the living space. "You could have three living areas here. What will go there?" She pointed to a long countertop beneath a row of windows with views of the circle drive and the cows across the County Road.

King took a deep breath and revealed, "A kitchen."

"What are you doing?" Jack asked, squinting with hands on his hips.

"Mom and Dad, this apartment is for you to live in. You can live here permanently or just stay here when you visit. It's up to you."

Ace whistled. "Damn, King, that's cool."

Rhonda dabbed at her eyes as she observed Jack and Kate's reactions. She touched Ace's arm and agreed, "It's cool."

Wiping tears away, Kate said, "Thank you, King. I don't know what to say. It's incredible."

"The master bedroom is this way," King said, ushering the group around the corner. The deck is not built yet, but the sliding doors will open onto a deck."

"My goodness! The only thing missing is grandchildren!" Kate said.

Ace threw up his hands. "Don't look at me."

Rhonda snickered.

King cleared his throat. "Well, there is a lovely woman downstairs that I plan to woo and someday marry. She won my heart the day we met."

Rhonda screamed, "What?" Oh my god!"

"It's between us, please. I have some wooing to do, remember?" King said.

"Oh yes, of course," said Rhonda apologetically.

Somberly, Jack patted King on the back. "Maybe we should go back downstairs so you can start that wooing program?"

When they returned to the dinner table, it was set with gorgeous glasses of chocolate mousse. Meagan could hear the comments about dessert from her hiding place in the mudroom.

The group helped themselves to coffee and condiments on a serving tray centered on the table.

Meagan entered the dining area to the shock and horror of the group.

King was stunned; he looked like he'd been slapped.

"Ah, ha!" Ace shouted, pointing to Meagan. "That's hilarious! I wondered if she was a freaking prisoner in this house. It's beginning to make sense." He laughed harder.

"Ace!" Kate gasped in a scolding tone. She deduced the baggy orange prisoner jumpsuit was the errand Meagan had to run earlier. Considering this, she hoped Meagan's short-temperedness would dissolve with this horrid display. Perhaps Meagan had been nervous about this all day…but to what end?

Meagan nodded. "A criminal shouldn't be ashamed of their crimes, right?"

"Oh, god," King mumbled. The slap had morphed into a punch in the gut. He was scrambling for a way to salvage a sinking relationship with Meagan now that he knew that she knew what he said to Dale. "Damn."

Confused, Rhonda said, "Meg, this really isn't funny. Orange was never your color." She laughed. "Seriously, why are you wearing that, and what did you do to your face? You look bruised."

"Jailhouse fight," Meagan said. She stood with arms crossed, her lips pursed. She had no intention of saying anything more.

King stopped stirring his coffee, set the spoon down, stood up, and cleared his throat. "Meagan is wearing this uniform to call me out, aren't you?" he asked, heeding the hurt in her ocean eyes as she stared at him.

"I made a huge mistake," he started.

"Not another one!" Ace blurted. "Shit, King, grow up!"

Jack snickered, earning a questionable look from Kate. "Let him talk."

"Yes, that's what I'm doing, Ace." King turned and directed his words to Meagan. "I'm growing up. The thought of Meagan in anyone's arms but mine drove me over the edge. So, to stop Dale from asking her out, I told him she was a felon." He winced and searched Meagan's eyes, ashamed.

Alarmed, Ace said, "That's harsh!"

"Oh, no! Brandon King Pullman!" exclaimed Kate, resting her hand on Jack's arm, shocked that King did such an immature and hurtful thing to Meagan.

King moved in close to Meagan, but she remained stiff. Nevertheless, he reached his good arm around her waist, tugged her to his side, and gazed into her sad eyes. "The reality is," he spoke softly to her, "Meagan is only a felon to me because she stole my heart."

Rhonda squealed in delight and covered her mouth with her hand.

"Dude, nice save," Ace declared. "Way to woo!"

Meagan covered her gasp with both hands. She dared not look him in the eye—she wanted more. King's words, his unexpected, candid honesty, were a soothing balm for her shattered heart.

King continued, "It was stupid. I'm sorry, Meagan. Will you forgive me?"

Jack reached for Kate's hand and held it in his lap.

"Yes," Meagan said, "I will forgive you if you tell Dale the truth."

"Hmm, okay, Meagan, would you like to know exactly what I'm going to tell him?" King grinned.

A shiver ran through Meagan's body. "No, that's okay; just stick to the truth."

"Wait," Rhonda cried, "I want to know. What are you going to tell Dale?"

King squeezed Meagan closer to himself and subtly inhaled the scent of her hair. "Hmm, I'm going to tell him, 'Dale, that beautiful woman in my house is not a felon, nor is she available to go out with you because I just asked her to marry me."

Rhonda's squeal was punctuated with a sigh.

"What?" Ace bolted up from his chair. "Dale's not an idiot. He's gonna ask if she said 'yes,' you numbskull!"

"What should King tell Dale, Meagan?" Rhonda prodded, passionately tuned into the developing drama in the kitchen. This was the most romantic proposal Rhonda had ever heard; she wanted to answer for her best friend.

Meagan's expression softened, and her eyes became dreamy. Turning to face King, she said, "Tell Dale I said, 'yes.'"

King mouthed, "Thank you," and pressed his lips on hers, kissing her like a lovesick soldier home for Christmas.

Meagan felt herself orbiting with him again. She wouldn't have known or cared if a thousand people had been at the table. She was riveted on King and memorizing the feeling of being held and cherished by him.

Amidst the cheering and toasting, Rhonda snapped a picture with her phone.

"You didn't think this one through, Son. You're supposed to give her a ring," Jack pointed out.

King had been moving the last gem piece from his shirt to his pants pockets, waiting for the right moment to return it to Meagan. He dug into the pocket of his sweatpants and presented her with the ring.

"Will this do temporarily?" he asked, slipping the amber heirloom on her ring finger. "I love you," he whispered in her ear.

"And I love you," Meagan returned.

The bandage still covering half of his face caused Meagan to wonder if King was winking at her or suffering eye spasms, but she winked back and returned his contagious smile. Rolling the amber ring around on her left hand, Meagan burst with gratitude for him.

Kate couldn't stand it any longer. Her curiosity was at an all-time high; she erupted, "Does this mean you're staying…moving in here?"

King answered for her. "Yes, Meagan is staying…but NOT in Mattie's old room."

"Cheers! Bro!" Ace held up his beer to toast in celebration. He leaned close to King and whispered, "I have a four-carat Marquise diamond ring you might want to look at."

The universe was converging for King in a new and excellent way. "Thanks. Hold it for me, Ace. There's a gentleman I want you to meet."

"Will do," Ace replied, shaking King's hand. "Congratulations!"

In that surreal moment, after acquiring the amber ring, Meagan realized her heirloom family was home and complete. She knew she was home too. This marvelous family and this wonderful man holding her were overwhelming. She wiped tears from her eyes and composed herself. "Sorry, I missed the tour. What's going in upstairs?"

In unison, Rhonda and Ace pointed to Jack and Kate, saying, "They are!"

King smiled at Meagan. "I want our kids to know their grandparents."

Jack gulped and stood up. "I need another drink."

"Me too, dear," Kate said, "But first, help me up from this chair so I can hug these two."

"Mom, please sit with Dad in the living room; you too, Ace and Rhonda. My fiancée and I will clear the dessert dishes and be there shortly.

Kate's eyes sparkled. "If you say so!"

Meagan tugged King by his good arm into the kitchen.

"I have questions for you…fiancé."

"Shoot." He pulled her to his side.

"How did you really get hurt?" Meagan asked.

"I found a cache, and some of your things were there, along with a couple of thugs. Please tell me your hunt is over."

She held King's free hand in both of hers. "You found the rest of my heirlooms! Everyone is home." Her voice cracked.

"Meagan, the question now is, are you?"

"Yes!" she exclaimed and kissed him. "Yes, yes, yes."

With Meagan smattering kisses all over King's face, he glanced heavenward and then squeezed his eyes shut.

I must talk to Conroy about his God because I must have had His help with the angel in my kitchen.

"Mom, are you sure you want to do this?" Gayla asked her mother as she entered the circle drive.

"I think so," Carol said, "It's long overdue, and I really should, for their safety." Hands shaking, Carol shut the car door, approached the front door, paused, then ran back to the car. Hyperventilating, she fastened her seatbelt. "I can't. Just go," she ordered. "Maybe someday, but not today."

The tires spit gravel as Gayla stomped on the gas.

Jack set his drink down on the end table next to his chair. "I hear a car out front."

"I can check, Dad," Ace said.

"I'll see who it is." His curiosity piqued, Jack opened the door and peered through the settling dust.

"Who is it, dear?" asked Kate.

"No one. Strange. I could have sworn I heard a car door slam."

The End

Leave a Review

To leave a review on Amazon, use this QR code.

To leave a review on Barnes and Noble, use this QR code.

Author Bio

Lauren Anne Davis was raised in Western Canada. She lived in Toronto and Michigan then moved to New Jersey. Texas is closest to her heart. Davis holds a BA from the University of North Texas. Although work has always been an important part of her life, she enjoys family time and playing with her hilarious English bulldog.

GRANTED

Emma

Hello folks, Justin Gains here with your Tulsa Monday-at-six AM weather report. We are currently looking at seventy degrees with a high of eighty-one by early afternoon. East of Tulsa, out toward Graystone, we are looking at the possible dark cloud-cover with rain for most of the area. If you are within the sound of my voice, you will likely get rain. It shouldn't last too long now, but those roads will be very wet. Be careful and keep your radio dial here on 1620 for weather updates every hour...."

"There are two things I dread in this life; horrible weather and doing a reading I don't want to do."

Shortly after five, Trish scurried from her Ford, Bronco toward Plaza South Shopping Center. On the sidewalk in front of A Ray Tan, she dug around in her purse for the shop keys while glancing at the sky to validate the weatherman's claims.

"Clear skies," she muttered, "I think you missed it today, Justin! Oh well, we all have an inaccurate day sometimes!" The remark excusing Justin's missed forecast was a self-serving comment to take the stress off herself. Her promise to Emma was already taking its toll.

The salon wouldn't be open to customers for another two hours. Trish had agreed to come in extra early to spend time with Emma and finally give her the palm reading her sweet young employee had been bugging her about.

"Where are you?" called Emma as she tossed her guard jacket onto the receptionist's chair.

"In the back making you a cup of 'Happy birthday coffee!'" said Trish.

Emma rubbed her hands together excitedly as though warming them over a comforting fire. "I am so excited. Can we please start!"

"Here is your caramel coffee with extra sugar." Trish handed Emma the oversized mug of gourmet brew. "Your hair is wet. Did you lifeguard this morning? I thought you were going to give that up?"

Emma sipped her coffee. "This is yummy. You are an excellent Barista. About the pool—I am leaving the job after I train these two high school kids. I'll miss swimming regularly, but I've registered for a couple of classes at the University of Tulsa."

"Ah, taking my advice, I see."

They walked down the hall to her office, where Trish had done readings for tanning clients on many occasions. The feeling of impending doom surrounded her today like fog, and she could not shake it. They walked down the hall to her office, where Trish had done readings for tanning clients on many occasions. The feeling of impending doom surrounded her today like fog, and she could not shake it.

"Alright, here we go. Let's see what's in store for my friend, Emma," Trish said, combing her fingers down Emma's palms and studying the lines. She smiled. "You, my dear, are in for a journey!

And I see love …" Then she frowned. "Ah, I hate this… but it's broken."

"What do you mean, Trish?"

Since the day Trish interviewed Emma for the job at A Ray Tan several years ago, they hit it off. Their mutually calm natures meshed, and they often finished each other's sentences. The eight-year age difference didn't make a hill of beans difference.

Emma knew Trish studied palm reading and that wealthy people often hired her for parties. One day at the salon, Emma overheard two clients in the waiting area talking about a reading Trish did at one of their homes.

"You know, her best friend, Meredith, refuses to let Trish read her palm—she's too accurate. The reading she did for me was freaky," the first woman said, "she said things about my husband…." She shook her head.

"Were they accurate?" the other client asked.

"Very. This was last year, mind you. Some things Trish said about the future have come true already, and it is weird because it all seemed so out-of-the-blue when she said it."

The other woman shivered. "That's exciting. I'm going to hire her if she'll do it."

"You'll be surprised." The first woman smirked. "By the way, if she sees that you're not happy about what she says, Trish will apologize and admit to probably being wrong—but she's not. Good luck!"

That conversation tipped the scales; now Emma wanted a reading for sure. She asked Trish to read her palm, knowing that Trish would have difficulty saying no since it would be Emma's day—it was all Emma wanted for her twenty-fourth birthday. Trish could only say yes.

Then she saw Emma's lines and wished she had said no.

Squinting, Trish studied the lines and continued, "Well, see this heartline? It's marred or split. Could it be you are or will be confused about who or what to love? I don't know. Hmm. It appears you will have an important choice to make between men."

Trish paused to look into Emma's eyes in a new light. "By the same token, with this marriage line in the middle of the Mount of Mercury, it seems you'll be married soon."

"What?" Emma said, shaking her head like there was water in her ears. "I don't even know one 'right' guy, Trish. And I'll have to decide between two? Marriage?" She laughed, mumbling, "Married soon. Wow."

"I'm sorry Emma. I'm probably wrong."

Emma's mouth hung open. She licked her lips. "It's okay. Don't apologize; I'm not freaking out. Just surprised, is all. Keep going."

Trish smiled, flipped her long penny-red hair over her shoulder, wiped the perspiration from her forehead with the sleeve of her blouse, and continued. "There's travel in your near future… and work. It appears you'll be working hard—toiling. Hmm."

"Toiling? That doesn't sound too great," Emma said. "I don't even garden."

"It doesn't refer to gardening, Emma, just hard work."

Trish tilted her head, looked deeply into Emma's hazel eyes, and then patted her hand. It disturbed Trish to see things in Emma's palm that might take her out of Oklahoma.

"Look, starting here, the love line is solid from here on out…and quite strong!" She smiled. "I would focus on that."

Trish didn't mention the death lines that she saw; they were as sure as gravity.

Emma was conflicted about the results of her boss's reading of her palm.

"So, my life will be this crazy, hard-working trip before I find this forever love—but I'll be married soon…after I choose whom to love?"

She now wished she hadn't asked for a reading. Lately, Emma had been feeling unsettled about her future. Her mother's boyfriend wasn't making things any easier. He was a horrible, mean man who caused her and her mother misery. Emma had hoped Trish might see a line in her palm indicating he would disappear soon.

"Yes! Isn't that exciting? A forever love?" Trish knew better than to paint a bleaker picture, even if that's what the lines told her. She had blurted out more worry to Emma than she should have, but Trish had never seen lines like that, and she felt worried for her sweet friend.

Trish was adamant about lines. They told about a person's life and disclosed secrets. Despite the grief and sadness in their future, she liked learning a person's secrets.

"Now, Emma, it's your birthday. You shouldn't even be up here at work," Trish scolded. "Go get a massage and take in a movie. Here, it's not much, but this should help."

She handed Emma a small blue envelope.

"Trish, you weren't supposed to get me anything. I came to the shop today for a reading, that's all, and thank you for doing that. Is someone I know going to disappear or die, by the way?"

The color drained from Trish's face.

"Kidding! I know you would have told me." Emma hugged the envelope to her chest. "I'll leave now…."

"Emma, get back here and open that card!"

She froze and grinned. Emma appreciated her thoughtful, funny boss.

The envelope contained a short, heartfelt letter which Emma read to herself.

"Thank you, Trish. "I'm going to get a massage now," she said excitedly, extracting the one-hundred-dollar bill from the card.

"Make sure he's a hot massage guy; you want your money's worth!"

Trish watched Emma jog to her junker in the pouring rain--- disgusted that a mother would let her daughter drive the decrepit Buick Skylark with its faded, chipped paint and backfiring engine. "That car looks diseased," she muttered. While she thought Emma looked ridiculous behind the wheel of that old piece of crap car, she admired her for having the audacity to drive it. It was the same with her mother; Trish thought Emma was crazy for living at Rose's apartment and getting wrapped up in her drama, but she was amazed at the girl's tenacity and concern for her mom.

She checked her makeup in the countertop mirror and wiped away a tear. "Be careful, Miss Emma; I haven't worked out who dies yet."

With thirty minutes of quiet before her shop would be busy with tanners and shoppers, Trish turned on music and picked up a rag to dust surfaces.

Emma's grandmother, Mrs. Lions had been a spectacular wife and mother, always throwing herself head-first to do whatever she deemed necessary for someone, always ready to answer the call.

When the doctor told her that Mr. Lions needed to be in a nursing home because of his dementia, she disagreed.

For the last two years of her life, Mrs. Lions lovingly cared for Mr. Lions in the house where they raised their two children, Grant and Rose.

Grant was sitting at his piano overlooking the ocean and writing music when he got the call from his sister, Rose, that their mother died.

An eighteen-year-old boy in a new pickup checked his email on his phone while driving down Interstate 35, swerved, and took Mrs. Lions' life, and everything changed that day.

Everything.

The young man who caused the collision barely survived the tangled wreck and was hospitalized with significant spine injuries.

When Rose called Grant about their mother's funeral, no one had to ask. No one had to mention it. Mr. Lions could not live alone.

Grant knew he would not return to California alone; his seventy-six-year-old father would be with him.

Little did he know he would be bringing three people back with him.

Grant was a private person who lived a secluded life, far from his parents and his sister. Until Rose called him from the hospital that day, and everything changed.

He had never been the one to bring Rose home from the emergency room and offer her safety and seclusion from her dangerous live-in boyfriend. That duty had fallen to their mother, Mrs. Lions, but she was gone now.

Since his sister, Rose, was eight years old, her number one topic of conversation was being happily married someday. Her first boyfriend hung himself from the gym rafters at school at seventeen. While Rose grieved, Grant thought she might not work so hard to find a replacement but rather be confidently independent for a while.

Instead, she slept with the next guy who told her he loved her, and the result was Emma.

Grant could hardly call Rose's actions 'a mistake' when he laid eyes on his gorgeous and clever niece, Emma. Every few years, when Grant made the trip back to Oklahoma, usually at Christmas, he most looked forward to talking to Emma, who occasionally slipped and called him 'Dad.' Who could blame her?

Emma's biological father abandoned her and Rose when Emma was one month old.

Years later, Rose met Gage.

Rose had only been dating Gage for three months when the emergency room personnel at Presbyterian Hospital knew her by name.

Still dressed in his funeral clothes, Grant ran toward Tulsa's Cherry Valley Emergency room with his fists balled up, ready to hit someone. Well, not just anyone—Gage. He'd like to pummel Gage for the way Gage had beaten on Rose. It made him sick to think his sister was hurting again at the hand of that sick son- of-a-bitch boyfriend. Grant dreaded the feelings that would well up in him at the sight of his pretty sister covered in bruises and bandages.

How Margaret Lions would have enjoyed seeing her son all 'doodied up.' The dark gray wool-blend Hugo Boss suit, white shirt, and black Cole Haan shoes were perfect for his mother's sunrise funeral. But now, hurrying across the hospital parking lot, he wished for sweats and Nikes.

Rose

The emergency room doors slid open, and Emma rushed to her tall, skinny, shaggy-haired Uncle Grant, crying.

"She's hurt bad this time," Emma told him through tears. "Uncle Grant, Mom was in so much pain because he dislocated her shoulder and broke her arm. The doctors are working on her now."

His arms went gently around his niece. "Did he touch you?"

Her cheek rested on his chest, nestled in Grant's leather jacket; Emma shook her head, 'No.'

She inhaled Grant's scent. It was lovely, like fresh air and cotton with a hint of sage.

Relief washed over him. "This is the last time, sweetheart. You and Rose are coming with me—unless you don't want to. Do you or your mother have any reason to return to that apartment?"

"No. The last time we moved, Mom rented a storage unit, so we wouldn't have to keep moving things we don't use often," Emma said, "Where do you live now?"

Grant disclosed, "I have a house in Santa Barbara, California. I can help you find a job. Want some coffee?" He pointed to a snack bar in the waiting area.

They helped themselves to a cup of freshly brewed Arabian coffee and sat in mid-century woven-fabric hospital chairs to wait for news about Rose.

Mulling over the events of the previous two weeks, Grant sipped the hospital brew and decided the job of caring for their wacky father would be suitable for Rose. Not only would his older sister be out of the public eye, healing, but helping their dad as well.

Even if Grant hired in-home care, he would still be alone with his father when the help left. This way, Rose would be there for Mr. Lions twenty-four-seven. Problem solved.

"I hate Gage," declared Emma.

Grant agreed, "So do I. How is school? Rose told me you are taking some classes."

"School is fine. My classes are online. I spend a lot of time at the library to avoid the jerk—Gage. Now I feel terrible…like maybe I could have stopped him from hurting Mom."

"Emma…I'm grateful you weren't there. There is no telling what would have happened," Grant said putting his arm around her shoulder in a half hug. "Where do you work now?"

Emma rolled her eyes. "Is this the speech where you tell me I'm wasting my life because I work at A Ray Tan?"

"No …" he stressed. Chuckling at the sight of his pale niece, he asked, "I guess you don't use the place yourself?"

"Very funny. I just don't want cancer … that way. My boss Trish pays pretty well, and I like working with her. In fact, you should meet Trish Felder!" Emma said excitedly.

Grant ignored the comment about meeting Emma's boss. He was curious about her cancer comment. His eyebrows flew up. "Cancer? What *way* is that?"

"Duh. Who wants to get tan in a bed? The beach is the best, that's all I'm saying. I would never fake-bake. I can tell when someone is bed-browned as opposed to beach bronzed. Plus, there's the smell."

One end of his perfect grin curled up affectionately toward Emma. The few times he had been around his niece, he enjoyed her direct, decisive manner—so much like Mrs. Lions.

"Smell?"

"Yeah, it's a disgusting combination of bed cleaner and roasted skin, whereas the beach tan smells like salty air and sunshine. You ignored my suggestion about Trish," Emma informed him with a no-nonsense look in her hazel eyes.

Grant tossed his Styrofoam cup in the trash and wondered out loud, "So, you won't miss Tulsa, Oklahoma. Is that what you're telling me? Is there a special guy whose heart you will destroy by leaving Oklahoma?"

"Yes, and no. I would miss Tulsa and Trish, but Gramps is coming with us, right? And no, I don't have a boyfriend! They are ridiculous."

His insightful, cocky niece had just done it again. Grant had not said anything about his plans for his father, yet Emma guessed it right.

"Yes, he's coming with us," Grant confirmed, mussing up her naturally wavy cashew-colored hair. "You're a mess, Emma. Maybe I should meet your boss and tell her about your terrible attitude toward tanning."

Emma rolled her eyes at Grant and texted Trish, "I want you to meet my uncle. What are you doing for dinner?"

The emergency room on-call physician, Dr. Brown, approached and lowered his mask, revealing several days' worth of beard growth.

"Rose is going to be fine. The arm is set and in a cast. Her shoulder is fine, and the bruises just take time. She has some other minor abrasions that will take some time to mend. She's ready to go when she wakes up. The release paperwork is finished."

Gazing wistfully at Emma, the chubby doctor took out his business card.

"Here's my card. Call me if there are any questions."

Emma smiled and pocketed the card. "Know a good doc in California? That's where Rose will be as soon as possible."

His smile disappeared. "Oh, no, I don't. Sorry," he replied, then left abruptly.

"Uncle Grant? You're meeting Trish for dinner at Caneli's restaurant at six. Her friend Meredith, whom she rents a room to, went to a funeral in New York with her children. Anyway, Trish is not busy tonight and is happy to meet you. Plus, I want you to tell me what she reads."

"Ah, reads? Oh, okay. Hmm."

Emma sipped her coffee. "Don't ask. Just wait, and you'll see!"

"How will I know it's her?" Grant asked.

"Trish is beautiful. She will be wearing a yellow flower in her hair… I told her to do that."

Grant smiled. "Thanks; very clever and old-fashioned. I like it."

End of sample

GRANTED is available in paperback at all fine retailers.

To continue reading GRANTED on Ebook, use the QR code for access on Amazon.